Praise for The Judas Line

10/12

...y stars

a ...gmatic

Ca... more

ur... ls, but

wh... ing for

he... on a

qu... p him

de... Along

th... g and

wa... with

th... When

M... Arch-

Fi... reader.

St... nd his

tr... ree-

d... g is

c... urpr...

...ers

...ed ...for ...ry or

a ...i ...cti... given

a ...hat ...still ...hout.

I ...hat ...you'... ...n Buter... *Files*,

... y M...rk Eve...ott's work R ...”

...e He...bert, Fanta... Book ...

...s ...novel

following... ...nind

him, special... ...assa... ...wn as

the silver. Jude Oliver must find the origins and stories of his family to be able to end the Silver's legacy for good, with only a single Catholic priest by his side. Blending paranormal and biblical ideas, *The Judas Line* is a riveting thriller that should prove hard to put down."

—Midwest Book Review

"I have come to expect a lot from this remarkably talented writer, but Mark manages to please yet again by bringing new elements to his latest work. *The Judas Line* is, as anticipated, a lightning-paced thriller that is equal parts non-stop action and intelligent musing. This is, in fact, a surprisingly introspective book that delves into many interesting questions about the nature of good, evil, and faith. It's an enthralling read certain to delight and entertain, a well-crafted gem worthy of a place on any bookshelf."

—Michelle Izmaylov, author of *The Galacteran Legacy: Galaxy Watch*

"Mark Everett Stone takes the classic good versus evil plot line and puts his own unique spin on it. He effortlessly merges bible canon with the world and people he's created, adding off-the-wall humor to help break the tension. This book makes you laugh while making you think about the nature of evil and the power of faith."

—Jamie White, author of *The Life and Times of No One in Particular*

★ ★ ★ ★ ★ "I found myself chuckling at some of the insane twists and turns of the plot and other times I was worried by the sudden turn of events .... A fast-paced read, with nail-biting moments and some humor thrown in. The characters were compelling, I often find myself picturing them in my head .... I can't recommend this book enough."

—Lisa McCourt Hollar, Jezri's Nightmares

"Once in a great while, a book comes along that challenges you to think outside the box. The Judas Line is one of those books. I was absolutely amazed at the way Mark Everett Stone has taken religious stories and beliefs and intertwined his own tale of power, evil, friendship, sacrifice and redemption. The action is nonstop and the characters will stay with you long after you finish the last page."
—M.E. Franco, author *Where Will You Run?*

"The pacing is flawless in every respect .... Never before have I found a work of fiction to be so captivating. It picks you up, sits you down, and it does not let you even think about getting back up. A word of warning: Hide your pocketbooks, because once you read this, you will spend your next paycheck on every Mark Everett Stone book available. And clear your schedule once you start, because, all of a sudden, that doctor's appointment doesn't seem so important."
—Grace Knight, author of *Sun And Moon* (2013)

Praise for What Happens in Vegas, Dies in Vegas

★ ★ ★ ★ ★ *"Things To Do In Denver When Your Un-Dead* was one of the most refreshing and original books I have read in a long time and the sequel is just as exciting as the first. In fact it may just be better than the first .... Exceptionally well-written and entertaining."
—Jerzri's Nightmares

"Vegas is non-stop action that will leave you with whiplash.... Stone leaves you gasping for breath by the end and of course, enjoys taunting the reader with the prospect of a third book in

the series, which I will be waiting anxiously to read."
—Shay Fabbro, award-winning author of the *Portal of Destiny* series

★★★★★"A cracking good yarn from first to final page, no question .... Mark has cemented himself solidly into the position of Master in my self-created niche of Paranormal Suspense Thriller writing. His command of his art grows exponentially with each work of his that I read ....Two very enthusiastic thumbs up for a job well and properly done."
—Jeffrey Hollar, The Latinum Vault

"Don't expect a minute of down-time, for Stone is a zero tolerance taskmaster who brings a complicated plotline and well fleshed-out characters to heel and makes it look easy. What you *can* expect is for Stone to surprise you repeatedly, satisfy you completely and leave you wanting more."
—AJ Aalto, author of *Touched*

Praise for Things to Do in Denver When You're Un-Dead

★★★★★"If you crave a really enjoyable Paranormal Suspense Thriller to read, THIS is your book. It grabs you from the very first page and drags you along (snarling for you to keep up) and dumps you at the feet of one of THE most unexpected plot twists of an ending that I have ever read."
—Jeffrey Hollar, The Latinum Vault

"If you like quick wit, sadistic charm, and bad-ass gadgets, then you will enjoy the hell out of this book."
—Shay Fabbro, award-winning author of the *Portal of Destiny* series

★ ★ ★ ★ ★ "This book was an absolute pleasure to read. It is witty, funny, dramatic and a well thought out paranormal with very fine storytelling. I couldn't put it down! That's a first for me in a long time."
—Clarrissa Lee Moon, author of the series, *The Nightwolves* and *Celeste Nites*

"I have really enjoyed reading this book .... The story could just be one of guns, blood and guts and magic, but ... Mark Everett Stone has made these characters seem real."
—Michele Herbert, Fantasy Book Review

"This is not a story for the faint of heart or stomach, nor for those wanting a plot with any connection to reality. Personally, I'm really looking forward to the promised sequel."
—Gordon Long, TCM Reviews

"A fantastic read and very easy to follow. The way Mark combines magicians, zombies and super ghouls with a Bogart-style ultra sarcastic officer of the 'Bureau' makes you want to keep on reading. I highly recommend this for everyone—not just those into stories of the un-dead."
—G.R. Holton, author of *Soleri*, *Guardian's Alliance* and *Deep Screams*

"Five stars, two thumbs, fantastic! From the moment I began the first page to the final flip of the last, I was hooked .... The writing is sharp, fast and engaging. The characters are fun and/ or not so fun in all the right places. Mark has captured the soul of his lead character so well that it's like the reader is sitting having a $300 bottle of vodka, chased with an aromatic and equally expensive cigar, while Kal spins tales of his heyday, punctuated by live action reenactments so real you wish you hadn't eaten dinner."
—Patti Larsen, author of *Fresco*, *Wasteland* (10/2011), *The*

Diamond City (2012), and *The Ghost Boy of MacKenzie House* (2012)

"The blending of dark twisted humor in this chilling tale is utterly perfect, written with a sure hand. Comedic timing is everything, and author Stone has perfected the classic one-liner.... Make no mistake folks, this isn't for the faint hearted ... the sarcasm is used as a brief respite in the fastest paced action horror that I have read in a very long time."
—Suzannah Burke, aka Stacey Danson, author of *Empty Chairs*

"In a first and quite brilliant novel, Stone proves himself equally adept at feverishly fast-paced action, edgy wit and banter, and the weaving of a richly satisfying and fresh world of mystery and intrigue. Write on, my friend."
—Michelle Izmaylov, author of *The Galacteran Legacy: Galaxy Watch*

THE
JUDAS
LINE

THE
JUDAS
LINE

Mark Everett Stone

PRESS

Seattle, WA

Published by Camel Press
PO Box 70515
Seattle, WA 98127
For more information go to: www.camelpress.com
markeverettstone.camelpress.com
www.markeverettstone.com

Cover design by Sabrina Sun

The Judas Line
Copyright © 2013 by Mark Everett Stone

ISBN: 978-1-60381-901-5 (Trade Paper)
ISBN: 978-1-60381-902-2 (eBook)

LOC Control Number: 2012935942

Printed in the United States of America

BOOK ONE

FRIENDS

Chapter One

Jude

Two air sprites flitted down the street, lifting random scraps of paper, tossing them about before moving on to the next bit of rubbish. Then they saw a little old man wearing a black fedora walking slowly down the sidewalk against the stiff winter wind, clutching his trench coat tightly to his skinny body. With whispery cries of glee they snatched the hat from his head, revealing a liver-spotted scalp. They tossed the fedora to and fro down the sidewalk.

I didn't want to interfere, but the old man's expression—sadness and frustration at knowing he didn't have the strength to run after his hat—tugged at me, so I whistled. Soft, like a breeze through aspens, the sound was still enough to distract the tiny elementals. Howling gusty cries, they dropped the hat and flew off. A scent like lemongrass tickled my nose.

The old man tottered to where his fedora had fallen and stooped to pick it up off the cement, damp with snowmelt. He carefully wiped off the brim and placed it on his bald head.

"What was that, Jude?"

I turned to the man sitting next to me. "What's what, Mike?"

"What was that?" he repeated, his shrewd blue eyes giving me a once-over.

"Just a couple of wind sprites messing with an old man's hat. I asked them to stop and they did."

My best friend for the past fifteen years snorted. A big man, still trim despite being on the wrong side of forty, he sported a black handlebar moustache and a flat-top haircut. His ski-slope nose jutted out under icy eyes that presided over high, sharp cheekbones and a chiseled jaw line. He was a classically handsome man still in his prime. That face had broken hearts all around the city, the reason being the accoutrement that rested comfortably around his neck: the collar of a Catholic priest.

"Always the crap artist, eh Jude?"

"Crap art is what I do best, man," I replied, watching the old man stumble away. "That's what you love about me."

Mike snorted and gave me a wry look. "You didn't call me all the way down from my warm church just to pull my leg while I freeze my butt off, did you?"

The park near Con Agra, normally so green and peaceful, looked dreary, brown and sad on this cold January day. It matched my mood perfectly. "I had something stashed down here I wanted to give you, Mike. You know, to keep it safe until the right time."

His gaze was skeptical. He knew me far too well.

"Okay, okay, man." I pulled a folded manila envelope from the inside pocket of my brown leather jacket. "This is very important, Mike, possibly dangerous, so if you accept it, know that there are those that wouldn't think twice about killing a priest to obtain it."

Alarm replaced skepticism. "What is it?"

"If you don't hear from me within a month, you can read what's inside and then do with it what you will, reveal it to whomever you wish. Consider it my confession. Until then, keep it at St. Stephen's. My Family and their lackeys won't violate the sanctity of the church; they're scared of it."

His eyebrows threatened to join his hairline.

I sighed heavily. "Don't ask because I can't answer. I need someone I can trust and you're it, man."

As usual, he saw right through me. "It's not just about your family," he stated flatly.

"Yeah, not just."

The bench shifted slightly as he leaned his bulk toward me. "Come to the church, Jude." A beefy calloused hand landed with surprising gentleness on my shoulder. "All this time you never entered God's house, even though you've told me you're a believer. It's time, long past time."

"Long past time," I murmured softly. "Long past time … long past time." I rubbed my face. "It has been long past time my whole damn life, Mike. It's not going to do any good now."

"God wants you to come to him. So just give in and come unto the Lord, Jude. He welcomes us all."

My smile was mirthless. "Me and the Family aren't on speaking terms with the Lord."

"Just because they don't believe—"

"Oh, they absolutely believe," I interrupted, shaking my head. "They just hate Him."

Mike stared at me, mouth agape. I don't know what made me reveal that fact. Perhaps my darkening mood, the feeling of impending doom, broke my give-a-shitter, but I spilled those few carefully hoarded beans with surprising ease. Things were going to come to a head and I desperately needed him.

"Do you hate Him, Jude?" Mike whispered, blue eyes holding a wealth of sadness.

"Aw, no, man. Of course not … if I did, my best friend wouldn't be a Catholic priest, and I wouldn't want with all my heart to feel God's blessing on me. Naw, Mike, I just think God doesn't care too much for me." Christ! I was starting to sound like a Danielle Steel character. Next thing you know, I'd pull out a monogrammed hanky and delicately dab my eyes as they leaked bitter tears.

"You know, that's the first real thing you've said to me in over six years," Mike mused.

"What did I say that was so real last time?"

" 'I'm buying.' "

"Damn, what the hell was I thinking, opening up like that? Sounds like I almost grew a vagina right then and there."

"No need to be a misogynistic prick, Jude."

"Sorry, man, it's been one of those centuries."

"Seriously, what is up with your family?"

"You know that's been a touchy subject for me."

The manila envelope slapped me on the chest. "Then keep your secret documents or whatever they are."

"What?"

A hard finger poked my chest and his breath, smelling of peppermint gum, washed over me. "You don't drop a bomb about your family hating God and His apathy toward you, then expect me to hold onto … whatever this is. I'm a priest, not an idiot."

Well damn, not how I wanted this conversation to go. Had I been prone to panic, I might have. A thread of unease rippled up and down my spine as I realized that even though my Family might consider Mike the enemy, I had no one else to count on. After all these years of hiding in plain sight, I saw Mike as the only person I could sincerely call a friend. Julian wanted to use me, while the rest of the Family wanted me dead and gone in the worst way. All Mike wanted was the truth. Could I handle that?

No choice … you take your friends where you can get them.

"Tell you what, amigo," I retorted, slapping the envelope back into his hands. "You go ahead and read what's in here. If you can handle it, if you think we still can be friends, then call me. The number to my new disposable is in there."

The fear that Mike would hate and revile me after reading the contents of the envelope blazed up inside, causing my stomach to clench. Nothing for it, however, but to trust him and hope for the best.

He clutched the envelope in one hand and stroked his ridiculous handlebar moustache with the other; something he always did when perched on the horns of a dilemma. "Okay, Jude," he said, folding and unfolding the envelope. "You got it, but I have to ask … what's going on?"

My eyes trailed up the side of Woodman Tower to where wind sprites frolicked on high. "What about the holy water I asked for, Mike?" I hedged.

"Having a courier deliver it to your place. Should be there sometime this afternoon. I don't know why you keep asking me for ten gallons of holy water every six months, but the donations are appreciated. Now ... answer the damn question."

"What's going on? Well, I have Family business to take care of soon."

Chapter Two

Jude

My place was a little white ranch-style affair on 61st near L Street, smack dab in a quiet middle class neighborhood where the houses are small, but the backyards are large. The kind of place you find newly married couples and the retired.

Omaha in winter is only slightly less windy and cold than the Ninth Circle of Hell, the frozen lake trapping the traitors to mankind. The previous day saw a wind chill of -65° F, cold enough to shatter the plastic quarter panels on my neighbor's blue Saturn coupe. I didn't mind the deep freeze, as long as the blessed cloak of anonymity covered me.

Before the keys left the ignition of my red Hyundai Sonata, my belt buckle vibrated slightly, sending a small thrill through my navel. The car filled with the aroma of lavender. Someone had tripped one of my many alarms. I had a guest.

"Damn." Just what the doctor hadn't ordered. My best guess … Family visit.

Magic was out of the question. If I used a Word, it would be detected, a scent that any mage within a hundred feet would pick up. That suited me fine. I could do without, and I'd spent a great portion of my Family's vast fortune on alternative methods.

Molecular thread, one of my best, most enjoyable toys. Linked iron molecules held rigid by an inch-long magnetic bottle attached to a six-inch slim cylinder. Not great as a weapon—having such a short blade—but perfect for detail work.

You may have seen movies where the canny thief uses a circular glasscutter on a windowpane, removing a perfectly round piece in just seconds with hardly a sound thanks to clever editing and the audience's willingness to suspend disbelief. The molecular blade requires no such flouting of physical laws. It cut through my bathroom window in a moment, allowing me to unlock it and slither in quietly.

With just the slightest whisper I drew my K-bar from its ankle sheath, readying it my left hand, right hand carefully opening the door to my bedroom, staying low. One of my few indulgences was fine furniture crafted out of heavy, sturdy wood and polished to a high gloss. If you look hard enough, you can find someone in any good-sized town who specializes in woodworking. I had found an elderly gentleman who had been crafting furniture for decades and commissioned several pieces to the tune of several thousand dollars. The centerpiece of the collection was a queen-sized sleigh bed made of stained red oak. The auburn wood gleamed to perfection and smelled faintly of the lemon oil I used to polish it. When I stepped into the bedroom, I detected evidence of a new smell—thus a new occupant.

It was the blood that confused my eyes, enough that it took several seconds for me to recognize Eliza, my next-door neighbor. A round, happy woman, the kind that minded everyone else's business. As long as she was awake, the block didn't need a neighborhood watch. Her short, frizzy blond hair was crusted in red; blood covered every inch of her naked, flabby body, as if a particularly twisted artist had painted it on. That same artist had ripped open her ample belly and festooned my bedroom with her guts.

The smell was horrible.

"Goddamn it," I whispered, tearing my eyes away from the corpse. She'd been dead for quite some while—the blood had coagulated, turning black—so why had my alarm tripped only a few short minutes earlier? There was only one answer.

Whoever did this *wanted* me warned. It was an invitation to a private horror show and I had front-row seats. This was Family work. From the violence and the brutality of Eliza's death, I knew which Family member waited for me.

Burke.

Shit, out of all of them, it just had to be him, the one guy I actually feared a little. Carefully, I lowered myself to the carpet next to the hall door. "Burke!" I shouted.

Four bullets tore through the door above my head, showering me with splinters and imbedding themselves into my oak armoire. There went another two grand.

The voice that drifted through my holy door dripped with contempt and amusement. "Did I get you, Olivier? Or should I call you Jude? That is the name you use now, is it not? Are you hurt?"

Sarky twerp. Family protocol dictated that no Family member commit violence on another, restricting assassinations to poisons and magic. Looked like things had changed in the last fifteen years. Burke was a cousin on the distaff line, unlikely to inherit the Big Title, but the only male of that branch in the past three-hundred years who had any real magical ability. That made him valuable to Julian, my father. That made him valuable to the Voice.

"You're still a lousy shot, Burke," I hollered back.

Four more shots, four more holes in my armoire. I gritted my teeth.

"You think you are oh so clever, don't you Jude? Always Daddy's little sm—"

My body blurred into motion as I voiced a Word that shattered the door into a thousand pieces, flinging the shards down the hallway. The woody projectiles caused Burke to raise his gun arm across his eyes for protection. The smell of burning insulation filled the air.

I was halfway down the hallway, legs pumping, empty left hand extended ready to grab, K-bar filled right hand held back, ready to stab the life from Burke's body. His gun hand came down, and his eyes widened at the sight of me barreling toward him like a defensive end going for the sack. I noticed a splinter cut on his chin. Thin lips skinned back from his teeth as he brought his gun to bear, certain in the knowledge I'd never get to him in time. He was right, I was too far away and not fast enough ... but my K-bar was plenty quick.

My arm flashed forward and the knife flew true, entering his shoulder with enough force to dislodge the silenced Glock from his hand. Grunting, I planted my shoulder in his breadbasket at the same time the 9mm hit the carpet. Both of us exploded into the living room and slammed hard into the couch, which flipped us over onto the coffee table. It gave way with a loud *crunch* under our combined weight.

Fortunately for my personal aesthetic, the living room furniture was little better than department-store specials, cheap cloth and pressboard, camouflage for a rich magus on the run.

Grunting, we stood staring at each other, me nursing a pulled groin muscle and Burke pulling the K-bar from his shoulder, letting loose a gout of blood that pattered to the floor. He spared the wound a quick glance and spoke a Word that sealed his injured flesh. A waft of cinnamon floated in the air.

I had to admit, he looked good for a man in his late thirties. Fit and trim, an inch over my own five-ten. Long lean muscles rippled under olive skin covered in a designer black t-shirt and silver/gray cotton slacks that swirled like liquid silk. Black handmade Crockett & Jones loafers caressed his feet while a Louis Moinet Meteoris tourbillion watch circled his wrist in a show of sinful steely opulence. He looked like a guy trying too hard to look cool and rich at the same time.

If someone were to see us together, they might mistake us for brothers ... the same unruly midnight hair, dark, dark eyes and strong, firm chins. The main differences were the perpetual sneer on Burke's full lips and the hooked nose that came to a sharp point. Mine was much shorter with a small arch high on the bridge.

"Why warn me, Burke? You could've had me dead bang," I panted after muttering a Healing of my own, adding to the cinnamon smell.

His smile was pure concentrated mean. "I wanted to see if you still had some mustard in you, Olivier."

"And?"

"The years away from the Family business hasn't made you completely incompetent, although your Botanical magic is second tier. Your alarm sprigs were simple to locate and bypass without dispelling the magic."

I stretched, working the kinks out. "And Eliza, my neighbor? Why her?"

Burke shrugged, performing a bit of stretching himself. "Why not? She saw me arrive at your door, so I invited her in for a ... bite." All fifty of his teeth flared at me, a jackal's smile carrying the devil's humor.

Suppressing the spike of anger that flared briefly through me took all my considerable training. Fight cold, not hot, that's how I'd been trained. Taking a slow, deep breath, I focused on my murderous cousin.

My face must've betrayed some of my anger because Burke smiled even wider, a shark ready for breakfast. My K-bar twirled between his fingers. "Where's the Silver, Olivier?"

"It's Jude now, Burke. Olivier was always so ... pretentious."

He snorted. "Have to agree with you there. Now, give it up, the Silver."

It was my turn to flash a hard and nasty smile. "You can search a thousand years and never find it, Burke, but something tells me that you won't be looking for too much longer." Quickly I reached down and tore off a leg from the cheap coffee table. "Let's dance, you and me."

He lunged, the razor edge of the K-bar whistling toward my chest. I blocked the knife with my improvised club, batting it aside and knocking Burke on the shoulder with the backswing. Stiffened fingers caught me in the throat and I stumbled backwards, gagging. Grinning savagely, Burke rushed in, stabbing for my eyes, but I fell to my knees and the knife swished above my scalp, missing me by millimeters.

Snarling, Burke slashed down, aiming for the join of my neck and shoulder, and I raised my hand, a silvery cylinder glinting between my fingers. The K-bar's blade parted and two thirds of the knife spun off past my ear, severed from the hilt. For a split second he stared at the ruined knife, the sheared two inches sticking out like a reproach; then I swept the molecular knife across the inside of his wrist, snapping tendons and slicing the Ulnar artery. Blood spurted from the damaged vessel as I leapt to my feet and quickly swept the inch-long invisible blade across his eyes.

Sobbing and shrieking he fell to the floor, clawing at eyes that leaked aqueous and vitreous fluid down his cheeks. Wasting no time, I scrambled over his body and pinned his arms with mine. "Where's your backup?" I yelled over his mewling sobs.

What I got was a Word that smelled like bleach: Pain. A tingle washed over my skin like the skittering of hundreds of spiders and another smell, like rotting meat, hit me like a brick as the unguent I had applied broke his magic.

I grunted. "Toadflax and Wintergreen, Burke, worked into a paste and smeared on my chest."

Burked cursed and spat. Knowing that further conversation was probably futile, I released his bad arm to run the molecular knife across his throat … twice. Arterial spray spewed across my face and clothes, coating me with warm, coppery saltiness.

Wasting no time, I reached under the couch for one of the many hold-out weapons. The cool feeling of the Kimber .45 ACP I'd stashed there met my fingers and I drew it out, ready in case Burke had backup. From the direction of my cousin I heard a gurgle and rapidly weakening thrashing sounds, but I ignored them. Blind and throat-cut, he no longer posed a threat.

No one burst through a window or door, no magic spells, no hail of bullets. Everything was … quiet. Slowly I let my breath out, lowering the ACP. When a cell suddenly rang, startling me, I nearly shot myself in the damn foot.

The tinny ringtone came from the front pocket of Burke's shiny pants. I fished inside and pulled out a sleek Windows phone. The tune was *Murder by Numbers* by the Police. It seems Burke had a macabre sense of humor. I was glad I'd killed him.

"Yeah," I answered in what I hoped was a good imitation of my cousin's deep, gruff voice.

"Is he dead yet, my dear boy?"

Oh lord. My stomach bounced off the low-rent worn beige shag carpet about seventeen times while my heart froze in my chest. It was Him. The Voice.

"I asked you if he was dead yet, Burke," the Voice intoned with a hint of exasperation. Deep, cultured, smooth and slick as motor oil—a sound that inspired trust, veneration and love. The second you start to *really* listen, fall under its spell, you're done. Put out the cat and call in the dog, it's over.

A faked cough bought me a few seconds as I considered my next play. "On the floor, unconscious," I said roughly.

The Voice became wintry. "Why haven't you killed him?"

"Need to find out where he hid the Silver."

"Good to see you aren't a waste of space, Burke. Wake him up and put him on, he'll talk to me."

Oh well, it had been worth a shot. "The part of Burke will now be played by a much more handsome and virile man." A note of sarcastic amusement wended its way through my voice, guaranteed to anger.

"Olivier." Low, solemn and loaded with spite, he turned my name into a curse. Yeah, he was angry all right.

"What's the matter, Voice, you sound unhappy. Were you really counting on *Burke* to take me out? Has it been so long that you forgot who you're dealing with?"

The Voice regained its smooth, cloying composure and his words came out sweet, mellifluous and warm, but with a foul, hateful undercurrent. Like honey-coated shit. "My dear boy, you had the potential to be the best killer alive, pure swift murder, but fifteen years *is* a long time to be out of the game and you never really had the heart for the hard work. Burke has had his nose deep in it since you left. We both thought, once you were found, you would come out worse for the experience."

"The more fool you."

"Careful boy." The Voice was now filled with such wrath that it literally blistered the skin of my ear. I threw the cell across the room just before it exploded into a million burning fragments, one of which cut a shallow groove across my neck as it whizzed by.

"Damn it!" I swore, clapping a hand to the cut. My fingers came away sticky. The Voice's pride kept him from being anything like a good sport and I had poked the old bear hard with a sharp stick.

Burke could lie like a politician and the Voice practically invented it, so it was conceivable that backup could be moments away. Snarling, I voiced a Word that hung the smell of peanuts in the air. I had ten minutes, more or less, to make preparations because my cover was blown big time and Hell was coming for me.

Tacky, covered in rust-red drying blood, looking like a tourist in Baghdad, I'd stand out wherever I went. My mind started working in overdrive as old habits, old reflexes started to come back online. The familiar rush I'd get when on a job, the adrenaline high, fizzled through my flesh like the hit of a really good designer drug. God in Heaven, I'd missed that feeling. For just a split second, barely the tick of a clock, I felt the seductive tug of temptation.

No. None of that. I'd done enough harm in my life, maybe more than I could make up for. Maybe enough to stain my soul black for all eternity, but I'd been given a second chance and I realized that I'd been pissing that chance away for fifteen years, hiding like a child afraid of the boogeyman.

Perhaps Burke's arrival had been fortuitous, kick-starting me out of my comfort zone, planting a metaphorical boot to my lazy backside.

Running into the kitchen, I opened the cupboard under the sink and carefully removed a large cardboard cylinder, the kind used for dishwashing tabs. I removed the plastic lid, revealing little blue and white plastic soap packets, a blind in case someone looked. Removing the concealed tray, I pulled out the tabs to reveal the compartment within. Ten inches deep, eight in diameter, just large enough to hold a plastic one-quart fishbowl, the cheap kind you see holding the feeder goldfish at the pet store. The bowl was filled with water and floating in the center—held there by a silver chain glued to a clear plastic lid—was a blackened leather pouch the size of a large egg.

Lifting the bowl, I noticed about an inch of heavy black liquid resting on the bottom, moving turgidly. As I watched, a drop of black liquid oozed from the leather bag and hung suspended for a moment before descending to mix with the sluggishly swirling fluid.

Squinting, I calculated it would be another twelve hours before the holy water in the bowl would become denatured enough for what lay in the bag to be detected by the Voice.

Time to go.

A quick wash, a change of clothes, two handguns (the Kimber .45 ACP and a Beretta PX4 Storm), a six-inch hunting knife and one twenty-six-inch collapsible solid-steel baton later, I was good to go. Over my shoulder I carried a large duffel with fifty grand in hundreds, the fish bowl (wrapped carefully and sealed tight), and five disposable cell phones.

On a side table next to an old red corduroy recliner sat a fat yellow candle with three wicks. They had never been lit and shone a dull waxy white. After moving the candle to the living room floor, I rolled cypress leaves in my palms—the crushing released a bold, earthy scent—and scattered them all about. Next I lightly dusted the wicks with powdered sulphur and lit them using an antique Zippo with a cross etched on its metal. As the wicks caught and sputtered, I said a phrase in a language that sounded like the pop of pitch in a flame and had the tang of hot metal.

Nothing.

I repeated the words, throat spasming, and was rewarded with an answering hiss. The flames dancing on the three wicks bent toward the center, elongating and meeting some three inches above the candle's center. More hissing and popping greeted my ears.

In the language of Fire, I gave instructions to the tiny fire elemental and it replied with crackling laughter.

Gravely I bowed to the sprite and it jigged in pleasure. I took one last look at the place I had called home for so long—a comfortable, nondescript haven that had suited me down to my toes. I really thought I had more time.

"Magus," the sprite cackled. "What do you want me to do with the bodies?"

I had to smile at its simple, honest greed. *"Burn them down. Down to dust,"* I answered gravely and walked away.

Chapter Three

Mike

What to do, what to do? I mused, staring at the manila envelope Jude had given me, my butt cheeks cold against the wooden pew. Christ stared with great sadness and pain from the large cross behind the altar, offering comfort, but not enough to sooth my turbulent thoughts.

Part of me wanted to read what was inside, but the other part was afraid of what I might learn about my friend. Jude was the most mysterious man I knew, and it seemed best to keep it that way.

After I'd returned from Germany, my time in the Army all said and done, the Call to the Church had pulled me into the Seminary and presto, change-o, a priest I became. Much to the dismay of my parents, who were lapsed Catholics to the point of being Protestant.

Then, fifteen years ago, on a clear summer's noon, after I—a young priest—had finished my second service ever, I had met a young man in black and tan, standing on the steps staring at the church with something like superstitious dread.

People in their Sunday best had avoided him as if by instinct, streaming around him as if he were a large, jagged rock. After I waved goodbye to my flock, I closed the door and approached the nervous young man.

He watched me warily, as if I carried a weapon under my robes and was prepared to attack. Up close I noted how young he looked—twenty or twenty-one—with long curly hair that fell to his shoulders, so black it seemed to drink the light. Olive skin, perhaps of Mediterranean descent, maybe Greek, with a short hawk nose and delicate features, almost feminine. His eyes were fawn-brown and he had the longest lashes I'd ever seen on a man. Black biker boots. The slacks and tan polo shirt were incongruous—a punk rocker trying to look respectable.

I pasted on my most sincere smile and held out a hand, which he eyed dubiously. "Hello, young man. Welcome to St. Stephen the Martyr Catholic Church, I'm Michael and you are …?"

He took the bait. "Jude. Jude Oliver." Hard calluses met mine. By the feel he was no stranger to hand-to-hand; his grip had some serious spice to it. "Who was St. Stephen and why is he a martyr?"

Taken aback, I blinked a couple of times before answering. "Ah, St. Stephen was a follower of Jesus, a prophet and miracle worker who was stoned to death after being tried for blasphemy against Moses and God."

"He blasphemed? Then why is he a saint?" Jude's intense stare was definitely disconcerting.

"It's believed that the charges against him were false, brought by the jealous and venal. Even though he knew he would die if judged harshly, he kept his faith and begged God not to punish his enemies for killing him."

Those powerful dark eyes moved past me to the church. "That is an unusual steeple," he noted quietly.

Okay, the attention span of a hummingbird. Got it. "Yeah, kind of weird new age. Not quite the traditional gothic, but I like it." The steeple was a hollow square tube that ended in a chisel-shaped skylight, a definite part from the norm.

"Does God love everyone?"

All right then; conversational whiplash was the order of the day. "Yes, my son, God loves everyone." Something about the way he spoke bothered me … his accent was flat, almost atonal, as if he'd learned English as a second language at an expensive European prep school. I'd met a few rich German and Swedish kids who sounded like that.

Those eyes once again fixed themselves on mine. "I am not your 'son,' you know."

"Figure of speech. It's a priest thing." Who was this kid?

"Even the evil ones, sir? He loves the evil?"

I stroked my moustache. "I'm not sure there are any truly *evil* people—"

"There are."

"What?"

Those eyes became even more forceful. "There are. Trust me."

Hmm. Maybe a bit daft. "Even them, Jude. Think of all people as God's children. You love your children, even the bad ones, you want them to wise up and come to their senses, rejoin the fold, so to speak."

Jude pursed his lips in distaste, as if he'd bitten something sour. "Not sure I can understand that, accepting the irredeemable, inviting them back into … the fold."

I took a step forward and his body tensed, as if preparing for flight or fight. My years in the Army had made me tough and I worked out regularly, a regimen that kept me hard, but somehow I knew this kid could kick my butt up one side and down the other if he chose. "Young man, no one is irredeemable."

For the first time something besides wariness flitted across his face. It looked like hope. "Can that be true?" he whispered.

"Of course, Jude. God *does* love us all."

"What about the Anti-Christ?" he asked suddenly.

"What do you mean?"

"The Anti-Christ, does God love him?"

Wow. I sure didn't see that one coming. "You go straight for the jugular, dontcha, kid?"

That earned a small twitch of the lips. So a sense of humor was hidden down there. Deep. "Well?"

Where was a rewind button when you needed one? I scrubbed my face with my palms and gave my answer some serious thought.

"You know, the Anti-Christ is Satan's expression on this world, the portal he uses to work his will. A finger puppet, so to speak. Satan is a fallen angel, created by God, and if God loves all his creations, which he does, then logic follows that he must love Satan, perhaps like a wayward son, and thus, by extension, the Anti-Christ."

"The Anti-Christ is a puppet?"

"According to scripture, he will be killed and his death allows Satan to enter him, to use his body like you would a pair of shoes."

Jude squinched his eyes almost shut as he considered my words. "I never *heard* that," he said slowly, carefully.

"Revelations."

"What?"

"The Book of Revelations."

"Where is this book?"

Now I was starting to get a little freaked out. "It's in the Bible. You've heard of the Bible, yes?"

A nod.

"Well, there you go, then."

Once more that squinchy look. "Where can I buy one of these Bibles? Is there a special store?"

Was he kidding me? Briefly I wondered if he had been living in a Buddhist monastery since birth. Holding up a hand, I said, "I'll be back." In my best Schwarzenegger voice. He just stared with a blank expression. "Never mind, classical reference. Wait here."

It took moments for me to snag a copy for the young man. He needed the Book more than anyone else I'd ever met.

Fortunately he still stood on the steps, staring at our squarish steeple. "Here you go," I said, handing him a black, leather-bound Bible. "It might be a difficult read, but it will answer many of your questions and raise some more."

He accepted the book, albeit with some hesitance, and flipped through the pages. "Thank you, sir."

My reply was automatic. "Please, call me Mike, everyone does."

That brought a genuine smile and transformed his face into something extraordinary. It was as if no one had ever extended him a simple courtesy before. "Well, one last question, if I may?"

"Of course. Go ahead."

"How can God love someone who was born evil?"

Obviously the kid had some major issues, but I felt that if I tried to dig, to stick my big nose in, he'd shut up tighter than a clam. Instead, I gave him the best answer I had, one supplied by John Steinbeck in *East of Eden*. "Thou mayest."

He staggered, gripping the iron railing for support.

"You okay, Jude?" I asked, alarmed.

Through clenched teeth he hissed, "Where did you hear that?"

"Hear what?"

" 'Thou mayest.' "

"A book called *East of Eden*, written by a man named Steinbeck. It's a retelling of Cain and Abel—"

"Who?"

"For goodness sakes, Jude, where have you been hiding?"

"Geneva."

"Really?" That would explain the prep school accent.

"Really."

I raised my hands in mock surrender. "Okay, I won't ask. Safe to say that John Steinbeck posited in his novel that when God spoke to Cain after he had slain his brother 'thou *mayest* chose between good and evil,' thereby conferring free will upon mankind. Now realize, this is what I remember from reading the book ten years ago and watching the mini-series."

"What's a mini-series?"

"Oh, Jude, you really have to go and read the Bible. Buy *East of Eden* and rent the mini-series. Take a couple of weekends to absorb them, then come back and we'll discuss."

"Really? You'd want to discuss literature with me?" he inquired in a slightly hopeful voice.

My heart went out to the lad because anyone with eyeballs could tell he was lonely. Possibly the loneliest man I'd ever met. I gestured to my robes. "And religion, always have to talk about religion as well. Part of the job."

He threw me a downward kind of smile and held out his hand, which I shook. "Ok, Mr.—"

"Engel, but call me Mike, please."

Once again he reeled. "That's … that's Danish … for … for—"

"Angel, yes. Trust me, I see the irony," I laughed, keeping it light, not wanting to do anything to scare the young man. God must have led this poor soul to me, and I felt it was my job, my calling, to render him whatever aid I could.

We made our farewells and I watched the strange boy walk away, thoughtfully turning the Bible over and over in his hands, a lost sheep in desperate need of a vigilant shepherd.

A thunderous *slam!* brought me back to the present with a start, nearly launching me out of the pew.

"Mike, there you are!" Jude cried, running down the aisle, dark eyes wide. "Tried your place first. I need your help."

Whatever words were about to pass my lips took a U-turn back down my throat as I drank in his appearance: hair matted and disheveled, slacks torn, a deep cut on his neck bleeding freely. "Lord, Jude … what happened?"

"Can't really talk about it now, Mike …"

I crossed my arms over my chest and glowered. "Make time," I rumbled threateningly. "You come into the house of the Lord reeking of blood and looking like that? You better start making time *right now*."

He could tell I wouldn't be moved on the matter and carefully laid a grimy brown backpack on the carpet. "My Family found me—at least one of them—and now they all know where I am."

"And the blood on your hands?" I pointed to the smeared rust-red stains, evidence of a poor attempt at cleaning up.

"Belonged to my cousin Burke. He doesn't need it anymore."

I sat down hard, the pew bruising my backside.

Jude knelt next to me and I could smell rank man-sweat and the coppery tang of dried blood. "Mike," he whispered urgently. "I had to, he came to kill me. It was self-defense and, let me tell you, if you knew my Family you'd understand."

My reply slithered softly past my lips. "Make me understand, Jude, please." I felt a jittery fear I hadn't experienced in a long time, not since the dry desert wind of Iraq stung my eyes.

"I don't have time, Mike." Jude's eyes seemed to grow larger and sadder, as if a great weight was crushing his soul. "Burke's death threw them off track for a little bit, but if I stick around, they'll sniff me out soon enough."

"They want to *kill* you? Why?"

"Because I stole something from … my father, something he'll do anything to retrieve. I have to destroy it before they find me again."

How come talking to Jude made me feel like I'd taken a big hit of some sweet pot? Always a rush, but accompanied by a sense of unreality. "What is it, what did you steal? Why do you have to destroy it?"

"If I can destroy it, this thing I've stolen, it will change humanity's fate forever, man."

Surprisingly enough, that clinched it for me because Jude did not lie. Sure, he'd withheld his story, had kept himself apart, but he'd never uttered a falsehood that I could detect and I consider myself pretty proficient at spotting fabrication. "What do you need?"

The relief that blossomed on his face soothed any lingering doubts I might have had. "I need about a gallon of holy water, Mike; then I'm leaving town. If the police come to question you, just tell the truth."

"What about the ten gallons I had couriered to your place?"

"I don't have a place anymore."

With an almost audible *click*, the tumblers of my mind ratcheted to a sticking place as I came to a decision, one that would change me and my view of the world forever. "Okay, Jude, I'll get you the holy water." For as long as I've known him he'd requested holy water, but wouldn't tell me why. To my shame, the donations he'd made to the parish had kept me from asking more than once. Things, however, were about to change. "But in return, I'm coming with you."

His brows furrowed. "Mike—" he began, but seeing the

determination on my face stopped him cold. Shaking his head, he laid on a tired grin. "Really, Mike?"

"Try and stop me."

For the first time in … I don't know how long, he indulged in a good belly laugh, looking younger than his thirty-six years.

Chapter Four

Jude

Mike's Corolla chugged south like an asthmatic jogger, a rusty shitbox on steel-belted radials. During the frigid Omaha winters, the city used salt instead of mag chloride to de-ice the roads—much more effective but infinitely harder on the automobiles. You don't see a car over five years old that doesn't have rust somewhere. Keeps the local dealers in business, though.

When Mike announced with such a serious face that he would be coming with me, I was surprised to hear myself say 'yes.' Just try saying 'no' to a priest with a full steam of stubborn going. See where it gets you.

By nightfall we reached a little motel on the outskirts of Florence, Kansas, the kind of place where you paid your forty bucks and received a room that actually had clean sheets. No liberated fluids to be found, thank goodness. It also had a shower with plenty of hot water and generic shampoo. No cable. No TV for that matter, but I didn't mind. What passed for entertainment in America made me wish for the good old days of gladiatorial combat. Or public executions. Now that's reality TV that would garner serious ratings.

After soaking in the shower for about a thousand years, I exited the tiny bathroom satisfyingly clean and pruny, toweling myself vigorously. "Your turn, big man," I told Mike, who eyed my Billy Idol-like wet hair with much amusement. By the time he finished his shower (while abusing my ears with "Puff the Magic Dragon" at the top of his lungs), I was dry and dressed in black boxer briefs and a loosely fitting Police concert t-shirt.

"Hey, Jude," he chuckled as he donned his own boxers. "What's up? Ready to talk?"

Always with the Beatles reference … that's what I get for choosing that name. "No, Mike. I'm ready to play show and tell, man." With that I opened the door, letting in the cool night air. Outside was the motel's cracked asphalt parking lot where Mike's sad little Corolla sat all alone with no automobile companionship. The halogen light that should have made the lot bright as day was burned out. The conditions looked optimal for my purposes and the zillion stars in the moonless sky lent a bit of extra magic to the still air. The January cold bit at my bare feet and ankles, but I didn't care.

"Show me what?" Mike inquired, pulling on a black t-shirt with the words HOLY ROLLER on the back.

Giving him an enigmatic smile, I began to whistle, much like when I dismissed the sprites that had taken the old man's hat, but instead of a breeze through aspens, the whistle emerged like the haunting moan of wind wending around an old, decrepit house. Once again the sweet smell of lemongrass soothed me.

Mike's mouth opened and I held up a hand to forestall any questions, keeping the eerie melody threading through my lips. One minute … two … my lips started to become numb and my mouth began to dry out. Just when I was about to call it quits and grab the stash of cypress leaves to help with summoning, I felt the smallest of air sprites wind around my legs.

"What is needed, Magus?" it asked in its whispery windy voice.

In the Language of Air, which was a trilling whistle, I said, "*I ask that you reveal yourself to this human, O marvelous free one.*" Fickle, mercurial air sprites, of all the elementals, were the most susceptible to flattery.

"And why should I do this, Magus?"

"It would fill him with awe and terror at your majesty," I replied, laying it on thick as library paste.

I could almost feel the tiny sprite's ego swell. It slinked its way over to a fair amount of rubbish (beer bottles, caps, gum and candy wrapper, etc.) and began to spin them round, swirling, cavorting in a fit of garbage glee. Motes of dust and dirt joined the two-foot tall tornado as it frolicked and danced toward Mike, whose eyelids had disappeared behind their orbs.

"J-Jude … what … what …?" he gabbled, pointing at the whirling garbage.

Usually I could shave with Mike's wit, so you can imagine how pleased I felt watching his remarkable intellect say sayonara. As for the sprite, it was having the time of its life.

Then it said something that ripped the smile off my face. *"This one smells of the Creator."*

"What do you mean, O wise one?" I whistled back in surprise.

Its laughter was the rustle of a zephyr across long grass. *"Those who dedicate themselves to the service of the Creator always smell different … pure."*

Pure? The smell of God? Or was it the smell of God's magic?

"Tell him I will touch him now." Its tone was perfunctory, commanding.

Smiling, I said, "Mike, hold out your hands. Slowly, please."

Gulping, he did as he was told. The dirt, dust and rubbish fell to the asphalt in a heap. Leaping on the hapless priest, it swirled around his arms, moving faster and faster until his hands shook as if palsied.

"Jude, what's going on?"

"He's shaking your hands, man."

"What is this? What is it? It's not going to do anything … drastic, is it?"

"It's an air sprite and it's checking you out. It's curious, I don't think it's ever been this close to a priest before."

"What do you mean?" he asked, trying to keep his trembling hands under control. "How does it know I'm a priest?"

"Smell."

"It smells my priestliness?" His voice took on a ragged edge as he strove to maintain his composure.

The sprite disengaged, whirled around my legs a couple more times and flittered off, whistling its breezy laughter.

"Mike, to a person sensitive to magic, a magus, Elemental magic, all magic, has a … well … *smell* I guess is the correct word. Every magus experiences those smells differently. When I do a Healing, I smell cinnamon, but another magus might smell antiseptic or chocolate-chip cookies. Elementals have the same kind of sense, but for them it's much more keen. When it 'smelled' you, it said you smelled 'of the Creator.' God."

He stared at me for perhaps five seconds before turning around and walking inside. I hurried to catch up. "What's wrong?"

Large muscles bunched and unbunched as he threw his arms up in frustration. "What's wrong? You just whistled up what you told me is an air sprite and that you and it can *smell* my priestliness! Also, you did magic. *Magic. Magic!*"

"Saying the word more than once doesn't make it any less real, man."

He responded to my sarcasm with a dyspeptic glare. "*Magic*, Jude. Not what our lot really believes in or encounters on a day-to-day basis."

I raised my hands, trying to placate the big man. "*Elemental* magic, Mike. Neither good nor evil, it merely *is* … like the weather. Elementals know of God, they call him the Creator and respect him. It's *man* they really don't care for."

"Oh, this is heavy," he muttered, sitting on the edge of his bed. "Elemental magic … creatures outside my ken." He looked up, face drawn. "Traveling with you sure is interesting." After a moment, he narrowed his eyes. "How can you see those things?"

Sitting next to him, I leaned forward and rested my elbows on my thighs. "Magi can see what you normal people can't. It's part and parcel of the whole magus bit. And don't worry, man, it'll get stranger than this because there's a lot more to this world than you can possibly imagine. Some good, some evil, but most of it neither."

"I don't know if I can accept it. Oh, I believe it, but accepting it is another thing entirely. I was taught that magic is the exclusive realm of diabolical forces."

It took heroic self-control on my part not to point out that I looked upon exorcism as a Catholic rite of magic, but I didn't want to open that can of worms while he still reeled from the night's revelations. How would you take it?

Sighing, I chose my words carefully. "Mike, God created the world and all the spirits and sprites within. The magic in the plants, the elementals ... all created by God in His infinite wisdom. As for the Words, that I don't know."

"Words?"

"There are Words that do things ... magical things, like healing and such," I sighed. "There are twelve Words of Great Power that a Magus can use. Most only master three or four, but they can do much with those. An Adept can master up to nine and with those he can achieve wonders you wouldn't believe.

"But Mike, the real, evil magic—the magic that can corrupt a soul and shatter the world—is in the Thirty Words." I held up a clenched fist. "Thirty Words of such virulence and destruction that their origin can only be infernal."

Moments passed as the priest considered what I had said. "What are they?"

I shook my head. "No one knows, unless they have the Silver. The Silver holds the Words and conveys them to the Magus, but not all of them. One, two, maybe three Words are all a Magus can handle because they are too much ... too alien for his or her mind to hold on to. As soon as the Magus releases the Silver, the Words leave." Memories I had long tried to forget surfaced. "It takes a very special kind of Magus to hold more than three out of the Thirty Words, and God help the world if that happens."

"The Silver?"

Lord I was tired! So much had happened today and a rush of fatigue washed hard over me, giving me a good case of the dizzies. I rose to my feet to get my blood pumping while addressing my best, and only, friend. "Listen, everything you need to know is in that envelope I gave you, the whole damn story. Just read it, please man." Normally I'd be happy shooting the crap with Mike for the rest of the night, but his look of dismay, his crumbling sense of certainty was painful to watch. Plus, I was more than a little afraid of how he would react to what he would learn. "I'm going outside for a second, just wait for me, please."

Cold air nearly robbed the breath from my lungs as I stepped outside, the door narrowly missing my butt as it slammed. The small sprite had gone, no doubt bored with hanging around a motel parking lot. Everything seemed peaceful, but we needed protection—an early warning system—and I knew the perfect one.

Diamond stars sparkled above my head and long grass filled with cockleburs and goatheads lay beneath my feet, pricking the tough calluses of my soles. I knelt and dug my fingers into the grassy ground, reaching, searching for fertile earth. Deep, deep, deep I dug, nails scrabbling, until the skin of my fingers found cool topsoil. Perfect.

The Language of Earth rumbled forth bringing the aroma of fresh-cut summertime grass, a scent I've always loved.

On and on the rumble issued from my aching throat, floating in the air like leaves on a pond. Despite the pain, the strain on my vocal cords, Earth Speech had always been my favorite; the slow rolling cadences, the patient tumble of vowels and consonants, the utter tranquility of the enduring soil.

Rustling and tumbling, rocks, dozens, hundreds, rolled toward me across the Kansas flatland, crushing grass; many splitting the ground as they spat themselves out of the earth in a rocky parade toward my position.

A rock the size of my skull rumble-tumbled to a stop in front of me. Round and almost smooth on one end, the other side jagged and ragged like a wound. Soon a couple more joined it. Then more and more, the latecomers rolling up on top of the dozen or so big stones on the bottom. The rustle of grass became louder and louder as an ever-increasing flurry of smaller rocks bounced my way and clacked to the top of the growing pile of stones. Within minutes it resembled a cairn, then the tall cast-offs you'd see at a quarry, before settling itself into an imposing ten-foot-high pile that loomed over my head.

Small stones shifted and moved in ways that defied gravity as the being—an Earth elemental—pressed its regard against my skin. *"You have called, Olivier Magus, and I have come,"* it thundered in the Language of Earth, a clackety rumble that shook bone. The fresh-cut lawn scent was nearly overpowering.

I blinked in surprise. *"You know me?"*

"All earth is connected, all stones and rock remember. You have talked to us before."

That was years ago! *"Good memory."*

Rubbly laughter. "Water has no memory, it only carves and babbles, while Air is flighty and Fire does not care, but Earth, dear Magus, Earth always remembers."

"Enemies search for me," I began. "Protection is needed. I would appreciate it if you could guard over our dwelling until the light of morning."

"Olivier Deschamps, your elder searches and has asked Earth for assistance."

Okay, that news hit like an ice water enema. Certainly set my stomach looking for destinations south. *"Julian?"*

"Yes, your elder, your brood sire. He has demanded that Earth search ceaselessly until you are found. He was quite adamant."

"How long ago was this?"

"What is time to stone and rock? What we perceive as gentle passing you humans see as ages come and gone, the rise and fall of what you call civilizations. To the round world, your species has barely begun."

Wasn't that a comforting thought? Mankind has always prided itself on being on the tippy-top of the food chain and it was a bit off-putting to realize that there existed those that not only might be a few links up from you, but outside the whole damn chain as well.

"Will you tell my ... brood sire my location?" I asked, more than a little uneasy. Things were worse than I thought.

"The brood sire Julian has no respect for Earth. He rages, demands and rails against It in ways that are unseemly. Had we been Fire and Air, his life would be forfeit. The Earth will not abide by his desires."

"Thank you."

"Your thanks are not necessary for you are respectful. Earth knows this, Magus. You will be protected until the light of the sun touches this place." With that the giant mound of stone and soil began to rattle, creaking and clattering, finally sinking out of sight.

With a sigh, I went inside, eager to sleep, but first I had to put more holy water into the fish bowl.

Chapter Five

Mike

Oh Lord, did I ever need a good slug of bourbon. Magic! Can you believe it? What Jude had showed me cracked the foundations of my reality. Elementals, Words, Silver … all these ran together in a jibber-jabber mishmash of nonsense as I attempted to absorb the enormity of the night's revelations.

Only one thing could ease my mind … prayer. My rosary slipping around my knuckles, I knelt and clasped my hands. I cast my mind out for a prayer to aid me in this situation and found that I couldn't think of anything. I drew a blank. At least three, perhaps four, minutes passed before the words of St. Alcuin of York came to mind. A prayer for comfort and strength:

> Give me O Lord, I pray Thee, firm faith, unwavering hope, perfect charity. Pour into my heart the Spirit of wisdom and understanding, the Spirit of counsel and spiritual strength, the Spirit of knowledge and true godliness and the Spirit of Thy holy fear. Light eternal, deliver me from evil …

That night I tossed and turned; sleep managed to evade me, chased away by a heady cocktail of adrenaline, fear and confusion that prayer was unable to dissipate. How was I going to resolve my faith and the use, not to mention the very existence of, magic?

I did get a few fitful winks in here and there, just enough to make me feel worse. In fact, my body felt so abused that I had Jude drive south on the 77, hooking up with the 35 to Wichita and down into Oklahoma.

"St. Stephen's going to be okay without you?" Jude asked suddenly after yawning hard enough to crack his jaw.

"Hm? Oh, yes," I replied, staring out the window at the miles of rich farm and pastureland. Black Angus cattle moved listlessly behind barbed wire fencing. "Fathers Anthony and Ray will carry on just fine. I wish you had let me call instead of leaving a note telling them I had to leave due to an emergency."

Jude snorted. "Not hardly. Couldn't take the chance, man. If you stop fiddling with that envelope and read what's inside, you'll understand why."

I gave voice to what was eating at me. "Little scared here, Jude. No, that's not right ... I'm a *lot* scared."

"Please Mike, just read it, okay?"

Hiding my amusement at how very American he sounded compared to that young, frightened man I'd met all those years ago, I opened the envelope (creased and frayed from my nervous hands) and pulled out a sheaf of cream-colored paper. Sighing, I began to read.

Family and Other Unsavory Things

If you were born into, say, the Ku Klux Klan and everything was 'nigger' this and 'spic' that, 'kike, lesbo, faggot, dago' etc., etc., all your life, would you think of yourself as a bigot? Let us consider the ancient Romans; they kept slaves with no pangs of conscience. To them a slave was something to be used, like a condom, and that attitude was *normal,* commonplace. Today if you talked about keeping a slave you'd be regarded as dangerous or criminal.

These are questions you should ask yourself before reading further because when you hear the details of my life, my upbringing, you may find my people to be almost as alien to your western culture as the Yanomamö tribe of the Amazon rainforest.

To start at the very beginning, I'd have to go back about two thousand years. My story begins in 1975, when I was born. That, however, is of no real interest, not even to me. Let's begin fifteen years later, 1990, the decade the Soviet Union fell so hard it bounced.

Fifteen is a cool age. Hormones rush through your veins with more potency than black tar heroin and time is your dearest friend because even a month seems like an age. Fifteen is a good place to start. Fifteen was the year I learned how to use Words.

"All right class," Professor Von Andor had said, holding several sheets of smooth white paper in one veiny, liver-spotted hand. His speech was precise, clipped, and delivered with a faint German accent, giving it an air of authority. "These are the Words. They are what you've been waiting for." Pale blue eyes under bushy white brows took us in. At over seventy, the Professor still stood as ramrod straight as he had as a young man in the Waffen SS. Steel-gray hair clipped to a savage crew cut bristled over his shiny scalp and a sharp nose hooked over near invisible lips. Wrinkles formed by both displeasure and spite bracketed both his eyes and mouth.

Switzerland in summer and the five of us were stuck in class, despite the perfect day—seventy-two degrees Fahrenheit (or about twenty-two degrees Celsius, which is how I measured temperature at the time) with small fluffy white clouds scudding across the sky and Lac Léman beckoning only a hundred yards away. Julian, my father, had a large estate near the lake, a summer home to retreat to from the office. Not that he ever used it for that purpose. Instead of retreating from the world, he had it converted to a school for members of the family who exhibited certain … talents.

On that occasion, the five of us who stood in the large, rather Spartan basement were learning our first Words and we couldn't be more excited. That five consisted of my half-brothers Henri, Julian II, Philip and myself, along with cousin Burke, who at that time displayed all the classic signs of teenaged angst and rebellion.

As the youngest to display an aptitude for magic, I was considered to be quite the prodigy, having already learned the Language of Air and Fire as well as coming along nicely with Water. Also, I had completed all the requisite courses in Botanical Magic far ahead of schedule. I learned so quickly, in fact, that Julian decided to lump me in with the other boys to see if I would sink or swim. And by sink, I mean die. Painfully.

In the Family there are many rules, but Rule #1 was: Survival of the Fittest. Julian Deschamps, billionaire businessman, enforced that rule with all the fanaticism of a tin-pot dictator in a third-world country. That is to say, brutally, savagely and without pity.

Training for Family began at the age of three. We went to school every day, given an education by the most talented, the most qualified private tutors money could buy, and a few who were lured by less savory means. By the age of ten you were either a cast-off (don't ask, not pleasant) or a graduate, receiving the equivalent of an American high school diploma. By the age of twelve you were expected to have finished the equivalent of a four-year University degree. It was at that point (generally puberty) that, if you were male, you either showed a talent for magic or you went directly into the business side of the Family. Either way, training in wet-work came next.

Male or female, at the age of twelve you were fair game, a target for your contemporaries, a sort of free-for-all training in assassination and survival. The one amendment to Rule #1 was: It must look natural or like an accident. No weapons, no obvious foul play. It was a lesson in subtlety and discretion, care and vigilance. By the time I'd reached my thirteenth birthday, I'd survived three attempts at poisoning and a balcony railing that had mysteriously corroded overnight. The only true safety from siblings came when they reached their majority, the time when they must cease all assassination attempts.

Does this sound terrible? To us kids, it was business as usual, the price of living in the lap of near-obscene luxury. Grow up fast or grow dead faster. And despite how brutal it seemed, being born female was worse, far worse. Mike sometimes calls me a misogynistic prick, and

I guess I am, but he's never met the Family, and God willing, he never will.

But I digress, so let's toddle off back to earlier in the narrative, magic training. Elemental magic takes years to master, but thanks to my facility, I blazed through at three times the normal speed. At age fifteen I was the youngest in my class.

The Professor handed us our assignments, twelve sheets of paper each, face down. "Here are the twelve Words," he intoned with somber intensity. "Healing, Force, Forgetting, Vigor, Avoidance, Strength, Truth, Vision, Clarity, Aspect, Pain, and The Walls. Arranged from easiest to most difficult, the Words will reveal themselves as they will, each according to your natures and aptitudes. Do not force understanding; it will do you no good."

Henri, a big brown-haired burly boy of seventeen, impatiently riffled through the papers before the Professor even finished. A scowl was fixed on his wide, brutish face. Of my three half-brothers, he was the one I hated most because of his boorishness and love of casual cruelty.

Julian II and Philip, the redheaded twins, turned their papers over in unison, thin faces pinched in thought and trepidation. Not only did they look the same, but their dispositions were identical as well, making them seem the same person split into two bodies.

Burke, well ... Burke is ... Burke. Brave, hard, fearsome, and a natural predator, a shark in human skin. He scared the ever-loving shit out of me. As a cousin on the distaff side, he was forbidden to seek my life, but that sure didn't stop him from torturing me at every opportunity, which was often. At sixteen and a few inches taller than myself, he showed an aptitude for magic not seen in his branch of the family since Vlad Tepes began his terrible rule of Wallachia in 1456. Julian had high hopes for Burke, who demonstrated the kind of ruthlessness most prized in my Family.

"I see the Words of Strength and Vigor," said Henri, a wide smile on his coarse features.

Well, shit ... my insides tried to make a beeline for the soles of my feet. Giving Henri more strength would be like pouring gasoline on a bonfire. It would only fuel the flames of his loutish, ham-handed ways.

As for the twins, their faces lit up with glee. "We have Aspect, Clarity and Vision!" they cried. Three Words, ones both could use with great subtlety, enough that they could possibly succeed in taking my life.

Burke, however, merely riffled through the pages, mouth twisted in what might be called both a smile and a snarl, and kept his peace.

"Speak up, Burke," the Professor said calmly. When he snapped his fingers under my cousin's nose to get his attention, Burke looked up, anger flaring in his dark eyes.

"Healing, Forgetting, Vigor, Avoidance, Clarity and Pain." That stopped everyone cold, shock rippling through all of us. Six Words! There hadn't been a holder of six Words since Rodrigo Borgia, who used his Words to help him become Pope Alexander the VI, the most corrupt and scandalous Christian religious figure of all time.

At that moment my fear of the twins disappeared in a flash because, even though Julian forbade Burke's hand in any assassination attempts, my cousin hated me enough that he could not stop himself from trying.

"What about you, Olivier?" The Professor's deep voice startled me out of my woolgathering.

Nodding quickly, I scanned the thick white papers in my hands, which had begun to tremble slightly. Each paper held a Word written in what I now know to be a mixture of squid ink, black hellbore and knotweed, a Botanical Magic brew. My eyes skittered over the first page, not wanting to acknowledge the black writing. In fact, for a second it seemed that there was no Word at all, just a blank page. Then it hit me like a pickaxe to the skull ... the Word. It crawled right in and made itself at home in my cerebral cortex, shoving aside non-essentials like Latin and Swedish.

Imagine someone using Vicks VapoRub on your brain ... that's what it felt like.

Page Two: it hit me the same way—hard and fast with a mental taste of tinfoil.

Three … four … five … *Wham! Wham! Wham!*

Done. I was done and the pages fell to the bare concrete around my Air Jordans. Twelve Words. I had all twelve Words rolling around my mind and I'm pretty sure I'd lost all functional use of Romanian.

Whoa …

"Well?" Henri asked, grabbing my black t-shirt in one huge hairy fist.

Okay … Risk Assessment Time. Henri's big pug-ugly loomed into view and in my peripheral Burke and the twins were staring at me speculatively. If I copped to all twelve it would be the same as painting a Day-Glo bull's-eye on my back and there would be no chance of dodging all of their attempts.

Good thing lying is second nature in my Family.

"Healing."

Silence. Five pairs of eyes met mine, incredulous. It was Burke who broke the tension by erupting in a full-throated belly laugh that shook his slender frame from head to toe. As if a new Word had been spoken, the Word of Mirth, it spread to my siblings quickly, doubling them over with laughter until they gasped for breath, hands to the hitching stitches in their sides.

"Very funny, assholes," I grumbled softly, but loud enough so they would hear and it set them to laughing again. The Day-Glo bull's-eye began to fade. I hid my smile in the palms of my hands.

"Oh, that's rich," Henri gasped. "Julian will be fit to burst. His precious prodigy can only Heal!"

During the laugh-fest, Burke had kept his eyes on me and I think he was probably taken in like the others, but I knew my supposed deficiency wouldn't stop him from tormenting me every chance he could. With the arrogance of six Words, he might find the balls to defy Julian and try for a kill.

Right then I knew that someday it would come down to him and me.

ဆ

I set the pages down on my lap, stunned, confused and more than a little afraid. If what Jude, or Olivier, whoever he was, had written here was true, then what other strange, menacing magics were out there? Who was his father, Julian Deschamps, and why would he let his children kill each other off? If it was all some sort of delusion, then a madman drove my car through Oklahoma into Texas.

"Remember, Mike, to me … all that was perfectly normal. I didn't know any other sort of life," Jude commented sadly, as if reading my thoughts.

I licked my lips. "It's unbelievable, but I saw what you did with that … that … air sprite, so I guess it's no great stretch to … this." I held up the envelope. "Now what?"

"Read the story."

"It's the strangest dang thing I've ever read, Jude … or do I call you Olivier?"

He made a face. "Olivier Deschamps wasn't someone you'd want to know, man. and I'm glad he's dead."

"But you *are* Olivier Deschamps."

Eyes sere and barren of hope glanced my way. "For both our sakes, man, you better hope not."

Chapter Six

Jude

Mike was shaken down to the roots. Oh, he hid it well, but I could see; we'd been friends long enough that I had his tells down pat. If he'd been a poker player, I'd have cleaned him out ages ago.

The Corolla chugged its way through Oklahoma and at Oklahoma City I switched off the 35 to the 44, taking us to Wichita Falls, Texas. As drives went, it rated up there with watching the grass grow. Mike was no help. He kept his eyes closed as though asleep or attempting to absorb what he'd read and seen.

Did I feel sorry for him? Almost. He may be a Catholic priest, but he's also one tough son-of-a-gun. The only thing that had kept him from becoming an outlaw biker was his calling, his faith.

He thought I didn't know about his wild side, but thanks to the Internet, I had found out a lot about Mr. Mike Engel, the Catholic priest. No father, mother dead of a heroin overdose when he was nineteen, one older sister—whereabouts unknown—and a stint in the army at eighteen to avoid jail time for boosting a motorcycle. Hoofed it over the sands in Desert Storm, ended his time in service with a couple of years in Germany. Finally, the call to God.

By all rights he should have exited the army a raving lunatic, hell-bent on wreaking havoc and drinking himself to death, but I guess he took to discipline in the service because he emerged straight as an arrow and left his past behind. Although he did keep a 1985 Harley FXWG 1340 Wide Glide in his garage that he'd been restoring for the past couple of years, a lingering reminder of his younger self.

The rest is, as they say, is history.

It ate at me, though, that I had let him come. Maybe the desire for company had overwhelmed common sense or maybe, better yet, he was the one man who might understand my whole sordid history. Hell, he helped me parse through the more difficult passages of the Bible (the Song of Solomon bored me to *tears*) and explained the Americanisms and obscure references in *East of Eden*.

"Where are we going, Jude?"

Mike's question derailed my train of thought. "West Texas." He was still leaning back, envelope in his lap and eyes closed.

"What's in west Texas?"

"A whole lot of nothing."

"Then why?"

I grinned. "It's what's under that nothing that I want to get at."

"What's under that nothing?" he asked patiently as Wichita Falls receded in my review mirror.

There was no harm in spilling the beans. "After I established myself in Omaha, I traveled all over America to secure some spookers."

"Spookers?" Mikes eyes cracked open and he stared at the surrounding countryside without interest.

"Stores of cash and false papers, just in case."

"In case you had to go on the lam?"

I laughed. "Lam? Who talks like that? Really, Mike, you should stop watching television. Rots your brain, man."

His icy blues rolled up. "You still haven't answered my question, smart aleck."

"Yes, in case I had to leg it. Passports, driver's licenses, cash, the whole lot. Enough to disappear again and land comfortably on my feet."

Mike snorted. "How very CIA-like of you."

"You've read a bit of what my Family is like, Mike," I said, voice cooling to just above absolute zero. "They would do, and spend, anything to find me, to get what I have."

"That silver thing of yours?"

"Yes, the Silver. One of the most powerful magical artifacts in the world, second only to the Grail and the Arc of the Covenant."

The explosion of incredulity I half expected didn't come. When I spared a glance from the road, it was to see Mike staring at me with eyes colder and more pitiless than the spaces between the stars.

"What?"

"The Arc of the Covenant? The Grail? Like the real ones, the ones Indiana Jones found?" The arctic tundra was warmer than his voice.

"When I left the Family, I liquidated my assets and I've used a lot of that to find something that would help me destroy the Silver."

"What about throwing it in the Laurentian Abyss?"

The vanishing point met my eyes as I answered. "You could stuff the Silver in a lead-lined box with a nuclear warhead set to detonate when it hit the ocean floor and you wouldn't even scratch it. It would reappear where someone in the Family would find it. No, the only way to destroy the Silver is to use a more powerful artifact."

Mike stayed quiet for quite some time, so long, in fact, that I began to worry. Finally he said, "So you're trying to destroy this silver thing by using an artifact that people have been trying to locate for centuries? Perhaps millennia?"

"Yes, Mike, I have to because the Silver is the biggest threat to mankind next to global thermonuclear war. It needs to go away and I should have investigated more thoroughly and taken action sooner." Regret tasted bitter in my throat. "Because I twigged onto the Grail six months ago."

A long pause. "Why didn't you?"

I exploded in a rush of verbal self-recrimination. "Damn me, Mike … I was too comfortable, man." When he didn't reply, I continued. "And maybe a little scared, too. Nebraska isn't the center of the universe, but it's a good place to be." Better, I felt much better. Maybe confession *was* good for the soul.

Mike stroked his moustache "So that's where we're going? To get the Grail?" I nodded and he blew a sigh through his lips. "The Archbishop will never believe this."

"I really wouldn't tell him if I were you."

Once again that cold stare. "Why?"

"The Family has … people in the Vatican."

I reckon that all the shocks to Mike's system must have aged him about five years, but he held strong, much stronger than most. What really touched me was his belief, not just in God, but also in me. He believed me and *in* me with no ulterior motives. I could see it in his honest features. Maybe God had put Mike in my way that day all those years ago at St. Stephen's and if He had, I owed Him big time.

Mike sat there in the passenger seat, idly rubbing his moustache and sucking absently on his front teeth, making a *ssssk sssskk* sound that would normally have driven me nuts, but for some reason didn't bother me at all in the moment. Then he pulled a rosary out of his pocket and began to pray.

Not big on prayer, myself. I always reckoned that God knew what I was up to, and he was busy enough without having to listen to my jibber-jabber. But, in the spirit of respect and fellowship, I kept my trap shut until Mike was done and had put the rosary back in his pocket.

"Listen," I began, reaching into the cup holder next to the hand brake for the open packet of peanut M&Ms I'd placed there earlier—my favorite munchies. Only the strict discipline I'd learned over the years kept me from gaining two hundred pounds. "In 1998 I'd traced a valuable artifact to Chicago, to a private collector named Mori Munakata, a wealthy real-estate investor who made serious money during the wild speculation of that time. Seems it was lumped together with other items of perceived greater value and he acquired the lot by rather dubious means.

"Without going into specifics that could be used against me in a court of law, I managed to liberate the artifact from his private vault and bring it to Omaha."

"I remember!" Mike interjected. "You said you went to Disney World. You lied to me, Jude."

"Well, just a little white lie. For your own protection, man."

Again he rolled his eyes, clearly unhappy.

"What I got was called the First Tablet. Ever heard of it?"

"I wasn't in school the day they taught 'Arcane Archeology.' "

"Just shows that you're a slacker. How about the history of writing, its invention?"

"Mesopotamia, right?"

Not bad. Mike was better read than I thought. "Until 1998 that was the conventional wisdom, however writing at the tomb King Scorpion of Abydos near Luxor was found dating back to 3400 B.C.E., four hundred years before Mesopotamian writing."

"Sounds like a bad movie starring The Rock."

I laughed. "In Pakistan, 1999, at the ancient site of Harappa, archeologists discovered writing that dated back to 3500 B.C.E. and that's generally considered to be the earliest known instance."

"How come I have a feeling that's not the case?"

M&Ms *crunched* between my teeth and I savored the peanut/chocolate flavor before I answered. "Because your instincts are sharp, man. The very first example of the written word was a stone tablet, about three-foot tall, that dated back to 5500 B.C.E., created by an unsavory character who *invented* writing so he could record his confession to God."

"What? Are you saying that there's written proof of writing that's over *seven thousand years old*? And proof that man worshipped God so long ago? Do you understand the significance of that?" he blurted, expression eager. Despite what he'd learned on this trip, this news seemed to shake him the most. Not surprising, though. Most people equate the formal worship of God to the Hebrews a little over three thousand years ago. Adding four thousand years to the mix would be a serious blow to the Agnostics and Atheists and would stand the religious community on its head.

"Sorry, but no one can read it. The language is unique and unknown. No Rosetta Stone to help translate, man."

"Then how do you know what it says?"

"Good question. Shows you're paying attention." *Crunch, crunch, crunch.* Whoever invented peanut M&Ms should be canonized. "The holder of Tablet understands all languages written and spoken."

"Sounds useful."

"More than *useful*. Imagine touching the Tablet and looking at a line of computer code. You'd understand it all. It's the Holy Grail for hackers, pardon the pun, and Munakata was using it to suss out his competition by hacking into their systems. Doubled his holdings in one year."

Mike snagged the green M&M I held between my fingertips and I felt a twinge of irritation … green ones are my favorite. "That is quite powerful, especially in this day and age where everything is computerized." He popped the M&M into his mouth and chewed. "So you said it was a recording of a confession to God. What did that person confess and who was it?"

And the hits just keep on coming. "Cain."

"Cain?"

"Yes."

"As in Cain and Abel?"

"Yes."

"Really?"

"Really."

"Cain?"

"You said that already."

"I know … it's still not digesting."

So I gave him a few minutes to absorb while I finished off the M&Ms. Thankfully there were still several green ones left. *Crunch, crunch, crunch.*

"Where is this revelatory Tablet then, Jude?'

I sighed. "Gone, Mike, gone. The reason I liberated it was because there might have been a slight chance that a much older artifact could destroy a more powerful one like the Silver." My voice trailed off.

"And?"

Well, damn. "It broke. I placed the bag that contained the Silver onto the Tablet and it shattered into a million pieces. Was combing pieces of seven thousand year old stone artifact out of my hair for days, man."

Not a peep out of Mike. I risked a glance out of the corner of my eye to see him staring at me and I began to sweat. When a Catholic priest starts giving you the old stink-eye, it really sets you back on your heels. Don't believe me? Give it a try. Bet you don't last two seconds before you get damp under the collar.

Mike took a long breath. "Are you telling me that you shattered one of the most valuable religious relics of all time ... on a hunch it would destroy this Silver of yours?"

"You're angry, aren't you?"

"Whatever gave you that idea?" he asked acidly.

He wasn't getting it. "I'm trying to rid the world of an extremely powerful, malevolent artifact here, man. Things happen ... magical artifacts break, you know."

"Harrumph!"

Great ... I'd been 'harrumphed' by a priest.

"Well," he said at last. "At least it proves that God created man a lot later than the archeologists thought."

Uh-oh. "Hm ... not quite, Mike."

His eyes speared me through the forehead. "What do you mean?"

"When God cursed Cain, giving him the Mark, forcing him to wander the earth and know no peace, he also cursed him with immortality. Cain had wandered for more than forty thousand years before creating the Tablet."

Mike just closed his eyes and rubbed his temples like he was trying to massage away a headache.

The Corolla stayed quiet as a tomb all the way to Midland, Texas, home of oil barons and the only skyline in that part of the state. Its sister city, Odessa, was the armpit of the Permian Basin, boasting only oil and an outstanding high-school football team. Other than that, it was the heart of darkness.

Late lunch, or an early dinner, came from Wienerschnitzel, where I ate greasiest, tastiest Polish sausage known to man. God bless

America. Mike ate three, slurping them down with a diet soda, and I could swear I heard his arteries hardening.

After filling the Corolla with gas, we headed out on Highway 20 westbound straight into the middle of miles of nothing except heat blasted white sand dotted with sad-looking scrub. A few small, worn hills provided the only change in altitude I could see and a single railroad track paralleled the highway, passing through the bleached and windswept bones of old towns that had once tried to suckle the milk of prosperity provided by a defunct railway.

The sun began to set before we reached the 10 to El Paso and pulled over onto the shoulder. Even though the Corolla's air conditioner barely functioned and the sun had just kissed the horizon, the outside air scorched my lungs dry as I took a deep breath. Just like I remembered.

"At least it's a dry heat," Mike joked as he fanned himself.

Wow … humor. He must have mellowed out about the Tablet. I tossed him a cheeky grin through the sweat beading on my lips and he returned it with interest. Good. We were all right again.

"If you're up for another display of Elemental magic," I remarked offhandedly, "then come on. Otherwise stay with the car. I won't be long."

"Oh, I wouldn't miss this for all the tea in China," he said.

"Be careful what you wish for, man, because I really don't want to freak you out any more than I have already."

"I don't think I can freak out any more, kid."

The sand and scrub absorbed my laughter. "Oh, Mike, you have no idea." My toe connected with a stone that looked to be half fossil while I wiped the sweat from my brow. "The world is filled with magics that the ordinary person never gets to see or is unprepared to see."

Mike stared out at the barren landscape, drinking in its desolation. After a moment the corner of his mouth crooked upward. He laughed softly at my look of annoyance. "It is my job as a priest to believe in things we don't or can't see, so I think I am doing well." A longer pause, then, "Why don't you keep your spooker in a safety deposit box?"

I glanced toward the sun half hidden by the horizon and throwing orange and red light into the darkening sky. "I put it somewhere safer than a mere bank."

By the time the last rays faded Mike and I had trekked about a mile from the Corolla. I whispered a Word and the night resolved itself into brilliant hues of green, gold and red, a psychedelic mash of colors. My hand found Mike's shoulder and I whispered the same Word in his ear. Vision always smelled of apples. Apple and pears.

With a muffled curse he stopped abruptly and crossed himself. Muttering an apology to God for the language, he rounded on me. "What did you do, Jude?" He rubbed his eyes. "Was this one of your Words?"

"Vision," I affirmed.

"Why the blazes didn't you warn me?" he ground out.

"Because you wouldn't have let me and then you would've spent the rest of our time out here hot, miserable and stumbling in the dark."

Grumble, grumble ...

"What was that?"

"I said, next time warn me!" he shot back. "You scared the ... wits out of me."

"But you can see, right?"

Mike craned his neck, sweeping his eyes across the sky then back to earth as he drank in this new vision. The flesh of his face went slack with shock. "Holy moley," he breathed in awe, crossing himself.

"That's Vision for you," I told him. "Gives you sight for distance, dark and even under water if needed, man. Pretty useful."

My home-grown holy roller continued to gawp at our tri-colored surroundings as I turned round in an effort to orient myself. Trying to find a specific spot in the middle of a west Texas empty was your basic needle-in-a-haystack exercise.

I knew I was in the right place, but even though the area hadn't changed much, it *had* changed. Fourteen years had passed since my trek around America hiding my spookers. Everywhere I turned the same vista met my eyes: sand, scrub and rocks.

"Must be going crazy," I muttered under my breath.

Mike piped up. "Talking to yourself is the first sign of a serious mental illness, you know," he agreed.

"Shut up, you," I retorted … quietly. Once again I eyeballed the landscape and still couldn't find a reference point other than a weather-beaten hill near where we had parked. I noticed that hill the first time because of the notch on top that made it look as if some Jurassic beast had given it a nibble.

Nothing for it but to try something a little more drastic. The Word slipped out of my mouth before I knew it. Clarity was one of the more subtle magics, but horribly effective in the right circumstances. And, for some reason, Clarity smelled like bacon to me.

Accompanied by a swirling sensation all my perceptions altered slightly and my thoughts contracted to a single, bright laser pinpoint. With Clarity you can recall anything, all memories in perfect detail without the stain of time's inevitable varnish. The storage lockers of my mind opened with a clatter to let all those old dusty recollections air out.

The hill, yes, the hill came back with a brilliantly sharp intensity that took my breath away. An image of how the land used to look superimposed itself on what it looked like now and, startled, I realized how much it *had* changed. Wind had scoured the sands over and around shrubs, while the occasional rainfall dug small ravines that were filled in again by the hot wind.

Footfalls that had scuffed across the landscape years ago came afresh to my ears, and the path I had taken renewed itself, bringing the old depressions in the sand into hard focus.

My feet led the way with no urging from the rest of me. I saw in the Clarity of the moment that I'd been off by a couple dozen yards … not too bad considering the amount of time that had passed.

There it was. I spied with my little eye something that began with 'B.' What in the past had been a large, white, humpy, craggy boulder turned out to be a patch of rock barely sticking up out of the sand, blasted and glowing red in my Vision.

Slowly I crouched a few feet away and dug my fingers into the warm sand near a shoulder-high, musky, earthy-smelling scrub.

The rattling, clackety Language of Earth ushered forth from my throat, tumbling out to land on the surface of the ragged rock. Almost immediately it vibrated, raising a cloud of dust and grit that tickled my nose.

"*Back so soon, scion of the Sicarii,*" rumbled the stone as it began to rise out of the ground, shedding sand and insects.

"*I am not of them, not for a long time.*" My voice was dry as the seared air, while the ground trembled beneath my feet.

"*Long time you say? Hardly such, I was not even fully covered.*" Humor belled through the boulder's voice in an explosion of subsonic mirth. When the rock finished rising, it stood far above my head, a scarred monolith leaning over far enough that I felt a twinge of fear for my precious self.

"*The box, you still have it?*" I asked through the smell of cut grass.

"Of course. Do you want it back?"

"Please."

Crack! The boulder split from top to bottom, a wide fissure yawning open and spitting out a black metal rectangle the size of a shoebox. It tumbled to the ground at my feet, landing with a heavy *thump!*

No seam, no hinge … nothing, just an iron box with a small handle welded to the long side. Leaning over I grasped the handle and put some starch into lifting the thing, which weighed a good fifty pounds. "*Thank you.*"

"A task to keep such a thing as crafted Earth safe is no task at all, considering the short amount of time served. I promised you a task, Sicarius, but it was over too soon. Some information, then, to help you."

"*I am no longer of the Sicarii,*" I clacked back, the hated name proving more than a little irksome.

"To the Sicarii you were born. Of the Sicarrii you will always be, whether you desire the name or not. Remember this, though:

Forgetful Water seeks you and Water talks. It always talks. It will never be quiet and will never stop searching, despite its dreamy, absentminded nature. Your brood sire has made sure."

"Why didn't you tell me earlier, when I summoned you in Kansas?"

"You did not ask."

"It is information I could have used then. Why tell me now? And how did Julian get Water to do his bidding?"

The elemental began to sink into the sandy soil, slowly disappearing. "You were owed. As for your brood sire, he has come into possession of Primal Water and has used it to make a bargain with all Water for its release."

Primal Water? One of the First Four Elementals? So ancient they had no language. Those First Ones were created by God and imbued with His divine spark. The knowledge that Julian had found Primal Water sent a shiver down my spine.

Before the boulder could vanish, I asked, "When did he find one of the Old Ones? When did he make his bargain?"

It was strange, hearing the grating Language of Earth grow soft. "A very short time ago. Not even long to humans. Less than a cycle of rain in this desert."

So, perhaps a few months back. That would explain how I was found. Wherever I had touched water, be it a puddle or a swimming pool, Water would know and inform Julian.

Water talks.

Chapter Seven

Mike

While watching a crooked pillar thrust itself out of the sand and growl at Jude, who growled in return, I kept worrying that my heart would stop. It's not every day that you hang around and chin-wag with the local geology. The strange thing about the whole incident was how used to it I was becoming.

Heck, the nighttime world had been rendered in glorious shades of green, red and gold, thanks to the Vision Word thingy, spell … whatever. Imagine looking at green sky with pinpoints of gold! A little garish for my taste, but nonetheless breathtaking. Who knew that three colors could combine to create such an amazing amount of variation?

My eyes still wandered over the landscape while Jude chatted up the talking rock, and I nearly jumped out of my skin at the sound of it splitting open and spitting out what looked like a black shoebox. For a while Jude talked to it in that strange tongue (it sounded like he was gargling with gravel); then it sank back into the ground.

Swinging the heavy box in one hand, Jude hustled us both back to the car. "I'll drive us to El Paso, man. We'll get a hotel room there."

In Kansas, Jude had said that El Paso 'was like Milwaukee, but without the charm.' I've been to Milwaukee … I was less than thrilled.

Lucky for me we arrived in the middle of the night, so the electric lights made the town glow with faerie fire and hid its less admirable face.

"El Paso might be a black hole," Jude said as we pulled into the parking lot of a Motel 9, "but it's a heck of a lot better than Juarez."

Our room in the motel was a little bigger than the one in Kansas, but the mattresses must have come from the same supplier because they were similarly hard as rocks.

While Jude took the first turn in the shower, I grabbed the manila envelope and crushed my backside on the bed's hard surface. Printer paper slid into my palms and I began to read.

The Happy Voice

It took weeks for me to adjust to the Words rattling around my cranium, the feeling of power they gave me. Meanwhile, my half-brothers and Burke contented themselves with verbal torment, but the assassination attempts had stopped, at least for a while. For the first time in years I found no taint of poison in my food or drink, no tripwires at the head of stairs and no weakened balcony railings. I had become irrelevant in their eyes, but that didn't stop me from exercising caution. There was no telling when they would grow tired of my presence and try erase me from the world.

Professor von Andor trained us in the uses of the Words. I do not know who had taught him because he was Wordless, yet he knew all about their uses—how intonation, inflection, volume and intent shape the power of the Words, shape their efficacy.

Of course the only Word I admitted to was Healing, the only one I could practice in front of the others lest they realize my deceit. Being the simplest of all Words to master, it required only volume to increase or decrease its potency. Strangely enough, despite the ease of use, it was the most practical Word of all. Nothing like breaking your arm and Healing it to convince oneself of that fact. Despite its usefulness, however, the one thing it could not do was regenerate lost tissue. You lose an arm; you've lost an arm, no take-backs.

I practiced the other Words on my own, within the confines of my room—in the walk-in closet with clothes taped to the walls to muffle any noise. I needn't have worried; the others were practicing in their own rooms and I doubted they would have heard a stampede of elephants considering the racket they made.

So, in the darkness of my closet, I rolled those Words around in my mouth like marbles, spitting them out with different inflections at different volumes, noting their effects and committing those effects to memory. Some Words, such as The Walls (which protects the magus' mind from tampering) could not be practiced alone; I needed others to hone my facility with them. Others like Aspect, Vigor, Strength and Clarity had effects that were readily apparent. Thankfully the others masked the smell of my magic as they exercised their own Words.

The Professor often chose me as a guinea pig so Burke could practice Forgetting. Depending on the volume and inflection, Forgetting had the potential to erase a full day's worth of memories. An Adept could fine-tune the Word to make the target Forget as little as the last five seconds.

"What?" I asked when I noticed everybody staring at me, wrinkling my nose at the smell of black licorice.

"Very good, Burke, you are down to ten seconds." The Professor's normally dry, avuncular voice contained a measure of satisfaction.

Had our Family been what passes for normal, Henri and the twins would have cheered Burke's accomplishment, but instead they glowered and looked uncomfortable.

"It worked then?" I asked.

"Indeed," the Professor stated. "He is progressing nicely."

A phone rang upstairs and the Professor slowly ascended the stairs to answer, leaving me in the basement with my half-brothers and Burke.

"Well, Olivier," Henri began, advancing slowly toward me in a half shamble. "You're pretty good at Healing, but what is Julian going to do with you now that you've got just one Word?" Dull malice filled his cow eyes.

Moving slowly so as not to spook the relatives, I reached into the front pocket of my black Levi's and pulled out a piece of wax paper folded many times. The twins and Burke moved in close to see what I had.

"Well, Henri, it's a good thing I've excelled at Botanical Magic," I said offhandedly as I unfolded the paper. In the center lay a sticky patch of grayish paste. I scooped a bit with a forefinger and applied it behind my ears like perfume. "Because now I can craft a defense against magic."

I experienced an immense feeling of satisfaction as realization registered on the faces of Burke and the twins. It took Henri a while longer to get my drift. They could try to use their Words against me, but it would do them little good if I were protected.

Henri moved closer, his breath foul in my nostrils. "You think you're so smart, do you little Olivier? Well, let me tell you something … as a near Wordless runt, you are of no interest to Julian. You're out of the running, little brother. Not even worth killing." His hands clenched and unclenched. I know he wanted to thrash me then and there, but the rules barred his way.

I laughed in his face, which mottled with fury. "Maybe so, *brother*, but he'll still have a use for me. Most likely to take care of his wet-work."

The assassins of the Sicarii (or Dagger Men) were—

"Hey Jude!" I yelled. "Hey, Jude! Got a question."

The door to the bathroom opened and he stood there in a towel. His wet black hair stood out like a ridiculous, puffy 'fro. "What is it?"

"Didn't you tell me that we had to avoid water? You just took a *shower!*"

He smoothed his hair down with slender hands. "I used the Word of Avoidance, man. Keeps attention off of me."

Oh. Good to know. "I'm a little puzzled by a name here. Sicarii. I know it is Latin for Dagger Men, but what is it?

His normally lively eyes darkened. "The first Sicarii were Jewish rebels in Judea some two thousand years ago," he informed me tonelessly, face closed. "They were assassins who slaughtered Romans and their sympathizers. Later, the Medellin Cartel had what they called the Sicarios, their version of the Sicarii assassins. The singular is Sicarius, or Dagger Man."

"Assassinations would have caused the Romans to retaliate harshly," I mused, more to myself than him.

"Yes. They did, all across Judea. The Romans slaughtered thousands to in an effort to find and discourage the Sicarii."

"Did your family have a connection to the Cartel?"

"My Family trained their assassins and took a large portion of the billions they made in the drug trade. Then, when things started heating up as the U.S. Delta Force, the CIA, and the Colombian National Police started hunting Cartel members, we withdrew our support and watched it die. It all ended in 1993."

"So, the Sicarii and your family...?"

His voice became hollow, as though his soul had been plucked out. "My Family are descendants of the Sicarii. In fact, I'm the last direct descendant of their leader. We call him the Founder."

"So—?"

"Yeah, Mike. We're a Family of assassins. The Sicarii are still around, still trying to destroy the Romans, man."

My mind wobbled. "But, Jude, the Romans are all gone. It's just a city now."

"No Mike," he claimed. "Not true. There's still the Roman Catholic Church."

Holy moley! I opened my mouth, but he had already turned and shut the door behind him. With a sigh, I went back to the manuscript.

The assassins of the Sicarii (or Dagger Men) were still a large part of our Family's legacy, although we had lessened the practice over the last century, preferring to let the media to do our dirty work for us in the form of character assassination. News hounds were quick to believe the worst in even the most honorable of people. However, our assassins were still the best-trained, most well funded, killers the world had ever known and even the most insane idiot (like Henri) feared them above all others.

All Family members were trained in wet-work, hence the title of Sicarius, even for those who did not practice assassination. Only a select few were chosen to join the ranks of the Dagger Men, the Sicarii Killer Elite. Once in, never out.

"You'd join the—" Julian II began.

"Dagger Men?" Philip finished.

Once again I gave them a grin well lubricated with nasty. "Why not?" It was a calculated risk, going from near Wordless half-brother to potential top assassin in their eyes, but sometimes you have to roll the dice and hope it doesn't come up snake eyes.

The Professor's slow tread preceded him down the steps. "Olivier, you father wishes to speak to you," he intoned gravely, a customary frown on his worn features. "He has sent an automobile, which will be here shortly."

Very much aware of the daggers glared at my back, I mounted the stairs to take a last look at Lac Léman before the car arrived.

The Grand Château du Lac Léman on the shore of Lake Geneva (aka Lac Léman) boasts the most expensive rates and the highest standards of luxury in all of Switzerland. It is also Family owned and operated.

The Sicarii, besides being a brotherhood of assassins, is also one of the world's largest multi-national conglomerates, ranking just behind the monster Hyundai for billions earned. Mining, bio-tech, computer chips, arms manufacturing, fossil fuels, construction and on and on and on … all with Sicarii fingers in the pie, all run by one man who lived in the Grand Château.

If you asked anyone who worked there, they would tell you that the finest room available would be the Presidential Suite. The finest *available*. What was not available in the small, but enormously opulent hotel, was my father's personal suite.

Not large by the standards of luxury hotels, only twelve hundred square feet, it had but one use … to cater to the whims of Julian Deschamps. Accessed by a private elevator, any visitor (especially Family) would be screened for weapons not only by the Elevator

Operator (a top Dagger Man), but also the most advanced technology available, all hidden in the elevator's mirrored walls and gold ornamentation.

Should you pass inspection (if not ... well, you can well imagine), the doors would open into the suite where Julian would greet you personally. Some might think that would be an unnecessarily high-risk situation for him, but you must realize he had been through the same training as all Sicarii and was seldom left alone without protection.

When I arrived and the doors opened, it was to the sight of Boris standing in front of the elevator. Dressed impeccably in a coffee-colored Saville Row suit, Boris was more a force of nature contained in cloth than a human being.

In 1971 Julian recruited Boris from the Soviet Union, where he was reputed to be the most feared, most vicious Spetsnaz (Special Forces) commando that had ever served that repressive regime. A master with a knife, pistol and rifle, as well as Sambo, their own peculiar brand of martial arts, he had all the qualities you could ask for in the perfect bodyguard.

Recruitment had been simplicity itself; all Julian did was dangle an obscene amount of money and offer to relocate Boris' immediate family to Switzerland. With that accomplished, Julian then paid a handsome amount to various officials in the Soviet government and records were conveniently destroyed and/or misplaced, erasing Boris from the annals of Russian history.

So there he stood, all six-six two-hundred-fifty pounds of chiseled, grizzled nasty, with a long face, shaven head, cauliflower left ear and flinty eyes deep-set beneath jutting brows. With a barely perceptible nod to the Elevator Operator, he moved to the side and ushered me into the suite.

"You look good, Boris," I remarked in passing. Actually, with his thick potato nose and scarred cheeks, he looked anything but.

"Thank you, Master Olivier," rumbled the behemoth in impeccable German, his voice so deep I could feel it vibrating the bones of my inner ear.

"Hello, son," came a cultured voice from across the room.

There, silhouetted before a large window looking out on the lake, behind a heavy, ornate desk, sat Julian. The light from the window erased the details and outlined his form in stark relief; he was darkness personified.

"Hello Julian," I responded, drawing near and standing at attention in front of the desk.

The shadow's head cocked slightly to the right. "The Professor has told me you only know one Word. Is this true?"

"No sir, I know them all." Lying to Julian was just another way to commit suicide … or worse.

If that confession caught him by surprise, his body language didn't show it, but I could hear the pleasure in his voice as he asked, "And why didn't you tell the Professor?"

"I didn't want the others to know."

A deep chuckle. "I always knew you were the smart one, Olivier."

The silhouette turned and the light from the window dimmed. Julian came into view, a starkly handsome man, skin a little lighter than mine, gray at the temples, taller by four inches and broader across the chest. Where my smile was wide and even, his had a sardonic twist.

I looked past him. "The window is new." A window might allow an ambitious son to remove his father from the Sicarii using a sniper rifle.

This time his smile held no scorn. "Not a window, but the latest in high-definition technology. Miniature cameras on the outside of the building record the actual view," he said. "Then they send it here, a near-perfect simulation."

I nodded. "Very nice."

"Not one for chitchat, are you, son?"

One of my eyebrows crept upward. "I am understandably curious as to the reason for your summons, sir."

His laughter held a note of genuine amusement. A surprise, considering that the last time I heard genuine humor from him was when the American shuttle *Challenger* exploded shortly after takeoff in 1981.

"The twins have no backbone, and Henri has no brains. The only ones with any hope of matching my standards are you and Burke." Boris appeared with a small snifter of brandy between his massive fingers. Julian nodded to the Russian and waved him off, inhaling deeply from the glass. "Want one, son?"

"No thank you, sir."

"Yes, you *are* the smart one," he mused quietly. "Just the perfect degree of paranoia. Like I said, it's down to you and Burke, and I prefer you because he favors the Harcourt side of the Family. However, when I heard from the Professor that you had only one Word, well …" his voice trailed off and he took a small sip. "I almost despaired.

"Imagine how I felt when I heard that the most promising fruit of my loins had turned out to be a magical dunce. Then, just this morning in fact, I said to myself, 'Julian, why is your most gifted son such a beggar with Words when he showed such promising, even amazing, talent at Elemental and Botanical Magics?' "

Julian drained half the snifter and swirled the brandy in his mouth for a moment before swallowing. "The answer, son, is that you are *not* a beggar with Words, that you were hiding your light under a bushel to keep a low profile from your bloodthirsty relatives, encouraging them to underestimate you."

"Got it in one, sir," I murmured.

"I twigged onto the truth in less than a week, son; it will take Burke less than two. So, if you think you can take the plunge, he should be your first order of business."

"Not too worried about Burke right now, sir."

Julian's pitch-black eyebrows shot up. "Why not?"

"He'll save me for last."

He pursed his lips. "Yes, I do believe you—as the Americans would say it—have his number, son. Very well." With that he reached for the phone (at this time, as you know, almost all phones were landline) and hit SPEAKER, then dialed a three-digit number.

"When I told the Patron about your marvelous duplicity, he asked to speak to you."

The Patron? My blood chilled to the point where the cells *must* have crystallized. No one but Julian talked to our mysterious Patron, the person who had guided the Family to the dizzying heights it had attained. Powerful beyond imagining, a being of myth and legend, the Patron would continue to guide us until the arrival of our Family's prophesied messiah, the Redeemer. At that time, the prophecies said, the Redeemer would cast down the Liar, the great enemy of the Family, of the Patron, and restore balance to the world.

"He wishes to speak to me?" I squeaked. I cursed my traitorous voice. A drop of sweat rolled into my eye.

The voice that emerged from the speakerphone took me totally by surprise and made me jump. A little bit, anyway. "Yes, I wanted to speak to you, Olivier. It is time I did so."

"Sir," I acknowledged, throat dry.

"You father speaks highly of your intelligence and cunning." Like a warm blanket the voice wrapped me and held on tight, a comfortable, protected feeling. Despite its rich, deep notes, it had an edge … an almost metallic undertone that grated against your nerves. It was at that moment I dubbed the speaker The Voice.

"Thank you, sir," I responded quietly.

"He's polite, Julian. I like them when they're polite."

Compared to the voice flowing from the phone, Julian's sounded tinny and grating. "Yes sir. I tried to raise them correctly."

"Young man," the voice continued as if Julian had not spoken. "There will come a time, if you survive, that we might work together. The fact that we are speaking tells me that you do know more than one Word, as was reported. I've been monitoring your progress closely through the years, so you can imagine my surprise when I heard 'one Word.' "

"Yes, sir." I wasn't sure where this was going, but I felt the sweat drenching my shirt.

"Julian," the Voice said, his delivery clipped and formal. "How many Words indeed?"

The head of the Sicarii's lips barely twitched in what might have been called a nervous smile. "All twelve, sir."

"Ahhh." A purr, the sound of a contented feline predator. "All twelve ... very nice, Olivier. Too bad Professor von Andor did not catch you out in your little lie."

"I can hold my own in a lie, sir."

A long pause. "No, boy, you can't. I know liars and you aren't one, not yet, which makes the Professor's oversight more egregious."

Julian spoke up, "I'll have a talk with him, sir. It won't happen again."

"No need to speak with him, Julian. I have received news that he suffered a terrible accident while speaking to his granddaughter on the telephone."

Julian's face gave the barest hint of shock before he quickly regained his composure. As for me, I was on edge. From the slight degree of smugness that had crept into the Voice, I *knew* that he had killed the Professor.

Mind you, no one much cared for the old Nazi. He was a cold, calculating, mean son-of-a-bitch who had a streak of bile a mile deep. I'd shed no tears for Professor Klaus von Andor, former employee of the Sicarri. Had I been given the job, I would have gladly killed him myself, but the Voice was more than capable of eliminating those in his employ.

"Anyway," the Voice continued. "Don't sweat the small stuff, Olivier, I will take care of that."

"Thank you, sir."

"Now ... I have a very positive feeling about you, young man. If you keep your eyes open and survive the next few years, I think you and I shall become close. Yes, close indeed."

That thought nearly stopped my heart. "Thank you, sir." I don't think I was capable of saying anything else at that point.

"Good. Good." *Click!* The line went dead.

"That's that," Julian muttered, lips pursed.

Redeemer, Liar ... prophesies of restoring balance to the world? I slipped the pages back into the manila envelope, more confused than ever. What the heck had I gotten myself into?

I looked over to the other bed and saw that Jude was fast asleep, snoring softly. A flick of a switch and the bedside light went out. For what seemed like hours, I lay in the dark wondering what terrible things might await us at journey's end.

Chapter Eight

Jude

After scrubbing away my morning breath with a toothbrush, I dressed in black jeans and a black Cabo Wabo t-shirt, along with black Converse sneakers. What can I say? I like black.

Speaking of which, when I exited the bathroom, Mike had on his black uniform, if you can call a priest's outfit a uniform. Still, he looked pretty snazzy for a big guy with a handlebar moustache.

I didn't bother to ask how much he'd read; he'd tell me when the time was right. The knowledge that would unfold for him, if it didn't drive him nuts, would allow me to see how far the Church's forgiveness extended.

Despite the Rio Grande only a few hundred yards away, the air was dry enough to suck the moisture right out of my skin, such a contrast to the turgid humidity of Omaha.

Maybe it was the contented lull that had slid eel-like through my brain, or the mental fatigue of being on the run, or even the lack of constant training, but five steps into the parking lot, my eyes fixed on the Corolla, I stepped into a puddle of water.

Where that puddle had come from, I don't know, but there it was in the middle of the otherwise bone-dry asphalt parking lot, soaking into my sneaker while dread clamped cold hands into my guts.

Unlike with the shower I had taken earlier, I hadn't used Avoidance to mask myself from the element.

Water talks.

I shouted, "Mike! We gotta go! Now, man!" Without waiting for an answer, I ran to the Corolla and made ready, trusting Mike would sense the urgency. A few seconds later my trust was rewarded as he opened the rear door and tossed our duffels in the back seat.

"What's going on?" he panted, snapping the seatbelt around his waist.

"It's Water," I grunted as the Corolla fired up. Tire marks followed us out of the lot as we sped away. "I told you that Water was looking for me; what I didn't tell you was how motivated Water would be in its search."

"Mind explaining?"

"When God created the world, He gave life to the elements, Earth, Air, Fire and Water, to help keep the world in harmony. Four original elements, the Four Old Ones, the Primals. Legend says they had no Language, only the feel for their kind. For millennia they were the caretakers of the natural world."

"Four old elementals. I would hazard a guess that they are powerful."

"Yeah, you could say that. Like the ocean is 'pretty powerful.' "

"Then where did the other elementals come from?"

"All I have is conjecture, gleaned from various sources." I turned onto the 10, racing north toward Sunland Park and Las Cruces. To our left, Juarez was revealed in all of its squalid and rotten glory, a gritty shame of a border town.

"Conjecture away," Mike urged.

"Okay. It seems that when an elemental becomes large, or great in power, it … buds, or splits, shearing off a part of itself, a new elemental. Mitosis on a magical level."

"So how did he find this Primal Water, if it so powerful?"

"That's what I'd like to know."

We passed quite a few miles of flat dry land in easy silence; then, just as we put a little town called Anthony in the rearview mirror, I felt a trembly sort of rumble from the front of the car.

"Damn," I swore through gritted teeth.

Mike jolted out of his meditations. "What?"

"Left front tire is about to go," I grumbled angrily as I braked and steered the car to the shoulder.

A quick inspection revealed a bubble in the sidewall of the tire, seconds away from blowing wide open. "Damn," I swore again.

"Don't worry, I have a spare," Mike commented as he came around the car. "A rubber donut."

A few minutes later saw us struggling with lug nuts rusted tight to the steel rim. Grunting and straining, we tugged on the lug wrench, shaking the little car back and forth.

Just as the third nut groaned loose, a voice hammered our ears, carried on the dry, dry breeze, "You gents look like you could use a little help."

Mike and I stood staring at the stranger in the light of the morning sun. "Just changing a tire," said Mike, extending a dirty hand.

The stranger was a big man with small piggy eyes, a red bulb of nose, an enormous belly that strained his green t-shirt and dirty jeans. A much-crumpled cowboy hat rested on his round head. "A priest, really?" He ignored the hand and began to laugh, round gut jiggling and jaggling.

"Yeah," Mike replied, puzzled, and slowly lowered his hand.

Still laughing, the stranger raised a fist the size of a dinner plate and, faster than I thought a big guy like that could move, punched Mike in the stomach. The priest folded like a bad poker hand around that big fist. Still laughing, the stranger lifted Mike by the back of his shirt with one hand as if he weighed nothing and threw him clear over the car to disappear on the other side.

A Word burst from between my lips, bringing the acrid stench of burning insulation: Force. I had summoned a two-by-three foot pane of energy, which was hurled with a velocity in direct proportion to the volume used. I had shouted at the top of my lungs.

And nothing happened.

Oh, a pained look spasmed across the stranger's face, but then he smiled, revealing teeth that were all canines. "Ouch."

"Demon," I spat, fists bunching.

The Hellspawn laughed again, human vocal cords ripping asunder beneath the vocal assault. "And they said you're a smart one. Can't see it, really." It spat a gobbet of blood onto the asphalt, as its eyes began to glow a venomous red.

No time for pussyfooting around. Strength and Vigor brought the smell of ammonia and peanuts. For the next ten minutes I knew I could lift a Volvo over my head, run miles without a hitch and, like Tony the Tiger would say, feel *Grrrrreat!* Smiling in glee, I leapt forward and threw a punch at the demon's midsection.

Craaaack!! It wasn't just the iron-like stomach of the demon that broke the small bones of my hand, but also the sudden deceleration as my hand stopped cold without budging that infernal asshole an inch.

Pain, like red-hot razors slicing through my flesh, stunned me for a brief moment, giving the demon a chance to deliver a blow to the chest that flung me into the Corolla's bumper hard enough to snap my spine. Shock, agony, an awful feeling as if my personal universe was collapsing in on itself condensed into a tiny, dense spot of spiritual matter that winked out in an instant.

"In the name of the Lord, I abjure thee!" A roaring, echoing voice brought me back, expanding that universe so that it encompassed my surroundings once again.

Ouch … that hurt … a *lot*.

"In God's name, I banish thee, Unclean Beast!" the voice hollered and I felt compelled to broach the spear of fire that transfixed me and opened my eyes.

My God, it was Mike! Filled with the fury of the righteous, he seemed to blaze as he held a crucifix in one hand and a bible in the other. Blood slid down his temple and his shirt was torn in several places, revealing skin scraped raw, but he paid no heed.

"You go, boy," I croaked feebly, drooling blood. It was then that I realized that the Corolla's bumper cradled me in a sitting position, that my arms lay lifeless at my side. "What the—" I began before sudden realization nearly made me pee my pants.

I couldn't feel my body. If it hadn't been for a car I would have fallen over. The one thing I did feel the throbbing ache high up on my spine.

Healing and cinnamon floated on the breeze, bringing with it a lessening of pain. Again ... and again ... the Word slowly restored sensation as my skin registered the hot asphalt and wasn't it odd to be in a place where January felt so bloody *warm*? Despite my mind's meandering, I uttered the Word a few more times and the ache in my back faded like a bad dream.

While I attempted to rejoin the world of the ambulatory, the demon, who by that time had black, chitinous spikes growing out of its forearms and shoulders, roared its hate at my friend. "Fool worshipper of a decrepit God," it hissed balefully, backing away from the crucifix. "Your time is coming to an end."

Mike took a deep breath, raised his arms to the sky, and shouted, "I command you, unclean spirit, whoever you are, along with all your minions now attacking this servant of God, by the mysteries of the incarnation, passion, resurrection, and ascension of our Lord Jesus Christ, by the descent of the Holy Spirit, by the coming of our Lord for judgment, that you tell me by some sign your name, and the day and hour of your departure. I command you, moreover, to obey me to the letter, I, who am a minister of God despite my unworthiness. Neither shall you be emboldened to harm in any way this creature of God, nor the bystanders, nor any of their possessions!"

In stunned disbelief I watched the demon fall to its knees, fear and loathing writ large on its face. I felt the bones of my back shift slightly as my legs twitched with new life, pins and needles tickling the skin while Mike, face beatific, continued his exorcism by reciting the King James version of Mark 16:15-18:

> At that time Jesus said to His disciples: 'Go ye into the whole world and preach the Gospel to every creature. He that believeth and is baptized shall be saved; but he that believeth not shall be condemned! And these signs shall follow them that believe:

in my name shall they cast out devils; they shall speak with new tongues; they shall take up serpents, and if they drink any deadly thing, it shall not hurt them; they shall lay hands on the sick, and they shall recover!'

Hands to its head, the demon gibbered madly, red eyes rolling in their sockets as Mike lowered the crucifix, touching the thing's forehead. With a final cry of misery and dismay, the demon collapsed facedown onto the ground. Black steam rose from the body and blew away in the slight breeze. Within moments its flesh began to bubble and sizzle, liquefying into a foul-smelling goop the same color as the asphalt.

"Jesus!" I breathed softly, then mentally apologized in case He had been paying attention.

"Don't blaspheme, Jude." Mike sounded exhausted, as if the juice of his life had bled out.

"Won't happen again," I muttered as I slowly heaved myself, groaning and grimacing, to my feet.

Despite the weariness that tugged at his face, Mike managed a tiny smile. "Don't lie, it's not nice."

"Right, got it." *Pop, pop, pop* went the bones of my back as I stood. "I'll do the best I can, Mike." Magical overload, backlash, ripped at my muscles, the result of too many Words used too quickly. I flogged my memory and realized that I'd used Healing at least ten times. With that came the cold awareness that I had come a gnat's whisker from death.

"You okay, Jude?" Mike asked, taking me by the elbow.

"I think so," I replied shakily, while taking mental inventory. Back … fine, arms, legs … fine and fine. Well, as fine as could be after kissing a bumper at full speed. "You should see the other guy."

His lips twitched for a brief moment. "I have."

Surprising enough, there were no other cars in sight. The highway was free and clear of impediments, the only vehicle a beat-up and dusty black Pontiac Grand Prix. Of the stranger/demon, only his clothes remained, floating in a puddle of noxious fluid.

"We have to go, Mike. I suggest we take the other car."

Mike worried at his lower lip. "That's stealing, Jude."

I rolled my eyes. "It's not like he needs it anymore, Mike. The man who owned that car died the second the demon took him over. It ate his soul."

My friend's eyes opened wide in shock and dismay at the horrible thought. "How—"

"Greater demons only have the capacity to eat souls that are corrupt and evil enough to act as a bridge between this world and Hell. I don't know who that man was, but he was no sweetheart, I can assure you."

We transferred our duffels and the metal box to the Grand Prix and made tracks as if the Devil himself dogged our heels.

Chapter Nine

Mike

Go to any town in America with a population of over three thousand and you can always find franchise hotels. Like weeds, they sprout up everywhere. That's where we ended up, beat down and worn out from the events of the day, though it wasn't yet noon.

Jude looked terrible, pasty white and drawn, the kind of terrible you see in cancer victims. When I asked, he shook his head and said, "The price of using too much Magic, Mike. It takes the starch out of you. It's called Backlash."

Funny, when you think of magic and all those fantasy books out there, you don't think of magic as having a cost to the magician unless it's misused. Maybe it wasn't the providence of Satan; maybe Jude was right and it was neither good nor evil, but a kind of natural force to be harnessed, like sunlight or wind.

Before my philosophical musings could distract me from the present, I helped Jude into bed. He hit dreamland before his head hit the pillow. Deciding that food was my personal priority, I headed out and purchased a couple of pizzas. Pepperoni for myself and a meat lover's for sleeping beauty, along with a two-liter of cola to wash it all down.

Back at the hotel, I set the pizza on a sideboard and took a slice, my stomach rumbling at the smell of cheese and grease. Before I could take a bite, Jude spoke up.

"Lord, Mike, that smells incredible." His voice was roughened by fatigue.

I set the box containing the meat lover's pizza next to him. "Try to breathe between bites," I cautioned.

Later, content and belching, Jude said, "What was that, Mike? I've never seen the like, man. What sort of spell did you cast to dismiss the demon?"

"It was a Roman Catholic Rite of Exorcism, from De Exorcismis et Supplicationibus Quibusdam, or Of Exorcism and Certain Supplications."

"So not a magic spell?"

I sighed. "No, Jude, although I can see how you'd think it could be." Taking a sip of cola, I shot him a glance. "When that ... demon threw me over the car, I think I blacked out for a second because the next thing I knew you hit the Corolla so hard I heard bones break.

"Jude, I saw red like never before, not even in Iraq during Desert Storm." Another drink from my cup. "It was the wrath of the Lord, Jude. His Spirit filled me and I knew what I had to do, what would drive it out. No spell required, only the glory of God."

Thanks to the food and rest some color finally crept back into his face. His hands, which had been shaking, had regained their customary steadiness. He licked his lips once, then twice before he said, "You were magnificent, Mike. That was one of the most incredible sights I've ever seen, man." Before I had a chance to reply, his eyes closed and he began to snore.

I grinned. "Lovely. Well, sleep tight." With that, I regarded the envelope next to me and realized it was a good time, as my younger parishioners might say, to 'get my read on.'

A Knife Worth Having

Three years passed quietly, or as quietly as time ever passes in my Family. Henri died shortly after my introduction to the Voice, choking on his own vomit after one of his customary heroic bouts of drunkenness. His death was so cleverly arranged that I could hardly believe the twins had done it.

When Julian II and Philip died a year later, their fishing boat capsizing in the Gulf of Bothnia, I realized that Burke had been a very naughty boy indeed. Those deaths certainly hadn't come at my hand. It didn't take long for me to realize that Burke wanted Julian to think that it was I who provided the three with their exits so that when I met with an untimely death, Julian would have to turn to him as the next Family patriarch. I felt the big DayGlo bullseye reappear on my back and heightened my vigilance.

When I turned eighteen, Julian, in a demonstration of paternal pride at my survival and my apparent 'terminal dismissal' of my siblings, put me in charge of a small underground research facility outside of Livingston, New Jersey, where nothing of great note had ever been produced. Run by an abhorrent little scientist by the name of Gillan, it provided me the perfect shelter from Burke's machinations, at least for a while. I'm not ashamed to admit that he scared the shit out of me.

My job was to make the facility productive, a test of my abilities and I wanted, no … *needed* to achieve something monumental, so I put millions into a few pet projects. Those projects, while potentially valuable, provided one more thing I desired above all else: power to take control of the Family.

When Gillan called and informed me that one of my projects had paid off, I immediately drove from New York to the lab. After I arrived at the complex (located beneath the Commonwealth Water Company Reservoir Number Three) I parked at the Cedar Hill Country Club (Family owned and operated) and entered the complex, where I dismissed the staff for the evening. I'd taken a golf cart down a steeply sloping tunnel to an elevator that was the main entrance to the compound. The three-story re-enforced steel facility had been started, and, nearly forgotten by, Julian. For me, however, it offered a glimmer of hope.

The first, and smallest, floor—the apex of the complex—consisted of offices for the researchers and myself. Floors two and three were larger—floor two almost three times as large as one and three almost five times larger than two—so the whole complex was shaped much like a ziggurat. Floor three housed the particle accelerator, used for our more esoteric research. Shiny white walls and floors echoed my footsteps as I exited the main elevator to find the fat doctor waiting for me. I don't know if it was lack of imagination or one of Julian's peccadilloes, but the entire lab looked like the set of a bad sci-fi movie ... all white on white with exposed metal gleaming silver in the harsh fluorescent light. Gillan led me to the lone conference room, a small space with a black table large enough to seat eight and a computer terminal the size of a flat-head V-8. Once the door was shut, he produced a small object from his pocket and handed it over.

I held the item up to the light. "Very nice, Dr. Gillan, very nice indeed. What is it? A mini Lightsaber?"

Dr. Gillan gingerly took the six-inch silvery cylinder from my grasp, an oily smile on puffy, bearded face. "Not quite, sir. It is molecular thread, or a molecular knife, if you will."

Excitement surged through me. Molecular thread! Previously it had existed only in the imagination of science fiction writers ... a chain of iron molecules that could cut through almost anything. Leaning forward, I gazed avidly at the cylinder. Less than an inch across, mostly constructed from titanium, one end appeared to be made of a glassy substance with a minute hole in the center. The body gleamed, having been polished to a mirror finish with a small, round, black button a couple of inches from the glassy end. "It doesn't look like much, Gillan," I remarked.

"The body of the cylinder, sir, contains twenty-five yards of molecular iron thread, to replace any that happen to break."

I gave him a look that brought sweat to his florid cheeks. "It breaks? Molecular thread is supposed to be able to cut through anything."

"Almost, sir. However if you move the thread too quickly through a hard material, such as a brick of iron, it will snap, which, of course, is why there is more thread, spooling out to replace the broken piece."

"What's the blade length?"

"One inch."

"One inch?" I blurted and sat back. "Only that?"

The fat little scientist licked his thick lips. "After an inch the magnetic bottle becomes unstable." A feverish light shone in his hazel eyes. "But just think, sir, the applications of just one small inch!"

I considered Dr. Gillan a moment. He was a rotund American with three chins, small eyes and curly, sandy-brown hair cut short and shot through with gray. An able scientist and wholly my creature, thanks to generous donations of young women to slake his unsavory lusts. It was not hard to find his weakness and exploit it, giving him the girls he craved, his vice placing him firmly under my thumb. An odious creature, but *my* odious creature and we both knew it.

"The specs?" I asked.

His smile could have lubed a Volvo. "Downloaded from the drive to a disk for you, sir."

"And the Crystal Drive?"

"On Floor Two," he said with an oily smile.

The desire to delouse right then and there nearly overcame me, but I fought the impulse, forcing myself to mirror his slick grin. The owner and CEO of the largest American computer firm must have been shrieking in anger at the loss of his precious Crystal Drive (an invention light years ahead of its time), the device and all data related to it having been stolen by my agents right out from under his nose. The developer, a man named Chandrahaskhar, now resided in our facility in Sweden. The device had cost—oh how it had cost—but in the end had paid off. It was my 'get out of jail free card,' as the Americans would say and I had jealously guarded the secret of its existence.

I took the precious knife back out of his hands and placed it in the inside breast pocket of my charcoal Brioni suit, ignoring his look of shock. "Give me the Crystal Drive, Gillan." My tone warned him not to argue, so he scuttled off to do as I asked. Once he was out of sight, I concentrated furiously, weighing the pros and cons of an idea that had formed once I'd laid eyes on the precious molecular knife.

Flipping a mental coin, I decided to take the risk.

With no time to waste, I entered his office, logged onto the lab computer and began erasing all traces of the molecular knife. Something like the knife was far too valuable to let Julian get his hands on and there was no way I would let Burke have a shot at it, considering his capabilities. No, this would be mine and mine alone. Within a matter of minutes all hard drives were wiped.

"Here you go, sir," Gillan puffed as he entered, a small black rectangle the size of a domino in his hand. "There is no other computer out there but the one we have here that can utilize this device." He handed the drive over and once again I was surprised at how heavy it was, not to mention slick from his sweaty palms.

"How about our other projects, Gillan?" I asked, not looking at him.

"Nothing has borne fruit, Mr. Deschamps, only the molecular knife. Why?"

"Where are the disks you mentioned?"

The fat scientist wordlessly opened the top right desk drawer, revealing a plastic bag containing a dozen three and a half inch floppies. I scooped the bag up and added the Crystal Drive to the small plastic squares.

"Thank you Dr. Gillan." I met the man's shifty eyes. "And the specs on the Crystal Drive?"

"On the drive itself. May I ask, sir, what is going on?"

"Only two projects have paid off, the molecular knife and the Crystal Drive—which we have successfully reverse-engineered—and there is only one other computer, my personal machine, that can accommodate the Drive. Everything else looks to be a wash-out, so I think it's time to close up shop."

"But, sir, why? We have the potential to do so much more!" Spit was collecting at the corners of his thick lips. He definitely did not want to give up his hot and cold running party girls. "Will you please give us some more time?"

Ignoring his question, I continued. "Do you realize, Gillan, that the girl delivered two weeks ago died of her injuries? Did you know that?"

His shiny forehead began to sweat even more. "Uh, n-no, s-sir," he stammered.

"I know she was an underage prostitute, Doctor, but, really, did you have to harm her so?"

He licked his lips. "You know how it is sometimes, sir, I get carried away. Really, sir … I'm so sorry." Fear spiced his speech like cayenne.

My eyes engaged his and I let my anger show through … just a little bit. He tried to back away, but my hand was quicker, stiffened fingers finding his throat. Cartilage gave way beneath my fingertips and he collapsed, choking. Once again I checked my watch and stepped over his thrashing body.

"The only consolation I've had these past months, Doctor," I uttered contemptuously as I exited the office, "was the prospect of killing you myself."

Gillan deserved much, much worse, having murdered several young girls over the years in his lustful frenzy. Add to that his obnoxious American attitude, and my self-restraint at not killing him earlier seemed heroic.

On the other end of the complex, nearly polar opposite to Dr. Gillan's office, was an unused hallway hidden behind a locked door that read ELECTRICAL. This hall (about two hundred yards long, made of plain concrete and illuminated by only a few bare bulbs) led to large steel door like a bank vault, complete with spoked wheel in the center and an electronic ten-digit keypad. After punching in the code on the pad, I spun the wheel and opened the door, revealing a shorter hallway that ended in an elevator door. Next to that door was a plain white button and another ten-digit keypad. I pushed the plain button to summon the elevator and then punched in a sequence of fifteen digits on the pad. A red light came to life behind the 0 and I knew everything was primed for action. Three minutes and counting.

Ding! The elevator doors opened and I plunged into a space barely wide enough to accommodate my shoulders, as long as I didn't take a deep breath. The doors closed and I pushed the only button available.

Less than a minute later the doors slid open and I squeezed myself out into the middle of what looked to be a gardener's shed; meanwhile the elevator vanished soundlessly, lowering a two-foot diameter plug of cement that fit seamlessly into the grimy floor.

I checked my watch. Less than two minutes left, plenty of time to catch the show. Pushing aside a riding lawn mower, I avoided the sliding, garage-type door, opting instead for a side door. Warm evening air caressed my face as my Barker Black shoes hit well-tended grass.

The long hallway and elevator had deposited me just north of the reservoir on the dam end next to Baker Road, smack dab in the middle of a grove of tall maples. I had a perfect view of the lake as the clock counted down to zero.

And ... *now.*

Not a ripple on the water, not a tremor to be felt, at least not yet. Not surprising because at that moment a few thousand magnesium strips were burning their way toward hundreds of tons of thermite built into the walls and floors of the complex. At the same time the ventilation system, housing hundreds of two-foot oxygen tanks, were unloading its gaseous burden. If the self-destruct procedure worked correctly, the thermite would burn at temperatures reaching 4500 degrees Fahrenheit, causing concrete and steel to melt like wax. When the oxygen reached the burning thermite, what I called Stage Two, things would become somewhat more... energized. The very air inside the complex would burn, tearing through all the corridors and through the ventilation system, exploding the remaining oxygen bottles that hadn't emptied their payload. Steel supports, three feet thick, would become taffy-soft and the whole shebang would collapse into Floor Three, which at that point would be hip deep in molten metal and lava. Dr. Gillan, by that time already transformed into charcoal briquettes, would disappear completely, becoming so much ionized gas.

Once Floors One and Two became vertically challenged and merged with Three, the topmost supports would give way, letting in millions of tons of reservoir. After that the fun would begin.

Leaning over, I dug my fingers through the grass and into the soil, rumbling the Language of Earth. The odor of cut grass slid into my nose as easily as my fingers slipped into the ground. Rumble, rumble the words burst forth, demanding, cajoling.

Under my feet, under my fingers, the elemental answered and did what I asked, humping and bumping the earth beneath me into a hill that grew and grew and grew. Soon I stood twenty feet atop an impressive berm that allowed me a clear view of the reservoir. The best seat in the house.

WHUMP!

Okay, I felt that right down to the roots of my teeth. The surface of the reservoir seemed to slump inwards before bulging up and rippling outwards from the middle in a shockwave that carried to the top of the berm and beyond, nearly hurling me off my feet.

Seconds later an explosion of water and steam erupted from the epicenter of the disturbance, shooting straight up, over a hundred feet into the evening air, carrying with it the faint tang of hot metal. The reaction was far greater than I had thought.

Quickly I whistled the Language of Air, bringing a bevy of sprites to my aid. *"Please, brothers!"* I implored. *"Let me join you in the sky!"*

"You are funny, Magus, wanting to join Air!" they laughed in return. "Why should we not drop you?"

Droplets began to fall and I could see an enormous swell surge out from the reservoir's center. It would be on me in moments. *"By the true name of Air, which is* (unpronounceable), *take me into your realm!"* I commanded. *"Now!"*

With a breathy shriek the sprites lifted me none too gently into the sky, nearly dislocating my shoulders in the process; however, I just set my mouth in a snarl and braced myself as best I could.

Just in time. A wave slammed hard into the berm, shooting a gush of water into the air high enough to ruin my $650 Barker Blacks.

From my vantage point, I saw a swirling vortex in the heart of the water, steaming and churning, bubbling and seething with savage energies. The burbly cries of Water came to me faintly as the sprites whisked me away toward the country club and soon I flew out of sight, leaving the hissing, boiling reservoir behind me.

Usually Air sprites are about as reliable as hummingbirds on heroin, but these particular elementals managed to land me in the parking lot of the country club without dropping me from too far up. I did twist my ankle when I landed.

"Well thank you *very much*, assholes," I cursed under my breath. Laughing merrily, the sprites fled into the sky.

Later, after a couple of shots of Glenfiddich and a Healing for my ankle, I called Julian.

"I am sorry sir, but the entire complex is a loss," I reported, fingering the molecular knife in my pocket. "We were under attack and I had to initiate the self-destruct protocol."

"Everything is lost, then?" A dangerous edge crept into his voice. "All the research, all that money sunk into that laboratory is *wasted*?" His soft words were as harsh as a scream.

"Not a total loss," I soothed, blinking rapidly as sweat poured into my eyes. "I have the Crystal Drive. The data of all the projects we were working on are stored on it, not to mention all the reverse-engineering specs for the Drive itself."

"So what, Olivier? It is just one invention out of many."

"So what? Julian, the Drive is *revolutionary*! It alone is worth tens of billions of dollars! Not to mention the tech from the Drive will help us build computers *generations* ahead of the competition. With this, we give ourselves the edge over the Liar's minions. A big edge. No computer system on the planet will be able to withstand us." Okay, a stretch. It would take years for us to develop the technology offered by the Crystal Drive, but he did not know that … yet.

When he spoke next, his tone was milder, but no less deadly. "Are you sure, son?"

"Julian … Father, I'm sure." A blatant manipulation, but I'm sure he appreciated the gesture. "Computers are the future. Everything will be computerized in the next twenty years, so think about us having the best, the fastest computers around. What will that do for the Sicarii?"

"Who attacked us?"

I licked my lips nervously but kept my voice steady. "My guess is the tech baron we stole the drive from. Only he has the kind of money to trace the theft to us. Whoever the attackers were, most likely mercenaries, they are dead now."

"I'll be in New York in a couple of hours. Meet me at my suite."

"Yes, sir."

Click. I sat there in the General Manager's office for a good minute until the annoying drone of the dial tone shook me out of my reverie. Julian was coming and that could mean one of two things: a) My ass was about to be turned into a lace doily or b) He wanted to commend me on a job well done. a) would give me a quick disappearing act while option b) allowed me to live a few years longer.

I sure hoped it was option b), because this was one meeting I could not afford to miss.

ༀ

Pages and pages of crisp white paper slipped through fingers numbed with shock. Jude had *murdered* a man! I looked at him sleeping peacefully on the bed, lips parted slightly. All these years I hadn't seen him as a person who could actually kill someone. Granted Dr. Gillan had been a slimy little toad, but crushing his throat and leaving him to choke to death? And *enjoying* it?

Who was the man whose story was recorded on these pages? Arrogant, cocky, cold and manipulative … not the person I traveled with. Was that what he *used* to be, or what he now hid beneath a veneer of friendship?

I knelt and began to pray, not just for my soul, but for my friend's as well. God had led me to Jude, I knew it like I knew the faces of the men I served with in the Iraqi desert, my brothers born of trial and blood. Therefore I would trust in God and my instincts to help me lead Jude/Olivier upon the path of righteousness.

But that didn't preclude keeping a close eye on him.

Chapter Ten

Jude

Showering came only after I used Avoidance, which, to me, smelled like hospital disinfectant. For a while the spell would mask my presence from ... well, everyone, but a lifetime of casting Avoidance every time I feared contact with water looked daunting. Something would have to be done about the Primal Water Julian possessed.

My Cabo Wabo t-shirt was a loss, so I made do with a dark gray, skintight, long-sleeved Henley. Mike still wore his dog collar and black duds, looking as if he hadn't gone to sleep at all. Which made me realize he probably hadn't; instead he had most likely read more of my memoirs. From the covert glances he shot my way, I thought I knew which part he'd just finished.

Damn.

How did you talk to your best friend about a man like Gillan and the contemptuous ease with which you ended his life? Could Mike understand? Would he? Hell, it's been years and I still didn't quite understand, and I was there!

"Mike," I began.

He held up a hand. "Not now, Jude." The look he gave me held buckets of disquiet. "I have to sort some things out for myself, okay?"

"Okay, man. Whatever you need." If he needed time, time he would get.

Mike held up the silvery crucifix that had dispelled the demon, twisting it to and fro in the harsh light of the room. Sighing, he placed the chain around his neck and let the crucifix dangle to rest between his pecs.

"Where to now, Jude?"

I rubbed my chin. "We go to see Leslie Winchester."

His icy blue eyes grew wide. "Leslie Winchester? *The* Leslie Winchester?"

"That would be her."

"*Cinnamon Relic* Leslie Winchester, one of the greatest rock bands of all time Leslie Winchester?"

"Yes, that Leslie Winchester?"

He sat down abruptly on the corner of his rock-hard bed. I hoped he didn't have hemorrhoids. "I used to listen to *Cinnamon Relic* all the time. I had their Greatest Hits record. Nearly wore the vinyl down to nothing listening to it."

"Well, you're sounding like a broken record, so there's some synchronicity there."

"Har-de-har-har… What's she doing in Las Cruces?"

"She lives here, well actually in Mesilla, in a castle she had built special."

"A castle?"

"She's crazy about them, fancies herself a noblewoman of the middle ages and wants to live as one, or some such nonsense."

Mike pondered the insanity of aging rock stars for a moment. "I'm keen to meet her, but why are we going?"

"I believe she has the Grail." I licked my dry lips and repeated, "The Holy Grail."

Mike shook his head ruefully. "Of course she does. How silly of me not to have known." He blew a sigh through his nose. "Well, let's go."

"That's it?"

"What?"

I scratched my head. "I thought you'd be more—"

"Flabbergasted?" he asked.

"As good a word as any, but yes."

Mike fingered his crucifix and stared at the ceiling for a beat. "Listen Jude, I've seen you summon elemental beings, use Words that give you amazing abilities, and I've read about an amazing device called a molecular knife that you say exists." Another sigh. "I am quickly running out of skepticism. It seems that my reservoir of disbelief is running dry."

Good point. Time to reduce the skepticism ratio even more. "Thanks for the reminder." I fished the knife in question out of my duffel and thumbed the button.

"Is that it?" Mike asked, drawing close, eyes wide.

"Yes." Approaching the metal box I'd recovered from Earth, I leaned over and drew a line around the edge of the box on the side with the handle. When the minute line met itself, I pulled hard and the handle side came free.

"Wow ..." Mike whispered in awe.

I flicked the knife off. "Yeah."

"Double wow."

My hands dipped into the box and pulled out fat wads of cash until I had three stacks of ten thousand dollars each. Next came audiotape, the old fashioned reel-to-reel kind favored in the '70s.

"What the heck, Jude?"

I held up the cash and the audiotape. "The audiotape is an original John Lennon Blues number he recorded in a little dive in New York, the only copy in existence. Combine that with the close to eighty grand I have, she'll sell the Grail to us."

"Why would she sell the Grail? It's worth a heck of a lot more than *that.*"

"Leslie Winchester doesn't know she has the Grail. Unless you are one of the few who can see the world as it really is—a magus, for instance—then you would not see the cup of Christ."

"So how do people see it?"

From my duffel I produced a plastic Wal-Mart bag and stuffed the money inside. "I don't know, Mike. You might see it as a crucifix, or a dinner plate, and it would feel and weigh like what you beheld, man." Once I had the contents of the box squared away, I grabbed the keycard to the room. "Walk and talk, Mike. Walk and talk."

He followed me down the hall to the elevators. "How do you know she has it, if it looks like something different?"

In the elevator I hit the button for the first floor. "A year ago I came into possession of a library belonging to a magus named Edgar Truesdale." At his skeptical look, I raised my right hand. "I swear it was all legit, part of an estate sale. The old man died of a stroke. With the library came his personal papers."

"A member of your Family, then?"

I shook my head. "Nope, he was one of the rare ones, a magus born outside of a magical lineage. Anyway, in his personal papers, he documented his sale of a job lot of ancient artifacts to one Leslie Winchester for a serious amount of money. He could have made even more money if he'd been able to establish the provenance of some of the more ancient pieces. It seems he was strapped for cash and sold most of his collectables."

"I thought you said a magus could make his fortune with just three Words?"

"Good, you've been paying attention. Yes, it's true, but Edgar had only one … Truth, and he wasn't very good with it, or so I believe."

"And?" Mike asked as our elevator doors opened.

"And included in his notes was a letter from Leslie Winchester stating that she did not receive the antique gold spoon as stated on the item list; however she said she did like the silver brooch he had sent. From that I put two and two together."

He nodded. "From that and the pictures of the items no doubt accompanied his personal papers."

I smiled as we strode briskly down the hall to the front doors. "Very cynical, Mike, but true. Yes, collectors take pictures of all the items in their collections and I had all his photos. One picture showed a small, worn bowl, like those used to drink from, say about two thousand years ago in Judea. Looking at the picture, and reading the letters, I knew straight away what he'd sold. He probably stroked out when he realized what he'd done, poor beggar." The threadbare hallway carpet blurred by in a nauseating pattern of blue and red. How is it that hotels know how to pick the worst wall-to-wall possible? They must have blind interior decorators working for them.

"How was the camera able to catch the image of the real Grail?" Mike asked, stroking his moustache.

"The Grail fools the mind but cannot deceive film or electronics."

Glass double doors opened and the semi-warm evening air filled our lungs. "You could be wrong, you know." Mike sounded almost smug. *How unpriestly*, I thought. "How do you know so much about the Grail, that it appears as different things to different people?"

I stopped and turned to my friend, who nearly collided with me. "Mike, buddy, when are you going to get it into your head that I once had access to almost limitless data and funds? Think about it, dude, my whole Family knew the secret of the Grail. They've been looking for it for centuries."

He blinked. "Got it. Powerful family, big connections, secret history."

We resumed walking toward the black Grand Prix parked a short distance away. "Good, you're getting it. Now, let's just hope Leslie still has the Grail; then we can figure out if it can destroy the Silver."

"What if the Silver is more powerful?"

"It isn't. Trust me, the Grail is the big banana, next to the Ark."

As we approached the Grand Prix, I held the fob up and pushed the trunk release button. The trunk lid obligingly popped open. When we got to the car, what we saw stopped us short.

"Holy—!" Mile blurted.

"That's a little disturbing," I agreed tonelessly.

Inside the trunk was the body of a woman. More of a girl, really, face sliced to ribbons along with her clothes. She had been small, petite, and probably pretty, with a fine bone structure and porcelain skin. Her small breasts as well as her sex had been cruelly slashed and I could tell that the killer had taken his damn sweet time at the job. Long strips of skin and muscle lay around her body like obscene, fleshy streamers. The sheer sadism of the act appalled even my jaded senses.

"This would explain why the demon chose that man," I muttered as, behind me, Mike became violently sick. The smell of puke mixed revoltingly with the corpse and blood stench billowing from the trunk. "The damn fool was a serial killer."

"How can you tell?" Mike burbled as he barfed again. His black loafers and the hem of his pants were spotted with his upchuck.

I pointed to the precise, almost surgical, cuts paralleling her face and breasts. "He took his time; he's done this before. Also, he appeared to have been in his forties, perhaps early fifties, and I'm guessing that would be a late start in the serial killing business. Most serial killers start when they're younger. Or, at least, that's what I've read."

Poor girl, she looked like any young thing fresh out of puberty and ready to face the world with a fresh supply of hormones along with a healthy dose of overconfident rebellion. From the blood that covered her head to foot, she'd been quite alive when that sick fuck had taken a savagely sharp knife to her, obliterating her sense of immortality and infallibility.

"We must tell the police, Jude," Mike moaned, staring at his shoes. "Her people have to be informed, so she can have a decent burial."

He was right, the cops had to be told, but the last thing I needed was to be taken into a police station and made to answer quite a few embarrassing questions, not the least of which was 'What happened to your house?' If Las Cruces PD was in the loop with decent facial recognition programs, then my Family would know where I was in an instant. We had pioneered the software, after all. That was the reason I avoided all airports. So … no cops.

"We find a burger joint and dump the car there, then make an anonymous call to the police." I slammed the trunk lid down, hiding the horror within.

Mike was aghast. "We can't do that!" He used his sleeve to wipe the puke from his lips.

I couldn't look at him. "It has to be this way. We can't get involved and maybe, just maybe, when they find this sicko's ID, they'll be able to solve other murders he's committed."

Swallowing a lump of dread, I turned to see what I had half-expected, a look of disappointment in my friend's eyes that made me almost wish I had those old, hard calluses on my soul again. "We go to the cops, my Family finds me. Us. After what you've read, do you really want to meet Julian?"

Righteous anger, fear and determination warred behind his baby blues for a few moments before his shoulders slumped and he nodded in resignation. It must have been a bitter pill for him to swallow, but at that moment necessity beat out the desire to assist the police and I couldn't be happier. However it did sting a bit to know how much that admission cost him, how badly it dented his principles.

Despite the blow to civic sensibilities, we meandered around the city until we found a battered blue Ford pick-up with a red and black For Sale sign in the front window. The rusted '80s vehicle rested on somewhat inflated tires in front of a respectable ranch style with a front yard containing three tons of crushed red and white rock.

When the owner cautiously answered the front door, he visibly relaxed at the sight of a priest on his front step. He was further reassured by Mike's willingness to pay his outrageous price for the beat-up old truck, although he lowered it a tad in deference to Mike's collar.

If franchise hotels are like weeds, then fast food joints are like cockroaches; when you see one, you know there are a thousand more just around the corner. Between a Wowzaburger (home of the greasiest cheeseburger in the Southwest) and a dilapidated white crack house lay a broken, dirt-covered drive that suited our needs perfectly. After parking the Grand Prix (carefully wiped of all prints) on the broken concrete, Mike picked me up and we were gone in far less than sixty seconds.

Mike stared out into the darkness, barely illuminated by the truck's anemic headlights. "Where to?" he inquired in a voice devoid of life.

"Time to see Leslie Winchester," I replied, more tired than I had been in a long time. When I worked alone, absent friends, the events of the past day wouldn't have fazed me one bit, but now, with Mike as my own little Jiminy Cricket, my energy levels had dropped somewhere south of zero. Who knew that a conscience could take so much out of you? I stared out of the corner of my eye at Mike as he drove, his jaw set in ferocious determination, and I realized I wouldn't trade places with my old self—that egocentric bastard—for all the safety and security in the world.

"Is there a Catholic church in Mesilla?" asked Mike.

I nodded. "A rather famous one, San Albino."

Big hands gripped the steering wheel until the knuckles shone white. "Right. Show me where."

How could I refuse?

Less than ten minutes later we reached the heart of Mesilla, a large plaza that held more tourist trap shops than you could shake a stick at, most selling 'authentic' Native American artwork and knickknacks. Hundreds of luminaria (small paper lanterns made of brown bags and weighted with sand in which a candle was set) were placed along the walkways illuminating the square, as well as the large wood and stucco gazebo in the plaza's center. Festooned in and around the gazebo were electric Christmas lights, contrasting boldly with the luminaria.

At one end, looming over the plaza like a patient father, stood the basilica San Albino with its twin rectangular towers bracketing the main body, a large white statue of the Virgin Mary out in front of the steps, staring at the stars.

We parked in a narrow lot just off the square and Mike quickly hopped out. "I'll be back," he said tersely.

Well, well, well … Feeling like a bad boy forced to stand in the corner for a time-out, I briefly experienced the need to follow. Instead I ground my teeth in frustration, sat on my fundament and waited.

And waited.

In the old days my natural impatience would have had me out of the truck in a hot second. This time, I sat and fumed.

Perhaps an hour went by, maybe more, but I didn't have a clue because in the middle of my fit of pouting I fell asleep.

Chapter Eleven

Jude

"Wake up, Jude."

They say you have to wake a trained killer from a distance because his first reaction would be to cause grievous bodily harm to the person doing the waking. In my case, that had been true, but fifteen years of relatively stress-free living had blunted my Spidey-sense somewhat so that I didn't even register Mike's presence until his loud voice startled me out of my slumber and caused me to mumble, "Whblet?"

He snorted, face craggy in the pick-up's overhead light. "Some ultra-dangerous wet work magus assassin you are." He sounded a lot happier than when he left.

Given enough time, perhaps ten minutes or so, I would've burned the flesh from his bones with a scathing remark. "What took you so long, man?"

"Confession."

Wow. I never studied the workings of the Catholic Church, but it made sense: even priests needed someone to talk to. "Almost wish I'd been a fly on the wall in the confessional."

For the first time since we'd found the body of the young girl, Mike smiled with genuine good humor. "He did recommend a good psychiatrist."

We both laughed, then he sobered. "The good father will contact the police anonymously concerning the body," he said.

Before my mouth could open wide enough to fit my size tens, I gave what he said some serious thought. Even if the police did manage to track the call back to the priest, the seal of the confessional would keep his mouth shut as to his source, so I didn't have to risk the Voice finding me in a police station. Mike must have seen all this in my face, for he just nodded, inserted the key in the ignition and fired up the tired old truck.

I nodded. "Let's go see a rock star." With that, we left the square and its shops made of adobe, brick and wood. The luminaria were a warm fare-thee-well in the rearview mirror.

Full night had descended and a fingernail moon lent scant light to the parched landscape as we pulled up to the estate of Leslie Winchester.

Unlike most construction in that part of the Southwest, the eight-foot wall surrounding the estate was made of large limestone blocks instead of adobe. It was too dark to see the castle; no light shone through any windows, but we did see a driveway guarded by a large wrought-iron gate with a speaker box set on a three-foot pole off to one side.

"What do you think?" Mike asked as we exited the truck parked across the street.

I handed him my duffel with the Silver in its holy water bath. "Let's ring the bell." My thumb pushed the button on the speaker box.

No answer. Again I pushed the button.

Soon after, a squinchy kind of warble came from the box. "Yes?" came a deep, cultured voice with a British accent.

Of course she'd have a butler or valet or major domo or whatever the Brits called them. I was willing to bet his name was Jeeves.

"Yes, sir, father Michael Engle and friend to see Ms. Winchester on some rather urgent business."

A roomful of snooty came back over the box. Jeeves must have been looking forward to a quiet night. "You must realize, sir, that it is after 8 p.m."

Tempting as it was to push a load of my own attitude back at him, I kept my voice respectful. "Father Engle desperately needs to talk to Ms. Winchester and it will only take at the most ten minutes."

"I shall inform the madam." Jeeves responded blandly. "One moment, please."

A hard knuckle rapped my arm. "Father Michael to see Ms. Winchester?" Mike sounded a little miffed.

"People respond to priests more positively than just an average Joe off the street."

"Harrumph."

I swear he must've practiced his 'harrumphs' in the mirror every morning.

Minutes later the iron gate slowly started to slide to the right and we strolled on through, up the driveway to the castle. Even up close it was barely visible, registering more as a darkly looming presence than a structure. Off to either side of the driveway I did manage to note that instead of crushed rock landscaping, Leslie Winchester managed to maintain a rather large yard of—if the smell was any indication—very lush grass. Tall trees formed ominous shapes here and there. They were most likely cottonwoods, the heartiest and tallest trees in the region.

Before we could get too close to the castle, floodlights came on with the kind of suddenness that has adrenaline pumping through your body in bucketfuls, and pinned us to the spot. We shaded our eyes to spare them from the blinding light.

Jeeves' voice emerged from speakers we couldn't see. "Please raise your hands above your heads and turn around."

We complied.

"Good enough. Thank you, gentlemen." With that, the drawbridge lowered.

Yes, a real-as-can-be drawbridge with clanking, rattling chains, the creaking of stressed wood and a tremendous *thud* that was felt right to the bones of our feet as it came to rest in front of us. Winchester was taking the whole ancient English castle a bit too far, I thought.

A garage. A big one well lit by fluorescents, holding half a dozen cars from Aston Martins to Audis. Standing in front, hands behind his back, was the one I assumed must be Jeeves. He confirmed my suspicion when he spoke.

"Father Engle," he said, staring up at Mike. "What is the nature of your visit?"

I took the moment before Mike answered to size up the butler. Short, maybe five-five, one hundred fifty pounds, very wide shoulders, black hair, big nose, weak chin and hairy eyebrows that looked like two caterpillars squaring off. All this was stuffed into a classic tuxedo complete with tails.

Mike took a slow step forward and I saw the butler's shoulders tense slightly. "Sir, my business with Ms. Winchester concerns both myself and my companion." Mike gently laid the duffel down onto the concrete. "It has to do with a certain antiquity she purchased a year ago." A hint of movement came from deep within the recesses of the garage.

Something tweaked my 'uh-oh' button. I noticed Jeeves stood on the balls of his feet and then I took in again the breadth of his shoulders and the fact that his hands still were hidden behind his back. This man knew how to take care of himself and I would've bet my last peso that he had a pistol in his hand. This was no ordinary butler by a long shot. Right then I knew we were walking into the lion's den smelling like prime rib.

Leslie Winchester came forward from the recesses of the garage into the light of the floods and I felt my eyes open wide in admiration. Not beautiful, but definitely a handsome woman, her once pixyish face had matured into a full blown representation of sensuality that age had not dimmed at all; in fact, my hot-o-meter was running into the red. Shoulder-length permed blond hair framed her face and her bust strained at a blue SOUNDGARDEN t-shit while her ample hips were encased in sprayed-on blue jeans. A pair of dainty white cowboy boots covered her curiously tiny feet.

"Nigel," she crooned through nibblesome, pouty lips. "A man of the cloth is always welcome here."

Nigel. Really? He would have been better off as a Jeeves.

"Really, madam, I must insist you stay back," Nigel warned, mouth set in a grim line. I felt danger spill into the air, the sense you get when lightning is about to strike. Surreptitiously, I slid my hand into the front pocket of my black jeans and palmed what was inside.

"Really, Nigel, I know a good man when—" Leslie began, eyes focused solely on Mike. Maybe I moved a fraction, or she caught me out of the corner of her eye, for she suddenly swiveled her head toward me and screamed, pointing a long, blood-red fingernail. *"Nigel! Watch out!"*

Not good, I thought just before shit hit the fan.

Both Nigel and I made our moves at the same time; he brought the gun he'd been hiding behind his back to bear and I flung what I'd palmed in a sidearm throw as I started forward. Two quarter-inch ball steel ball bearings flew at Nigel's skull, propelled with all the desperate strength I could muster, my heart trip-hammering in fear. The business end of his silenced pistol looming toward me like a tunnel to Hell. A Walther PPK, I observed offhandedly, how very James Bond. My lizard brain gibbered as fight-or-flight hormones flooded my bloodstream.

A quarter-inch ball bearing doesn't seem like much—an itty-bitty little thing—but if you ever hefted one, you'd be surprised at its weight and smooth perfection. Then throw it … hard. That little ball bearing will pound into your average piece of drywall and stick. Now, imagine getting hit in the head by one. Ouch, lights out.

Unless you unload one with a wrist-rocket, it won't kill your target, but if it hits the skull, it could put your enemy out of commission for about a week.

Nigel the Brit had better reflexes than I thought. As the two bearings left my hand, he took a half step to the side, aiming the PPK while I propelled myself forward on legs suddenly energized with adrenaline.

His first shot went wide, spoiled by a bearing hitting his left cheek with the sound of a ball-peen hammer hitting a side of beef. It rocked his head back. His second shot took a chunk out of my right ear as the other bearing sailed over his head to ricochet off the garage ceiling.

There wasn't time for Words and if I had tried for one, Nigel would have used that pause to put two in my chest and one in my head. As effective as Words are, sometimes they're just not fast enough.

Before the pain from my mutilated ear had time to register, I was within range of the short Brit, reaching for his gun hand. Without flinching he dropped the weapon and sidestepped, bringing his other arm to the party holding a fistful of K-bar.

As Leslie continued to scream in an ever annoying, piercing pitch, I dodged Nigel's first swipe with the knife and punched him in the chest with a palm strike that should have knocked him ass over hat; instead it felt like slapping a brick wall. He gave perhaps an inch and smiled nastily.

Something about the way he held himself set alarm bells jangling up a storm. "SAS," I guessed.

He nodded, not even breathing hard, the bastard. "Retired. You?"

"Sicarii, also retired."

His eyes widened briefly. So, he'd heard of the Family business. Not surprising, considering that the U.S., U.K. and Russian intelligence agencies had known for generations, but it did speak volumes of his former clearance levels. You know, the kind usually reserved for heads-of-state.

"I've 'eard of you wankers," he confirmed, all trace of upper crust dissolving into something that would never pass in Buckingham Palace. A nice little mouse was forming under his left eye. "Real bad arseholes, ain't ya?"

"I do all right, Jeeves."

He flicked a glance at Leslie, who had stopped screaming and stared at us in mute fascination. "The lady wants a proper butler, don't she? So I gives it to 'er, an' she pays well for it."

"Jude!" Mike warned. "Don't do this!"

"No dice, man," I countered. "This has to be."

Nigel's grin contained enough purified wickedness to stun a rhino.

"Too right, mate." The tip of the K-bar moved in little circles. "Too right."

Mike sighed and held up his hands in surrender. Leslie took a couple of steps toward the priest, as if his godliness would shield her from collateral damage.

The K-bar blurred toward my throat the same instant Nigel tried to grab my right arm with his left hand in an effort to draw me close for the finishing stroke. I slapped his knife hand away, earning a cut to my forearm, and managed to weasel away from his grasping left hand. Dull pain erupted from my leg where the toe of his shiny lace-ups had smacked against my right shin.

I hopped back, favoring my left leg, and took the full force of his evil smile. We had just tested each other and he was better. For the first time in a long while I faced an opponent I actually feared and, from the satisfaction in his eyes, he knew it.

Damn, I hate having to cheat.

Healing ... cinnamon ... Vigor and Strength ... ammonia and peanuts ... All the fatigue from the day vanished. Good times.

My first strike, a knife hand to the tricep, numbed his arm while my second, backed by Strength, thudded into his solar plexus, robbing him of breath. Poor Nigel stood there, bent over and trying to catch his breath when I used my hole card ... Force.

I sneezed the aroma of burning insulation out of my lungs as Nigel found himself flying through the air, landing with a jarring crash on the hood of a silver Aston Martin. The hood crumpled like tinfoil and his spine starred the windshield before he flipped over the car out of sight.

"Aw, damn," I moaned to myself. "Not the Vanquish! I love that car."

"You bastard!" came a piercing shriek. I turned toward the source just in time to catch a full on slap from Leslie Winchester that had a heap of heat behind it. "You've killed Nigel!"

Mike rushed up and tried to calm the hysterical rocker down, placing his body like a shield in front of me. Enraged, she still tried to brush past for another go. He managed to capture her in the cage of his arms.

"He's alive, lady!" I shouted back at her as she screamed more imprecations at me, most of which were anatomically impossible.

Instantly she deflated. "Alive?" Her voice, when not shouting or screaming, was very throaty, sexy.

"Yeah." I motioned toward the damaged Vanquish while rubbing my stinging cheek. She'd hit hard enough for my teeth to cut the inside of my mouth. For an older lady, her arm had surprising strength.

A low-pitched moan came from behind the Vanquish and the former rock diva produced a tiny *eeep* and ran to check on the damaged Nigel. "She sure can hit a ton, man," I told Mike.

He arched an eyebrow. "You did mangle that poor butler."

"Poor butler!" I exclaimed. "He's former SAS. If I had given him an inch, he would've taken a mile of my precious hide."

Shiny whites cut through his moustache. "Never saw you scared before. I have to admit, you sure looked like you got knocked down a peg there for a second."

Leslie, who was crooning sweet nothings in Nigel's battered ears, was helping the groaning butler to his feet. "You think there's something going on there?" I whispered, holding a hand to my stinging ear. A hole the size of a dime had been torn open by Nigel's bullet and was bleeding freely.

Mike stared at the couple staggering toward us. "If there wasn't anything before, there will be soon." He squinted at the limping Brit while handing me a white hanky. "Can you do something for him?"

"You asking me to perform magic?" I raised my eyes toward the heavens while holding the hanky to my leaking ear. " 'And the sun will be darkened and the moon will be as blood.' Surely this must be the end times."

A ham-sized fist punched me in the arm. "Don't be a dick."

I shook my head and rubbed my arm where he'd hit me. "Didn't know priests could be so violent." Leslie and her pet butler made their way around the Aston, him sporting a bruised and bloody face while she kept a death grip on his arm. Briefly I pondered the strange things that bring us humans together and why it seemed that only when things were at their worst were we at our best.

Nigel and his new love bunny headed deeper into the garage, so Mike and I followed, catching up to the pair before they could reach a large oak door banded with iron that looked as if it had been a prop in a Robin Hood movie. "Wait a second," I urged, cutting the two off at the pass.

"Don't you hurt him!" Leslie hissed. I mean, really hissed. You read about people hissing their sentences, but this was the first time I'd experienced it. Kind of cool in a scary, creepy sort of way.

I held up a hand while cupping my ear with the other. The hanky was heavy with blood. "Easy there, Ms. Winchester. I only want to help Mister ... Nigel here, if you let me."

"You tried to kill him!" she screeched with enough force to drive nails through my ears.

Nigel stared at me with the one eye that wasn't puffed shut. "Mum, if 'e wanted to kill me, 'e would 'ave, wouldn't 'e?"

"Your Liverpool is showing," I grinned.

"Well, it's me old home, innit?"

"Love your accent." Before he could reply I clapped a palm on the top of his black hair (gray at the roots, I saw) and used Healing.

The result was dramatic, to say the least. Back arching, he stood on his tippy toes for just a second before slamming his heels back onto the concrete.

"Nigel? Are you all right? Did he hurt you again?" Leslie shrieked. I'd begun to wonder if this voice was the norm, if she reserved the sexy one for special occasions. If so, I didn't envy Nigel.

Nigel waved her off. "It's okay, mum. Whatever he did, I feel ruddy marvelous. It's a miracle!" he marveled, hopping from foot to foot. I noticed that his speech had reverted to the oh-so-proper Jeeves mode.

Leslie stared at me with wide, wide eyes. "What did you do?"

Mike came up from behind. "Why don't we discuss everything over some tea?"

Nigel nodded. "Yes, that is brilliant."

Muttering a Healing that stemmed the flow from my damaged ear, I nodded in agreement.

Chapter Twelve

Jude

"Why did you scream when you saw me?"

Righteous question, I thought. Usually women don't react to me like that. Sighing, I blew softly into my cup of Earl Gray and waited for an answer. Thanks to Healing my ear was fine, not even a scab.

The butler, happy to be healed and saying that I'd cured his bad knee as well, had led us through the Robin Hood door and into the house/castle.

Leslie might have fancied herself a fourteenth-century lady, but her place belonged squarely in the twenty-first. Black and white checked marble floors, Persian rugs, warm wood and glittering crystal. And the kitchen, oh my! The kitchen would have Bobby Flay drooling like a bloodhound. A stainless-steel fridge the size of Buick, a pantry that could double as a bedroom and a separate freezer unit large enough to hold a cow or three.

"I've been having … dreams. Bad dreams and you, or someone who looks like you, was in them." Leslie took a sip of her tea. She rested her elbows on the polished surface of a mahogany table large enough to seat twelve comfortably. "They started about a year ago, but stopped about five months ago."

Mike, who sat next to Nigel, nodded. "They started after you bought that job lot of artifacts from Edgar Truesdale, is—"

"One moment," Nigel interrupted, comfortably out of his Jeeves persona. "I was my employer's purchasing agent."

Leslie nodded. "I don't travel much and Nigel is the only person I trust, so he was sent to procure the antiquities. He emailed the photographs to me of the different lots and I chose which one to buy."

I rubbed my temples in an attempt to forestall a headache. "Lovely, but what were the dreams you had of me? Was I the villain of your subconscious?"

She couldn't meet my eyes. "Every time I dreamed of you, I felt overwhelming danger," she said timidly.

Strange things, unseemly and unnatural things, had been happening to me all my life, so that bit of news barely registered on my Strange Crap-O-Meter. However, Mike and I did exchange a look or two. "The Grail?" he asked.

I shook my head. "Had to be."

"What? Do you mean the Holy Grail?" Nigel's body tensed.

"Yes, like the Holy Grail," I replied with a sigh.

Leslie's head wobbled around like a bobble-head doll's. "Seriously?"

Mike placed his hand on hers. "Yes, Ms. Winchester."

She turned from him to me, finally able to look me in the eye. "Who are you? Why did I dream of you?" I noticed the fine crow's feet fanning from the corners of her eyes.

"Tell them, Jude," Mike said with a sigh. "They have what we're looking for, so they deserve to know."

"Mike ..." I warned. "They'll sic the men in white with the butterfly nets and wraparound jackets after us."

"No, Jude. I'm going to have to insist on this one." His face settled into familiar stubborn lines. "It's the decent thing to do. The *right* thing."

I groaned, "I was afraid you were going to say that."

"What?"

"Well, Nigel," I began. "Let me start by saying that I *love* your accent." Nothing. Not a smirk or chuckle. Tough castle. "Okay, this story begins in Omaha …."

Mike filled in the blank spots with what he'd already read, allowing us to keep the story to less than two hours. Through it all, Nigel and Leslie's mouths opened and closed several times in surprise.

"Oh my word, I heard of the Sicarii beggars before, but we always reckoned they were a small for-hire group only," Nigel remarked, his tea cold and forgotten. "Either that or they were affiliated with those South American drug blokes."

"How high was your clearance?"

"Been with the SAS for near thirty years, so I heard many things."

"Gad, I nearly got my ass handed to me by an old man? I'll never live it down."

Leslie beamed, running a slim hand down Nigel's arm. He didn't seem to mind at all. "Not so old to me." She said. An answering grin blossomed on his homely face, which handsomed him up considerably.

Mike cleared his throat. "We think the silver brooch, which is really the Grail, somehow gave you those dreams, maybe as a warning, or to prepare you for Jude's arrival. Interpreting dreams is not an exact science, you know."

"Leslie, you said it was me or someone who looked like me." I took a sip of cold tea. "Think, was it me? Look at me now and think back to your dream … Are you sure it was me?"

"I think so … It's been so long." She worried her bottom lip in such a way that I wanted to add mine to the mix, but I'd probably have to fight Nigel for the privilege.

"Leslie, why did the dreams stop?" Mike asked.

When she didn't answer, Nigel spoke up. "Because she doesn't have the bloody artifact anymore," he whispered sadly. She nodded.

I laid my forehead on the table. "Aww … Jiminy Christmas … I'd hoped this would be easy."

"Easy? Easy?" blurted Mike. "You think what we've been through is easy? Elementals, serial killers and Nigel the British Mike Tyson? Not to mention that fresh notch in your ear."

My felt like a lump of lead. "Yeah, Mike ... considering that my Family is involved, this has been a cakewalk."

"Which means?"

"It's only going to get harder."

"I knew you were going to say that."

"You guys sound like Danny Glover and Mel Gibson in *Lethal Weapon*, you know that?" Leslie hid her smile behind a slim hand.

The bloom must have faded from the rose of Mike's teenage crush because he gave her a rather crusty look. "Thanks tons, that's so comforting." He snorted. "At least I get to be Danny Glover."

"Okay, as amusing as this is, let's get back on topic." I pierced Leslie with my own hard look. "The brooch ... the Grail. Nigel said you don't have it anymore, so where is it?" It wasn't as if I was surprised. For most of my life, Murphy's Laws have been a constant I've never been able to escape or dodge. Believe me, even Words are of no use in avoiding them.

Nigel bowed his head and Leslie toyed with her teacup for a moment before saying, "My son stole it."

Mike goggled. "Your son stole the Holy Grail?"

Nigel bristled at his tone while I just put my head in my hands. "What? It did not look like the bloody Holy Grail."

"All right, all right, everyone. Chill out," I said into the palm of my hands. "Tell me what happened, please."

Leslie sighed. "My boy, Alexander, came 'round about six months ago in an old '82 Pan Head that his father had given to him for his fifteenth birthday, said he wanted to come to see his mom, but what he really wanted was to take whatever he could fit in his backpack."

"Of course." Artifacts like the Grail have an unsettling habit of eluding those who search for them. I think God reckons that man should not muck about with them, at least not the ones who know their power. I passed my thoughts on to the group.

"So you think God made my son take the Grail?"

I phrased my reply carefully. No need to irritate mama bear. "I think God provides the opportunity and lets us talking monkeys decide if we want to take advantage." The last of the tea slithered its way down my throat. "But let me put it to you this way: there are dozens of powerful artifacts in the world, all loaded with their own special powers, so why doesn't mankind know about them all? Why hasn't there been an amazing discovery, documented and publicized?"

Nigel squinted at me. "Because they don't want to be found, do they?"

"Got it in one."

"So what now?" Mike asked.

"Now we go have a word with Alexander."

Leslie bristled in full mama-bear mode. "Don't you hurt my boy! He's not perfect, but he is mine."

I donned my most sincere look. "Not a problem, ma'am. Just want to have a word or three with him. If you want, I'll let Mike do the talking."

Nigel patted Leslie's hand. "You won't find the little bleeder without his mother. He rides with a motorcycle gang. Moves around like a gypsy."

"Do you know where Alexander is now, Leslie?" Mike asked gently.

She nodded. "I can find out. He gave me a number to call if I needed to get in touch. But first I want reassurances." Her face shut down hard and fast.

Looking at her, I knew she wouldn't budge and from Mike's expression, he knew it too.

"What do you want?" I asked cautiously.

She held up a fist and her pinky rose. "One: I want your promise you won't hurt my boy." Another finger joined the pinky. "Two: I want to see that Silver you've talked about." The third finger made an appearance and she leaned toward us. "Three: I want to *see* some more magic."

Mike and I exchanged a look. "Done and done," we said in unison. Strange that the spontaneous Healing of Nigel hadn't been enough for her.

"Bloody *Lethal Weapon*, indeed," muttered Nigel under his breath.

I ignored the comment, but inside was pleased. Obviously I was the Mel Gibson character, Riggs. Dipping into my backpack, I pulled out a plastic liter bottle, empty except for a little dribble at the bottom, and the cardboard cylinder containing the Silver. I removed the top, the camouflage tablets and pulled out the fishbowl. Only a few drops of black fluid rolled around on the bottom like maleficent mercury. Just looking at it prickled the hairs on the back of my neck.

Nigel peered at the bowl. "That bag? That's it?"

"It's what's inside that will shrivel your *cojones*." I held the near empty bottle out to Mike. "Can you bless some more water? This is all that's left." He nodded as he grabbed the bottle and headed toward the tap.

Leslie took a deep breath. "What's that black liquid?"

I considered the foul fluid. "Denatured holy water. Call it unholy water."

Behind me I heard a clatter as Mike dropped the plastic bottle. "What do you mean 'unholy water'?" Nigel asked.

"When the Silver comes in contact with holy water, it begins to transform it, turn it into something that doesn't ... irritate it, I guess. As its nature is infernal, it changes it to something that suits its nature."

"What is it, exactly, then?" Leslie asked.

A private part of me wanted to tuck the Silver back in its cylinder and shut down that line of inquiry, but a promise was a promise, no matter how annoying. "It's exactly what I said it is, Silver."

"Okay, that ... Silver thingy is bad, evil, but why keep it in holy water? Does that neutralize its power?" I could tell she wanted to touch the bowl, but I kept it out of reach.

"Kind of," I replied slowly. "Mainly it's to keep my Family and the Voice from sensing it, and thereby finding me. You see, I stole it from them."

Mike began to speak softly, blessing the tap water, I guess.

I got a wide-angle view of Leslie's eye as she stared through the bowl. "How powerful is it? What does it do?" Nigel stood very close to her and I hid my smile by half turning away. Oh yeah, those two were going to hook up or I was a blind man.

"The Silver had been the ... crux, I guess, of my Family's power for the past two millennia. When a Family member who's a magus holds it, he has access to very powerful, even devastating Words."

"What kind?" asked the butler.

I met Nigel's eyes and something in mine gave him pause. "Trust me, mate, you don't want to know."

"So the Grail—" Leslie began.

"Will destroy the Silver, I believe," I finished, setting the bowl down. Mike walked over, pressed the now full plastic bottle into my hand and gave me a reassuring pat on the back.

"Well, kids, it's been a swell ride," I grinned, hoping it would hide my fatigue. "But we really have to boogie."

"You're not going to tell us any more, are you?" For some reason Leslie looked a little sad. I guess she wasn't comfortable with a little mystery.

"Some things are best left unsaid and some things are best left unknown. 'Ignorance is bliss' is not just a catchy phrase, man."

Mike nodded. "He hasn't even told *me* what the Silver is."

I nodded. "But he'll find out soon enough."

Chapter Thirteen

Mike

Despite the strange and unusual circumstances, not to mention the outrageous story Jude and I had spun, Leslie was a gracious hostess. Heck, if it had been me, I might have called the nearest mental hospital for a brace of straitjackets and a pair of big Iowa farm boys to help strap them on.

I must admit that, upon first meeting Leslie Winchester, my adolescent fantasies from the early '80s dimmed somewhat against the harsh light of reality. Even so, she remained a fine figure of a woman, lush and emanating enough sex appeal to make my collar feel tight. It was the first time in a long while I heard the siren call of the opposite sex.

Leslie was kind enough to offer us a bed for the night, but we declined, our business being too urgent for us to lose any more time. Sighing, she found her smart phone and tapped an icon. Obligingly, she hit the SPEAKER and let us listen in.

A clicking noise as a gravelly voice answered, "Ma? Is that you?"

"Yes, Alexander, it's me," replied Leslie with a melancholy smile.

"Look, if it's about the glass rose, I'm sorry, I couldn't help myself." Alexander, despite his deep, gruff voice, sounded petulant and childish.

I looked at Jude. *Glass rose?* I mouthed silently. He nodded once, affirming that the Grail's camouflage capability was at work.

"It's okay, sweetie," Leslie purred. "It's not about that. Where are you?"

"At our place in Bend."

"Good. Honey, a couple of friends of mine want to talk to you. It's important."

Alexander's voice became even rougher. "I don't wanna talk to anyone, Ma."

"Sweetie," she soothed. "It's all right. They're good people. One's a priest."

"And the other one, Ma, is he a slim, darker man, dark like an Ay-rab or Jew?"

I felt a prickle down my spine. Jude shook his head, eyes hooded with concern. This wasn't going to end well.

"Yes, his name is Jude. I believe he's a good man."

"Ma, I see either that priest or that Ay-rab Jew up here and I'm gonna put a hole in 'em. That also goes for that uptight Limey bastard you got waitin' on you hand and foot."

Leslie's face became a study in apprehension. "Alexander, please!"

"The name's Baphemaloch, Ma." Behind me I heard Jude swear softly. Later, I'd have to talk to him about his language. "Me and the Demons are going to Keep the Glass Rose Safe." I could hear the capitals in his voice. "So if you see your two pals, tell them Baphemaloch is waiting." The line went dead.

"Shit," Jude muttered while Leslie moaned and began to weep, laying her head on Nigel's shoulder.

"Language," I admonished. Still, I couldn't put any heat into the rebuke because of the creepy feeling skittering over my skin. Alexander/Baphemaloch's voice had carried a diamond-sharp edge.

"What? What's going on?" Nigel said, perplexed and angry.

Jude sighed. "Alexander is under the influence."

Nigel raised an eyebrow through the curls of Leslie's hair as she dampened his tux with her tears.

"What, Jude?" I kept my tone neutral. "What kind of influence? Drugs?"

He shook his head, avoiding our eyes. "Who are the demons he was talking about?"

"The biker gang he belongs to, Demon's Blood," Leslie's voice was muffled by the stiff fabric of Nigel's jacket.

"Mate, the priest asked you a question. What influence is Alexander under?" Nigel inquired calmly, features set in stone.

He fingered the notch in his ear. "Drugs, man. Probably meth."

Jude's lie caused a wave of nausea to sweep through me. His terrible poker face was visible only to me because he was half turned away from Nigel. He knew I'd caught him out.

Leslie sobbed harder as Nigel stroked her hair.

A few minutes later the couple escorted us through the front door/garage/drawbridge affair all the way to the wrought-iron gate. Jude turned to the shaken Leslie and said, "I'll do what I can to help Alexander."

A spark of hope caught behind her eyes and blazed. "You promise?" she begged in a little girl lost voice.

"Hey!" Jude said suddenly. "I still owe you some magic." He turned to Nigel and me. "Give us a moment, gents."

Obligingly we moved away, watching curiously as Jude leaned in and whispered into Leslie's ear.

I looked at the butler. "Nigel, do you mind if I ask you a personal question?"

He grinned impishly "You want to know what a former SAS chap from Liverpool is doing in the States acting like a proper butler to her nibs?"

"Well, yeah."

"Not too ruddy hard to figure. I retired from service and was dithering around my flat when a chum of mine who runs an employment service calls and informs me that *the* Leslie Winchester was looking for a real gentleman butler." He sighed, staring at the woman talking softly with Jude. "My friend knows I have it something bad for the lady, always have since I bought my first *Cinnamon Relic* back in the '70s. So I donned my best high-end accent and he puts me into the job. That was six bloody years ago and I've been happy bugger ever since."

One thing puzzled me. "Why the upper-crust dialect?"

"Americans expect the snooty, snide type of talk they see in Merchant Ivory productions," he said as if that explained everything. At my look of incomprehension, he said, "I must of watched *Remains of the Day* at least a dozen times so I could sound like Anthony Hopkins."

I nodded sagely, wondering if Leslie realized how much he cared for her.

A few seconds later Leslie gave Jude a tight hug, her face bright and happy, while he surreptitiously rubbed his nose.

"Thank you very much for your generosity, Ms. Winchester," Jude said with false good cheer. "I'm sorry for any ruckus we might have caused."

"Nonsense, Jude!" she said, dimpling prettily. "I'm sorry for all the screaming. And please, it's Leslie."

"Leslie it is, then."

"Hey, I still have to call Alexander for you, just a sec." She began toward the castle, but Jude put himself in her way with one swift move.

"No need, Leslie, I'll find him. I have my ways and it will be just fine."

Nigel and I gave each other a puzzled look but kept our traps shut.

"You still owe me some more magic," said Leslie.

"Right you are!" Jude ran his slender fingers though her hair and said a Word.

I've heard Jude use Words and, like all the others, this one slipped into my ear and nestled in the frontal lobe like a happy cat before screeching and tearing off out the other ear. The sensation wasn't unpleasant.

Whatever Word he whispered in her ear hit like an electric shock, causing her to tremble violently. Her eyes grew so round, so wide I thought that they would pop out.

Nigel rushed forward, body poised to lash out with lethal force, but suddenly the tension went out of Leslie as if someone had blown out the candle of her rigidity.

"Oh, wow ... what a rush," she breathed, face flushed and streaming with sweat.

"You all right, mum?" Nigel asked, voice tight.

She grabbed him by the shoulders and planted a long wet one on him that carried so much heat that even the neighbors must have felt it.

"Good lord," I said, crossing myself and pulling Jude away from the two and their frantic embrace. "Jude, what did you do?"

"Hit her with a Forgetting, erased the memory of the conversation with Alexander." The happy couple continued their clinch, Nigel giving as much as he got and adding a bit of interest. "I also gave her Vigor, which is a lot like a super dose of caffeine without the tremors." He eyeballed the two for another moment. "I think it tore down the barrier that has kept those two apart."

I whispered out of the corner of my mouth, "Was a Forgetting necessary?"

"You saw how broken up she was," he whispered back. "This is much better, although I hate messing with peoples' minds. The smell of licorice makes me want to barf."

"How's your ear, by the way?" I asked, pointing to the notch right above the lobe of his left ear.

He fingered the gap. "I wish Healing would regenerate lost tissue. But I'm okay, man."

The two lovebirds hadn't come up for air yet, so I grabbed Jude (who seemed enthralled by their embrace) and led him out the gate. "You need to find a nice girl, Jude."

"If I find one, I hope she can hold her breath like *that*," he remarked with a smile.

"Don't be a perv."

The smile slid from his face. "Least of my sins."

Jude did the driving from there, heading out toward 25 North, but before that we stopped at a Circle K, where he asked me to gas the truck while he went inside to pay. As the digits on the pump climbed, Jude exited the store with a small plastic bag and a donut in one hand.

"You got twenty bucks for gas," he slurred through a mouth of day-old pastry.

"Cool. Get me one?"

He shook his head. "Last one, but I did you one better." Smiling through powdered sugar, he handed me a Mountain Dew. "I know it's not sacramental wine, but—"

"It'll do." Ah, the sweet caffeinated brew caressed my throat like an old lover. I so missed the buzz of stimulants, the only vice I really subscribe to. "That hit the spot," I belched. "Now what?"

"Now we drive a while."

"Then?"

"We make a phone call."

Lovely. Great time to get all mysterious on me, but pushing him wouldn't get me jack-squat, so I sat next to him, basking in a comfortable silence that only good friends can generate.

Before too long we passed a wide spot in the middle of the road called Socorro, a flash of neon and halogens that met our eyes briefly before it became a quickly fading memory. It was about five miles north of that little town that Jude pulled over and eased out of the car, taking the bag with him. He left the engine running and the headlights on.

"Jude, what is it?" By the dim light of the sliver moon and the stars, I saw him hold up a plastic case and drop the bag to the ground.

"Don't litter," I snapped, picking up the bag.

"Saint Michael." The smugness in his voice was thick enough to cut.

"Smartass. Now what gives?"

"Phone call." He turned toward me and ripped the plastic case open and held up a disposable cell phone. "I have some things to tell you that are going to seem rather … fantastic. You have to stay strong."

Uneasy, I nodded. "I think I have heard a few fantastic things already."

"Oh, and get my duffel, please."

After I set the duffel at his feet, he rummaged through, pulling out the liter bottle of holy water, a plastic sleeve of Dixie cups and a small make-up case. Opening the case he removed a small fat jar with a white label.

"What's going on, Jude?"

He unscrewed the cap and took a sniff. "This, my friend, is a mixture of dill seed, edelweiss and foxglove. Mixed properly they provide protection from magic." The bottle flew through the air and I caught it reflexively. Inside was a whitish paste. I brought it to my nose and smelled a kind of electric tang. I tossed the bottle back.

"You see," Jude continued, setting the bottle carefully on the ground and picking up the sleeve of Dixie cups. "Herbs are at their most potent when fresh; however, keeping a greenhouse with you wherever you go puts a damper on your travel plans. So I mixed these while fresh and made a paste out of them using a mixture of agar-agar and holy water." He pulled seven tiny cups from their sleeve. "Can't use corn starch or tapioca starch to thicken the mix— they unbalance the ingredients—but agar-agar is almost perfect." A slim finger dipped into the jar of paste and emerged with a tiny glob, which he smeared on the top inside inch of the first Dixie cup.

"Mike, when God created the world, he used a Word. *The* Word. First there's nothing, then *poof!* God says the Word and there was light. Then he says the Word again and *poof!* Our happy little planet. All the Words are mere reflections of the Word, like copies of a copy of a copy *ad nauseum* until all you can see are a few smeared, broken letters.

"Elemental and Botanical magic are different, man. They are leftover divine sparks when God spoke the Word bringing life to this world. The elements had their Primals to keep the balance just so, while plants grew into their potential, each one with a capacity for a kind of magic ... Protection, Purification, Healing, Wisdom, Strength, etc."

Soon all seven cups had their smears of paste and he laid six in a circle with the seventh in the center. Then he poured the holy water into each cup until it barely touched the white paste.

"Botanical magic is the most versatile," he said quietly. "The subtlest. So many uses for the spark of divine magic in each plant. The Family has always regarded Botanical magic as the weakest, because it requires so much preparation and the ingredients aren't conveniently located in one spot. However, with a little discipline, a little patience, you can achieve miracles Words or Elemental magic can never touch.

"Now, as you've read in my … memoir, only males in my family can use the Words. In fact, the magi not related to my Family are all male, at least as far as I know, my exposure to magi outside the Family has been rather limited. However, the use of Botanical magic is not gender specific, nor does it require you to be a magus. All you need is a slight … *sensitivity* to magic. Male or female, if you have that sensitivity to magic, you have the ability to use Botanical magic."

Like firecrackers on a string, words popped out of his mouth faster and faster while I listened, rapt. "That's where Wiccans come from, you know. Back in the day someone stumbled onto their magical heritage, usually by accident, and formed a religion based on nature." The words trailed off. He looked up at the clear sky, staring at the slew of stars overhead. "Nature's not a bad thing to worship, really. It's all about balance and acceptance, realizing that things have their time to live and die. There are worse things to worship … much worse."

I couldn't keep quiet any more. "Why are you telling me this, Jude?"

"I love the stars, man. Always have. People look at the stars and think that Heaven must be there, despite what the Hubble telescope shows." He laughed and the sound was like cracking ice. "Did you know that Christ had two brothers and a sister?"

The conversational whiplash nearly spun my head about. "What?"

"God used the Word to impregnate Mary and she was still infused with the divine spark when she gave birth to the other three children. Not surprising really, considering zero birth control, and what kind of a loving God tells people to go forth and multiply, but leaves them without the ability to do so? That doesn't make sense, considering she was married. So that little bit of divine spark got passed to her kids. The line of Joseph and Mary has some of the most powerful magi that have ever existed. The Sicarii have been trying to eliminate them for two millennia, man. And failing miserably."

"Jude—"

"No, you have to hear this, man. Please. It'll prepare you for what's to come." A deep sigh. "You know Luke 22:3-6 and John 13:27 … the Gospels that said Satan entered Judas and that led to the betrayal of Jesus?"

"Of course."

"Of course … look who I'm talking to. Think about this: Satan never enters anyone else in the Bible, does he? Not until Revelations. Whom does Satan merge with in Revelations, Mike?"

An easy one. "His son, the Anti-Christ."

"Good. Now put two and two together here, man … Satan only enters his son, or relative maybe because they are strong enough to be entered, to be able to contain Satan's might. Reasonable, yes?"

"Yes, but—"

"So logic dictates," Jude broke in. "That he can *only* enter a family member, like his son, or grandson, someone with resilient flesh."

I stroked my moustache. "That's possible, I guess."

"When Christ comes at the end times, who comes to oppose him?"

"The Anti-Christ."

"Good, we're getting somewhere. Okay, big question here … so who opposed Christ two thousand years ago? Who betrayed him? And who is most likely to be seen as a kind of Anti-Christ?"

Oh, my … his words tumbled about in my head like pachinko balls ding ding dinging against my skull and knocking about everything I'd ever learned in Seminary. "Judas …" I breathed.

His look was bitter as vinegar. "Yeah. And because he was entered by Satan and, in the end, opposed Christ …?"

I wanted to puke. "The Anti-Christ?"

Jude nodded. "Yeah, he was Satan's first born son, the one sent to betray Christ."

The ground was warm and sandy under my butt; however, something prickled my left cheek. A thorn perhaps, but I didn't feel it, not as pain, more as a minor irritation. That pachinko ball continued to bounce off the soft gray matter, scattering my thoughts, so I fell back on the only thing that could offer any comfort.

"'Our father who art in Heaven, hallowed be thy name …'"

I guess it was a kindness that Jude let me finish.

"You okay, Mike?" he asked when my voice trailed off.

Centered again, I nodded. It came to me that anyone else would haul Jude away to the laughing academy, even if they believed in magic, but in all my time in the army, as a priest, I *know* when someone is lying to me or delusional. Jude was neither. I just wished he was. "I'm fine."

"Good, because here comes the fastball. Judas Iscariot … do you know the origin of the name Iscariot? It's not a family name. Judas claimed to be the son of Simon. No, the name comes from the band of rebels he formed, fanatics who would do anything to drive out the Romans, led by a man who practically foamed at the mouth. A group of assassins called the Sicarii."

"Judas Iscariot is—"

"The Founder. Founder of the Sicarii and of my Family. Except the spark that created the magi in the Family is not quite divine, is it?"

"Oh, dear Lord." Ding ding ding. Why was he hitting me with all this? Was the sand shifting under me? No, I was lying flat on my back, staring at the stars. They winked at me, impervious to the shock my system had just received.

"Trust me, *He* has nothing to do with it." There came a soft *thump* as Jude sat down beside me. "Sorry to hit you with all this, Mike, but you had to know. It wasn't all in the memoir and we're about to enter the lion's den. It's here, right before the plunge that you have to decide whether to fish or cut bait, man."

Kind of him to give me the option, although it wasn't needed, not by a long shot. Some things you feel right down to the bone because the people you share your strange little worlds with, the people you let inside the walls of your life and who let you into theirs, deserve the benefit of the doubt. But one essential truth shone like the light of the Lord:

He was my friend.

"Let's see what we catch, then," I said.

The phones little LED cast a harsh light on Jude's features, turning them a ghastly green. *Dit, Dit, Dit* ... He dialed, pressed the SPEAKER button, and gently balanced the phone on the center cup inside the ring.

Only three numbers? I thought.

Three numbers or not, a tinny ringing noise came from the cell. Two, three, four then five rings without an answer.

"Olivier, my boy, I am so glad you called."

Oh my ... that voice, *the* Voice. It had to be ... It rolled out of the tiny speakers as if thrumming from the very atmosphere we breathed, bypassing any mere mechanical contrivance built by man. Smooth as silk, almost greasy, deep and vibrant with a paternal undertone that set my teeth on edge.

John Noble, I thought. The voice sounded like that of John Noble, the actor who played a crazy scientist on a sci-fi show called *Fringe* (a priest who watches and reads sci-fi, who'da thunkit?). The Voice had the same cadence and inflection, but there was a deep ... *wrongness* to it that reminded me of a shark swimming just below the waves, dorsal fin breaching to declare its menacing intentions.

"Hello," Jude said distantly, as if he didn't care a whit about the Voice.

"You've blocked me. I'm impressed; no one has ever done that before. It just proves to me once again how special you are."

"Yeah, well, I don't need you tracking me or blowing a phone up in my face."

"You'll just have to forgive me that one, boy. I lost my temper. Won't happen again." It sounded sincere, but I could see the big muscles at the corner of Jude's jaws clench.

"I think I'll have to opt out of believing you this time."

"No problem, my boy," the Voice purred. "Come on home soon. All is forgiven, you have my guarantee. No one will gainsay me, you know that."

"That's true."

"For fifteen years you've evaded me and the Family. That ought to prove to anyone with half a brain that you're the One we need, my boy, despite the fact you have the Liar's talking monkey traveling with you."

Jude's alarmed gaze met mine. "What?" he asked. "You talking about the priest who tried to help me fix a flat when one of your gate crashers attempted to trim my hair down to the neck? He was just passing by."

"I think you're using him to help you find the Liar's Cup."

Jude grimaced. "No, I'm not, but something tells me it's no longer where I think it is. You've got it, don't you? Or, I should say, one of your party boys has it."

"Ah, so you've spoken with the lovely Ms. Winchester, have you?"

"Not really *spoken*. More like she screamed all she knew before I bled her out like the pig that she was." I shot him a surprised glance, but he shook his head slightly.

"Good boy, nice to see that all your years in America have not dulled your killer's edge."

"Yeah, talk to Burke about it, man."

"Burke was good, no doubt about it, no doubt at all." A brief moment of silence. "You sound so very American, Olivier, the cadence, the inflection. It doesn't suit you."

"I spent a long time trying to blend in. Cultural camouflage."

"So come home to us, boy. Tell me where you are."

"I don't think so, sir. I'm not strong enough yet to take on Julian."

The laughter that burst forth from those speakers made my hair stand on end. "Boy, you have the Silver. With that you can remove Julian handily."

Jude scratched his head. "Yeah, but I don't have the Silver anymore."

If the laugher was unnerving, the silence that followed was

horrifying. In place of menace there was a thick, gelid sense of evil that froze the breath in my lungs and drained all electrical impulses from my brain, leaving me in a senseless limbo.

That limbo stretched to infinity and back before the Voice spoke again. "You are lying," he said, breaking the pregnant pause with a snap.

"No," Jude refuted. "I'm not. Three years ago in Libya I located the Ark. Took some working, but managed to smuggle it home in a tramp freighter out of Benghazi named Star of Rawiah. I had placed the Silver inside so you couldn't track it, surrounded by all that holiness, but somewhere off the coast of Sardinia the ship went down with all hands. For all I know, the Ark is at the bottom of the Med with the Silver still inside."

Oh, *Lord* ... I felt it before it happened.

Screeeeeccchhhhhh! Razor blades slicing through skin, fingernails on chalkboard, the ripping of tin and high pitched whine of a stressed turbo as it headed toward failure. The sound that leaked through those tiny speakers was all those and more; a mix of noises so ghastly it was if someone had stuffed them into a blender and hit frappé.

Mere seconds passed, but to my poor tortured ears it seemed a lifetime. Just when I thought the fine bones of my middle ear would shatter, the cell's LED screen cracked with a soft *pop* and let out a curl of dark smoke.

"Well, that pissed him off."

If that was an example of being pissed off, I sure didn't want to be around when the Voice gave vent to some serious anger issues. I stared numbly at my friend as he removed the phone and threw it out deep into the desert before empting the cups of holy water. Surprisingly, there were only a few drops left in each.

Jude caught the edge of my curiosity. "The presence of holy water acts like buffer between the real world and the Voice so he can't track us, but the sharper his focus, the more holy water is dissipated."

"Jude," I said slowly, my brain refusing to engage past first gear. "That ... that *Voice*, the Patron of your family ... he is, is he ... ah ..."

My mouth didn't want to work right and I felt unyielding pressure bearing down upon my shoulders.

"Yeah, man." Jude nodded. "It's who you think it is. My many time great-grandfather, Lucifer."

I watched the hardening of his tortured features, his expression more eloquent than a scream. I didn't respond. Words wouldn't suffice to console a man with Hell in his blood.

Chapter Fourteen

Mike

Late that night or early next morning—depending on how you wanted to look at it—we paid our freight at a hotel in Las Vegas, New Mexico, that had beds with mattresses only marginally softer than limestone. Both of us moved as if on autopilot, the events of the past few hours having drained us so much that the beds could've been made of razor blades and rusty nails and we wouldn't have noticed.

Before Jude could crash for the night, I asked, "What did you mean when you told Leslie that her son was 'under the influence' and why did you tell the Voice all those lies?"

He showed me his molars in a jaw-cracking yawn. "Told the Voice lies because I don't want him knowing exactly what we're about. Best thing to do is to keep him thinking that I want to gather my own base of power. As for Alexander, I think he's under the influence of Hell, Mike. Baphemaloch is the name of a parasite, like a demonic tick. Instead of sucking blood, it infects the host with negative emotions. The longer it's attached to the host, the more control it exerts until the host's soul withers and dies."

I could have gone the rest of my life without hearing that. A parasitic ... what? Proto-demon? The image of an evil virus slipping into Alexander's cells and replicating, bursting forth in a black flood to infect more cells with damnation made me shudder.

"Why call the Voice, Jude? Why take that chance?"

He replied through lips numbed by fatigue. "You had to know what you were really up against, man. Not just in your head, but in your gut. We could die trying to destroy the Silver and I wanted to give you the chance to walk away." He paused. "I thought it might be best for you to let me face the crap festival I bought tickets to alone."

Fat chance of that happening! I bit back a sour retort, realizing that he wanted me to go, that he was trying to protect me, like a good friend would. Another question reached my lips, but remained unvoiced. Jude had fallen asleep, a forearm draped over his eyes, soft snores bubbling through his lips.

No way I could've slept, so it was time to continue my journey into my friend's past.

Tripping the Silver

Wham! My butt and back hit the mat at the exact same time; knocking what precious breath I had left out of my lungs.

"You have got to do better than that!" bellowed Sarge.

At five-eight, a hundred sixty pounds, Sarge didn't look like much with his short, bone-white flat-top haircut, round face and gray moustache that was so perfectly level I swore that he used a ruler to trim it. In fact, Sarge looked more like an athletic accountant stuffed in camo pants and khaki t-shirt than a wet-work instructor. You got the impression he would rather be petting Chihuahuas than slitting throats and I'm pretty sure a few of his victims thought the same thing before they died.

Julian had confided that Sarge was indeed ex-U.S. military. That and one of the most successful serial killers the world had ever seen, racking up a body count somewhere north of three hundred. A killer so effective that for twenty-five years he had the FBI and Interpol scratching their heads in bafflement, astounded by the preternatural ability he'd displayed at eluding them.

He didn't elude Julian, though, who was so impressed by the man's skills that he made an offer the aging murderer couldn't refuse: teach wet-work skills to the young Family members. In return he would be well paid. Also, he could kill whenever he wanted, as long it was on his own time and didn't lead back to the Family.

For ten years that arrangement had worked quite well.

From my vantage point on my back, staring up at Sarge's angry face as he yelled at me, spit gathering at the corners of his mouth like silt at the bottom of a river, I thought that he just might break his promise about permanently harming Family.

"Olivier, you are about as useless as a sack of smashed assholes, you got me, boy?" Sarge yelled. "Now get up off your flabby ass and at least *try* not to embarrass yourself when fighting your cousin!"

The aforementioned cousin was not Burke, who routinely kicked my ass up one side and down the other with great frequency and enthusiasm in these little practice bouts. No, this cousin was someone who could actually give Burke a run for the sadistic money—Cousin Annabeth.

While my Family is terribly misogynistic, there are those women who showed such promise in the red side of the business that instead of being used as honey traps or breeders, they were allowed to work as true Dagger Men.

I considered Annabeth as I groaned my way vertical under Sarge's disappointed gaze. An inch shorter than myself, tall for a woman, her shoulders were strong enough to carry all my troubles with room for a couple of hundred pounds. Her slim hands were calloused to hammer hardness and her muscles slithered under her bronze skin in all their chiseled perfection. Underneath a cap of short black hair, her dark eyes blazed out of a heart-shaped face, smoldering with subtle contempt at my contemptible fighting skills.

"Good throw, Anna," I croaked, forcing air into tired lungs.

"Stuff it, Olivier," she answered in a surprisingly smooth and dangerous voice, like velvet over steel.

Sarge's craggy, hard face came nose to nose with mine. "You kick her butt, boy. If you can't then you aren't worth pissing on." Hate, bitter soul-hate like a cancer, shone out of his eyes. I guessed it was the thing that drove him to kill and kill again. None of those kills would never, *ever* be enough, even if the blood of his victims eventually drowned him. "She's a woman," he whispered fiercely. "A *whore!*"

I suppressed the rush of contempt for him that suddenly surged through me, although it must have shown because his face shut down with an almost audible slam and he turned away, trembling slightly.

"Ready, Olivier?" Annabeth's smooth voice came from behind, carrying a wealth of smugness.

"Stuff it, Annabeth," I said, spinning, fist flying out to catch her on the chin and dropping her to land sprawling on the practice mat.

Needles of hot water attacked my scalp as I positioned myself beneath the showerhead, shedding sweat and grime in rivulets down my torso and legs.

Two hours of sparring, an hour of weapons—both hand and pistol—followed by meditation to calm the nerves, to keep them on an even keel though the most stressful situations.

Hands harder than flint touched my back, ran up the ridged lines of my shoulder blades and caressed my neck. I turned and met Annabeth's hot mouth, our tongues dueling with the same fervor we'd demonstrated on the mat. My hands found her butt, lifting her in the air with a grunt and I slid into her, her warm wetness inviting, welcoming.

I fell back to the cold tiles of the shower as we tore at each other in our mutual torrent of lust. Thrusting, clawing, we bit and ripped, our young bodies suffused with enough hormones to allow us to survive the rush. The old, I reckoned foolishly in my naïveté, only had memories to console their twilight years.

Afterwards we soaped each other's backs in the quiet post-coital lassitude. "You sure Sarge and Burke didn't see you come in?" I asked.

"Burke left for the hotel and Sarge disappeared to wherever that creepy American creeps off to.

"Good. I want to keep you all to myself."

When she laughed it gave my ears an orgasm. "No way I could bed

Burke—he's too cruel, a vicious bastard. And Sarge doesn't screw, he kills. That's how he gets his rocks off."

All true. Just thinking about Sarge having sex seemed like a violation of all natural laws. With Sarge and Burke in the wind, we had the whole villa to ourselves.

"What do you have planned for the day?" she asked later as we toweled each other off.

"Off to see Julian," I answered through the tangle of my longish hair.

"What's he got planned?"

"I have no clue." It had been a year since Julian had 'torn me a new one,' as the Americans like to say, over that business with the Lab. The aftermath of the Lab's destruction had lowered the reservoir by three feet and raised more than a few eyebrows. It had even made the national news in the States. Julian had to scramble to find experts who would testify that it had been an 'unforeseen seismic event' of low magnitude that 'nonetheless had unfortunate consequences to the local bedrock.' A somewhat outrageous claim, but a generous pile of cash will convince people to believe or say anything. If our Family had a motto, that would be it.

Good thing for me the Crystal Drive proved to be every bit as useful as I said it would be. Unwilling to take advantage of global production of that new tech, Julian instead had sunk considerable sums of money into creating computers and networks that far outstripped anything even the superpowers could invent. That alone saved my life, just as I knew it would.

Annabeth ran her short nails up and down my chest, bringing new life to my nether parts. "Well," she purred. "You keep your hide intact. I have uses for it."

Just before I closed her lips with mine, I said, "Good, it's all yours."

If anything, Boris looked even more dangerous than the last time I'd stood in Julian's office. Still big, still chiseled out of the same gutrock as all the other extreme hard-asses necessity and money had created to do the jobs no one else could do.

"Looking good, Boris." I tipped the big man a nod.

A soft grunt and barely perceptible tilt of his head was the only answers he deigned provide.

"Glad you could come, son," Julian said, back to me, facing the window/monitor.

"You called, I came," was my reply.

"Indeed." A tilt of his perfectly coiffed head to the desk. "Sir?"

"Yes, Julian. Do it." The Voice sounded almost bored, but I could tell there was an vein of anticipation running through those glossy tones.

Boris came into view carrying a portable safe, one that looked like a tiny beige suitcase, and set it flat on the desk, hinge side toward me. Julian reached out with one well-manicured finger and punched what I supposed was a keypad I couldn't see. A hiss of cold air puffed out from within as the safe opened, ruffling the carefully arranged stacks of papers. He pulled out a small, worn leather purse or pouch, the kind people used centuries ago. It chinked softly as he placed it on the desk.

"Open it," he said.

"What?"

His scowl transformed his handsome face into something bestial. "Don't be dense, Olivier. Open the damn pouch."

Shrugging, I took a step forward and picked it up.

It was heavier than I thought.

"What is it?"

The Voice answered, "Your final test, Olivier. The test to see if you are worthy to be the next head of the Family. Open it and see if you can use the Family Silver."

Uh-oh. The Silver had been legend in the Family for millennia. An artifact of such might and baleful power that only a Family member could even touch it. It was said that if one outside the Family were to handle it, a gruesome death would ensue.

And there it was, resting in the center of my palm like a spider's egg-sack, pregnant with untold malignant possibilities. Not wanting to drag the whole macabre thing out, I teased open the puckered opening and poured the contents into my other hand.

Coins. Silver. The size of American nickels.

Thirty of them.

ॐ

"Holy shit!" I gasped, dropping the papers. In the other bed Jude snored softly, content in his sleep. Quickly I crossed myself and silently apologized to the Lord for my cussing.

Thirty pieces of silver, the same thirty pieces that had been used to bribe Judas into betraying Jesus? Had to be! According to Jude (oh the irony!), Judas was the son of Satan, an Anti-Christ *born to oppose* Christ, and that would certainly explain the Silver as an evil artifact. The story of Christ painted Judas as one of the most infamous characters in history.

According to Matthew 27:3-10, Judas had returned the money and committed suicide by hanging himself. In the Acts of the Apostles, he'd used the money to buy a field, but he fell and burst asunder like an overripe melon. That field was known thereafter as Akeldama, the Field of Blood.

Obviously, if Jude was correct (and I had little reason to doubt him, considering all that I had experienced in last few days), then his ancestor had *not* died shortly after the crucifixion, but instead had founded a dynasty of assassins and power brokers whose main goal was to foster the Anti-Christ.

My brain hurt.

So much information, so little time. If I were a drinking man, I'd be three sheets to the wind already. Smiling ruefully, I envisioned the members of my Ranger chalk in Iran and what they would say. "Suck it up, Soldier," quickly came to mind. So suck it up I did, gathering the pages of the memoir and taking up the thread of the story.

ॐ

Each silver coin shone in the soft light of Julian's office, perfect and unblemished, yet roughly cast and stamped. A likeness of a man adorned one side while an eagle stood on the left side of the reverse, right foot on what appeared to be a ship's ram with a palm frond behind. If I remembered correctly, it was the type of coin called a Half Shekel, a Temple Tax Coin.

Cold. Very cold. Almost cold enough to sear my palm, and greasy, sliding effortlessly over one another as if they were magnets with the same polarity. Quickly, before they could spill to the floor, I clamped my other hand over them, trapping them in the cave of my palms.

A hammer-blow to my brain rocked me backwards. Pain, pain like nothing else I had ever felt. Pain I couldn't describe because it had no frame of reference in my world. Burning, drowning, disemboweling, impaling. All these and yet none of them; maybe it was a new elemental, a Pain elemental and I was experiencing the Primal.

On and on for days it lasted, searing my mind with acid and fire, robbing me of all other senses. Blind and deaf I lived in a world of unending agony, of flesh slowly being stripped from bone and nerves sliced with razors of fire, no end to the suffering in sight. If a knife had been put in my hand I wouldn't have known how to use it, so lost was I in that universe of anguish.

When it finally stopped, I fell to my knees and sobbed with relief. Over. I didn't care about the tears that fell to the floor, nor the snot that dribbled down over my lips and chin, I just reveled in the near orgasmic feeling of *no more pain*.

The first Word slid foully, sinuously into my mind like a snake, or a curl of smoke from a campfire that catches you unaware, accompanied by a feeling that my brain had been invaded by maggots. "Hate" was the Word that settled in for a visit and a cup of whatever my brain was offering. With that Word I could set brothers, lovers, anybody to fighting, exaggerating the smallest imaginary insult. "Hate" was the first Word the Silver had for me.

Next came "Enslave." Bend others to my own ends, strip them of all free will and make them wholly mine, body and soul.

"Plague." Cholera, smallpox, Ebola, you name it; I had it all in one little Word.

More and more Words tumbled into my poor head. Thirty of them, one for each itty-bitty coin that jangled in my hands. With those Words I could become the Four Horsemen of the Apocalypse on steroids, Ragnarok squared, Armageddon on a stick and pass the ketchup, please. There was nothing that could be kept from me, nothing I couldn't do.

With those Words, I could end the world right then and there.

It was then that I began to doubt the Voice. Doubt Julian.

Maybe I wasn't made of sterner stuff, but as the Words clamored like an unholy choir in my mind, I began to be afraid. The Words were not just baleful magic at my disposal, but a power that not only hated the world but hated me as well and would discard me like a candy wrapper when its purpose was served.

Two thousand years earlier the Voice had promised his only son Judah (only in the Greek is he called Judas) that there would be born unto his line the Redeemer, the one who would topple the Lying God from his Throne and set the world to rights. That Redeemer would rule the world and all would be perfect.

Blah, blah, blah.

I knew then, with utter certainty, that it would be the Patron, the Voice—not the Redeemer—who would rule. Just as the Voice had entered Judah all those years ago to rid the world of the Lying God's son, the Voice would enter the Redeemer, but this time, unlike two thousand years ago, that possession would be permanent.

Perhaps it was the gift of prophesy, or clairvoyance, some prescient notion, but I knew that the Voice would tear the Redeemer's soul from the moorings of his body and fling it to the farthest corners of the Abyss.

And I knew, without a doubt, with the acquisition of all thirty of the Words, that I would be the Redeemer.

I would be the Anti-Christ.

ॐ

There are times in your life when you have an 'oh no!' moment, usually in a microsecond before something bad happens, like a car crash. You say 'oh no!' then *wham,* your brand new Lexus introduces itself to a tree at forty miles an hour.

For me, my first 'oh no!' moment was when I realized someone was actually trying to kill me my second day in Iraq. A 7.62 mm slug whizzed past my ear at 2,346 feet per second, upsetting my whole outlook on life.

Finding out that Jude had the potential to become one of the greatest evils that had ever walked the earth was my third 'oh no!' moment and definitely the worst.

More "oh no!" moments awaited me before our journey's end.

Time for prayer.

Chapter Fifteen

Jude

"You have that look on your face," I observed as I finished packing the duffel.

Mike thinks he can look innocent, but his poker face is almost as bad as mine. "What look?"

"The look that says 'I just found out that my buddy Jude was destined to become Satan's puppet on earth.'"

He sighed, shoulders slumping. "You have to admit, it's a lot to swallow," he mumbled, not looking at me.

"Yeah, I wasn't bursting with joy when it first occurred to me, Mike. Believe me, it isn't easy to cope when all you believe has been stripped away in an instant. At least you've had the benefit of a couple of days of prep, man."

He grabbed the keys to our beater truck from the side table. "Still, Jude, it's a load, a big load, to handle. I feel like I should hate and revile you, but I still love you. Despite all that I have learned." Tears clogged his throat and I knew a conflict of Catholic dogma and personal feelings raged within him.

So I did the only thing I could think of, the only thing I could do. I grabbed him in a big bear hug and held on as if he was my only port in a storm.

For a moment or two he resisted, his big shoulders tense, hard as basalt, but slowly he melted in my grasp and hugged back. Laughter began to rack his body, hitching the big muscles of his back and stomach, an explosion of ironic mirth that leapt from him to me until we both stood shaking in each other's embrace.

"A priest and the Anti-Christ walk into a bar …" I began.

Mike disengaged, wiping his eyes, and punched me lightly in the gut. "You're right, it sounds like a bad joke. Humor from the Apocalypse." He held a hand up, dangling the truck keys from a finger. "Come on, let's go."

That day we arrived in Denver, where I had hidden another spooker buried deep in the earth in a vacant lot I owned on Colfax Street just west of I-25. This time, instead of summoning an elemental and having a nice confab, I just had Earth bring the box to the surface where I used the molecular knife to cut it open. Halfway through the thread broke and I had to spool more out. At the rate I broke the threads, I guess I had another three hundred years before I needed more.

Inside the box was another thirty thousand dollars. However, the money wasn't the prize; the false ID was. The previous spooker had a phony ID I'd created in '97, but it was for Tariq al-Muhammad, which would be a red flag in the post 9/11 world, so I needed a new one in case I came under scrutiny. The Jude Oliver persona was burned and I needed to become someone new.

Say hello to Morgan Heart.

Morgan had a SSN, passport and even an old Colorado driver's license, as well as a Mastercard and Visa. The cover was flawless, the best money could buy.

"Can I see that?" asked Mike, pointing at the knife.

I handed the cylinder over. "Careful. You'll slice yourself up a treat if you're not careful."

"Been kind of curious about this." He pushed the button. "Don't see anything."

"One molecule thick is far too small for the naked eye, but it's there." I smiled as Mike gingerly handled the cylinder.

"What powers it? I imagine it must use a lot of juice, keeping the thread carefully spooled and contained in the magnetic bottle." Mike handed the knife back.

"It's surprisingly energy efficient, actually. Runs on two watch batteries and they only need to be changed once a month under normal usage."

He stood and brushed the dirt of his knees. Instead of his usual black outfit with collar, he had dressed like a lumberjack—blue jeans, red-checked flannel shirt, boots and a brown Gore-Tex jacket. We had plenty money to spare. I could have dressed us in Armani.

"I'm surprised, Mike. You haven't asked me what's next."

"We're going to get the Grail, I know that," he said quietly. "Now that I understand what's at stake, I know we have to see this thing through."

"Yeah." I pocketed all the IDs except the driver's license and stood, leaving the box where it lay. "Just making sure."

"No worries, Jude."

"Morgan."

"What?"

I held up the outdated driver's license. "It's Morgan Heart now. My Jude Oliver persona is history now."

"Morgan Heart?"

"Yeah."

"Morgan *Heart*?"

"You said that already."

A cheesy smile spread across his face. "That is the lamest alter-ego I've ever heard. Sounds like a porn name."

"It's what was available." Grumble grumble. "What do *you* know from porn names?"

"I had a life before my calling, *Morgan*. You would've been better off with Bruce Wayne or Clark Kent!" His laughter bounced off the tired brick buildings that surrounded the garbage-strewn lot. People walking by on the sidewalk paused for a moment to stare at the big unshaven man with the funky moustache.

"Laugh it up, Mr. Funny Guy," I mumbled, flashing a rueful smile.

Whatever may come, Mike was still my friend and all was right in the universe.

The laughter wound down like a spring that was slowly losing tension. "Okay, Morgan, where to now?"

"To finish what we started, man." I stared at the cold gray sky, watching the plumes of my breath billow forth. "We go to Bend."

Bend, Oregon. Why did it have to be Bend? Personally I would've rather gone back to Odessa, and that place was a pit. Bend parks itself on the high plains desert area east of Eugene and just north of the Deschutes National Forest. In the summer, the grass is dry, the juniper trees look scrofulous and the only thing growing that's not a bilious sage green lives right next to the river that runs through town where all the expensive houses are located. Living in one of those makes you the elite among cockroaches.

Okay, a little harsh, a little pessimistic. But not by much.

The old truck trundled past downtown where the touristy shops and restaurants are located, catering to whatever yuppie trade there might be and took us to the outskirts, where the real people with real information could be found. The information we sought couldn't be provided by the drinkers of appletinis and cosmopolitans.

Feighan's stood on the crossroads of Hopeless and Helpless, catering to people who liked their beer cold, their TV sports played at volumes even rock bands would cringe at and prided themselves on the thickness of their chest hair. That included the women.

We walked into a room lit by bad fluorescents and cheesy neon beer signs. Even though it was a hair past noon there were at least twenty people drinking, playing pool or watching satellite TV, drinks clutched in fists, complexions sallow and tired. Mike and I moseyed up to the bar (always wanted to say that) and sat with elbows resting on a none-too-clean bar top.

"What can I get you folks?" asked a youngish bartender whose ponytail barely contained his curly black hair. A yellow t-shirt with FEIGHAN'S stretched tight across his broad shoulders and chest.

I held up two fingers. "Buds, please."

When the bartender came back, I held up a hundred dollar bill.

"The change is yours for some information."

He smiled, revealing very even, very white teeth through the scruff on his face. "You cops?"

Mike shook his head. "Nope."

The young man took my hundred. "You guys watch too many cop shows. I would've been happy with a ten." Chuckling, he made change and stuffed the bills in his front pocket. "It's good business to cooperate with the cops. What do you want to know?"

"Wonderful," I groused. Mike took a sip of bear to hide his smile.

"Really, mister, bartenders aren't like in the movies. We're just average Joes looking to make a few dollars here and there. Just ask your questions."

A soft sniggering came from my left. It was a wooly old man in a Red Sox ball cap sporting a walrus moustache. He seemed to find the whole conversation humorous. A second later Mike joined in.

Red faced, I asked, "We're looking for a biker gang by the name of Demon's Blood."

The bartender's tan faded. "You don't want to mess with those idiots, dude. Not if you want to keep your nose attached to your face."

Mike piped up. "Bad guys?"

"The worst," the old fellow next to me chimed in, his voice made husky by cigarettes. "They don't come into town much, don't shit where they eat, you know, but them boys like to raise a ruckus all through the state. Heard they messed up a fella in Lebanon so bad he can't walk no more."

I kept my eyes on the bartender. "Where do they hang their hats?"

"Mister, you're committing suicide and I won't help a man kill himself." Two fingers dipped into his front pocket and started to pull out the folding change he'd stuffed there.

It was Mike who put an end to the bartender's resistance. "Son," he drawled. "If we don't take care of the business we have with the gang, a lot of people are going to wish they committed suicide." From his flat top to his boots, he radiated confidence and resolve.

It was enough for the young man, if just barely. The change

disappeared back into his jeans. "In Terrebonne. Their leader owns a bar up there."

Mike's eyebrows shot up. "Their leader? Alexander?"

"No one knows his name," the old man jumped in. "Calls himself Shiv."

Not anymore, I thought darkly. "What's the name of this bar?"

"The Hard Way. That's all I got, dude." The bartender left to pour a beer.

Mike shot me a look. "The Hard way?" he whispered.

My voice was equally quiet. "Lousy name."

"So how do we handle it?"

I shot him a toothy grin. "I have the beginnings of a cunning plan."

"Oh, Lord."

Chapter Sixteen

Mike

If I were a cursing man, I would've laid a blue streak all the way from Bend to Terrebonne, but I had put that part of my past behind me when I left the Army. Morgan's (funny how easily I'd stopped thinking of him as Jude) plan had me scared spitless, but to save Alexander's soul from the infernal parasite, I had to put fear behind me. Just like in Iraq.

Danzinger's handled the distribution of beer and liquor in the area, including the Hard Way. It didn't take much to find out when the next delivery of beer would be heading to the gang's club—only a judicious use of ten grand of Morgan's cash, mainly, a bribe to the dispatcher for a uniform and a temporary assignment as a delivery driver. The next scheduled delivery was for the next day, so we holed up in a hotel until it was time for action.

Once my cover was in place, Morgan disappeared to "arrange for backup" should I need it. That had me worried, but there was nothing for it. I just had to trust him.

The beer truck handled like a pig on a skateboard, but I managed to steer the darn thing all the way to Terrebonne, a blip on the road so small that if you blinked, you'd miss it. Thanks to the jolly dispatcher, I had an easy-to-read map to get me to the bar.

If Bend had a hope of green, Terrebonne abandoned that hope a long time ago, some time just before the dawn of Mankind. The only thing that separated it from Las Cruces was the winter wind that howled down the flat land.

Toasty in a dark blue Danzinger's jacket, I pulled up to the back entrance of the bar. The dispatcher had given me the code to the surprisingly sophisticated electronic lock that safeguarded the back door. Made me wonder why such a crappy looking little place needed one.

I try not to be judgmental, but the Hard Way looked like the kind of place where the bartender swept up teeth as well as trash at the end of business. The patchy roof needed re-shingling; the parking lot resembled the surface of the moon while most of the windows contained wood, not glass. Nevertheless, the front and sides of the building had enough Harleys packed together for a Sturgis rally—a border of chrome, steel and rubber.

After opening the truck for delivery, I started to punch the code for the back door. Halfway through the sequence, it opened. A bearded, grimy man in dark biker leathers and a scraggly beard leaned out.

"Where's Dave?" he asked gruffly, beady eyes narrowed.

I kept my tone noncommittal and shrugged. "Not available today."

He gave me a squint while I studied him in return. Big, flabby, tattoos on neck and chest, biker leather ripped at the shoulders so the fat arms could swing free. Long, tangled brown hair. Not a boss, just a flunky, I surmised.

His study of me was mercifully brief. After all, I was wearing the Danzinger uniform—the navy-blue pants, short-sleeved shirt and ball cap. Despite that, I could feel his cold appraisal. Apparently I passed muster because he pushed the door open wide and propped it with a cinder block.

With a smile and a nod to the troglodyte, I unloaded a keg that I placed on my shoulder with a grunt and carried in.

With the big lummox in the way there was barely enough room in the dimly lit storage area for me to maneuver the keg around. For some reason he was staring at me, his thick lips parted.

"What?" Was my fly undone?

"Most guys use the hand truck," he uttered softly, pointing to a once blue dolly.

I silently berated myself. This was supposed to be a recon mission and I had just showed off by hauling a 156 lb keg of beer on my shoulder like it was nothing. Smiling, I asked, "Where's the cooler?"

The fat man pointed to the right and I made my way among the boxes of liquor and bottled beer, stacked high. Covertly glancing here and there, I noticed no window to the main room, just a battered wooden door painted black. There had to be some way to scope out the main bar.

On my third keg trip, I hit on an idea. "You want me to take a keg up front? Maybe clear out an empty?"

Just as I reckoned, here was a man who had no problem with someone else doing the heavy lifting. "Sure," he said with a gap-toothed smile that did nothing to improve his looks. "Follow me."

Keg perched on my shoulder, I complied, trailing him through the black door and into the bar proper. Not much, really, just a typical one-room place with a dozen tables, two pool tables and a grimy counter that ran the length of the room. Bikers of every size, shape and color crowded the place (apparently the Demon's Blood was an equal opportunity gang), causing such a ruckus that my ears threatened to shut down for good. Fat guy led the way to a trio of lonely looking taps lined against the wall.

Then the place got quiet and I felt the first shiver of dread trill through me. Carefully I set the keg down and looked around. Dozens of eyes were upon me, some speculatively, some apprehensively.

"Can I help you folks?" I kept my voice mild, light.

More silence. I shifted uncomfortably from foot to foot then turned my attention back to the keg, which I stowed in the cooler underneath the taps. An empty in one hand, I was headed toward the door to storeroom door when I was stopped by a voice I recognized.

"How did you do that, man?" The voice was hard-edged and growly, with a deep undercurrent of menace. When I'd heard it last, it had come though Leslie Winchester's cell.

"Do what?" I asked, not looking up.

"Look at me when I talk to you!" Alexander screamed and I jumped like I'd been goosed.

Alexander Winchester had his mother's nose and eyes, but little else. Rangy and lean instead of bulky and muscular, with long dirty blond hair and acne-scarred cheeks. The leader of the Demon's Blood didn't look like one. Oh, he was tall enough and had the sleek grace of a panther, but there was no look of ... competence in his face. Instead he had the air of a petulant, spoiled child who had been given everything he wanted and hated the givers because it was never enough. Cold, cold green eyes sparkled like pools of viridian cruelty. A purple Crown Royal bag was tied to the belt of his dirty blue jeans and one veiny hand caressed it like a lover.

I knew instantly what was in that bag.

My eyes must have lingered too long. "What you looking at, asswipe?" he snarled. There came a sudden stillness from the other bikers and I knew that the wrong word, the wrong gesture, would see me buried beneath a stack of kicking, stabbing bodies.

So of course I took the road only the proud and foolish follow. "Your purse, ace."

Not good. Don't know why I said that. Something about Alexander really rubbed me the wrong way. Looking at him made my eyes itch, as if I could see *into* him, capture his subtle wrongness with sight; hence the suicidal response.

A busty woman standing next to the pool tables, blue and black tats on her large breasts, pointed out the only window as Alexander brought his hands up, knife flickering between his fingers. "What the hell?" she cried.

Everyone looked, even Alexander, who was poised to jump the bar. I could see two snowplows enter the lot at high speed; one dove out of sight to the left and one to the right.

Alexander snarled, "What the f---?" Just before a rending crash shook the building, a tearing, grinding noise boomed from both sides of the bar.

"Our bikes, man!" someone yelled, horrified.

Almost magically the bar emptied, people running out to save their motorcycles in a flood, shouting and screaming imprecations. Alexander spun around and fled with the mob, but not before spearing me with one last baleful glare. "I'm gonna kill you," that glare told me. "Your guts are mine!"

I've never been so grateful for Morgan until that moment, saving me from my stupidity, my fat mouth. Pride is a sin that we all are susceptible to, so maybe I owed the Lord a few Hail Marys and a little time spent in reflection.

Time enough for that later, if I lived. I hurdled the bar in pursuit of the bikers, eager to see what Morgan had cooked up. I made it to the door in time to hear a few bikes power up along with the scrape and screech of metal as the plows came back into view, dragging parts of motorcycles behind them like so much metallic confetti.

"Hey Mike," came a voice from behind. My heart leapt as I spun. Morgan! He stood behind the bar with a smug look on his face. Smug look or no, I could've kissed him right then. "See if you can get Alexander inside," he urged. "Alone, if possible."

Great, how was I going to get the attention of a psychopathic—

Never mind. Stupid question. Steadying my nerves, I stood in the doorway and shouted. "Hey, Alexander! We haven't finished talking about your sissy little purse yet!" Not much as insults went, but in my line of work, cultivating effective verbal ripostes was not high on my "to do" list.

Hey, it worked. While the two snowplows gunned for the road with a handful of Harleys in pursuit, Alexander came high-stepping around from the right of the building, knife in hand, trailing his own cadre of out of shape but lethally dangerous followers who would have no problem festooning the place with my guts.

Two hasty steps back and I was inside. "Get ready, Morgan." Behind me I heard sneakers hit linoleum as he vaulted the bar. I guess he'd already taken care of the fat guy.

Alexander/Baphemaloch tore through the front entrance like the door wasn't even there. Its tempered glass shattered into a million shiny bits as he/it tore through the backstop and hit the wall.

Alexander's fist, clutching six inches of knife, flashed toward me. Army training kicked in before I knew it and my fingers grabbed his knife wrist and pulled while twisting my body to the right. A brick-hard fist slammed into my kidney, bringing a searing ache that locked my muscles for a split second. As the pain tore through my torso, I still managed to fall back far enough for Alexander to stumble forward and tangle his feet with mine.

Both of us landed on a table, collapsing it. Splintering, it dropped to the floor as Morgan shouted one of his Words that hurled Alexander's followers around like tenpins.

Alexander's head swiveled wildly from our position on the remains of the table. "The Ay-rab Jew!" he screamed in panic, spit flying from his mouth.

Morgan was among the rest of the bikers, some five in all, moving like a ballet dancer, sinuous and deadly. Every punch, every stiffened finger hit with lethal precision, dropping gang members left and right.

Alexander twisted like an eel, shrieking, hands scrabbling for the knife that had dropped from his fingers when we landed. I grabbed a handful of dirty denim and squirmed my way up along his body until I came face to face with a demon.

Bloated features, a gaping maw showing rows of shiny white teeth. Red eyes wept black blood that flowed down to the hideously long canines, only to drip drip drip down its chin. Curling ram's horns sprung from a wide brow. It took me a second to realize it was an artful rendering on the back of Alexander's leathers.

That moment of shock, that split-second hesitation allowed Alexander to surge forward and grab his knife. Roaring in triumph, he leapt to his feet, throwing me off and planting the solid heel of his black boot in my gut.

Okay, that hurt. My breath gushed explosively out of my mouth as paralysis gripped my torso. I folded around that boot and held on, hands clenching Alexander's leg like it was a lifeline.

Alexander's head swiveled toward me, face stretched in a terrifying smile, his mouth pulled wider than human muscles are capable of. His eyes, once a shimmering green, now glowed black, like the absence of hope.

"Oh no," I gasped with what air I had left.

"Oh yes," answered the thing wearing Alexander's face. Baphemaloch? Probably.

With uncanny strength, he/it kicked out, prying my fingers free from his leg and launching me like a soccer ball across the bar. I had time enough to think *This is going to hurt*, right before I hit the beer taps.

My 220 lbs hit those three steel taps hard enough to bend them, but not hard enough to break. Before the searing agony in my back rendered me unconscious, I fell to the floor behind the bar, landing on something that gave way with a muffled *pop*.

Fade to black.

Chapter Seventeen

Jude/Morgan

"Look at me when I talk to you!" shrieked the voice from the cell in my hand. The other was in the breast pocket of Mike's uniform. Two disposable phones purchased the day before, a quick and easy way to eavesdrop on Mike's encounter with the gang.

I started. From beside me, Jim, the owner of the local snowplow service, swore. "Let's go, man!" I urged, slapping the dash. "This isn't going to end well for Mike if we don't get there on time!"

The young bartender, who introduced himself as Trev, along with walrus mustache man and a donation of a few hundred dollars, had given me the lead on the dispatcher at Danzinger's and the snowplow guy.

Bernie, the dispatcher, had just been for sale, but Jim and his brother/co-owner Dale, were enthusiastic haters of the Blood. Seems like Jim's youngest son was a victim of the meth the gang was slinging and was a friend of Trev's. The two brothers, both with Popeye-style forearms and the beginnings of beer guts, would've worked for free, but when I shoved fifteen grand into Jim's hand for his son's rehab, I not only had the use of his two plows, but a friend for life.

Several phone calls later and the rest of my plan had come together. I just hoped no one would get killed. Especially me.

While Jim put the truck in gear (we were a few hundred yards away, parked at a truck stop along the Dalles-California Hwy), I raised Dale on the CB and told him to get his ass in gear.

Both plows were almost to the Hard Way when I heard, "Your purse, Ace."

Was Mike suicidal? Wasn't killing yourself frowned upon by Catholics?

"Dale to the left, Jim to the right," I shouted into the CB as we made the turn into the bar's parking lot. Motorcycles were parked in a big U around the building. It wasn't hard to spot Alexander's Pan Head; it was the only Harley that had a wide clearing around it on the right side of the building. "Jim, you and Dale going to be okay?"

Jim's wide face smiled savagely as the blade of the plow hammered into the row of motorcycles, twisting and tearing bright chrome and polished leather. "Don't you worry about me, son," he shouted above the din. "We got this! Oh yeah, we got this!"

Metal grated and ground underneath the plow's tires and I could imagine sparks flying. Bits of chrome and steel were flung sideways into the building, rattling the whole structure. My smile matched Jim's mean for mean and the ride along motorcycle corpses was quickly over, the plow peeling off behind the building. I saw Dale maneuver his truck on the gritty flatland just outside the lot coming the other way, raising a cloud of gray dust.

Without a word, I opened the door and leapt out, taking the duffel with me (no way I could leave the Silver out of my sight now, not while on the run), tucking and rolling then bounding to my feet, making tracks as the plows made their turns toward the exit. The back door stood wide open, a cinderblock standing in for a doorstop. That made my life a little easier.

Inside, two precious seconds were wasted determining left or right. Left. Splintered black door. Shouts, screams from behind and I cursed myself because I'd promised Mike I wouldn't use guns; the Kimber and Beretta lay nestled at the bottom of the duffel with my underwear.

Through the door, a fat guy behind the bar, shotgun in his hands, aimed at my friend's back. No way in hell. My kick took him under his raised arm above his kidney and the shotgun dropped from his spasming hands. My fist hit the side of his lardy neck, then his jaw and he was *down*. The urge to finish him off burned like acid through my veins, but that's not what I did anymore, not what I was about.

Breathing hard, I said, "Hey, Mike, see if you can get Alexander inside. Alone if possible."

Mike grinned at me and went outside to poke the bear. "Hey, Alexander, we haven't finished talking about your sissy little purse yet!"

My feet hit the ground at the same time Alexander hit the door so hard it shattered and began to have a little hoedown with Mike. I reckoned he could take care of himself, so I went after the few who had followed their master inside.

Time to play.

It's funny how your muscles remember old patterns, old moves. I fell into the same routines of Krav Maga and Aikido that I'd learned all those years ago. A wrist trapped in my hands snapped so easily, the sound a crack of pain. Spinning, I threw an elbow into a screaming man's face that smeared his nose across his face in a spray of blood.

A low kick broke an ankle while I turned a punch coming at my face into a hip throw that flung the man headfirst into one of the pool tables. He fell and lay very still.

Three down. Stiffened fingers jabbed hard against a throat. Four. A punch landed solidly on my chin, but I rode with it, despite the pain. I've taken worse. My response broke the man's elbow across my knee. Five. Anger slithered through me like a snake of fire, but I didn't give into the passion; instead I used it, let it fuel me, although desire to use magic nearly robbed me of my senses. *No magic,* I thought. *Save it, keep it handy just in case.*

My hands grabbed a man's ear and pulled. An ear is held on by skin and cartilage, and I peeled it off like a decal, tossing it aside. Six.

The last man stared into my eyes and ran. He must have been the brains of the outfit.

A crash came from behind, startling me, and I spun in time to see

Mike fall out of sight before a flash of steel focused my attention on a knife slashing toward my throat. I leaned away and the tip missed my neck by a fraction of an inch.

"Baphemaloch," I growled at the demon wearing Alexander's face. "So you've come into your own."

"A Baphemaloch no more," he hissed, lips curling unnaturally. "With sentience comes a new name. I am Cazzizz."

Alexander was gone, or at least, the thing that made him Alexander, eaten by a spiritual parasite that had become a demon. Leslie's son was gone and that hell-thing was going to pay.

"Well, Cazzizz, let's have some fun." With that, I struck.

And missed. *Fast*, the demon was faster than anyone I'd ever met, even Burke, and he was the quickest form of death I'd ever met.

Horny black knuckles hammered into my cheek, knocking me sideways. A boot to thigh sent a bolt of pain up my hip and knocked me to the floor. Cazzizz's toe took me in the ribs, breaking several, spraying my torso with needles of pain and driving the breath from my lungs.

While I choked and gasped, Cazzizz walked slowly around my thrashing body, savoring his victory as if it were heady wine. "You have no protection against demons, Olivier." He smiled even wider, the edges of his lips touching his ears like an obscene clown's. "Oh, yes. I know who you are. Hell is full of those looking for you; I can hear them clamoring their envy and rage. Your death will bring me great power, such great rewards." He raised a leg, boot heel hovering over my head. I closed my eyes. It had been a good run, longer than I thought.

The blow never came.

"Demon, you looking for this?"

Mike! My eyes snapped open.

My friend stood behind the bar, bleeding from his mouth and ear. In one hand he held a purple bag with gold thread, the kind expensive scotch comes in and I knew what lay inside.

"Mike," I choked with what breath my lungs had left.

Too late, the demon attacked

With a bloody smile, Mike held up his cross—a small, silvery thing that didn't look like much, but was empowered with the unshakable faith of one simple man. That alone imbued it with the strength of the Lord.

The greater demon in New Mexico had been a real bad ass. It had taken a rite of exorcism to banish it. Cazzizz was a newborn, a demon newly formed from the soul of an evil man.

It took only one command.

"Begone."

Like a pressure wave caught on high-speed camera, the sound, the force of the command rolled over and through me in a swirling, argent flow, but I felt no pain, just a sense of warm comfort.

The demon, however, didn't get off so lucky. Howling, it was caught in mid-leap like an insect in silvery amber, frozen for one millisecond before simply vanishing with a faint pop and a hint of whitish smoke, leaving the whole bar trapped in a moment of perfect peace.

Oh, God, that felt good.

And then pain. Lots of it, buckets and barrelfuls, almost more than I could stand, coming from near every part of my body. Hurriedly, I let off with a Healing that took just enough edge off the agony for me to push out another one. I sneezed with the scent of cinnamon clogging my nose.

"Oh, I don't want to do that again," I moaned, finally levering myself upright. Staggering over to where Mike lay half on the bar, I clapped a hand on his back and smacked him with Healing. Then another, because he looked white as a sheet.

"Thanks, Morgan," he sighed in relief, stretching. After a long bone-popping moment, he held up the purple bag and teased apart the puckered-shut opening. Long fingers dipped inside and pulled out the Holy Grail.

Sure didn't look like much—a small green, ceramic bowl with a beige rim and a small crack, more of nick really, on the rim. It fit snugly in the palm of Mike's hand.

"This is the Grail?" he said skeptically, turning it this way and that.

"Looks like a high school art project you'd make for your mother, not the cup of Christ." Still, despite his hesitation, I noticed he cradled it very, very carefully.

I smirked. "Nine out of ten people used pottery for their wine cups. It was the norm."

He stashed the Grail back into the purple bag. As the cup disappeared, there came a faint ringing sound from his clothes. Mike patted his pockets and eventually fished out the cell.

I grabbed the phone before he could answer and threw it through the broken door, sending it clattering and shattering on the cold asphalt outside.

"Why'd you do that?" he exclaimed.

The look I gave him could've fried eggs. "You know anyone who has the number of a phone I bought *yesterday*?" How the hell did the Voice find us? The newborn demon?

Mike had the grace to blush. "But why didn't he call *you*?"

Reaching into the pocket of my coat, I pulled forth several shards of broken plastic. "This is why. Must have broken when the demon kicked me." Not bothering to linger, I vaulted the bar and grabbed the duffel I'd set there before my encounter with the demon Alexander. Wetness filled my palms.

"Oh, no," I muttered, ripping open the bag, fear rushing through my body like a tidal wave. There, in the middle of all my clothes, was the cardboard cylinder that held the Silver, crushed and shapeless. "This isn't good, man."

Black fluid coated the bundles of hundred dollar bills, unholy water spilled from the fish bowl. I could smell an acidic tang as the foul liquid ate through the money like an evil acid.

"Morgan, I'm so sorry, I must have landed on it when Alexander tossed me at the bar." Mike rubbed his lower back at the memory.

"No problem, man, but this, this is how *he* found us." I tore into the crushed cylinder, careful not to touch the black fluid, and extracted the small black bag, dangling it in my fingers by the leather straps. "No holy water to mask its signature."

"And that means what?"

"Means we run, and right *now*!"

Out the back and into the delivery truck. For the first time in I don't know how long, panic had a good hold of me with icy claws and wasn't letting go. Truck and axle nearly parted ways as I took a curb too hard and too fast. A trickle of blood ran down my throat from where I bit my lip, but the only thing I could think of was *Get to Bend*.

"What's going on, Morgan?" Mike yelled while the truck bounced up and down. He was definitely a little green around the gills.

"It's thirty miles to the church in Bend," I hollered back. "That's where we can destroy the Silver." The truck smoothed out some and the noise level decreased. "Right now the Patron can track us because the Silver is out and we can't afford to stay still for any length of time or we could be hip-deep in fiends. We *have* to get to holy ground ASAP."

I could see Mike trying not to be skeptical, but he just shrugged and said, "What's going on with Jim and Dale? How are they going to get rid of those bikers?"

"You realize the bikers aren't a threat now, right? It's what the Patron will send after us that's the threat."

"What aren't you telling me, Morgan," he said in a voice filled with gravel.

I knew that tone, was dreading the question and didn't want to answer it. "Jim and Dale are at the Sun Spot Drive-In."

"And what are they doing there?" he urged.

"Ambushing the remaining bikers."

"What?!"

"After you went to bed last night, Jim and Dale called some family and friends and arranged a welcome for the remaining bikers at the drive-in. Seems like there were a *lot* of people willing to take a swing at the gang. The list of people included the deputy sheriff, who said he wanted 'run those bastards out of town on a rail.' "

"What are they planning?"

"What do you think? A picnic? Some fish and chips and a screening of the new *Batman* movie?" I shook my head. "No, the gang's pissed off a lot of locals from Terrebonne to Bend, and most of them want to join in on the action. I think at last count there were a hundred fifty people signed up and they are going to beat those bikers black and blue and trash their bikes."

Silence. And more silence.

I risked a glance at Mike. He was stroking his ridiculous handlebar moustache. "Normally I'm opposed to violence, but the gang has done a lot of harm and if the sheriff won't help, then I suppose the people must take matters into their own hands." I was so shocked I nearly hit an old Hyundai chugging down the highway toward us. "But," he continued. "I hope they don't kill anyone."

Shaking my head, I said, "No, the plan is to turn them from psychopathic bikers to beaten and bruised psychopathic *pedestrians*, and then run them out of town."

He nodded reluctantly. "I just wish you would've informed me of your plans."

"Sorry, man, I didn't want to strain your sense of law and order."

"Morgan, one thing you should know: the Church has been struggling with secular laws for as long as it has existed. I see no problem with using violence against evil when all other recourses have been exhausted." He spoke as if we were chitchatting in a mall rather than in a truck zooming down the highway at seventy. I shook my head in wonder at Mike's ability to surprise me even after fifteen years.

Smiling, I snagged the CB. "Dispatch, this is 183."

"One-eight-three, go," came Bernie's staticky voice over the radio.

"Dispatch, be advised that we are en route to the Chamber of Commerce." That was my way of telling Bernie he could pick the truck up there. It was merely a hop, skip and jump from there to the Holy Redeemer Catholic Church.

Squawk! "Be advised, Olivier," Bernie said in a voice as cold as the grave. "You're never going to make it."

My insides nearly became my outsides as terror spiked through me. That wasn't Bernie. Beside me, Mike crossed himself.

We'd been found.

Chapter Eighteen

Mike

Can't say I was too terribly surprised that Morgan kept the ambush from me. Most people think priests are passive, pacifist bead rubbers. Most of the time we are, but in my case I had been a warrior, a man used to blood and death, armpit deep in both.

Moreover, most Americans don't realize that the Church has a militant order, The Military Corps of the Order of Malta, part of the Sovereign Military Hospitaller Order of St. John of Jerusalem of Rhodes and of Malta (better known as the SMOM or Knights of Malta). The Military Corps of the Order has the official title of Auxiliary Military Corps of the Italian Army.

The Catholic Church may be a peace-loving organization dedicated to the teachings of Christ, but it's not stupid. Faith is one thing, but I believe God *does* help those who help themselves.

When I heard the Voice emerge from the CB, its tone mocking and contemptuous, I decided it was time to fight fire with fire.

In the space between our seats rested our duffels, filled with none too fresh clothes and other small essentials. My hand reached for the floor where Morgan threw his weapons and emerged with a .45 ACP. A Kimber, nice, but I prefer the H&K. Along with the Kimber I found a Beretta (which I gave to Morgan) and two extra clips for both. In my bag was the manila envelope, which I stuffed in the inside pocket of my Danzinger's jacket.

"What do you mean?" Morgan asked the Voice. "We've already won."

"Boy, you must think I'm five kinds of stupid to fall for the 'Oh, I've lost the Silver' routine. Julian had an SS Team deployed in the area ever since the Baphemoloch became aware enough to recognize that the host he was eating carried the Grail. My associate found you near Las Cruces. With the host's memories, it was child's play to deduce what you were doing in the southwest, Olivier. This is the last time you will receive this offer; shoot the Holy Roller in the head, give up and rejoin the Family."

"Understood, sir," Morgan said through clenched teeth. Rolling down the window, he wrenched the CB off its moorings with one hand and threw it out of the truck. "Damn, his mouth runs like a fucking river. Pardon the profanity."

"Pardoned." I said, then, "SS Team?"

"Special Services Team. An elite squad, much like the Israeli commandos, but much, much worse. Basically Dagger Men Special Forces."

Stomach hitting the floor, I stared out the window for a couple of seconds. "You think he's lying? It's what he does, you know."

His look was bleak, barren of hope. "I don't think so, Mike. The Patron is a Power and Intelligence like you've never encountered. Amp up Stephen Hawking's brain by a thousand and you might come close. He's touchy, mean, controlling and unimaginably evil, but he's no dope. Yeah, I think we're in big trouble, because he knows we're going to a church to destroy the Silver." He shuddered. "Down on the floor should be a small black shaving bag. Get it."

Black shaving bag. Right … eight by four inches of simulated leather zippered shut. "Okay, now what?"

"Inside there are six metal vials and a small glass jar. Open the jar and smear some of the contents on your forehead and chest. It'll protect you; then give me one of the vials."

Outside the window, we passed Redmond, barreling south toward

Bend and a team of commandos waiting to kill us. In the bag I found the vials, the small jar and what looked to be several silver cigarette cases. The small jar contained a pinkish-white paste that smelled like charbroiled ugly. Grimacing, I applied the paste and tried not to puke; it smelled so bad. After wiping my hands I handed Morgan one of the six silvery vials, the contents of which he gulped in one swallow.

At my inquiring look he said, "Pennyroyal, Master Wart and Blessed Thistle herb. For that little extra kick, you know." He grinned like a skull grins, with horrifying knowledge and lost hope. Then the smile faded, replaced by an angry scowl.

"Shit!" he swore suddenly. "Why the hell am I driving to Bend when there's a Catholic church in Redmond?" He said a word I won't repeat. "I'm such a damn *idiot*!"

Noon traffic on the highway was fairly light, but there were still enough cars to cause concern as he yanked the steering wheel hard to the left and spun the truck, tires squealing and smoking, into a one-eighty. I kissed the side window in time to see an old, red Saab hatchback miss us by a hair and rumble off the road into the sandy, scrub-filled flatland. In the side-view mirror, as we sped back north, I saw the driver of the Saab raise a finger in a gesture as old as man.

"Please don't do that again," I rasped through clenched teeth. "Please, please, please!"

"No promises, but if it will make you feel better, take a drink from a vial."

Sounded like good advice, so I did.

If someone had peeled back my skull, exposing my brain, then poured white lighting on the vulnerable gray matter, that wouldn't even come close to the feeling that coursed through my skull.

Wow.

"A kick in the pants, eh Mike?"

"It's not my pants that have been kicked." I shook my head in an effort to chase away a sudden case of double vision.

"I should have planned to stop here first," Morgan grated after turning onto a residential street. "But noooooooo, I had to think of returning this stupid truck first." His fist smacked into the steering wheel three or four times, his anger pulsing through the cab like heat waves.

"You're only human, Morgan."

"You sure about that?" he snarled.

"Of course I am, you nitwit, now shut up and drive," I barked out like every Drill Instructor in history—hard, fast and loud. He tried to hide it, but I caught the telltale beginnings of a smile.

Smirking myself, I stared out the windshield as we pulled into a large parking lot. The brick building dominating it looked more like a high-class no-tell motel than a church, but the cross on its peaked roof gave lie to that impression. The sign in front declared it to be the St. Thomas Catholic Church.

Screeching to a halt under the overhang between a pair of pillars and the front doors, we jumped out, scrambling, stumbling, only to find both of the main doors locked.

Undeterred, Morgan shouted a Word and the right-hand door shattered, the pieces flying inward in a shower of deadly splinters.

"I'll pay for it," he panted, propelling me into the church and up the nave.

It took a second or two for my eyes to adjust to the gloom and by the time we reached the altar, the dancing spots of light in my eyes had faded somewhat. "What now, Morgan and why a church?"

He led me to the altar. "Because no demon will enter holy ground, and no elemental would dare perpetrate violence in what they call 'the Creator's footprint on the earth.' This is where the Grail is strongest, in the hands of a true believer." He leaned in and whispered fiercely. "You banished *two* demons, Mike, and I can tell you see the Grail as it really is; you weren't fooled for one second. It has no reason to hide from *you*." My eyes widened in shock as I realized he was right. It didn't look like a silver brooch or glass rose; it looked like what it was, a simple cup. He dug out the Silver from the front pocket of his jeans and I decanted the Grail from the purple bag. "We could just dump the coins into the Grail," he continued. "That might work, but it also might destroy both of them, and I won't be the person who broke the Holy Grail, man."

Understandable. "Now what?" A strange, distant *thap thap thapping* sound came to my ears and we both shared a nervous look as we realized its significance. A helicopter was hovering above us.

"Crap," he muttered, sweat beading his forehead. Hurriedly he emptied the contents of the little black bag into the Grail, which was nestled in the palm of my hand.

Cha-chink. Tiny, innocuous coins, gleaming bright, flooded the bowl. Roughly circular, they had a shining brilliance that drew the eye and their weight was a steady pressure in my hand. It was one of the most beautiful—and most terrible—sights I'd ever seen.

The Silver made me sick to my stomach; a burning bile collected at the back of my throat and my skin crawled. Maybe the Lord had graced me with prescience, I didn't know, but I knew that if I touched those glittering, malevolent coins, something bad would happen, something biblical.

Rotors cleaved the air outside the Church. The copter would be overhead any second now, I realized.

"Mike, all you have to do is exorcize the coins," Morgan breathed. "That's all you have to do, man." He gently placed his hands on either side of my face. "You can do it, Mike."

A Ritual of Exorcism on the fly, just like that? "I don't know the words to exorcize an … an artifact." *Thwap, thwap, thwap* … much closer.

Morgan's breath, slightly sweet, caressed my cheek, his lips only inches away. "My friend, it's not about words, it's about *faith*. Now, duck!" The Beretta appeared in his hand as if by magic, while his other pushed me down behind the altar.

Thwap, thwap, thwap … then deafening reports as Morgan fired several times. A scream of pain. More reports and splinters of altar rained down upon me.

Faith, it's about faith, I thought, staring at the beige-rimmed bowl with its terrible contents. *Faith. Faith.* Faith in myself, faith in Morgan, and more importantly, faith in the Lord. But what word could contain such faith? Faith that when our backs are up against it, the Lord will be there lending us strength as we falter, courage when we have none, and peace when our time has come. What words could convey all that? I'd fought demons, seen/felt elementals and trusted in a man who, had things been different, would have been my greatest enemy instead of a man I'd come to think of, not as a lost soul, but as a brother. What choice did I have?

As slivers of wood rained down and bullets tore gaping holes in the cross hanging on the wall above my head, the words came to me—timeless in their simplicity and love. Not an exorcism, but a simple prayer:

> The Lord is my Shepherd; I shall not want.
> He maketh me to lie down in green pastures:
> He leadeth me beside the still waters.
> He restoreth my soul:
> He leadeth me in the paths of righteousness for his name sake.

Another scream of pain split the air along with the sound of hundreds of rounds tearing the pews into matchsticks. There came an agonized groan and I knew Morgan was hurt. I heard someone, a woman, yell, "Give it up, Olivier!"

> Yea, though I walk through the valley of the shadow of death,
> I will fear no evil: For thou art with me;
> Thy rod and thy staff, they comfort me.
> Thou preparest a table before me in the presence of mine enemies;
> Thou annointest my head with oil; My cup runneth over.

It filled me, the Lord's grace, a peaceful feeling that transcended everything, and I was filled with the knowledge of what must occur next. As if guided by a will not my own, my free hand hovered over the cup of Christ and settled delicately on the rim.

Surely goodness and mercy shall follow me all the days of my life,

And I will dwell in the House of the Lord forever.

The flesh of my palm grew warm, then hot, but there was no pain, just a sense of *rightness* and distantly, as if from a half-remembered dream, I heard a low-pitched, agonized scream that echoed through the foundations of reality. Light came from the Grail, blazing through my hand as if the tissue was transparent, light that shot up to, and through, the roof, a beam of pure silver that speared the sky.

With the abruptness of a summer squall, it vanished. I removed my hand from the Grail to reveal … dust. Grayish, grainy dust that puffed up at the slightest breath. Silence gripped the church, broken only Morgan's triumphant shout, "You did it, Mike!"

I would've smiled, but at that moment a man dressed in a desert camo, covered in body armor, wearing a black helmet and mask, burst through the door that led from the back of the church to the baptismal font. A wicked-looking MP-5 SMG, all matte black and deadly as a spider, was clutched in his hands. As if in slow motion he aimed the weapon and pulled the trigger.

Bullets streaked their way toward me, my death assured.

Then a power and fury filled my eyes with glory.

Chapter Nineteen

Morgan

Through the front door I saw zip lines descend to the parking lot, SS commandos dropping like arachnids on silken threads. My feet thudded on the dark green carpet of the nave as I ran toward the door, Beretta raised. My first shot went high, I'm pretty sure over the shoulder of the first commando, but my second shot took him in the throat, tearing out chunks of spine through the back of his neck in a red mist, dropping him like a rag doll.

I flung myself to the left, landing between pews just as bullets stitched the air I had occupied. Close, but all I had to do was stay alive long enough to keep those idiots off Mike's back so he could do his job. After that I really didn't give a damn, not anymore, I was just so *tired* of it all. At least I could make that SS team regret their arrogance and give the Patron a big shitburger to eat.

Bullets took large pieces out of the top of the pews as I rose to my knees, keeping my head down. A silenced SMG, I'd bet. From a crouch I lunged back into the aisle, the Beretta spitting lead though the shattered doorway, miraculously catching another heavily armored commando in the shoulder. A good hit; there are a lot of functioning bits in the shoulder and a bullet will really screw up your century. I completed the roll, landing between more pews directly opposite of where I had been.

"Good shooting, Olivier," came a soft, female voice from outside, one I knew oh so well.

Shit. Annabeth. Just what I didn't need. Julian and the Patron knew exactly how to get under my skin. Zero to irritating in two seconds flat.

I knew better than to answer. She wanted me focused on the front door, so I spun, catching sight of a man coming through one of the side doors. Two shots in the groin had him on the ground shrieking and spewing blood.

The first bullet hit my spine, the second my kidney. Two more flung me around to catch the fifth right above the heart. I caught Annabeth's incredulous look as the flattened, crushed lead nuggets fell to the floor around me. The Beretta spoke again, two rounds into her armored chest. Tit for tat, I suppose.

She should've paid more attention to Botanical Magic, although very few do. It doesn't promise immediate rewards, but it packs a hell of a wallop. The potion I'd drunk earlier not only provided me some much needed strength, but it was the magical equivalent of Kevlar.

Staggering, backing toward the altar, I emptied the Beretta out the door and slammed home a new clip, the pain from the rounds I'd taken a furious spike to my tender flesh. I was sure I would pee blood for a week.

Two more rounds, stomach and chest, each harder as the efficacy of the potion began to wear thin. Snarling, I fell to my knees, sure I was a dead man kneeling.

"Give it up, Olivier!" Annabeth shouted above the roar of the helicopter, keeping herself inconveniently out of sight.

My reply was as inventive as it was profane. "Sorry, God," I mumbled as I remembered whose house I was in.

Stained glass shattered, coating two bodies as they flew into opposite ends of the church. Soon, I knew, it would be over. *Hurry Mike*, I thought, *Running out of options*. As I levered myself upright, I shouted a Healing and Vigor, going for the gusto but they were poor imitations of their potential. I'd used too much magic and it was beginning to drag me down, a spiraling descent into Backlash.

One commando fell, brains splattering the inside of his helmet as I twisted and spun, spraying bullets. I felt a blow to the ribs like the kick of a horse and I knew the potion was done for. The next ones would tear me apart.

It started as a low-pitched whine, a deep vibration that hit the edge of perception, teasing the ears. Slowly it built into a bone chattering buzz that held a wealth of anger and frustration, rage translated into sound.

I knew what that sound was.

It was over, done. I'd won. Or, I should say, *we* had won, Mike and I. My only regret was that he would soon follow me in death. But I'd probably take the express elevator down, down, down to a reward that no soul had ever been subjected to. I had no doubt that the Patron would set aside a special place for me in Hell.

It didn't matter. "You did it, Mike," I cried victoriously.

A ragged furrow appeared on my chest as the gunman to my right, the one I wasn't able to kill, fired his weapon. I held out my arms like a benediction, mirroring Christ on his cross behind me. It was time.

In tones of righteous fury, I heard Mike shout. "Thou Shalt Not!" I spun to see him stand up from behind the altar, tall and proud, a vision of anger and judgment, the Grail cupped in one big hand. He stared at a gunman, who emptied a full clip at the enraged priest.

Every bullet missed. Instead the altar shredded apart, splintering into a thousand pieces, as if the hand he held palm outward in front of him had *shoved* the bullets aside. The commando, no fool I guess, dropped his emptied weapon and hightailed it out of there.

More wood splintered around Mike as he turned, the Grail in one hand, the other still stretched out before him. I thought he was a blazing pillar of wrath in New Mexico, exorcizing the first demon we encountered, but that was a flickering candle compared to the bonfire that burned behind the shattered remains of the altar.

His black flattop fairly gave off sparks as it waved slightly, as if affected by an unseen ocean current. Thin shoots of silver colored his otherwise night-black hair at the temples, while his presence, always a commanding one, drew the eye like a magnet and gripped the mind with implacable golden fingers.

Behind me an SMG roared and I knew I was a dead man, but the only thing that happened was the formation of new craters as the bullets slammed into the wall behind Mike.

"What the fuck!" Annabeth breathed from behind me.

I couldn't help grinning, although she couldn't see it. "Kind of puts the Patron into perspective, doesn't it?"

Mike's eyes bored into mine and I felt an electric thrill. "Run."

I stepped forward. "Hey, man, I can't do that!"

His voice became a Command. "Run, my friend. They will not stop you." His smile filled me with hope. "Go now, out the back."

My feet refused to obey my orders, instead following Mike's. I risked a look behind to see Annabeth and three more commandos; all staring in rapt fascination as Mike slowly descended the stairs to the aisle toward them.

Out the back, still taking the lead, my sneakers slapped on asphalt then dry, brown grass. A couple hundred feet directly ahead was a fence, a barrier between the church property and track housing, and from behind and above, the helicopter, a UH-60 Black Hawk.

Heart thudding, I ran toward the fence line, hating myself for abandoning my friend but knowing I had no choice. At fifty feet from the church parking lot, the first round grazed the outside of my left thigh, leaving a burning trail of blood. The second powdered the earth in front of me, throwing up a softball-sized divot.

Face and chest hit the ground at the same time as 50 mm rounds stuttered across the area around my body. Whoever was firing was either playing with me or had orders to bring me in alive. Since "mercy" isn't in the vocabulary of Dagger Man or the Family, my guess was on the former.

With a growl, I rumbled into grass, the Language of Earth tumbling from my lips like stones and the smell of hot metal overcoming the scent of dry grass and dust. Faster and faster I gabbled, pleading, begging as the helicopter circled above me. I could almost feel the 50 cals sights on the back of my neck.

Surprisingly, Earth responded much quicker than I had anticipated with an interrogative shake of the ground around my navel.

Thwap, thwap, thawp ... The copter started to land and I risked a glance. A helmeted commando sat at the open port training the muzzle of a 50 cal at my head, the three rotating barrels ready to spit a quick and messy death. I tried not to piss myself.

Earth rattled, shaking under my prostrate form, demanding a startling price. A steep price, but at that point I was in no position to negotiate. Firing back an affirmative, Earth shook harder as the Black Hawk landed not more than twenty feet away, spraying me with sand and grit.

Suddenly, the ground swallowed me whole.

BOOK TWO

SECOND MAN

Chapter Twenty

Mike

I opened the manila envelope once more with every intention of finishing Jude's, now Morgan's, tale. I wondered if he was well.

A Forest of Trouble

Of course, back before I stole the Silver, I didn't know the term Anti-Christ; that came later after Mike gave me a copy of the Bible. Instead, our prophecies spoke of the Redeemer, the vessel for the Patron and I knew there was no way I wanted to be anyone's damn vessel. The thought of losing my free will was abhorrent to me. I would tolerate it no more than a parent would put up with an unrepentant, enthusiastic child rapist teaching in a grade school.

Eyes full of the Words that thudded against my gray matter, I held out the Silver to Julian, arm shaking with the stress of holding the coins. Julian took them from my hand and poured them back into the pouch.

The moment the Silver left my palm, the Words oozed away, all thirty of the malignant things, flushed free from my overburdened brain. Let me tell you, I nearly swooned with relief. Apparently those Words were too powerful to be permanently placed in the mind

of man. "S-six," I stammered, eyes glued to the floor. "Six Words."
Please, please, please, I thought. *Please be satisfied with that.* Not quite
a prayer, more of a desperate plea to anyone but the Patron.

Julian beamed, the first time he'd ever thrown a smile my way. The
Voice was conspicuous in its silence.

"Well done, Olivier," Julian said, sounding … happy. That alone
nearly made me wet my pants. "Your grandfather controlled the
Reich with just four, the weakest four at that. With six you can
destroy nations."

The Voice spoke up sounding mildly disappointed. "I had expected
more, Olivier. I expected so much more."

"Sorry to disappoint, sir." Please, oh please, be content with six
Words!

"Oh, well, Julian, there's always Burke." If that was meant to
provoke a reaction, it didn't work. I'd half expected the response, so
I managed to school my expression into something resembling rage
and frustration.

Julian moved his lips into an unkind smile. "Don't worry, Olivier,
you have so much to offer the family. With all twelve lesser Words
at your command you will rise far in the Sicarii, most likely to the
rank of Dagger Man Grand Commander." He sounded as if he were
throwing me a bone instead of informing me that I could be the
leader of all our forces in the world, second only to him. However,
in his eyes, anything less than top dog was unacceptable and I knew
that if Burke became head of the Family, my time on earth would be
severely … limited.

My answering smile was as close to absolute zero as I could
manage. "Thank you, Julian."

As soon as I could, I bowed out, but not before hearing the Voice
say to Julian, "Send for Burke."

Andre, Julian's driver, dropped me off at the estate, mercifully
vacant except for Annabeth. Her mouth, hot and hungry, greeted me
with enthusiasm as I walked through the front door.

"Hello, lover," she purred when we came up for breath.

"Hello yourself, beautiful." Again I dipped my mouth to hers and for a long, long while we forgot about the world around us.

Later, caught in the tangles of post-coital bliss, we held and stroked each other. A small island of peace in the ocean of my life.

"What are you thinking, Olivier?" she breathed while nuzzling my neck, a caress I'd always found irresistible. "Something's bothering you."

"I may have to kill Burke."

The nuzzling stopped. "Why?"

"The Patron and Julian are looking to him, now. They're going to test the Silver on him." No one from the female side of the Line had ever been tested with the Silver before. Only direct Line members were guaranteed to survive the experience, while those from the more distant branches tended to die gruesome deaths. Somehow I knew that Burke would survive.

"Why don't they look to you?'

"They tested me," I said, running my fingers up and down her arm. "I only drew six Words. I think they were hoping for more." The lie slipped easily from my mouth. I lusted for Annabeth, but that didn't mean I would trust her with a secret.

She propped herself on one elbow and looked deep in my eyes. I saw gold flakes in the brown of her irises and it struck me as unusual that I'd never noticed before. "But you have all twelve Words and are a natural at the other two branches of magic. Why would they choose him over you?"

"Burke has the respect of the entire Family, from the assassins to the bureaucrats. He's a natural leader and as ruthless as they come. I think Julian sees me as too ... soft."

Her hand dipped under the covers. "You don't feel soft to me," she grinned as her lips met mine. I responded immediately to her touch.

My troubles disappeared. At least for a little while.

New Hampshire, just outside of Durham on an estate at the edge of Great Bay, near the Adams Point State Wildlife Refuge. It was Julian's favorite place outside of Switzerland, the only place in the

United States he could tolerate for more than a week.

The night of one of the worst blizzards to hit the region found me, Annabeth, Burke, cousins Fergus, Anton and Simone in a Huey copter flying over the white bones of trees, the snow so thick it seemed a swirling fog of white. This was the final test, the final toughening point. If I survived, I would be part of an SS Team, a member of an elite brotherhood of assassins that only the most lethal and skilled Family could join.

Two days earlier, I had received the summons from Julian, a summons I couldn't refuse and one that surprised me. As the last male in the direct Line, it was understood that I would not have to undergo the rigorous final test. I guess my inclusion was a testimony to the Voice's displeasure. What really piqued my interest was Burke's involvement. He had never evinced any interest in wet work, preferring to run his highly successful R&D department of Wellington Arms Manufacturing—one of the Family's largest companies, in fact—which was producing his design of the new repeating ballistic knife prototype that had been touted as the next big thing in urban warfare.

The mission was simple: all of us would attempt a high altitude drop at night and must survive the next four days in the forest on our own. If we encountered another, we attempted a 'kill' with a paintball gun. Those who struggled back to the estate alive were SS. Words were not allowed and the Professor supplied potions we were forced to drink to block our access to all magic, so for the next few days, we were effectively "normal."

Fergus, a wild-haired blond from a distant Scottish branch, grinned sourly at us just before leaping out of the helicopter. Next came Burke, then Annabeth, Simone, myself, and Anton.

I gave my French cousin a cheeky grin, which he returned with enthusiasm. A short twenty-year-old, he had an infectious good humor that made him my second favorite cousin after Annabeth.

On a summer's day, twelve thousand feet slaps your face with a chill you won't soon forget, but in winter—with the winds approaching 50 mph, in the dead of night where the demons of imagination roam—

it is like having your skin removed, layer-by-layer, by a sadist with a cold iron knife. The wind's passage clawed at my ears and I was extremely grateful for the thin plastic goggles that shielded my eyes, certain that they would otherwise have frozen solid on the way down.

At three thousand feet the altimeter automatically deployed my parachute and the world became silent except for the gusting of the blizzard. After the terror of the fall, even the storm was a relief.

No night vision, no magic, no relief from the fear of not being able to see where I was going as the parachute was buffeted remorselessly by frigid winds. Not for the first time I cursed Julian for his sadistic streak.

Branches and twigs slapped and scratched me, tearing with woody fingers. A ragged piece as big around as my thumb punched into my left bicep, not ripping though my protective clothing, but hitting with enough force to sear the muscle with a pain that momentarily paralyzed the arm.

I flexed my knees just in time to absorb the bone jarring impact that even a foot of snow didn't lessen. My right hand slapped the chute release as the shock of my landing traveled straight up to my balls and set up shop for a few painful moments.

Teeth gritted, I unclipped a glowstick, bent it to break the glass capsule inside and shook it hard, letting the phosphorescent chemicals mix. A cool green glow lit the immediate surroundings. Stark sentinels—beech trees bare in the harsh winter climate—surrounded me along with tall hemlock and creek maples. Not what I needed. If I were unable to find shelter, all that would be left would be my corpsicle.

Not wanting to abandon any resource or leave telltale signs of my arrival, I searched for and found my 'chute, tugging it out of a grasping hemlock. With the white fabric tucked under one arm, I went in search of shelter, flexing my left arm to work out the pain of the growing bruise.

By the green light of the glowstick I finally found what I was looking for—a white spruce, its bottommost branches so heavily laden with snow that they touched the ground. Perfect. Imitating a snake, I slithered underneath the branches to find myself in a sheltered cone next to the trunk, a spot safe from the clawing wind. Withdrawing a small packet from the pocket of one arm, I worried the plastic apart and unfolded a thin Mylar blanket. That along with the 'chute would keep me alive until morning. Rolled up like a burrito, I took calm, even breaths to ease the burning in my lungs, the plumes of frost from my mouth hanging like the spirits of the dead in the eerie light of the glowstick.

Despite the howling wind and freezing cold, it was surprisingly easy to fall asleep.

Footprints, poorly hidden and leading west. The diffuse morning sunlight oozed through the wooden bones around me, faintly illuminating the drag marks that failed to fully conceal the passage of what I assumed was one of my cousins. Slowly, carefully, I followed those drag marks, alert for the possibility of ambush.

According to my watch I had been following those marks for forty minutes and it was only a handful more before I rounded a maple and saw my target, heavy white winter coat and leggings blending almost seamlessly with the pristine surroundings, the same kind of camouflaging winter gear I wore. The figure crept along, evergreen branches dragging behind.

I smiled, lifted my paintball gun and fired. Alcohol and blue dye spheres tore through the air to *splat* onto the figure's back, knocking the person down.

"Kill to me," I called softly.

Grunting, the person rose, sky blue blotches marring the formerly white coat. "Yeah, you got me," came a voice I knew so well.

"Annabeth!"

She turned, arching her back in discomfort and raised an eyebrow. "That's the problem with you, Olivier, you lack the killer instinct."

"What?"

Her smile was mirthless. "You followed my tracks. I meant for you to find me."

The smile that had so beguiled me was wrong. That situation

was wrong. My danger sense kicked in too late to avoid three sharp impacts along my spine ... the last thudding home with a hollow sound that tore my body away from conscious control.

Cold on my face, needles of frost that melted and reformed with every hitching breath. Coppery blood filled my mouth, my nostrils. A lung was punctured, quickly filling with blood, but I could not feel the wound. A numb feeling of horror gripped me as I realized that my spine had been severed near my neck and I was insensate to the cold stealing through my body.

I was dying.

No Words, no potions, no elementals. Cut off from all help, I could only lie there and feel my life slowly drip away.

Abruptly my perspective changed and the cold left my face as light flooded my eyes. Someone was kind enough to turn me over. That someone was Burke, also clothed in heavy white winter gear.

"Hello, Olivier," he smiled nastily, holding up one of his prized repeating ballistic knives.

I grunted painfully in reply.

"You really are a simple creature," he continued. "So easily duped." Annabeth came within view to stand next to him. Her grin was anything but nice.

"Bitch," I bubbled, spraying blood from my lips in a red mist.

"Opportunist," she corrected haughtily. "I always go with a winner and we know who the real winner is, don't we, Olivier?"

Burke's teeth shone as white as the snow around him. With one gloved hand he casually reached through the opening of her white coat and cupped her left breast. Fury ripped through the blood in my throat as I vented a sharp whistle of a scream, soon followed by Burke's laughter.

Annabeth's sweet voice floated toward me. "So what do we do with him?"

"Nothing," came the contemptuous reply. "Let the forest swallow him up."

Gray skies and snow flurries. A cold wind brushed my face with icy fingers and blood steamed on my lips as I desperately struggled for air. I couldn't feel it, but I knew my body was starting to get colder and colder as I slowly froze to death. That is, if I did not bleed out first.

Burke and Annabeth. Annabeth and Burke. I should have seen it, should have at least *felt* something, but I had been blinded by my lust, my passion. At least my wounds did not hurt, not compared to the pain of Annabeth's betrayal. I had actually started to *trust* her and she used that to help Burke get the drop on me.

I wondered if she was Julian's idea. It had been one of his cunning, sadistic plans and I had fallen for it hook, line and sinker.

Nose and cheeks started to go numb, and it would not be long before I gently slipped into my final slumber. Well, at least I would not be the Vessel for the Voice, the Family's precious Redeemer. Death was far preferable to being someone's puppet.

Oh, who was I kidding? Burke had pulled my strings, so had Annabeth and no doubt Julian. I had been a puppet all along … the best kind, one who did not know he was a puppet.

The soft, golden glow slowly coloring the bones of the beech trees hovering over me matched my feeling of weary lassitude.

Golden glow? What? A pique of interest pierced the veil of my drowsiness.

It stepped into view. No, not an *It*, but a *He*, a perfectly built, golden-hued man with lustrous, long black hair that flowed to his hips. Dressed in a white wrap of silky material that encircled his waist, he seemed impervious to the biting cold.

"Who?" I coughed, spraying more blood.

Then the wings unfurled, eagle-like pinions banded in white, bronze and silver. It came to me that I knew this being … one of the Liar's messengers, a winged servant whose charter was to deceive the true believers into accepting the gospels of the Lying God. Fear like nothing I'd ever known clawed at my mind and I smelled the urine I couldn't feel.

As if reading my mind, the messenger, the deceiving angel, smiled sadly and crouched, laying an aureate hand on my cheek. Even up close his perfection blinded me, rendering me unable to recall his simplest features.

"Know this, young Sicarius, and decide," he said, voice like the music of the world.

And the heavens opened up to me.

I heard the first Word and saw the creation of everything. *Everything.* It all came together in a clash of sound so immense I couldn't even really define it as sound—more a vast feeling too intense for mere mortals to conceptualize.

The world came into being, with Primals to maintain the delicate balance of nature. They fought, they struggled, but always with a harmony that made the struggle beautiful to watch, a ballet of violence and joy. With the creation of the Primals came the Angels, and none so powerful, so beautiful as Lucifer. He was the sun, the light that eclipsed all others. Then came plants and animals, growing, rising and falling quickly as time accelerated faster and faster.

It was almost too much for me to bear, this kaleidoscope of imagery that unfolded like an origami rose with millions of petals in my mind. Faster and faster the visions whirled and danced until the Word was spoken again—softer this time, a mere breath of celestial magic—and Man was born.

I felt the joy of the Creator as the divine spark flared inside Man, a spark that became the Soul … and I felt jealousy, the jealousy of an Angel. Lucifer. He saw in the Soul something that was lacking in him, a callous joke mocking his perfection. For the first time something new had been born in the universe that was not fashioned by God.

Hate.

Lucifer's hatred for all men, their lack of perfection, their Souls, infected many Angels until they banded together in discord and tried to use their Words, the Words of their jealousy and hatred, against the Throne.

A struggle raged in Heaven as angel fought angel, the dead winking out of existence forever. Angelic blood ran in rivers along the splendid silver streets of the City of God and the Creator wept, unwilling to raise a hand to stop His children. It was a struggle that had to be decided by angels, a painful evolution of their moral hearts.

The angels of hate and jealousy were defeated, falling flaming from the heights, beautiful wings taken from them, bodies stripped of their perfection not because they defied the Creator, but because they wasted all that they were, all that they could have been, on Hate. They let it consume them and shape them into something horrific to behold.

Lucifer fell the farthest—far enough that God's grace no longer touched his wounded, burned body. In that place, the Abyss, he began to craft Hell, a trap for the souls of Man whose evil denied them Heaven.

The Morning Star began to disguise himself with many Names, the foremost being Satan. In the world's infancy, he walked its surface, often in disguise. Serpent, Dragon, Leviathan, all forms and names he used to bedevil man until Lucifer's Hate gave him such power that the world could no longer contain his power, his form. He had grown swollen and pregnant with abhorrence. In his attempt to foster hate, he was denied the earth; he had no portal to give him access save in dreams.

But the damage was done. Man had defied the Creator, maturing too quickly, the divine plan thrown awry, and Man was cast out of Eden, which was removed from the boundaries of Earth. So they would not toil in loneliness, the Word was spoken again and more Men came into being, filling the earth with their industry. Satan's stain still wreaked its havoc, though, as the first murder was committed, brother killing brother.

Satan laughed and he plotted.

"I am Harachel," said the being softly, his breath a faint tickle against my face. "Angel of Knowledge."

Back. I was back and aware again of my surroundings. The vision that had held me faded like yesterday's dream, but that vision left one certainty in its wake: the knowledge that it was the *truth*.

The Voice wasn't the victim of an insane, lying God, wasn't the poor oppressed savior of mankind, the one who would provide much needed order. All my life I'd been lied to. My life was a lie.

I began to cry at the injustice of it all, wiping my eyes.

Wiping my eyes? My arms ... they moved! I could feel. Sure, I felt so cold that I'd bleed ice cubes, but I *felt!* Shakily I stood, swaying for a moment with pins and needles pricking my feet. I looked up to thank the angel (an angel—one of the good guys!) and was stopped cold by the look of compassion in his eyes.

"You have the choice, Olivier Deschamps." The angel smiled and it was the most glorious thing I had ever seen. "Thou *mayest* choose between good and evil." That said, it vanished, as if it had never been, no sign, just a lingering tinkle, like fairy bells. Not even footprints in the snow.

For a long time I wondered at the archaic verbiage, but it was not until I met Mike that I realized those words were the equivalent of a smack to the back of the head.

Sighing, I headed deeper into the forest. I had some planning to do.

Thou mayest.

℘

Wow. I could hardly believe what I had just read. Morgan/Jude met an angel! The concept stunned me, almost left me breathless. Silently I praised the Lord for showing Morgan the truth and letting him decide for himself.

Carefully I tucked the pages of the manuscript into the back pocket of my uniform and drank the cup of tepid tea that had been left for me. Once again I pondered the lonely roads we find ourselves on.

Back in the church, I had looked down a barrel of a gun and felt God's power fill and sustain me. I knew that Morgan had to escape, that a sacrifice for his safety had to be made and that it would be me. No problem ... trust in the Lord, right?

Not just a saying anymore, not for me.

Bullets missed, guns jammed and my friend made tracks. Once he left, the power slowly drained away, leaving me with a curious sense of calm and a cool detachment. Nothing could bother me.

Unfortunately, the lady (who turned out to be the infamous Annabeth) decked me a good one on the jaw and I dropped like a rock to the floor of the nave. Oddly enough, it didn't hurt all. I smiled at her redly, blood dripping from a split lip.

"Take the Liar's trash to the chopper," she sneered. I had to hand it to Morgan; she definitely was a knockout.

Strong hands zip-tied my hands behind my back and hauled me to my feet. "So this is a priest?" said a deep voice from beneath a beige helmet. "Looks like a dumbass hick instead of one of the Liar's butt-boys."

A few choice words came to mind, but I made do with my serene smile and soon found myself airborne. After a few seconds a needle pinched into my flesh and the world went away for a while.

I came to in a little ten-by-ten room, empty save for a cot and a bedpan. My captors had done a poor job of searching me because the manila envelope was still tucked into my jacket pocket. A little light reading during my time in happyville.

No worries though; the Lord was on my side. But I sure could have used a gun right about then.

Chapter Twenty-One

Morgan

Rock flowed around me, pliable and thick as liquid cement. The bubble of air I rode in was only slightly bigger than my body, but the air remained sweet, pure. Light, dim and diffuse, lit the bubble as it floated through liquefied bedrock. Farther and farther I traveled until even the sight of rock stretching like taffy became … tiresome.

It wasn't like flying, more like slowly body surfing on a wave of cool caramel, but without the sugary smell.

Bump. My nose smacked against stone that didn't flow resulting in a wash of pain that exploded behind my eyes. Before I could cry out, I oozed into the rock, birthing through to the other side.

Ow! Shards of something sliced into my hand right down to the bone and sharp points stabbed at me moments before they melted into a hard, smooth surface. Stale air clogged my nose, but I managed to whisper a quick Healing. Blood slicked my hands as the gashes covering my fingers and palms slowly closed, flesh knitting together until not a seam of damage remained. Only my chest still bled from a half dozen slices and punctures. Whatever had cut me sliced my shirt and jacket to ribbons. Another Healing and the fetid air was replaced by cinnamon, a vast improvement.

Shuddering as the pain subsided, I sat cross-legged on whatever hard surface I found myself on, forearms on knees, forehead on arms.

"You are safe here," rumbled Earth. "Although you have lost water."

I answered back, trying not to cough as the Language clogged my throat. "*I ... I am well. I have healed myself, although the air is bad.*"

Almost immediately the atmosphere sweetened. "Son of the Sicarii, you may rest here before you have to go. No magics can sense you in this place. Earth will keep you safe here."

Here? Where was here, except in the belly of the planet? I looked around.

Holy shit! A cave ... I sat in a cave made of crystal daggers a foot long, deep purple and perilously sharp. All around, ceiling, floors, walls, that hundred-foot sphere pointed violet death at where I sat and I was amazed. It was a geode, a damn geode the size of a large house with amethyst daggers cropping up everywhere except for the smooth purple floor I sat on. Earth had melted the crystal down to a flat pane some five feet on a side.

"Wow."

"You will pay the price agreed upon, yes, Son of the Sicarii?"

Apparently my time to marvel at nature's wonder was up. I thought back to what Earth had asked of me. "*Take back the First Water from your sire, Sicarii,*" Earth had demanded. "*And you will be saved.*"

I had racked my brains while the chopper circled overhead, readying for a landing. First Water? It hit me like a tsunami ... Earth wanted the Primal Water in Julian's possession.

Awww, hell.

Of course I'd agreed. Rather die on an impossible mission later than be taken captive by Annabeth sooner. At the thought of my once-lover I remembered Mike. Mike! In my time surfing through stone, I'd almost forgotten him. My best friend was in the clutches of my Family. I had to save him from whatever unimaginable fate Julian had planned. Well, not unimaginable to the Voice.

"*I will pay the price.*" What choice did I have? Didn't want to piss off, oh ... the whole planet ... literally. I hoped I could kill two birds with one stone: find the Primal, find my friend.

"Why do you want the Prim—ah … First Water? Earth, Water, Fire and Air always seem to be in conflict."

"Not so. What you see as conflict, we see as the eternal dance, an expression of the Song."

"Song?"

"What you humans call the Word. The Word the Creator used to bring all things into being. Fire hungers, Water talks, Earth abides and Air flows. All struggle with the others, but without them, life cannot be. So, in our eternal conflict, we help maintain the balance and the Song."

Perhaps the idea of the Primal in Julian's hands made Earth chatty because this was the longest conversation with Earth I'd ever had. Whatever, I was all ears. *"What does this have to do with First Water?"*

For the first time since I learned the Language, Earth sounded irritated. "The Power in First Water is great. If your sire were to somehow harness that power, he could upset the balance, add a discordant note to the Song and thus destroy it."

"And if he destroys Song?"

"He destroys the Word and everything will cease to be."

That didn't sound promising. Who needed the Silver when Primal Water had so much more potential for devastation? Pictures of vast tidal waves and floods strobed in my imagination and a headache started to burn behind my eyeballs.

"Julian will have the First Water with him at all times, then. I just have to find him. This may take a while." I laughed. "By human standards, that is."

"First Water is close, on the mound of human-made earth you call a city. The large one to the east next to the ocean."

A few seconds deciphering led me to conclude that Julian was in New York. Wonderful. I hate New York, it is too … intense. *"All right, but it will take some planning. The Sicarii are careful and well protected. I am just one human."*

"There is another who will help." I had the impression Earth wanted this done Right Now. "Second Man always looks for new challenges and has no love for your ... family. It remains up to you to convince him."

Second Man? My head throbbed even harder and I toyed with the idea of Healing it, but I'd been too cavalier with my Words lately. I wanted to avoid a serious case of Backlash, the state a magus finds himself in when too much magic, too quickly, is used, draining the magus dry. If he survived the coma, the outcome was usually loss of Words, some or all, with no capability to relearn them. It was as if the part of the brain where they were stored became permanently damaged, burned out.

"Who is Second Man?"

"Second Man is Second Man," Earth rumbled placidly, as if that explained everything.

"That does nothing for me. Second Man ... is he a magus like me?"

The geode shook, a mini-tremor that had amethyst crystals chiming. It took me a few moments to realize that Earth was laughing. Belling crystal laughter had the amethyst shaking so hard I was soon covered in purple dust.

"Oh, Son of Sicarii!" Earth groaned happily, a sound like the slow rubbing of flint. "Second Man is so much more than a mere magus. He is a magus like none other alive.

"You will rest here until you feel well enough to continue; then you will be taken to Second Man. Speak to him, convince him to aid you and return First Water."

"Where?"

"To Water. Pour First Water into Water and it will be free."

"And if I can't get it? What if Julian resists my best efforts to free the First Water?"

"Then Earth will take action."

Uh-oh. *"Action."*

"Earth will swallow the mound of man-made earth and ensure the return of the First Water, should such means prove necessary."

Swallow New York? It wasn't hard for me to envision Earth tearing the city apart, flinging shards of cement, steel and glass into the sea.

Millions would die and the responsibility of saving them was on my shoulders.

Sounded easy enough.

I emerged from the frozen soil next to Hwy 50 just outside of Gunnison, Colorado. Not that I was any great shakes at geography; Earth had placed me right next to the town's "Welcome To" sign.

Gunnison in January ... and I thought Omaha was cold! The breeze that flowed down the mountains into the little valley sheared right through my torn and bloodied jacket, raising goose bumps all over my quickly cooling flesh.

Earth had given me a rough idea where I could find this so-called "Second Man," my potential ally against the Family. A couple hundred long, cold yards later I came across a gravel road that intersected Hwy 50. It was the one I'd been told to take, so take it I did.

The sun slipped below the horizon before I'd gone too far and things got *really* interesting. Hands stinging, lips numb, I stumbled along up a steep slope that only the best SUVs or mountain goats could climb. Soon I was wishing for a Sherpa. Before my skin turned too blue, I came to a copse of evergreens. Nestled there in the center like a spider in its web was a genuine log cabin. It looked like something out of a maple syrup ad. The gravel road became a driveway, which housed an old, battered, Jeep Wrangler, a menacing lump of darkness on four rugged tires.

The light streaming from the window looked warm and inviting, and I knew if I didn't find shelter soon, my Family would be the least of my worries.

Knocking on the front door felt like it would break my poor frozen flesh and shatter my knuckles like glass. My breath fogged and I shivered uncontrollably.

The door opened, spilling golden light into my eyes that caused them to water. I blinked a few times to clear the tears away. "A shivering man bestrides the portal to my home with the appearance of the lost and forlorn," uttered a deep voice with a heap of *gravitas*. "Stranger, why do you attempt such a perilous night without adequate clothing?" When my eyes finally adjusted, I took in the sight of a tall, handsome man, with slightly weather-beaten, deeply tanned skin. He was lean, with short, curly auburn hair streaked with blond, the same color as his jawline beard and moustache. His most striking feature, however, was the Glacier-style mirrored sunglasses perched high on his hawk nose. Who would wear glasses like that in the dead of night? Was he blind? "Please do the honor of granting forgiveness," he continued. "Guests are rare and should be well received. It has been far too long since my eyes have beheld a fellow traveler." Nope, not blind. The smile he laid on me shone with a wealth of highly polished teeth.

The Second Man mystery I'd been pondering on my cold and miserable walk up the gravel road became, in a flash of those pearlies, a mystery no more. My heart thudded so hard it felt like my ribs would crack.

You see, I'd seen that face most of my life, the Sicarii's Most Wanted, most feared boogeyman, the Man With No Eyes. He had many names, but they all boiled down to just one: Death. Sicarii Dagger Men had targeted him as the Legend Maker: whoever managed to kill him would be the greatest assassin of all time.

Earth called him Second Man because that's what he was, the second man to ever walk the earth, born thousands of years ago after the expulsion from Eden. The First Murderer.

Cain. Yeah, *that* Cain.

According to the Bible, Cain was cursed to be a restless wanderer and God said that any who slew him "will suffer vengeance seven times over." So of course, if the Lying God said he should not be touched, the Sicarii had to try some touching With Extreme Prejudice, confidant that the Patron would have their back.

All those thoughts, those emotions, must have flitted across my face because the smile died from his. "Walter," he called softly.

I frowned. "Walter?"

"Not you." He pointed into the darkness behind me. "Him."

Twisting around, I had just enough time to grunt in surprise before two large, rough hands clamped down on my shoulders hard enough for my bones to creak in protest and hoisted me effortlessly three feet in the air. A blank dark slab a foot square regarded me impassively.

"Stranger, you have the misfortune of regarding Walter, a bodyguard of no mean capability," Cain said smoothly, without heat.

I blinked a few times because what I saw my brain couldn't quite translate, as if my visual cortex had gone bye-bye. When comprehension finally struck, I sagged despite the numbing pain from his viselike grip. What I took to be a rough-hewn giant (at least ten feet tall) dressed in black turned out to be a creature made of wrought iron. Shaped like a man, all the joints were well articulated, delicately crafted; however, that's where any semblance of precision ended. Where a face should have been, there was only a rough, flat, rectangular surface like the bottom of an anvil. Torso, thighs, forearms, anything that didn't have a joint looked cobbled together, welded from whatever scraps of black iron could be found. I recognized the U shape of a horseshoe welded to its stomach, connecting foot length pieces of rebar. The thing was so massive that I couldn't help but wonder why I hadn't heard it approach. A stealth monster?

On the spot where its forehead should have been I saw an inscription, just one word: תמא or *emet*, the Hebrew word for "truth." A cold chill that had nothing to do with the pain in my shoulders ran down my spine. A rough-hewn monster like that hadn't been seen in centuries—a Golem.

A little background: In Prague, Josefov, the Jewish Quarter, the late sixteenth century, Rabbi Judah Loew ben Bezalel created a golem to defend the Jewish ghetto from anti-Semitic attacks and pogroms. Constructed from clay taken from the banks of the Vltava River, it was brought to life with Hebrew incantations and lengthy rituals. The golem became so violent in defense of the Jews, its attacks so heinous, that the Holy Roman Emperor, Rudolf II, begged the Rabbi to stop the golem in return for leaving the Jews alone.

The Rabbi rubbed out the first letter of the word "emet" from the golem's forehead, leaving the Hebrew word "met," meaning "dead." Thus the golem was deactivated and stored in the attic of the Old

New Synagogue, where it has remained all these years.

When Rabbi Judah died, he took with him the secret of how to create golems. It looked like he wasn't the only one privy to that secret.

"So am I to assume by the reaction so nakedly writ across your face upon beholding my countenance, that you are truly aware of my provenance?" Cain remarked as he poured himself a shot of Glenfiddich.

Seated in the kitchen area of his cabin, the golem's large iron paws still clamped to my shoulders—albeit with less force—I nodded. Provenance? Really? Who talks like that?

"So am I to assume that when you embarked upon the path leading to my humble abode you had not a whit of a notion as to whom you would meet?"

I shook my head.

"May one inquire what business brings you to my house?" he asked, sitting down and taking a sip of scotch. His glasses winked in the soft lamplight.

I stared at my twin reflections. Glacier sunglasses are popular with the skiing crowd, keeping the sun's harsh glare from reaching the eyes by placing pieces of leather between the sunglasses and the corners of the eyes along the stems. Instead of leather, Cain's glasses seemed to be constructed of densely woven metal mesh. "I was told Second Man would help me."

He tilted his head to one side. "Second Man? That name has not reached these delicate, shell-like ears in centuries. I must conclude then that this person, or persons, who put you on the path to my doorstep, are powerful indeed, but unable to aid you in your endeavors. So, my newfound guest, who sent you?"

"Earth."

"Earth?"

"Yeah, man, Earth."

Cain took another sip from his shot glass. "What would drive an elemental to have you enlist the aid of the most notorious human in history?"

Since I wasn't going anywhere—the golem had made damn sure of that—I plunged in. "The Sicarii have Primal Water. Earth wants it freed to restore balance and if I can't retrieve the Primal, Earth will swallow New York to make sure it doesn't remain in Sicarii hands."

From his reaction, you would've thought we were talking about the weather. "And?"

Despite the heavy iron hands enclosing my shoulders, I managed to lean forward. "Are you nuts, man? Or should I say, 'Do you find yourself in the mouth of madness, surrah?' "

His laughter startled the hell out of me. Deep and booming, it sprung like a tidal wave from his lips, breaking against the rocks of my surprise. A minute or two later, as the laughter ebbed, he turned his head and wiped his eyes, saying, "It is a joy to my ears to hear the heat of your response, young man."

"You wanted me to lose my temper?"

"Indeed. The truth of your statements needed verification and the dismay painted on your face gave me proof of your candor."

"So can you call off your metal pet, please?"

Cain's smile quickly evaporated. "Not until I am apprised of the fullness of your story."

Mind racing through my options, I realized I didn't have any. How Cain would react to the story of my origins, I didn't know, but considering the Sicarii had been trying to kill him for two thousand years … probably not well.

I glanced at the giant's hands and sighed. This was going to suck.

"Well, man, it all started in Omaha …"

Chapter Twenty-Two

Mike

Despite being in the clutches of Satan's earthly minions who viewed me as a lackey of a lying God, I was being treated pretty darn well. Three hots and a cot until the next day, or what I assumed was the next day (the room had no windows), when I was bound, gagged, and a black bag lowered over my head. A short car ride later and the lot of us were airborne. By the soft texture and spaciousness of the seat, I assumed we flew by private jet. Too bad about my trussed-up condition, I could've used a nice comfy ride.

Maybe they were afraid I'd call down the wrath of the Lord to blast us out of the sky because shortly after takeoff I felt a sharp jab to my neck and it was light's out for the priest.

If I had dreams, they didn't travel with me to consciousness, but pain sure did. My eyeballs screamed at me as pressure forced them deep into their sockets. When I began to struggle and moan the pressure eased.

"Wake up, Mr. Engle."

"Wha—?" Holy moley, that hurt! My eyes watered fiercely as I shook the cobwebs out of my head.

"Boris, if you would." Once again large calloused thumbs rammed into my closed eyelids and the pain ricocheted around my skull. That time I screamed. Loud.

"Ah, good to see you awake, Mr. Engle," the voice said as the pressure eased. I was learning to really hate that voice. Belatedly, I realized I was bound to a chair that was none too comfortable.

Focusing proved difficult—my eyes were still smarting and everything was all light and shadow—so I shook my head once again to clear it. Slowly the world came into focus and I saw, standing in front of me, an elegantly dressed older man perhaps in his fifties with streaks of white in his once dark hair. He bore such a startling resemblance to Morgan that I knew it had to be Julian.

His smile contained enough wickedness frighten angels. "You do not look like a priest, Mr. Engle." Julian began to walk slowly around my chair. "More like truck driver. Yes, a truck driver. It is that ridiculous moustache. Is that not right, Boris?"

The mountain of well-dressed muscle named Boris (whose expression registered no signs of humanity) grunted once, the sound seeming to come from the depths of some lightless cave.

I stole a look at my surroundings. A large art deco space with a white baby grand that Liberace would have loved to play, a black leather sofa and loveseat, natural wood surfaces and a plush carpeted staircase leading to a second floor. What really took the taco was the floor to ceiling windows with a panoramic view of what I believed was New York City. From the scale, I guessed we were at fifty plus stories up. Outside the rain sheeted down—a perfect counterpoint to my mood and aching eyes.

Drinking in the full kitchen and dining room behind me, I cast my eyes to Julian and kept my trap shut.

Morgan's father, still smiling wickedly, stopped inches away. Boris loomed like only the massive can loom, the flat, soulless chips of his eyes conveying the message that any misbehavior on my part would be dealt with harshly.

"Mr. Engle, you delayed my people with your rather … potent magic in order for my wayward son to make his escape. What I want to know is …" He leaned forward, his breath washing over me as he whispered, "Where is he?"

"I really don't know," I sighed, not meeting his eyes. "The Lord provided the opportunity for his escape, but where he went was up to him. But I *will* tell you is this: you need a new brand of mouthwash." Almost before the words left my mouth I knew what would happen. Boris placed a large thumb under my ear in the space behind my jawbone. At Julian's nod he pressed. Hard.

Instant, remorseless pain, like an iron spike slowly pushing into my throat. My muscles contracted as I tried to veer away from the digging thumb, but Boris' huge hands kept my head steady as a rock.

When he let go I almost sobbed in relief. It took a few moments, but I managed to control my labored breathing.

"Where is he, Mr. Engle?"

I screamed into Julian's smug and wicked face. "I don't know!"

Another nod to Boris, another round of pain for me, but this time digging under the other ear.

By the time the former Spetznaz finished, I had given up being brave and shrieked my agony to the uncaring world until my throat shut down. Head throbbing and body slick with sweat, I sobbed like a child while the zip tie holding my wrists together behind my back dug into my skin, tearing it, covering my hands in blood.

"Where is my son, Mr. Engle? Where is the Grail?"

I did my best not to start in surprise. The Grail? I had no clue where it could be. Last thing I remembered was facing Annabeth empty handed. Either the Grail had fallen or I'd set it down near the altar. Either way, it could protect itself. By the time I was airborne and on my way to New York, it had probably landed in the hands of some old lady who was using it as a paperweight. "Sorry, Julian, but I'll have to stick to 'I don't know' on both questions." I licked my lips, tasting the fear-sweat coating my face.

Julian quietly spoke into my ear. "I know you know all about us, Mr. Engle. I've read that silly memoir of Olivier's that you kept in that coat." He laughed at my startled look. "Oh yes, Mr. Engle, I have read it and found it rather droll. There's nothing in there that can aid you, but at least you are aware of the kind of man I am and what I am capable of. I let you keep it so you know what you are up against in the hopes that you will see reason.

"My ... employer knows you destroyed the Silver, but that does not matter much now as we have other sources of power. Yes, you and my errant son have inconvenienced us somewhat, but we are powerful and you are not. So ponder that for a moment and then tell me where my son is hiding. Believe me, the rewards for aiding the Family are ... vast." The last was breathed with such amusement that I knew I'd never live to see such rewards should I betray my Morgan.

This wasn't going to end well. I cast an eye at Boris, the perfect sociopath, and then at Julian, the perfect ... well, I'd rather not swear, but you can fill in the blanks. They could torture me for months and I couldn't tell them anything. Heck, I wouldn't tell if I could. Morgan was a friend and damn near the only person I considered family.

"You know, Julian," I rasped, smiling a crooked smile. "This is going to be a long day."

Oh yeah. It was a very long day, indeed.

I was tortured for hours, maybe days, I don't know because my brain had gone on overload the first few minutes after my show of defiance. Boris went at me without once breaking the skin and I had to give the big man credit, I felt more pain than I thought possible and still live. Arm locks, fingers jabbed at my throat, nerve centers in feet and arms pinched, poked and punched. Twice he dislocated my shoulders and twice the pain of the ball joints popping back into their sockets hurt more than the dislocating.

Either Julian finally grew bored with my screams, or he finally believed my protests. I was carried to small room that on second glance was actually a large walk-in closet and dumped on a plain air mattress. At that point I considered consciousness superfluous and passed out.

When I woke, there was no pain, no bruising, just a quiet lassitude and a feeling that something was amiss. Well, more amiss than usual, that is. Someone had been kind enough to place a tray of food by the bed. Cold cuts, bread, cheese, strawberries a bit past their prime, and bottled water. Wasting no time, I dove in and finished the whole spread—including the water—in less than five minutes.

A Healing, I mused. Must have been. It explained why my muscles weren't screaming bloody murder and why I felt pretty good.

With a sigh and a groan I knelt next to the bed and clasped my hands in front of me in a pose of supplication. Words tumbled from my lips with comforting familiarity: "Our Father, who art in heaven…"

Once done I felt much better, renewed. It had been a while since I had prayed and the lack had made me feel … itchy. One of my younger parishioners once asked, "Does God really listen to our prayers? And if so, why doesn't he answer them?" I believe he does. I believe he answers those prayers that absolutely need to be answered, that it is His judgment, His foresight that determines which prayers are the most needful. I've heard so many people say that if there is a God, He wouldn't let bad things happen: earthquakes, mass murders, fires, plagues, etc.

My take on God is that he is a loving, patient father and we are a bunch of snot-nosed rebellious brats. In the infancy of our existence as a race, He was there to help and guide us, instructing us on how to behave. He punished us when we needed to be punished and rewarded us when appropriate. As the society of man began to age, we depended less and less upon the aid of our Lord, like adolescents learning to fend for themselves. Now, many thousands of years after our creation, we are at the point where we must stand on our own two feet and rely on ourselves to get the job done. However, that doesn't mean God doesn't watch over us, providing sage advice and a gentle nudge or two.

We call the Lord "Our Father," but it is up to us to become self-sufficient, to stop harassing him all the time for all the little things. As for the bad things that happen, most of the time we—our own selves—bear the blame.

So when I pray, it's for the souls of my congregation, for the souls of my friends. I also pray that mankind as a whole will just grow up and start taking responsibility for its own actions instead of passing the blame off to God. We should just have faith that, ultimately, God has our backs.

I understand that sounds kind of preachy, but that's part of the job description.

Shortly after my prayers Boris came, holding the door open and, with a nod of his head, indicated I should follow him. Big and tough as I was, he could still handle me like I was a third grader, so I followed him back to Julian. Long hallways with expensive carpeting told me we were in a hotel, and a ritzy one at that.

"Ah, Mr. Engle," he purred from his seat on the black sofa, a glass of red cradled in one manicured hand. The cityscape twinkled with a million varicolored electric stars. "Please sit." His other hand pointed to an ugly, cold steel chair facing him.

Deciding that compliance was the better part of valor, I sat.

A big man long since gone to flab descended the stairs behind Julian. Short gray hair and beard framed a face dissipated by drink, the pug nose red-veined, the cheeks streaked with burst vessels. Despite his obvious deterioration, he was impeccably dressed in a dove-gray suit, presumably Armani. He held out a folder to Julian, who took it with casual indifference, flicking his fingers at the front door behind me. The chubby man left without a word.

"My son wrote that he believed he was the Redeemer, the prophesied one." Julian took a sip of wine. "He couldn't be more wrong, despite having access to all thirty Words provided by the Silver. You see, Mr. Engle, the true Redeemer would welcome the touch of the Patron. No, my son is woefully weak, despite his capabilities." He finished the glass, placed it on the glass-topped coffee table and stared at me intently. "Enough about Olivier, let's talk about you."

Julian flipped through the folder. "Intensive interrogation reveals so much about a person," he began, eyes scanning pages and pages of computer print out. "Your interrogation was witnessed by Dr. Silvestri." He flicked a finger at the door chubby had exited. "The report he compiled tells me all I need to know. Hmmm …" Flip, flip,

flip. " 'Loyal to a fault and has an over-inflated sense of right and wrong.' No surprise there. 'Aggressive tendencies buried beneath the teaching of his deity.' Once again, no surprise. Look at this: 'A suitable candidate for martyrdom.' Well, well, you are a true follower of the Liar and his brat." All this uttered in an unheated, avuncular tone.

"Let's look at your military file," he continued. "Hmmm ... Two tours in Iraq during Desert Storm, very bold. Wounded twice, Purple Heart with clusters ... very nice. Bronze Star for meritorious service while engaged in an action against the enemy. That means you are a genuine war hero." He set the folder aside. "Which begs the question: how does a war hero become part of a pacifist brotherhood of celibate weenies?"

I couldn't help myself; he tickled me to no end. He just didn't get it ... the faith, the rigorous discipline required to become a priest in the modern age and hold true to vows willingly taken. He didn't get that there is more than one path to the Lord, more than one way to serve Him. Soldier, seamstress, surgeon, senator ... all could find God in their own way. People like Julian refused to believe that the Lord's heart is big enough to encompass the world in all its glorious diversity.

Like I said, I couldn't help myself ... I laughed in his face.

The next word out of his mouth was so predictable. "Boris."

What that big Russian did next took a long time and hurt like hell.

Chapter Twenty-Three

Morgan

"What a tale you have spun whole cloth out of the fabric of fantasy, Mr. Sicarius!" Cain declared as I finished my story. He took a sip of whisky and flashed a gamine's grin. "I fancy that you have had quite some time to concoct such an elaborate fabrication."

My throat was dry and I had a headache. The whole story took over two hours to relate and my shoulders had long since cramped up under the iron hands of the golem. "Listen, it's the truth, man," I snapped. "I didn't come here for my health."

"The truth is a slippery thing, too subjective to be boilerplate for all mankind."

Who talks like that? I asked him again.

"Today's language offers no music or grace," he laughed. "When LOL and OMG are considered the soul of wit, I must needs revert to a more intelligent method of conveying meaning."

"You have got to be shitting me." The golem's hands flexed slightly, enough for me to feel it.

Cain lost his smile. What came out of his mouth next was a Word. Truth. It carried a cloying hit of garlic. "Is the story you related a factual one?" he asked, becoming very still.

A familiar vise-like pressure filled my head and it felt like my brain was about to squirt out through my ears. "Yes," I gritted my teeth. "It's a true story." With that said, the pressure eased.

"Hmmm."

I had to smile. That was the shortest, least convoluted sentence he'd uttered since we met.

"It is at this point, Mr. Heart, that I am presented with a quandary. There is no love lost between me and the Sicarii, but I confess to an overweening fondness for my skin and its placement upon my frame. That said, you should provide me with a suitable argument to sway me."

This guy was going to give me schpilkas. "How about saving millions of people from Earth?"

"That reason does hold merit, but as I see very little chance of success against the Dagger Men, it is not good enough."

I'd been holding back one last card, one that could get me dead at the hands of a golem right quick. "Cain," I said, licking my lips. "My real name is Olivier Deschamps." During my story, I'd left that little bit out, fearing that it might lead to sudden iron poisoning. With my eyes shut, I waited for ferric hands to crush my torso.

There was an expectant hush, as if the universe was waiting for the other shoe to drop, then, "Deschamps?" Soft, deadly.

Eyes still closed. "Yes."

"You are the son of the current head of the Sicarii?"

"Yes I am."

"Excellent!"

What? No painful death? I opened my eyes to see that, once again, Cain grinned from ear to ear.

Seeing my confusion, he explained, "Nothing would provide me with more joy and satisfaction than tweaking Julian Deschamps's nose by aiding his *son* to foil his nefarious plans."

Nefarious? "Okay, great. Now can you tell the Incredible Hulk to let me go?"

The golem's hands did just that and I nearly passed out as the blood rushed back to my shoulders. Muscles began to spasm and that awful pins-and-needles sensation traveled up and down my arms. The lumbering monster clank-clanked to the door and gently turned the knob with an intricately jointed hand. Freezing wind rushed in as it disappeared into the darkness, closing the door behind it.

"Th-thank you."

Cain nodded and retrieved a bottle of vodka from the refrigerator freezer. Pulling a tumbler from a cabinet, he poured two fingers worth and held it out to me.

Liquor splashed my wrist as my hands shook, but I managed to put the glass to my lips and take a long pull. The burn slithered all the way down and warmed my belly.

"Oh my," I breathed, "I needed that."

Tap, tap, tap, went Cain's fingernail against the kitchen table as I finished my drink. *Tap, tap, tap.* "One question, young Deschamps, if you would be so kind. For two millennia the Sicarii have endeavored to shorten me by a head, to end my ceaseless wanderings upon this troubled earth. Why would they undertake such a trying and perilous task? Everyone has met a swift end at my hands, or the hands of my protectors." He gestured to the golem. "Such as the formidable Walter."

"They want to spit in the eye of God and prove that they're the best."

He raised a bushy eyebrow.

I sighed. "You were cursed by God and marked, so no man would kill you lest they suffer His vengeance. The Sicarii don't fear God, so killing you, the world's oldest man and strongest magus, would be quite the feather in a Dagger Man's cap. It would make him or her a legend."

"Then they are foolish indeed."

"Indeed, but you already know all this."

"It has evolved into a force of habit to inquire about the motives of the Sicarii, imprudent as they may be. You are such a stubborn lot."

"Stubborn or not, I'm a tired man who needs a good night's sleep."

"Of course, young man, I shall provide you with that very thing." He pointed to the opposite end of the cabin, to a sofa next to a fireplace where a few persistent embers glowed. "My domain is small but comfortable, as you will discover. Liquid good cheer I have supplied and the couch offers generous comfort to ease you to slumber. My room is beyond yon piney door. Should the occasion arise for my assistance, you need only call." That said, Cain walked through the "piney door" (made of rough-hewn timbers and glowing with beeswax) and returned a few moments later with an armload of blankets and a pillow. I stoked the fire, coaxing it back to life with more wood.

"Between that comforting fire and warm quilt, you will find that night passes most satisfactorily."

I nodded, noting that he stood a good head taller than me. "Didn't think early man would grow so big."

Once again those teeth blinded me with reflected firelight. "In the beginning, God crafted the first men well. My own father topped my own height by a handspan."

I translated that into at least five or six inches. Added to Cain's own six-five, possibly six-six, Adam would have been close to seven feet tall. "Holy shit!" I blurted.

"Indeed, we were all giants in those fabled early days," he said. "And long lived. Most men had the capacity to live well past twenty-five score years, although I am the current record holder in the category of longevity."

Five hundred years? Maybe God crafted men *too* well back then. Cain appeared to be not a day over forty. What must his life have been like, all those years of wandering, knowing that everyone he cared about would die long before he met his own fate? The loneliness must have been overwhelming, the strain of such longevity eating at his sanity for millennia. Or maybe that was the real curse God inflicted, forced sanity in an insane situation. Suddenly his archaic, perambulating speech patterns didn't seem so odd; perhaps it was a defense mechanism that helped him cope with the sheer weight of time.

"Cain, I have to ask …"

"Why do I encumber my visage with sunglasses?"

"You have to admit, it's a little odd, unless you live in the *Matrix,* man."

"That is not the first time I have heard that interrogative." Cain pursed his lips, as if considering some internal landscape and then removed his shades.

Whoa.

Ever see a Siberian Husky? A beautiful creature with a nice thick furry coat, well suited as sled dogs. Many of these dogs have white-blue eyes that give them a ferocious, almost alien, appearance. Cain's eyes were like that, the whites blending seamlessly into white-blue and centered with the fathomless black of the pupil.

A small gasp escaped my lips as I felt the remorseless heat of his gaze, the stress of his attention that was like a constant pressure wave from an eternally exploding bomb. I took an involuntary step backward and the sofa's edge hit the back of my knees, dumping me unceremoniously on my butt.

That insidious pressure abruptly cut off as the glaciers slipped back over Cain's eyes and air rushed back into my lungs because I'd finally remembered to breathe. "Damn."

Once again he flashed a smile. "Quite correct, Mr. Deschamps, I am damned for as long as the Lord desires me to be so. Despite the excessively extended lifespan, not to mention the near ceaseless wandering, I am content that my punishment is a just one."

"Ceaseless wandering?" I inquired. "Looks like you've put down roots here rather well."

Cain handed me the bedding. "No matter how remote the locale or friendly the neighboring folk, circumstances always arise that force my evacuation from whatever plot of land I have called home. The Mark of Cain assures it. My tenure near Gunnison has endured for nearly two years—long by the standards of my curse—so it is with heavy heart that I recognize the imminent end of my stay."

I didn't bother to debate the merits of his punishment. There were murderers aplenty—the Family and myself were prime examples—but maybe it was because he was the first murderer that caused God to punish him so severely. That, and his attempt to lie to God about his crime. Whatever the reason, I could see in his half-hidden face that even after thousands of years, he still had not forgiven himself.

What stopped him from committing suicide? I marveled at his discipline.

Cain turned and walked to the door of his bedroom, stopping only for a moment to say, over his shoulder, "My circumstances presented me with the most difficulty those years preceding the twelfth century. It was then the Chinese invented sunglasses, mere smoky quartz lenses to assist in concealing their expressions in court. That simple device has brought me more peace than any other in the countless millennia of my travels." His voice dropped to a near whisper, his sadness clutching at my throat. "That was the last time I prayed to God, to thank him for his infinite capacity for creativity."

"Good night, Cain."

"Good night, Mr. Deschamps."

As I lay down, snuggling into the blankets and enjoying the warmth of the fire, Cain's door opened a crack.

"Did you really destroy my Tablet, Mr. Deschamps?

"Call me Morgan. And yes, I'm afraid so, but it wasn't on purpose."

An infinite sadness colored his face for moment. "Pity. I should have liked to have held the old stone once more, if only for a moment."

Chapter Twenty-Four

Mike

Wake, eat, pray, talk to Julian. Boris would beat me to a pulp, then send me back to the room so I could be Healed by a man I never saw because most to those times my eyes were swelled shut.

Not what you'd call a summer vacation.

Each day I managed to endure the bone-breaking sessions with Boris and each day I prayed to God to give me the strength to do so because each day I survived meant that Morgan remained free. If it hadn't been for the Healings, I would've died the second day, but I guess Julian wanted this to last and last. His reputation for cruelty was well deserved.

I wondered if his entire family were sociopaths from birth, or if their criminal insanity had been carefully nurtured. Either way, it was a miracle that Morgan remained sane.

Julian had read Morgan's memoirs and seemed unimpressed, calling them "the ineffectual ramblings of a weak-willed man." If he really understood Morgan's willpower, he would have been very afraid. I just hoped my friend wouldn't do anything stupid, like try to affect a rescue. Unfortunately, I knew better. In any case, he had not bothered to take them away from me.

One day Boris didn't come for me, a reprieve of sorts, or Julian wanted to concentrate his efforts on his wayward son.

So, with nothing to do but pray, I pulled out the tattered memoirs from my ripped and torn Danzinger's jacket and began to read.

My Life No Longer

The angel had given more than food for thought; he'd supplied a banquet, which I dined on as I waited, hidden under another spruce. Julian expected the rest of the SS hopefuls to wander in after the next three days, so I had time to meditate on my situation.

What should I do? What were my options? If I returned to the mansion after the allotted time, it would spur Annabeth and Burke on to new heights of plotting. They couldn't afford to let me live and if I did return, I could not afford to let *them* live. As much as I craved revenge, what the angel had revealed undercut my thirst for blood.

The Voice (I couldn't bring myself call him Satan or Lucifer) would eventually know of my change of heart and his response would be the same as Burke's, just more immediate and efficient.

There was only one option that really worked for me: run away.

Do it soon, I thought. Then, *do it before anyone makes it back. Grab what you can and sneak out like a thief in the night.* And then it hit me. Thief. If Julian could have seen my smile at that moment, he would not have recognized me.

Only a few hours had passed since Burke used the ballistic knife on me, perforating my back, and the blood had frozen to my white jacket, leaving three ragged red splotches to mark the impact points. It did not matter, I wouldn't need the jacket anymore, but what I did need was a good read on where the mansion lay.

Exiting my shelter, I began a look around and spotted the perfect tree. An old growth eastern Hemlock big enough that two people couldn't span it with their arms. It towered high above the other trees, even the old-growth maples, a pillar reaching high into the sky before branches erupted like woody fingers.

Reaching into a thigh pouch, I removed a plastic vial, thankful that it hadn't broken when Burke attacked. It was my ace-in-the-hole. The liquid inside swirled with reddish brown flakes, the potent mixture something I had never attempted before, something I thought might be new under the sun.

A mixture of toadflax, wintergreen, bamboo, chili pepper and poke root, herbs used in the making of anti-magic unguents. I had added sage white for cleansing and gum Arabic for purification. The potion had taken over two months to brew, the herbs steeped in water melted from 3,500-year-old ice. I worried that the mixture might be magically toxic and kill me quicker than strychnine, but ... desperate times and all that. Taking a deep breath, I unscrewed the vial and downed the contents.

Actually not bad. The chili pepper gave the mixture a nice kick. It would do quite well as marinade if I added honey.

One minute ... two ... I still lived. Very nice. I let Vigor past my lips and reveled in the feeling of well-being and energy that flooded through me along with the smell of peanuts..

Yes, I cheated. In my Family, that's worth bonus points.

Checking my compass, I located east and softly muttered a word ... Strength. The sharp, chemical smell of ammonia assaulted me and I began to climb, fingers easily gripping the hemlock's gnarled bark, gouging handholds. Halfway to the first branch, my boots began to split and tear as I kicked toeholds into the tree, seeking purchase in the soft wood. If I had chosen a hardwood, I might have had some difficulty.

Strength, however, did not mean I could ignore the splinters the slipped under my finger and toenails and the sticky resin that began to coat my hands. Just before my hands started to bleed in earnest, I reached the first branch, levering myself up with my magically enhanced strength. Sitting on my precarious perch, I teased splinters from my stinging fingers and mumbled a Healing, watching the flesh re-knit.

High enough, the old-growth conifer gave me an advantage I had so desperately needed. While my cousins hunted each other (knowing Burke, he wouldn't try to find the mansion until he had bagged his limit), I would wend my way back. There were things I needed to do to ensure a good head start.

Scanning the horizon above the spiny spikes of beech, cedar, ash and hawthorn, I eventually spotted what I thought was the clearing that housed the mansion, its roof buried behind the barren branches of the forest.

As I reached the ground, hands and feet a bloody mess, someone let out an "ahem."

Heart beating wildly, I turned just in time to take three shots to the chest, green paint spattering my face. "Bloody hell," I groused.

Fergus laughed. "Saw ya up in tha' tree, cuz and decided t' be a mite sportin' and wait till ya reached bottom before shooting ya."

"Mighty kind of you, Fergus."

The Scotsman laughed and I pounded a Forgetting into his brain, almost gagging at the licorice odor. Fergus's pupils dominated his eyeballs as he stared blindly ahead.

"Turn around, Fergus, and forget you ever saw Olivier," I said in slow, even tones. Forgetting placed the subject into a mild hypnotic trance. "Travel west for ten minutes and start searching for your cousins."

Fergus nodded dumbly and turned around, slowly shambling west.

An hour later I found myself on the Mansion grounds, silently slipping into the servants' entrance. Only one chef was in attendance in the kitchen, no doubt whipping up something tasty for Julian and Boris.

One Forgetting later and I was ghosting to the second floor, reaching my room—which, fortunately, was empty of any cleaning staff—and finding that my suitcase had remained untouched.

As befitted a scion of the Judas Line, my room was plush, 1,400 square feet of white harp seal fur carpeting and a four-poster bed big enough for a battalion, coated with navy blue silk sheets. Satiny fur swished between my toes after I ripped off the remains of my boots and discarded my much-abused outerwear. The desire to shower pulled at me, but time pulled harder. Donning designer blue jeans, a black turtleneck and Timberline boots, I almost felt human enough for travel.

I did not need much, just some basics, but first, a little preparation. Two jars had been secreted in a compartment of my suitcase. One contained a whitish paste, which I smeared on my chest and forearms under the turtleneck. The other went into my front pocket.

From another compartment in my case I found my cell phone. I flipped it open and dialed.

A tinny voice answered. "Vance, this is Olivier Deschamps." I kept my voice smooth and urbane despite the thudding of my heart. I wiped sweat from my brow. "Yes, thank you. I need you to liquidate some assets for me …"

Once my exit finances were taken care of, I eased down the obscenely long hallway to Burke's room. Julian, knowing full well the animosity between Burke and me, had always made sure we were quartered far apart. Not out of any consideration for our welfare, I am sure, but to keep the mayhem to a minimum.

His door was locked, of course, but that proved a minor obstacle. The molecular knife made short work of the lock plate and bolt. Burke's accommodations were nearly identical to mine except for the Panda-skin rugs strewn almost carelessly across the floor.

Burke was paranoid and cunning, an almost perfect assassin, so where would a perfect assassin keep his secrets? The armoire? Nope, empty. Next I tried under the bed and came up empty. Chest of drawers … nothing. Same for the toilet tank and all the ventilation registers. I cast my eyes about as I considered what hidey-holes that Burke would use. Where, where, where?

Eventually I focused on the armoire, an enormous cedar-lined affair about seven feet tall, constructed of white oak and covered in beautifully intricate scrollwork. However, it wasn't the craftsmanship that drew my attention, but the space between the bottom of the armoire and the floor. The thing must weigh a ton, I mused. Muttering Strength, I crossed to the wooden monstrosity and heaved, lifting it high and settling it down onto one of the panda rugs. Nothing.

I cursed and was about to move the armoire back when another possibility occurred to me. Lowering the armoire down on its back, I inspected the underside. Stuck to the wood with silvery duct tape was a padded manila envelope.

Bingo.

Ripping it free, I eagerly tore at the seal and emptied the contents onto black and white fur. A CD in a thin plastic case, one black credit card, one of his prized ballistic knives, and four strips of photo negatives in protective plastic sleeves.

I held the negatives up to the light. Annabeth … me … the shower. Crap. Cursing, I stuffed the negatives into one pocket while the rest of the items went into others. I wanted to kill Burke and I wanted to hurt Annabeth like she'd hurt me—run the knife in and twist—but I had bigger fish to fry.

Seconds later, I headed upstairs to Julian's office, small duffel the size of a bowling bag in one hand, a black leather jacket under one arm and fear hammering spikes through my temples. The audacity of what I planned had me shaking in my boots. I took no notice of the teak flooring save to walk carefully to avoid telltale sounds. After an eternity of climbing, I reached the third floor and Julian's room, which was located behind double doors made of oak; their intricately carved panels sported scenes from a bacchanalia and polished bronze knobs.

I placed the duffel and jacket on the floor and knocked softly.

Boris opened the door, craggy face impassive as a death mask.

"Hello, Boris. I need to speak to Julian." I was surprised how nonchalant I sounded.

He shook his head slightly.

"He is busy?"

A barely perceptible nod.

"Ah, well tell him this." As loud as I could, I hit him with Force.

It was a risky shot, one that could backfire if the big Russian carried protection. Which he did. With a grunt that sounded like an echo from the Abyss, he took two steps back, flinging one large, knobbly hand up in front of his eyes to ward off splinters as both doors were torn apart.

Leaping, I hit him in the solar plexus with the heel of my right boot. I might as well have hit a tree. The big man didn't even grunt; instead he gripped my leg and pulled me through the doorway, throwing me ten feet in the air, over a settee and into a heavy as hell coffee table made of polished redwood. I felt ribs break as I bounced and landed hard on the floor.

The first bullet hit the coffee table, throwing up a shower of burgundy splinters. The second grazed my ear, the bullet passing with a flat *crack* to gouge a furrow in the hardwood floor. The shot itself had been a quiet *shht*, the sound dampened by the best suppressor that money could buy.

I kicked the coffee table on its side just in time for it to catch the third bullet, my boot absorbing some of the shock, but a fragment of pain flashed through my ankle. Another bullet thudded home and I thanked my lucky stars that Julian loved heavy wooden furniture.

Boris was on the move—I could hear his patent leather shoes swish along the wool carpeting—so I ground out another Strength and heaved the coffee table upright, as I stood, using it as a shield.

Before the giant Russian could score a lucky shot, I straightened my arms, hurling the table at him with my augmented strength. The table flew straight and true, hitting Boris flat and hard, knocking him back to smack against a wall, a 9 mm flying out of his hand.

For the first time I saw emotion register on Boris' face, and that sight sent a cold worm of fear wiggling its way through my bowels. Those hairy brows had drawn down and thin lips settled themselves into a savage snarl that shone redly through the blood that ran from a newly broken nose. Boris was *pissed* and I knew that if I didn't do something quick, I'd soon be on my way to my final descent.

Silently, I charged, fists jabbing. I parried a fist hurtling toward my jaw and drove two knuckles into his solar plexus—like hitting an anvil. Even with Strength, I could barely keep up. I took a knee to the hip while I connected with an elbow to the point of his chin. Boris' head rocked back maybe an inch, and my elbow screamed at my stupidity.

Too close. I should have stayed outside the range of those monkey arms because those two rock-hard limbs shot out and pulled me to him, crushing me to his chest and driving the air from my lungs.

No air, no Words. Big and ugly doesn't mean dumb.

Next thing I knew my feet left the floor and he *squeezed*. What breath remained made a quick exit and black spots began to form in my vision. In desperation I brought my knee forward and connected.

Boris coughed, gagging through the pain that must have burned from his testicles, freezing muscles all the way to his throat. The two pythons crushing the life from my torso loosened their grip and I rammed my head forward, my hairline meeting the bridge of his nose with a sickening *crunch,* smashing his least attractive and already mangled feature into a pulpy mess. Blood spurted from both nostrils, wetting my chest.

Once again those great arms loosened and breath rushed back into my oxygen-starved lungs, allowing me to break free. I dropped to a kneeling position and swung an elbow into the side of Boris' left knee.

Boris howled his agony to the ceiling, a raw animal cry that raised the hair on the back of my neck. His knee had *cracked* violently, bending the wrong way.

I rolled away, out of reach, as he collapsed onto his good knee, holding the other out to the side, crooked in all the wrong ways. My hand brushed something hard, cold and I reflexively grabbed hold, risking a look to see what it was.

Boris' 9 mm. Hallelujah. The weapon swung around, impelled by a force that seemed not to be my own and pointed right between the big man's eyes. To this day I still do not know if I would have pulled the trigger; there was a split second of hesitation as I held his eyes prisoner with the barrel's cavernous hole. I had him dead bang, he was mine and he knew it. I could see it in his eyes, in the little twitch at the corner of his mouth.

A wash of burning agony in my ears, my mind, my chest and arms. A Word, spoken behind me, compressing my brain with the savagery of its power, my mind shrieking in protest as a black force swept over me. It drowned my soul in a miasma of spiritual sewage right before the chest and arms of my turtleneck exploded in blue flames. The unguent I'd smeared on my skin had overheated from absorbing too much power.

Twisting, the flames slapping at my throat and hands, I turned to see Julian with the Silver in one hand, a bright sheen of sweat on his face. He'd used one of the Thirty Words on me—Enslave, I believe—trying to turn me into a brainless automaton.

The fire ate at my skin. I could only ignore it for a second before the blistering pain became all-consuming. I saw Julian sway slightly, one hand braced on a mahogany desk as his mouth began to form a Word that would blast my brains into jelly. The 9 mm swung up, spitting bullets that stitched Julian up from thigh to shoulder. The Silver fell from his slack fingers, the heinous metal bouncing in a delirious dance across the carpet.

Frantically, I ripped the turtleneck from my body, along with a few patches of skin; the pain was so nerve-tearing, so awful that I sobbed like a child. The burning garment fell unheeded to the floor as I blurted one Healing after another, a soothing balm flowing along my seared chest and arms.

Sobbing in relief, I swung around and put two rounds into Boris' ankles, spraying bones fragments and blood across the floor.

ରୁ

A knock on the door interrupted me before I could continue and I stuffed the pages of Morgan's memoir under the air mattress.

The door opened to reveal Boris' large frame. He gestured briefly for me to follow. Nodding, I stood and bowed my head in brief prayer. A beefy hand on my bicep interrupted me.

I stared down at the sausage-like digits encircling my arm and I felt something I thought long-since purged from my soul. Fury.

His grip slipped off as I suddenly raised my arm high and a slight look of shock appeared on his face. I decided to add to it by hitting him with an overhand right to the face.

The big man dropped and I snarled down at him, "I'm not tied to a chair now, Boris." Panting and flushed with heat, I gritted my teeth in an effort to control the rage within. Not since Al-Qurnah, during Desert Storm—bullets buzzing around thick as bees—had I felt anger so hot, so pervasive that it threatened to slip from the chains of my self-control.

"Next time you interrupt me at my prayers, Boris," I snarled as he stood, looming over me with ham-hands clenched. "Bring a weapon."

Six, seven, eight seconds passed as the red slowly faded from the Russian's eyes. Finally, with a grudging nod of respect, he once again gestured for me to follow.

Chapter Twenty-Five

Morgan

"Are my ears deceiving me?" Cain whispered in amazement as he poured imitation maple syrup on his pancakes. "Did you impart to my shell like protuberances that you have designed an artifact of small puissance using naught but Botanical Magic?"

I nodded. "My belt buckle alarm. Took me six years."

"And you undertook such an endeavor without the benefit of the Word Create? With such an utterance, that commission would have cost you but a few minutes."

A plump middle-aged waitress arrived to refill our coffee. Cain gave her one of his brilliant smiles that had her blushing like a schoolgirl. The man was far too handsome for his own good. He may have been an eternal wanderer, but I had the sneaking suspicion that he hadn't lacked for company.

That morning he'd woke me up by whistling a merry tune. He was far jollier than a person ought to be at six a.m. and it took every iota of willpower not to curse him up one side and down the other. Despite the loan of too-big clothes, forgiveness came only with the first cup of coffee at the Dove's Egg in downtown Gunnison.

I tapped my head. "All twelve Words known by the Sicarii are nestled in here, big man, and Create isn't one of them."

"All twelve, you say?" Cain grinned into his steaming cup. "All twelve?" He began to laugh.

"What's so funny, Methuselah?"

Cain shoveled a good heaping of pancake into his mouth and chewed noisily before answering. "The very world teems with amusement for my pleasure, my young friend, but what tickles my fancy to the extreme is the knowledge that the Sicarii have a paltry twelve Words when there are total of twenty-five."

I choked on a piece of syrup-drenched buttermilk pancake. Twenty-five Words? The concept was mind blowing! How could there be twenty-five Words when the Sicarii magi only had access to twelve?

"Ponder upon the origins of these Words of power, these pale reflections of the Word God employed to bring reality as we understand it into being. Now consider … what magus created these verbal instruments? How did he or she create such wonderful utterances?"

"She?"

"Ah, are the Sicarii so gender-biased? By your question it must be so; however, very little could surprise me when it comes to your kinsmen. Let's us harken back to the topic at hand. Consider this, the Lord created the world and all therein, so if magic is part and parcel of creation …" his voice trailed off.

"Then magic comes from God? The Words, too?"

"Indeed there remains hope for you, yet. When my legendary parents partook of the Fruit from the Tree of Knowledge, the Words sprang new born into their minds, a mighty power they were unable to appreciate or utilize with sufficient wisdom. It was Pandora opening the box of lore, or Prometheus bestowing fire upon a shivering mankind. It was not only for disobedience that God banished man from the fruitful Garden, but for tapping into a power they were not ready to wield."

My whisper was fierce. "Adam and Eve were the first … first … *magi*?"

"Yes."

"And they passed these Words off onto you?"

"Yes."

"Then why are the Twenty-Five less powerful than the Thirty provided by the Silver?"

"My young friend, God employs a screwdriver, not a sledgehammer."

I would've commented further, but I saw a man at a booth across the way reading a paper, the front page facing me and featuring a large color photo.

The photograph was of me; taken so long ago I almost didn't recognize myself. "We have to leave, man," I said slowly, peeling off a couple of twenties for our breakfast. "Now."

To his inquiring look, I said, "Trust me."

Fortunately, there was a newspaper dispenser outside the diner, so I purchased the *Denver Post* and read the article while Cain peered over my shoulder, a big grin on his wide face:

> Swiss billionaire philanthropist Julian Deschamps announced yesterday that his son, Olivier, has disappeared while on vacation in the U.S.
>
> A spokesperson for the Deschamps family announced that longtime friend and spiritual advisor, Father Michael Engle of St. Stephen's Catholic Church in Omaha, Nebraska, flew to New York to meet Mr. Deschamps to offer spiritual and emotional support.
>
> Although no ransom demands have been made and no group has taken credit for Olivier's disappearance, authorities are not ruling out foul play.

There was more, but it didn't matter. It was a message meant for me, confirmation that they had Mike.

And they were taunting me.

Before I could crumble the paper in my furious hands, Cain deftly snatched it from my grasp. "Look here, Mr. Heart, an 800 number, a hotline for information as to your whereabouts." A long finger stabbed the paper under the number.

I muttered a spiteful curse that caused Cain to raise an eyebrow. "They *want* me to call in. They're messing with me, man."

"If that indeed is their nefarious plan, perhaps you should establish communication to ascertain what it is they desire."

"My Family is rich and powerful enough that they could trace even a cloned phone, and Avoidance doesn't work on tech."

Cain just smiled and led me back to the Wrangler, fired it up and started out of town. Before too long we passed the turn to his cabin, and before I could comment, he reached into the pocket of his black leather jacket and tossed me a cell.

"What your father and his Dagger Men fail to realize is that I am the oldest man in all of history, which has not only given me a unique perspective on life, but has allowed me to, with a touch of foresight, amass a fortune of almost inconceivable magnitude."

I looked at the phone, the newest and best from Apple. "So what you're saying is that you're bucks up?"

A flash of teeth. "Bucks up? My good man, such a term does not do justice to the resources available to me. Why, if Julian were to know the true extent of my resources, no doubt he would suffer from an immediate and quite fatal stroke."

"If you're so damn rich, why haven't you taken out the Sicarii long since? You could have hired thousands of mercenaries."

We drove in silence for so long that I thought he wouldn't answer, but finally he spoke. "I have beheld your kin and have been content to let them be. It is not for me to steer mankind in the right direction as End Times approach. Besides, throughout the millennia, I have been responsible for enough death and am not eager to add to that burden on my soul."

"Then why help me?"

"I pondered that very question as I lay in repose last night. I have come to one inescapable conclusion."

"You don't really know?" I guessed.

"I don't really know," he agreed. "Despite the reasons I disclosed earlier. Perhaps my curse tugs at its leash and I must again go a-wandering. But that is neither here nor there. It is imperative you use the cell phone. Not to worry, I have invested quite a sum of capital to obtain a phone that not a soul on this earth has the wherewithal to track." His grin almost blinded me. "It is good to be rich."

Why not? I dialed the 800 number, the phone rang and an androgynous voice answered, "Deschamps tip line; what do you have for us?"

"I'd like to speak to Julian Deschamps, please." In my mind's eye, I saw a voice recognition program chugging away in an effort to study and verify my vocal patterns as well as tonality from the sample taken when I was younger—compensating for the differences that age and environment would have wrought.

Must have been a match, because the androgynous voice asked me to "Hold, please." Less than a minute later a voice I never wanted to hear again came on the line.

"Hello, son."

I licked my lips. "Hello, Julian. The newspapers, very subtle, so what do you do for an encore? Set fire to the Pentagon?"

"We needed your attention and subtle does not do the job. Your priest is here."

"Funny, I don't have any ownership papers. Must not be mine."

"Very droll, son. If you want him back, you must come to me."

"You know what, Julian," I smiled savagely into the phone. "Keep him, man."

"How American you sound, son. Do you think you sound like John Wayne? Gary Cooper?"

What a perfect straight line. What? He never saw *Die Hard*? "Everyone wants to be the Duke, but I kind of like Bruce Willis. You know, yippie-ki-yay, motherfu—"

"Enough!" shouted Julian, his normally calm voice thrumming with anger. "You are beginning to tire me. Come back and I will let your Liar's pet go. Stay hidden, and I will hand the white collared boy-lover over to Boris for some face-to-face time."

I could feel the phone-casing tremble in my clenched fist, but eased back before the glass facing could shatter. "Go ahead, give him to Boris. I hope that Russian maniac chokes on him."

"You are quite serious, aren't you?" Julian asked in surprise.

"As a heart attack."

"I do not believe you."

"And I don't believe you will let the priest go if I turn myself in, so it looks like we're at an impasse, Julian. Oh, and don't bother to trace this call, you won't be able to."

"You have some impressive technology, boy, and a bad attitude."

"Keeps me young. Tell you what, Julian, you let the priest go and I don't come and kill you, Boris and everyone else. Just like I killed Burke."

There was silence for a few seconds and when his voice came back, it was low and dangerous. "You did surprise me by killing Burke, son. He showed so much promise, but there are more. There are *always* more." I heard a long breath slide over the connection. "Today is Tuesday. Thursday evening I will give the priest to Boris and he will die horribly. You have until then to come to New Hampshire to turn yourself in."

It was time to hang up, so I did. "Bastard," I growled.

Cain plucked the cell out of my hand. Without taking his eyes from the road, he touched an icon and said, "Dial Otto." After a few rings he said, "Otto, this is Evan. Get the plane ready." With that he disconnected.

At my look, he grinned. "Let us depart to plan mischief upon the enemy."

Sounded damn good to me.

We drove to a private landing strip housing one plane, a Beechcraft Baron. There an old man took the keys to the Wrangler, and soon I found myself airborne, with Cain at the stick.

"I can only imagine having the wings of angels," he said as we headed east. "The freedom of flight has been my utmost joy since the invention of the hot air balloon."

"What's the plan, Cain?"

"The plan is, my young friend, to assail the mighty fortress, rescue the advocate of our Lord, and wreak such havoc upon your estranged family that they will hesitate, nay, *quake* at the thought of ever assaulting their most wayward member again."

I gave that some thought. "I can live with that. Only problem is, how are the two of us going to pull it off?"

"Simplicity itself!" he said after a spot of turbulence shook the plane like a maraca. My stomach thankfully kept the pancake and sausage breakfast secure. "We will build an army. The only question that remains to trouble us is: where on earth have they secreted the priest?"

It was my turn to flash him a grin. "That's easy!" I said over the roar of the engine. "In the New York Grand Hotel."

Chapter Twenty-Six

Mike

"It seems that my son does not value your life," mused Julian as he paced around the room, glass of red balanced in one elegant, manicured hand. "For your sake, let's hope I'm wrong."

Boris hadn't bothered to tie me to the ugly steel chair this time; instead he handed me a glass of whatever Julian was having. I took a sip—Petite Sirah and a very good one, too—and waited for Julian to clarify.

I didn't have to wait long. "I've offered Olivier your freedom if he hands himself over to us." Eyes dark and deep with hatred stared into mine. "He refused."

"There's no way he'll consider it, Julian; he knows you'll kill me anyway."

Julian whirled, striding forward and stepping close, his face a bare inch from mine. I could smell the wine on his breath, sour and acidic. "What makes you think I'd go back on my word, priest?" Malice and loathing suffused his voice, the first deep emotions I'd detected in him. "Why do you think you know me so well??"

Something snapped inside me, most likely my patience. That can happen when you've been brutally beaten and healed too many times to keep track of. My snarl matched his ounce for ounce. "By now everyone knows I destroyed the Silver, so you can't afford to let me go," I whispered, my tone scalding. "You *have* to kill me or lose the respect, the fear, of your troops."

A twitch told me I'd hit home. "Also, you have in your possession a man of God who banished two demons, proving that the Lord God is mightier than your so-called Patron."

I'll give Julian one thing; most people would've slugged me by then, but he just smiled slightly and said, "Can't you call him by his name, priest? Or is fear of his wrath stilling your tongue?"

"Satan, Lucifer, Abaddon, The Adversary, Little Horn, The Dragon, The Beast, The Serpent … It doesn't matter. *He* is the Liar, not my God." What was that? The muscles around Julian's eyes tightened slightly and suddenly I *knew*! "But you know that, don't you? Not like the rank and file, who believe all that Lying God foolishness, you *know*!

"What? Was it something you learned when you became head of the family, the dirty little secret of the Sicarii? That's it, isn't it? Did that make you feel foolish, weak? Did all your vaunted dreams come crashing down around your ears when your father told you the truth? Ha! The truth, that's rich! You found out about the Patron and you peed your pants, didn't you?"

For a man in his sixties, he could still hit like heavyweight. His fist took me square in the breadbasket and I doubled over. At least I splashed my wine on his $3,000 suit.

"You pissant!" he screamed, olive complexion mottled with fury. "You are *nothing!* Your precious god weakened himself so much by creating reality that he is but a shadow of what he once was! On the other hand, my lord Lucifer has grown *strong*, mighty beyond comprehension and is ready to assail Heaven to throw down the weak Throne!" It cost him, but he finally, with visible effort, brought himself back under a semblance of control. "He keeps his promises, our Patron does, and the promise of sitting at his right hand when the battle is won will be kept. That is the Covenant of the Sicarii, foolish priest of a weak god, that is what sustains us, gives us the will to go on and achieve victory."

Gagging and retching, I sat in that damn ugly, cold chair, curled around my bruised muscles. Dimly I heard Julian say, "Boris, continue your instruction. He needs to learn a lesson about who is mighty."

With a grunt, Boris went to work.

It's never the beatings that make me feel puny, afraid. It's *after* the beatings when the bones creak and the muscles pop, sending glassy shards of pain up and down my spine. My teeth wiggle loose and the hot, coppery blood slides down my throat to nestle warmly in my stomach. The feeling of flesh so badly mortified, the assault so blatantly horrid that I lie on my mattress, curled up in a ball, trying to deny those sensations—the hurt, the gut-wrenching humiliation of it all.

When Boris dumped me back on the air mattress, I lay there softly weeping while the blood bubbled from my nose. Eventually the tears dried as reason slowly stole upon me.

For a split second, one infinitesimal moment, I had hoped Julian would have me killed, just so I could go to my God, to Heaven, and know a perfect peace, but a stubborn part of my soul refused death. I had too many things yet to do, people to guide to God's love and glory. I had never been one to shirk responsibility before and I wasn't about to start.

I took a sip of tepid water from a plastic bottle left for me and tried to relax, but the pain was too much. Every which way I tried to turn brought more shards of glass scraping across my nerves—a symphony of agony and Boris was the conductor.

Heck with it, I thought, reaching under the mattress for the papers hidden there. It took a few tries—my eyes refused to focus—but soon I was able to pick up where I left off.

My Life No Longer

Sobbing in relief, I swung around and put two rounds into Boris' ankles, spraying bone fragments and blood across the floor. He had stopped screaming, instead curling himself into a ball, body hitching and spasming as he wept.

Cinnamon wafted to me as I heard Julian grate out, between clenched teeth, one Healing after another. My own Healing took the bite out of the burns covering my chest and arms.

My eyes swung back to the leader of the Sicarii in time to see bloody bullets spit from his body. The barrel of the 9 swung up. "Don't," I mumbled unsteadily, the constant use of Words hitting me with a rush of fatigue. "I'll just shoot you again."

Eyes so much like mine regarded me from the floor as he snatched back a hand that had been reaching for the scattered Silver. "You may not believe me," he replied evenly. "But I am actually proud of you, son." A tongue flicked out to lick blood from his lips.

"Be a good boy, Julian, and scoot over to the wall, under the Chagal. There you go, good." Muttering The Walls (and inhaling the smell of pine) I knelt and began scooping Silver with one hand. Words, foul and slimy, tried to force themselves into my mind, but with the added strength of The Walls, I kept the loathsome things at bay. Eventually I had all thirty and placed them in the pouch Julian had dropped on his desk.

"What are you doing?" he asked.

"Do you have a Zippo, you know … for your cigars."

"You do not light a cigar with a lighter. You use wooden matches to preserve the flavor; I have told you that before. Why?"

Matches. Right on the desk in a crystal cup. Feeling the looming presence of time at my back, I vaulted Boris' writhing body and grabbed my leather jacket from where I'd placed it next to the door, whipping around, pistol raised, before Julian had a chance to commit mischief. The angry glint in his eye told me he had been planning just that.

"Ah-ah-ah," I admonished as he glared cold death. "Stay seated and I will not shoot you through the head."

"You kill me, boy, and another will take my place." Julian's chest heaved with fury. "There is *always* another."

"Yes, I know," I muttered, surprisingly sad as I placed the small crystal cup of matches in my pocket. It was time to ... tie up loose ends.

Not more than ten minutes later I walked toward the large detached garage that housed everything the Family needed to motor about in New Hampshire. I wore a new shirt, black silk this time, under my jacket.

I had left Williams, Julian's chauffer, trussed like a Christmas goose with the chef to keep him company. The cleaning staff also had been detained, albeit in Burke's bedroom. Hoped they liked the bed; it sure looked comfy.

As for Julian and Boris, they were in a bedroom closet, bound and gagged and none too happy with yours truly. Instead of wasting a Word on the Russian, I smeared his ankles with a salve designed to promote swift recovery. It took longer than Healing, but I had begun to feel the first nibble of Backlash at the edges of my mind and did not want to push my luck.

The garage lights flickered on the second I entered, revealing a variety of automobiles, motorcycles (my favorite being the 1922 Indian Chief in satin black), and a few snowmobiles.

I examined the keys hanging on a pegboard mounted to the far wall and smiled when I found what I needed: a brand new Land Rover, perfect for the snowy weather, smooth, comfortable and, better yet, it was Burke's.

Once I had the garage door open and moved the Rover, I poured a small puddle of gasoline in the middle of the garage floor and struck one of the matches I had pocketed. The puddle flamed up instantly.

The Language of fire crackled from my throat and was answered almost immediately. *"What do you need, watery one?"* As usual, the fire elemental sounded ravenous.

"Do you know where you are?" I asked.

"Fire knows well the machine it drives," it answered. "Is not Fire what man needs to make these Earthen contraptions move?"

"Well, what do you see here? Sixteen, no ... seventeen cars, plus some bikes and such. You look hungry, so take them all and feed well."

"What do you wish in return, generous one?" I could almost feel the elemental's eagerness.

"Nothing yet. Just keep your feeding confined to this building. Nothing else but this garage and its contents."

"Done!" it chattered gleefully, growing to the size of a bonfire.

I put the burning garage in my rearview mirror, speeding down the road away from a life no longer my own.

In Portsmouth I found a pet store that sold just the plastic container I required. Next I stopped at a Catholic church and helped myself to just enough holy water to fill the container and drown the cry of the Silver. That would confuse any who would use it to track me to ground. Avoidance was used to thwart scryers.

Penn Station, the next day ... the Rover safely ditched and money wired to an account at Chase Manhattan Bank under an alias I'd established long ago, Jude Oliver. Enough to start me out in luxury. A hard bench beneath my butt offered no ease as I stared at the train schedule in my hands, not really seeing the words printed there. My mind was brimming with chaotic thoughts.

My only problem was deciding where to go. LA? Chicago? Miami? All good places, plenty of people to hide among, but not quite right for the purpose I had in mind. All the major U.S. cities were rife with Sicarii agents. I had to go where no would think to look.

"You look lost."

I started. A pretty brunette, brown curls covering her shoulders, stood just behind and to the right. Sensible flats, dark no-nonsense skirt and white blouse. A fair face framed with dark horn-rimmed glasses. She had nice dimples, too. "What?"

"I said you look lost. You've been sitting there for a half hour staring at nothing."

My lips curled in what some might call a smile. "I am a bit lost, I guess."

The woman leaned forward and I smelled ... hyacinth. "What are you looking for?"

What indeed? "A place big enough to lose myself in, but not too big. Big enough to have the comforts of city life. Some place forgotten by man."

Her laughter reminded me of sleigh bells. "Are you running from the law?"

"No, just from Family."

"Omaha," she said brightly. "Yes, definitely Omaha."

"Omaha? You mean Nebraska?" I scratched my chin. "Really? Nebraska?" Who the hell lived in Nebraska?

"See? Even you are surprised at the thought. Don't worry; it's a nice, peaceful place, a good place to raise a family, if a bit boring."

"Nebraska? Omaha?" I rolled the words around in my mouth a few times. Yes, that just might work. I put on my best smile. "Thank you. Yes, that should work. Thank you very much."

"Don't mention it," she said over her shoulder, heading toward the exit.

I called after her. "I didn't get your name!"

She turned around, walking backwards, and said, "I didn't give it." With that she strode purposefully toward the door.

For some reason, as I watched her depart the station, I heard the sound of bells.

ॐ

I smiled as the last page slipped through my fingers to float gently to the floor. What a story. Angels, Words, Satan, The Silver, everything Morgan had endured and the family that had twisted him. It was amazing that he was relatively sane.

My eyes closed and I fell into the most peaceful, deep sleep I'd had in weeks.

Chapter Twenty-Seven

Morgan

Next stop, Omaha, (the irony was not lost on me) where we boarded a private jet. Cain spent the entire trip on the cell, calling several people in what I realized was his huge organization, and by late afternoon we landed in New York, where a stretch limo waited for us as well as plenty of fine food. The ride was smooth enough that we didn't spill a drop of the cabernet, which went quite well with the venison.

By the time the calamari vanished into my growling stomach and the bottle surrendered its last drop, we had arrived at our destination, an old warehouse in Clinton near the water. Cain led the way in and the limo silently rolled away, sticking out like rose in a compost heap in the former Hell's Kitchen.

"What do you use this place for?" I asked, following Cain up a steep set of stairs to the second floor.

"Truth be told, I am not sure," he answered, keys jangling in one hand. During the second leg of our trip his attitude had changed; he had become more commanding, almost imperious and businesslike.

Cain found the right key and inserted it into the lock of a plain white door marked OFFICE. We entered a largish square room roughly twenty feet on a side, containing several old wooden chairs and an oak desk. Sitting at the desk was a youngish man with coal-black hair cut short and a ridiculously cleft chin. His unibrow rose in surprise when he looked first at me then at my companion.

"Cain, thank God," he said, striding forward to engulf the man in a ferocious hug. "I was getting bored out of my mind."

"It does my eyes good to behold you again, my friend," Cain said, returning the hug hard enough that I heard ribs creak. "Come, give a hale welcome to a new friend discovered mere hours ago." He disengaged to gesture my way. "This is—"

"Morgan," I finished, shaking the man's hand. "Morgan Heart."

That earned me a strange look, but he smiled brightly and in a slight southern twang, "Alan. Alan Mendomer, good to meet you."

Cain took a seat behind the desk. "Alan is apprenticed to me, a magus of no small talent. He has agreed to assist us on our perilous quest in exchange for a Word."

Alan snorted. "It's about time y'all gave me another Word, boss. Been a dog's age."

"And earn this Word you will, Alan. But let us attend to other matters."

I leaned in close to the southerner and whispered, "Does he always talk like that?"

"Ever since I met him," he whispered in reply.

Cain ignored our byplay and asked, "The supplies that I had ordered en route, have they reached this facility? And where, pray tell, is the lovely and fearsome Maggie?"

"Yeah, boss, they got here an hour ago. I had them placed. As for Maggie, we all got ourselves a gen-u-ine problem."

I raise an eyebrow. "Maggie?"

Cain nodded. "Yet another apprentice who toils to earn more Words."

"Maggie's got herself in a patch of trouble with that ijit crowd she hangs with," Alan said. "Talked to Haime and he says he's not givin' her up. Says she owes big time."

"She has angered the League? That news bodes poorly for our venture."

"The League?" I asked.

Alan shot me a glance. "The League of Valhalla. Bunch of damn-fool boneheads who like to dress up as Norsemen, fronted by a bigger bonehead named Haime."

"Haime? Really?"

"S'what he calls himself."

"Well, let us tarry no longer, lest we grow roots through the soles of our boots." Cain rose and stretched. "Alan, do ready our supplies and weaponry for a battle most dire. We shall return shortly with the delectable Maggie."

"Sure, gotcha boss. It'll be a laugh riot."

"What's the plan, Cain?" I asked, following the tall man back down the stairs and out into the street.

He sighed. "You will have a rare opportunity to meet a god."

I had the feeling that things were spiraling out of control. Fortunately, I was used to it. "So, where to?"

"We have the good fortune to find ourselves in the same locale as the gathering place of the League. Our dear delicate Maggie is a long-standing member of the League and it is that very reason I chose this warehouse as our staging point." We walked down the canyons of Clinton, the old buildings a testament to a craftsmanship lost to those who now constructed buildings of glass and steel. "It had occurred to me that she would be otherwise occupied, but of all my apprentices, she is the most capable of undertaking highly dangerous tasks. Make no mistake, Alan will be an asset, but Maggie ... well, you shall see."

I nodded absently, feeling a little uncomfortable. New York City affected me like that, its vibrancy and ferociousness eating away at the slow paced, smaller town comfort I'd grown so used to in Omaha.

Before long we found ourselves on the waterfront, amid more industrial looking warehouses. Our destination proved to be a plain, whitewashed affair complete with loading docks and several glass doors with signs that read: USE OTHER ENTRANCE. All the doors sported the same sign. Cute.

Cain made straight for one and knocked on the aluminum frame. A man like a monolith in a bad black suit with a nasty look plastered to his pug ugly face answered, blocking the opening. "What you want," he rumbled from some deep dark place.

"My good man," Cain began with one his patented smiles. "I have come to this location drear to enjoy the hospitality of your employer, who, I am sure you know, has been a good and true friend of mine since time immemorial."

We waited while the rock that talked deciphered Cain's complex dialogue. Apparently the effort proved to be too much because he swung that massive head side to side and said, "No."

"Wait, wait, hold on a minute, Ralphie!" shouted a voice with a thick English dialect. Squeezing around the giant, a skinny man in a gray suit with a dog puke colored tie dusted himself off and offered us an insincere smile. Lank brown hair hung to his lapels. "It's grand to see you again Mr. Canus. Please don't give Ralphie here no mind." He patted the giant on the shoulder.

Canus? I raised an eyebrow at my companion who just smiled blandly and turned to the newcomer.

"Oh, I understand Ralphie must suffer from an over enthusiasm for his profession and his dedication to his employer, which I find quite commendable. Thank you all the same, Stephen." Cain replied smoothly, his smile not slipping a millimeter.

Stephan continued to grin, the strain of it visible in every line of his pockmarked face. His dishwater hair was swept back from a high forehead that helped to balance a potato-like protuberance of a nose. "Well, Mr. Canus, it is always an honor to have you join our little group. Mr. Haime's awaitin' for you in da smoking room with brandy and cigars and whatnot. You and your guest will follow me, please?" With that, Stephan did his best to lever the reluctant Ralphie out of the way. The big man obliged, but I think mostly to avoid getting hair oil on his cheap suit.

As we walked down a long, dark, wood-paneled hallway, the sounds of a raucous good time originating from far off in the warehouse assaulted our ears. The noise up close must have been deafening. Bright blue, red, and yellow banded the carpet that covered the hall floor, lines of cheap shag color leading us to the heart of the warehouse. We eventually came to a plain wooden door with a silver knob. Stephan knocked three times.

"Enter," said a deep voice from the other side.

We entered to find a largish man sitting in an overstuffed leather recliner, sipping brandy from a snifter and smoking an expensive cigar in front of an electric heater designed to simulate a fireplace. The room was done up in Warm Wood Library circa 1875, all toasty and comfy. The only light radiated from the flickering electric fire that lent the room its air of cut-rate cheeriness.

Dressed in a burgundy-colored smoking jacket and jeans, the man rose gracefully from his recliner. His short beard sparkled honey in the dim light. "Thank you, Stephan," the man said, sounding like a weary, down-on-his-luck British lord.

Stephan turned without a word and closed the door behind him.

"Cain, good to see you. Want a brandy?" The blond man turned to a slightly battered sideboard to fetch a decanter, showing us a long golden braid that hung to his waist.

"As much as I enjoy your fine liquor, Heimdall, my companion and I are here for reasons that are not social."

Heimdall? "You're Haime?" I asked.

"That I am, as well as Heimdall. I have so many names." He tossed me an inquiring look, his irises winking with gold.

I took in his hair, his height and the slight gold hue to his skin that didn't come from the faux fireplace. The pieces clicked together. "You're an angel."

Heimdall/Haime nodded with a rueful twist to his lips. "Fallen, but one of those who decided *not* to rule in Hell."

"Let me guess: you and your brothers and sisters were worshipped as gods in your own right."

Heimdall smiled, showing over large teeth. "Of course. Hell is so dreary and mankind is so accommodating to me and mine. We were still mighty then." A faint look of sorrow flitted across his face. "Earth provides so many comforts, but we still remember Heaven and curse the day we heeded Lucifer's silver-tongued arguments." He shook his head. "And who might you be?"

"Me? I go by Morgan Heart."

"Pleasure to make your acquaintance. Would you like a cigar? They're Dominican."

To me, most cigars smell like burning turds. "No, thank you." While it was surprising to find the fallen in NYC, it only made sense. They had to go *somewhere* and why not the City That Never Sleeps? "So, if you're the mythical Heimdall ..."

"I am," he interrupted smoothly, his teeth shining with enough wattage to rival Cain's. "Trust me."

"Quite. Then what is this warehouse? Asgard? Valhalla? If I remember, Heimdall guarded the Bifrost, The Rainbow Bridge, the only entrance to Asgard. I take it that ugly shag outside represents the Bridge?"

The fallen angel turned to Cain. "Look who's the bright penny. Where did you find this one?"

"This intrepid lad located me. I merely tolerate his company because we have formed an unlikely but mutually beneficial alliance."

Those golden brows shot up. "Since when do you *ally* yourself with anyone?"

"Since now." All the humor had left Cain's face. "I do hate to be a bother, but we have urgent need of the fair Maggie. Please produce her."

"I can't do that, old friend."

No smile, no humor, remained on Cain's face. Instead, his expression was so neutral that it scared me more than a show of anger. "And why, pray tell, can you not?"

Heimdall stuck a cigar between his teeth and the end flared to life. "Because she broke the rules in a fight. She used magic, the stupid twit."

"Are you not a lord of Asgard? Can you not, with a snap of your perfect fingers, set her free?"

"I'm just a broken-down old angel, a Potentate who's had his wings burned off. No one really believes in Asgard anymore." He waved his snifter around the room. "All this is window dressing. If I let her go, the League will lose faith in the Council have to shut the place down."

I raised a hand like a third grader in class. "And the League is what exactly?"

It was Cain who answered. "The League is comprised of mortals disenchanted with today's hustle and bustle world. They wished to be a part of an atavistic society unburdened by the confines of technology and, unfortunately, good hygiene. The Asgardians wished for worshippers and these disaffected souls proved most malleable to persuasion, forming the League of Valhalla."

"Right now they're partying," Heimdall sighed. "Drinking, screwing, eating and fighting. They go at it hammer and tong with authentic weaponry and Eir, the goddess of healing, tries to keep the damage to a minimum."

I was thunderstruck. "They're trying to kill each other?"

Heimdall nodded. "Controlled bouts in full armor. I'm proud to say we haven't had a death in over five years."

"That is the stupidest damn thing I've heard in ... hell, *forever!*"

The faux-god growled and pointed a finger the size of one of his cigars at my head. "Listen, asshole—" he began.

"He is entitled to his opinion," Cain said smoothly. "But for now I must beseech the rest of the Council of Asgardians, perhaps they can see to it that Maggie is temporarily released into my custody. I will return her forthwith."

"Personally, big guy, I don't care if you return her fivewith. It ain't my call." Gone was the cultured speech, revealing coarser influences. I guess he'd been in New York long enough to become acclimated.

Cain remained unperturbed. "Then let us repair to the council chambers, where I could sway the Council to view circumstances more favorably."

"What do you need her for, anyway?"

"Careful, Haime," I smiled. "Your Hicksville is showing."

He tossed me a golden glare. "Wise guys. Always wise guys. Okay, Cain and you—Mr. Smartypants—let's go see the Council." Consciously reverting to his more cultured speech, "But I can tell you, it will do you no good."

I whispered to Cain as Heimdall led us back into the hallway,

"What made him lose his cosmopolitan veneer?"

"That happens when angels grow weary, they become a little more … human," Cain replied quietly.

"I heard that," the angel said, "it's not nice."

"Although his hearing does remain unparalleled."

Shortly, after that eye-watering hallway turned several times, we came to another door, this one also plain, whitewashed wood. Heimdall ushered us through.

Big room. Big enough to play football in and have enough space for fans. Lengthwise down one wall was a television as big as a movie screen. Showing on the enormous plasma was a movie, a classic, playing at a decibel level that would have had *The Who* screaming for mercy. *Bridge over the River Kwai*. And there, bigger than life, was Alec Guinness, much younger than his Obi-Wan days in a much better movie.

Arranged in a semi-circle in front of the screen were dozens of Lazy Boy type recliners, most of them occupied by people drinking champagne or eating what looked like cucumber sandwiches.

All of them angels.

This just kept getting better and better.

Most of the avid watchers were true to type, although not dressed for their roles: a huge, burly man whose beer gut strained against the buttons of his blue flannel shirt and whose huge bushy red beard stretched to his belt had to be Thor. A lean gent with white hair and beard sporting an eye patch and Saville Row suit had to be Odin. The rest, Freyr, Freya, Sif and others reclined in indolent luxury, although the only one who seemed to be genuinely enjoying the movie was Thor, who grinned at every gunshot and laughed at every explosion.

"Is this what mythological beings do when they retire? Watch television and go to seed?" I ran my eyes over the lavish rugs on the teak floor and the full bar a few short steps away. The other side of the room held a kitchenette where, if I wasn't mistaken, Balder the Beautiful was prepping a BLT.

Heimdall muttered, "Oh, bugger me," as one of the faux deities paused the movie.

Cain closed his eyes. "Now you've done it, you've hurt their feelings."

Perhaps I should have remained silent, but the sight of all those angels, those sad, pathetic creatures, lounging in idleness and sloth drove a spike of anger into my brain They had *Heaven*, they had *God*, and instead of trying to get back into His good graces they did *nothing*. "What? Sensitive Cherubim and Seraphim?" A dull heat throbbed behind my eyes, the frustration of the past few days, my worry for Mike and the sheer ridiculousness of it all finally snapped the tether of my sanity and self control.

"What is the meaning of this, Loki?" thundered Odin as he shot to his feet, giving Cain the old stink-eye, which was impressive considering he only had the one. "You dare bring an insolent *human* to a gathering of the *gods*!" A low rumble of righteous anger came from the assembled angels as they rose to their feet and, as one, strode toward us.

"Loki?" I whispered.

"It was a long time ago," retorted Cain, composure shot as he held up his hands toward the advancing Asgardians. "I am vilified everywhere."

I should've known, was my only thought before I decided to add gas to the fire. "Am I to understand that Maggie is illegally incarcerated here for the use of magic in an unlawful fight?" I bellowed.

The question stopped the angels in their tracks. "She broke the rules and she has to pay the price!" thundered Thor. A belch followed his shout of outrage. He reminded me of a rough-hewn lumberjack straight out of Ken Kesey's *Sometimes a Great Notion*.

"So you *are* detaining her against her will. Illegal imprisonment, or did you fail to realize you were in the United States and that's not considered kosher?"

Thor and the others just stood and stared, looking confused while Odin strode purposely toward me. "Human laws have no validity here," he said.

I set off a wide, nasty smile that showed plenty of teeth. "What I have, *fallen*, is a hidden microphone that, when I give the command, will have plenty of *humans* with plenty of guns waltzing in here to ruin the party I hear coming through these walls. Somehow I don't think losing your worshippers is in your game plan. Also, something tells me you aren't bulletproof." A that time I was praying fervently for the fallen not to call my bluff.

"You're lying," Odin accused, narrowing his eye dangerously.

I laughed, a harsh, evil sound. "No, man, I'm *Sicarii.*"

Odin, the supposed father of the "gods" and the rest of his angelic crew drew back, naked fear on their golden faces. For the first time in my life I really understood the fear my Family generated.

"Loki," Odin hissed at Cain. "You brought one of *them* here?"

Cain snorted, with disgust or resignation, I wasn't sure. "Oh please stop the histrionics, Jophiel, it is unbecoming in a being your age," he admonished, using the fallen's true name. "I find myself concerned only with the return of my lovely apprentice. And the name is Cain. I shed the Loki persona centuries ago along with those temperamental Vikings who disgraced Norway with their rapacious ways."

"But—"

"Heed this advice, Jophiel, and acquiesce to this formidable young man's demands. If he can summon the strength to coerce *my* assistance, then you must believe in his ability to carry out his diabolical threats. Besides, you have long ago squandered what little power you had and can no long be labeled 'mighty.' No doubt it is by sheer numbers alone that you and yours forcibly persuaded the formidable Maggie to remain as an unwilling guest."

"Do you really have to talk like that, man?" I asked quietly, keeping an eye on Odin who signaled to Freya.

"I'm afraid so," came the whispered reply.

The Father of the Norse Gods stared at me with pointed hatred for a brief moment before nodding to Freya, who left through the only other door, located next to the kitchenette. Thor and the others, weary and defeated, walked back to the recliners, doing their level best to ignore us now that their impotence had been proven. Soon WWII continued on the giant screen. Moments later they were joined by Odin, the tattered rags of his dignity wrapped around him like a shroud.

Minutes passed as Heimdall shot dirty glances our way and pouted, biting a thumbnail. When Freya returned he left in a huff, face closed and stormy.

The former goddess of fertility brought with her a woman big enough to double as the statue of liberty, a buxom lady with muscles on her muscles and long blonde hair twirled in a braid. She was dressed in chainmail and leather leggings, a double bitted axe in one hand and a wooden round shield in the other.

"Holy crap," I breathed.

Cain shot the approaching woman a grin. "Did I not mention that she is more woman than any one sane man can handle?"

"She's a one woman big brass band. A blonde mountain with tits."

"Don't be vulgar."

"Am I wrong?"

"Well ... no."

When the larger-than-life Maggie saw Cain, she lumbered forward like an out of control locomotive and slammed him in a hug that would've flattened a lesser man. He tried to give back as good as he got, but I could tell it was a losing battle.

"Woman," he gasped into her neck. "You are damaging me irreparably."

Maggie let him go and planted a wet one on his lips. "Thanks, boss."

I kept my hand in front of my mouth to hide a smile while fielding covert dirty looks from the disgruntled Asgardians.

"Well, well, who's this?" Maggie's voice came dangerously close to my ear. A large, shapely hand landed on my back with enough force to stun the average water buffalo. I gulped.

"This young man is responsible for your deliverance from Valhallan hospitality, my dear." Cain's voice was smug. "His convincing and erudite arguments swayed the so-called gods to remand you into our custody. He is the one who should fully enjoy your appreciation."

Next thing I knew a warm mouth and chainmail-covered pillowy breasts were pressed firm against my chest while soft lips devoured mine. Part of me, the unthinking beast, had no problem with the estrogen assault and I instinctively wrapped my arms around her strong shoulders.

Finally the kiss ended, but my mind still traveled on paths more lusty than lucid. I did notice that when she smiled, her face dimpled prettily and there was small cleft on her chin that gave her a somewhat raffish look.

"Oooo," she breathed into my mouth. "I like him, Cain. Can I keep him?"

"Wha—?" Not my most intelligent question.

Cain winked at me over her shoulder. "My dear, I am afraid that if you were to retain possession of this gentleman you might break him."

Long fingers ruffled through my hair and I fought the urge to purr. "We'll talk later, tall dark and sexy," she laughed throatily. To Cain, "What's the job, boss?'

"Let us repair to a more amenable locale and discuss the task at hand. Safe to say the current endeavor will help you garner your fifth and final Word."

Abruptly, Cain and I found ourselves in the hallway, pulled along by Maggie whose long strides and strong grip gave us no choice but to exit the warehouse forcefully. Even the monolithic Ralphie gave way without a word to the storm of feminine purpose bearing down on him.

Once outside, Cain extricated himself from Maggie's iron hard grip and rounded on me, his face stormy. "What was that about?" he roared, all pretensions gone the way of the Dodo. "You humiliated them, emasculated them! And for what?"

Despite the desire to scream right back at him, I kept my cool. Instead, I stared into his mirrored glaciers and said, "They weren't going to let her go."

"You don't—"

"Yes I do. You do, too." I rubbed my eyes. "The only person I've ever called a friend is being held by my sadistic bastard of a father and those role-playing dickheads were standing in the way." Breathing hard, I puked forth all the rage and frustration I'd been feeling at the one man I was sure could kill me without breaking a sweat. Didn't give a damn, though. "A bunch of angels scrabbling for tidbits of power by throwing a rager Norse-style party and lording over a lot of disillusioned misanthropes like Roman emperors desperate to ignore the fact that the barbarians are at the bloody gates.

"Those idiots would have wasted our time just like they've squandered whatever miniscule portion of their divinity they retained after the fall. No, I won't suffer morons who don't even *try* to act like the angels they once were."

Cain did some serious looming while Maggie bit her lip, afraid we were about to throw down the gauntlet.

The oldest man in the world poked an iron-hard finger in my chest. *Poke, poke, poke* ... "You, my friend, have lost all reason ... and I love that about you!" His face split nearly in half with the force of his grin. "Twice in two days you have managed to surprise me. Me! And I thought the world had naught else to offer to shake my equilibrium." Cain leaned close, both hands on my shoulder. "You are dangerous, unpredictable and that is why I reason that we may yet live through this madness!" With that he strode away, hands in pockets, whistling a happy tune.

Maggie and I shared a look. "Is he always like this?" I asked.

She shook her head and hooked her armored arm in mine. "I've never seen him this happy, handsome."

Chapter Twenty-Eight

Mike

It wasn't Boris who opened the door to my closet. Instead a statuesque brunette with a chip the size of the Chrysler building on her shoulder stood in the doorway skewering me with her eyes. The line of her sleek black body suit was spoiled by all the weapons Velcro-ed in strategic locations and suspicious bulges that indicated she had still more pocketed away.

Great … Annabeth.

"Get up, priest," she huffed.

"Where's the Russian?"

Apparently she didn't care for my attitude because the next thing I knew there was a strange, bulky looking knife pointed between my eyes. It had to be one of Burke's repeating ballistic knives.

Intrigued, I rose unsteadily to my feet, wincing and hesitant as my muscles protested every movement, while my ribs, bruised, sent lancets of pain to the back of my skull. Stretching didn't help, but I did it anyway, playing for time as I studied the woman. Annabeth, beautiful yet opaque, like the space between the stars. Black hair cut to a page-boy bob, broad shouldered, well-stacked, but standing with an air of languid grace that told me her body, while lush, had been honed to perfection like a straight razor. Steel covered in cream.

"Lay on, McDuff," I said, teeth clenched in torment. At that moment I would have begged Julian for a Healing.

A contemptuous snort, a wave of one slender but strong hand and we were off down the corridors of … wherever the heck we were, the thick pile carpeting and tastefully rich yet understated wallpaper testifying to the magnitude of the Sicarii fortune.

My guide-slash-captor stopped at a door indistinguishable from the one to Julian's suite and produced a key card, swiping on the lock plate. The telltale glowed green and we entered.

We entered a suite identical to Julian's, including the wall to ceiling windows that looked out onto nighttime New York, except that all the furniture had been removed from this suite. Gym mats had replaced the sofas, chairs and tables, turning the large space into a sparring room. Only one piece of furniture remained: the ugly steel chair, the same chair I had spent so many thrilling hours on. They hadn't even bothered to clean off the blood.

Half a dozen men and women, all in black skintights like Annabeth's, stopped their combat training to stare at me as I sat. All were in their thirties, with the physical and psychic hardness of people who had been breaking bones and ripping flesh most of their adult lives. All had Annabeth's lethal grace. They scared the spit out of me.

My captor nodded to a youth who bore a striking resemblance to Morgan. He moved toward me with the grace of a panther, raising one long-fingered hand to brush my shoulder. He whispered a Word that I felt from the soles of my feet to the top of my skull, one that removed most of the aches and pains of Boris' beating.

"Thank you," I said sincerely. "I needed that." My body was once again more or less in good shape and my ribs felt less battered. Not a full Healing, but a massive improvement. "God bless you."

The youth paled, taking a hasty step back, and one of the older men, short with a round face, started forward, a wooden practice knife gripped tight in one hand and a ferocious scowl on his face. Perhaps he was offended by the blessing. Annabeth flicked her fingers and he stopped short. From the way her hands moved, I reckoned she used some sort of sign language. I didn't care ... As far as the Sicarii was concerned, I was a dead man whose body hadn't received the message yet.

"We might as well carry on a civilized conversation, Annabeth," I murmured. "That is, if you are able."

She didn't bother to look at me. "Why should we talk?"

"It couldn't hurt. Anything you tell me I'll be taking to my grave."

Her mouth quirked into a half-smile. "True enough."

"Did you ever love ... Olivier?"

"I didn't know you were going to get personal, Michael." My name was a curse from her perfect mouth.

"Olivier wrote—"

"I know. I've read it."

"And?"

"No." Firm, resolute.

"I think he really cared about you."

"He was a means to an end."

"So you were working with Burke all that time."

"Of course."

"Burke's gone and with him your meal ticket. What do you plan to do now?'

Anger broke through her mask and the back of her hand found my bruised cheek, hitting just hard enough to flame my face with pain, but not hard enough to break the skin.

Instead of shooting a snappy, snide remark that would've earned me a few more contusions, I watched the Sicarii dream team practice. They moved like liquid death, using combinations of several martial arts with an effectiveness that took my breath away. I could've watched them try to beat the crap out of each other all night, but I had to poke the bear.

"Sooooo ... Burke was more than a meal ticket." I rubbed the aching flesh of my cheek "You cared for him."

"Shut up," she hissed, cheeks crimson.

I lowered my voice. "Oh, you Sicarii don't subscribe to love."

"This conversation is over."

"Too bad, it was just getting interesting." I considered her beautiful face for a moment. "Sorry for your loss." It surprised me how much I meant that.

The result of my empathy was not what I had been hoping for. Maybe it was because I was a priest of the 'Lying God' or because I showed compassion, but she drew close to grab the lapels of my tattered uniform in preparation for delivering a good butt-kicking.

"Is this your gun?" I whispered into her face, pressing the barrel of a 9 mm into her side out of sight of the others.

"How did—?"

My tattered smile was unbecoming for one in my profession. "Your outfit is cute, but using Velcro to secure your weapon is a terrible idea, as well as getting it within my reach. Now, I'm going to stand up slowly and you will move slowly with me. If you don't, you will find out the hard way that I was an army Ranger long before I became a priest, got it?"

Her mouth barely moved. "Got it, but realize this, shitwad: I am going to kill you."

"Then I can't be used against my friend. Now, stand up … slowly."

Almost made it. My hand was on the door when, out of the corner of my eye, I saw round-face start forward, catching the drift and sounding the alarm.

I shoved Annabeth away, clipping the back of her skull with the butt of the pistol before bringing it to bear and shooting twice, catching her in the calf—shredding flesh and bone—and firing a second round into round-face's hip. While he stumbled to his knees, clutching at the hole four inches from his crotch, I ducked out the door and ran down the hallway. My feet slammed almost soundlessly against the lush carpeting while my heart thudded painfully against my screaming ribs. Behind me I heard the door open … only three steps from a turn … drywall powdered beside my ear as I turned the corner, the round missing me by less than an inch.

Spinning, I hit the floor behind the dubious safety of the wall as more rounds showered the air with plaster. Not waiting for the Sicarii to come to me, I scrambled forward on hands and knees far enough to see around the corner and empty the 9's clip, catching an unlucky assassin in the stomach and forcing the others to duck back in the room. I'd bought myself a few precious seconds.

Would they stop to help their comrade? Normally I'd say yes, but with this lot, that might not be an option. The only thing that mattered, though, was getting away or making the cost of taking me down a dear one. I knew—sure as I was running hell bent for leather—that Morgan was coming. I could feel it in my heart.

Two more turns and I hit pay dirt. Elevators. Not much time; the killers would be on me in moments and I knew they wouldn't hesitate to kill me. I forced fingers into the seam of the doors, straining and grunting, slowly pulling them apart, slicking the crisp white paint with sweat and blood until they finally opened just far enough for me to slip through into the dimly lit shaft and grab oil-slick cables.

Down into the dark ... the doors above closing, shutting off the light from the hallway. Wouldn't be hard for them to find me, so I had to move fast. By the shaft's dim light I saw a ladder bolted to the wall, but that route was too slow, so I let the slick cable slide through my hands, my skin burning despite the thin coating of grease. One floor, two ... then another as I slid, palms catching steel splinters, driving deep into flesh. I gritted my teeth and prayed for strength as the flesh of my palms seared away.

Fourth floor down and light from above tagged me. A shot rang out and a burning pain erupted from my left arm as a bullet scorched me from shoulder to elbow. Lord that hurt! Panic lent strength and I grabbed for the ladder with a desperate lunge. If I missed, massive deceleration trauma would be my fate. Despite a slick of blood and oil coating my hand, I managed to hold onto a rung long enough for my body to slam against the ladder, raising a cloud of dust from the steel. My foot hooked the side rail and I thrust an arm up to the elbow between rungs, hugging the ladder close to me with frantic energy. More shots rang out, but thankfully they missed, only spraying cement chips in my face.

Elevator doors above and to my left. They seemed miles away, but I had to go for it. Flailing, knuckles smarting against rungs, I tried to ignore the bullets that tore around me. The cable behind flapped and I knew someone was coming.

Four inches of space at the elevator door, barely enough for my clodhopper boots to find purchase. Another round grazed my calf and the ricochet buried itself into the heel of my boot, almost hurtling me off the ledge into the darkness of the shaft.

There! My fingers found a grip and adrenaline lent me strength, allowing me to force the doors open … and push through … falling into an empty hallway, battered and bleeding. Behind me, the door dimpled outwards with rounds that sounded like hammer blows. I breathed a sigh of relief that it was taking what had been meant for me.

Not much time … All my training kicked in and I rose to my feet, wounds throbbing but almost forgotten. Fear and anger fought for control in equal measure, but it was the voices of every man and woman I had the honor to serve with that spurred me into action: "Get off your ass, you sonofabitch and take the fight *to* the enemy!"

Right.

A priest is a man of peace as well as a man of God. The teachings of Christ provide the foundation of our beliefs, but I've always known that deep down, I could take the life of an evil person if I deemed it necessary and now it seemed very necessary. I'd started with Annabeth, goading her with kindness into becoming angry enough to drop her guard once within reach. Where it would end, well … I wasn't sure, but I knew it would get bloody.

Behind me the doors to the elevator began to open and a grimy hand thrust through, followed by a shoulder, then a head. A tall man with sallow features … the Sicarius I'd shot in the belly. I guess that skintight outfit had a bulletproof torso. He saw me a split second after I moved, too late to bring his gun to bear. My kick took him in the hip and I *shoved* as hard as I could, sending him hurtling down the shaft. The doors closed on his shriek of dismay. His chest might have been bulletproof, but it wasn't splatterproof.

Eyes burning with tears, I turned and ran down the empty hall, every step ringing out the same word: *murder … murder … murder …*

I knocked on door after door. I kicked and screamed and no one answered or screamed back at me to get lost. For some reason the floor was deserted and the knowledge I was running out of time weighed heavily on me.

Stairs! A way out. Hand on the knob and shoulder to the door, I rammed it open. Shouts echoed from below and the thuds of hurried footsteps came my way up the stairwell. No good. Up, however, seemed clear. I guess I didn't have a choice.

Thudding up the stairs, one floor then two … and I made the decision to keep going, back to the floor I'd just come from, reckoning they wouldn't search for me there. Soon, panting and bleeding, I came to what I believed was the floor I had fled. Next to the steel door was a sign that read 53.

I put my ear to the door and heard nothing, so I went through. Nothing. All quiet. Through the door into unfamiliar surroundings. Left or right? I flipped a mental quarter and went left.

Good thing because I quickly came upon blood smell, the source of which was smeared on the wall. I located the suite by the blood still wet on the door handle.

I cursed then crossed myself. The door was locked and I had no key card, but the point became moot because down the hall, around the corner, one more of the Sicarii boys came into view. Options flickered through my mind in less than a second, moments before his eyes would rise to see me standing by the door.

The best option was also the most dangerous, but I was sick of running away. So I ran *toward*.

Muscles cried in agony and bruised bones added their voices to the cacophony of pain that rang in my ears. The Sicarius looked up as I raced toward him. Almost in slow motion he went for the pistol Velcro-ed to the chest of his black one piece, a look of surprise flitting briefly across his face.

Closer, fifteen feet and his hand reached the pistol.

Ten feet … the weapon ripped free with the sound of paper tearing.

My feet left the carpet as I dove at a dead run, the pistol rising to meet my eyes.

Click.

I hit the man full on, shoulder in his midsection, the pistol with safety on flying from his hand as I drove him backward to land in heap, both of us kicking and scratching, punching and biting.

We rolled, grappling, the Dagger Man's teeth buried in my shoulder, and I screamed in hot pain as his bicuspids tore into soft tissue. My knee came up, but he expected the play and twisted so I hit his thigh. A calloused knuckle rammed my jaw, followed by an elbow that had me seeing stars. That elbow made a comeback and I turtled, letting it hit the top of my skull. I sagged as my neck compressed and the Sicarius screamed.

I rolled away from the noise as the Sicarius kept at it, holding on to what I assumed was a broken elbow. People always said I was hard-headed and the proof lay moaning on the hallway carpet.

I kept my back to the wall, using it to support me as I stood shakily, every nerve in my body firing at once. The Dagger Man finally came to grips with his pain and also came to his feet, a grimace of hate on his long youthful face.

Sweat stung my eyes as I watched him reach into a pocket with his good hand and pull out a butterfly knife, which he opened one-handed with the ease of constant practice. My foot lashed out but he dodged the halfhearted attack with ease. The assassin might have been injured, but he still had skills.

So I dove for the pistol, hoping that my battered body would prove quick enough. It didn't. The Sicarius kicked, catching me in the stomach—folding me in half and wrenching my midsection—then he fell on top of my writhing body with thrust a knee to the kidney that momentarily paralyzed my body in torment.

But I had the gun.

He grabbed my arm and through the haze of suffering that clouded my eyes, I saw the light of understanding reach him. Despite his one-handed grip, I was stronger. As breath struggled to enter my lungs, my thumb stroked the safety and I pulled the trigger. Twice.

Blood. Brains. Bone. All sprayed upwards and settled back down to coat my face as the body of the Dagger Man settled on my chest.

Oh, Lord, forgive me.

Sobbing for the dead man, mumbling prayers for his soul, I clumsily searched his body, my tears wetting the black one-piece. My eyes strayed to the small, round holes on his forehead, knowing that the exit wounds had torn the back of his head off. Eventually I found a key card in a hip pocket. No use trying to hide the body, the hall gave plenty of evidence as to what had happened, the walls being decorated in red and pink. Sluggishly, I trod toward the door to the suite. My hands were on fire with pain; metal slivers and friction burns had tattered the palms into raw meat. My blood slicked the pistol, dripping down the barrel.

Heart thumping madly with guilt and relief, I swiped the key card at the door. I needed to get clean. I needed to tend my wounds, needed to rest, if only for a while. The door opened and I stepped inside.

A man stood by the floor-to-ceiling windows, staring out into the night. At the sound of the door shutting behind me, he turned.

Boris smiled.

Oh, hell.

Chapter Twenty-Nine

Morgan

"**D**id I forget to mention that this idea of mine is seriously insane?" I shouted at Cain over the din of the rotors. Fear ate at my guts.

Night, three thousand feet in the air, the Bell 430 helicopter remained stable as the pilot waited for us to jump. Flashbacks to another night jump fifteen years ago kept flickering before my eyes, but this time we would jump into a city rife with thermals and strange wind shears that could flip a parachute topsy-turvy in an instant, not to mention that it was cold as hell. The black sweater, Kevlar vests, and heavy black denim pants offered some protection.

"A young man with your history of rash behavior and rebellion against the most powerful criminal organization in history thinks *this* idea is mad?" Cain shouted back with a grin. "Once again you manage to surprise!"

Right, that's me, Mr. Surprise.

Six hours earlier Cain, Maggie, Alan and I had stood together in the dark warehouse, a single bare bulb from a small lamp providing a ring of light that perfectly illuminated the round table it rested upon. Alan had handed out Kevlar vests and provided a spread of weaponry large enough to take out the Latin American country of your choice.

Alan handed a laptop to Cain. "Here's the schematics to the hotel, boss."

Cain regarded the computer for a brief moment. "Once again you do not fail to impress, my boy."

"You won't need that, man," I commented as I picked up a .45 and checked the sights. "All we need are the top three floors, 53 to 55. Everything else is the ordinary rich and famous."

"You're cute when you're all authoritative and shit," Maggie smiled as she struggled out of her chainmail and shrugged into her vest, her large axe resting on the table. I couldn't help it; I stared at her charms out of the corner of my eyes. She caught the look and gave me a satisfied smile that heated up all my naughty bits.

Man, I'd been without proper company for far too long.

My eyebrows danced in her direction. "The Sicarii own the place and I made sure to learn everything I could about where Julian would hang his hat."

Cain replaced his sunglasses with thick, black goggles, briefly revealing his disturbing Husky eyes. "What do you suggest, then?"

"A roof access would be best. There will be guards, but with our magic and a little surprise, we can take them down."

"Four of us storming the battlements." Maggie holstered a 9 mm and picked up a Tec-9. "I love it."

Cain frowned. "Not to impugn your knowledge of all things Sicarii, but are you certain that is wise?"

I shook my head. "There are only two access points to the upper stories—a heavily defended private elevator that they can shut down in an instant and an equally well-defended stairwell. Then let's consider the innocents staying in the hotel who could be killed or hurt by stray bullets."

Alan piped up. "So what do we all do? I'm no frontal assault guy, no soldier. I'm just a realtor."

Not just a realtor. Not with three Words. "We parachute down to the roof and take the access stairs to the suite levels."

"How many Sicarii guards will there be," asked Maggie, curling her braid around the top of her head and covering it with a black wool cap.

"At least two dozen."

The two apprentices stopped what they were doing and tried to pick their jaws off the floor. "Two dozen highly trained assassins?" Maggie squeaked. It was off-putting to see a woman so big squeak like a mouse.

"At least two dozen."

Cain grunted. "Then the need for a two pronged attack is paramount. One to provide a much needed diversion, the other to strike at the heart of the enemy."

"How are we going to manage that, boss?"

"It comes to me that we must seek aid elsewhere," Cain declared. "Perhaps a conversation with our employer would prove beneficial."

"Second Man, Sicarius, what do you want?" Earth grated. The elemental towered over us, a vaguely human-shaped mass.

The alleyway between warehouses was dark enough to hide in, but there was enough light to see the elemental that had joined us.

Both Cain and I had used the Language of Earth to summon this creature, a being formed of concrete and brick that had a strange, plastic quality to it, allowing it to move without cracking or powdering. Normally it takes a while for Earth to answer a summons, but when we called, the elemental had come quickly.

"Shortly we will attack the Sicarii stronghold and retrieve First Water," I answered, tasting the smell of the Language on my tongue. "We need to you to shake the ground beneath the building they hide in."

A blobby head swung my way. *"Shake? You wish to tear down one of your human-made earth structures?"*

"No. We want you to move the earth around the building just enough to create a distraction. The building must still stand when you are done."

"When?"

It was Alan who answered. *"When I give the signal."* His vocabulary was good, but I wondered if Earth cared that a human butchered its Language with such a horrible accent.

"This will help secure the First Water?"

I nodded. *"Yes."*

"Call. Earth will come. Then tell me which dwelling to … shake."

Back inside the warehouse, Cain made some calls while the rest of us readied our gear.

Maggie gave me an inquiring look. "Why would the Sicarii worry about evacuating the hotel, handsome?"

I smiled, hefting a pair of half-inch ball bearings. "While the Sicarii are powerful, the hotel is filled with those they do business with, including former dictators, captains of industry, drug lords, etc. They can't afford to let any harm come to their guests. No, after the first few tremors, the hotel will be evacuated for safety's sake and the normal staff sent home. They will lock the place up tight as a security precaution." I put the bearings into a pocket on my left arm.

"Then why attack? We'll get slaughtered."

"That's the beauty of it. They might prep for it, but they really don't think anyone would be so foolish as to try an assault. Julian has no idea that I've recruited Cain for this; he thinks I'm all by my lonesome, and that has made him complacent. They'll be ripe for a surprise attack."

I felt the heat of her as she came close. She smelled of female musk and lemons. "I love the way your devious little mind works, handsome."

My grin was predatory. "The rest of me works pretty well, too."

Her eyes grew wide and her voice husky. "Promises, promises," she said.

Alan held up a disk of whitish putty, the size of an American silver dollar. Mounted in the center was a small, flat black box with a small metal ring set on the side. "If y'all could stop the foreplay and tone down the pheromone levels, I'd appreciate knowing what this is."

I had no clue and Maggie just shook her head.

"That, my dear apprentices and colleague, is what most would affectionately call a 'door buster.' " Cain stepped in to the light of the lamp, a cell phone glowing softly in one hand. "A disk of Plastique with a timed detonator. Simply attach the explosive near the lock plate of whatever point of egress you wish to harm, pull the pin and in five seconds any locking mechanism will yield."

"When he talks, he gives me a headache," I whispered to Maggie.

"I know. I'd consider giving him a shag if he could keep his words to one or two syllables."

"If you children are quite done with your sophomoric rantings, we have other pressing concerns. Alan, has our shipment of re-enforcements arrived?"

"While you were out earlier, boss."

Cain nodded and pulled a small stack of three by five cards out of the pocket of his red flannel shirt. "Good. I think it is time for my fine friends to receive compensation." To each of us he handed a card.

Maggie and Alan snatched at theirs eagerly, while I took a more cautious approach.

My eyes found the Word written there and it slid into my mind like a lover into an embrace, warm and gentle. Things shifted in my mind and I felt some part of me, part of my memory, evaporate like ice under the hot sun. I didn't know what it could have been. The Word, however, stuck fast.

"Create. This is Create," I breathed. A thirteenth Word! I immediately knew what I could do with this Word, the capability of making artifacts and wards. I knew that when I used it, it would smell like the ocean.

"Peace, you gave me Peace!" Maggie nearly screamed, outraged. She flung the card onto the table.

Peace? I immediately felt a near-overwhelming desire to snatch her card and add the word to my Vocabulary.

Cain simply smiled and said, "If you did not have the facility for it, my dear, the Word would not have taken root in your mind. While the Word might not have any offensive capabilities, never underestimate the power of a Word properly used."

I gave Maggie speculative look.

She threw it right back at me. "What?"

My grin was sheepish. "Never met a female magus before, man; it's such a new experience. Sorry."

Smiling, she picked up the axe and whirled it around her body. Slowly at first, then faster and faster, the axe humming, a steel blur with a sharp edge. Alan and I backed up before we could suffer an amateur tracheotomy. After a few seconds she slowed then stopped, setting the axe gently on the table. "When it comes to me, buster, you ain't seen nothin' yet." Her grin was toothy and savage.

"Damn," I breathed, curiously aroused. "That's for sure, Blondie."

"Can't read this one," Alan said morosely, holding up his Word card. "Sorry, boss."

"Not a bother," Cain replied, unfazed by the Maggie's demonstration. He handed another card to the stricken apprentice. "The magus's inner landscape and talent determine the amount and type of Words that can be accessed."

Alan took the card and read. A few moments passed before a beatific smile spread across his face and dimples appeared at the corners of his mouth matching the one on his chin. "Grace … it's Grace."

Cain flashed teeth and gathered the cards from both apprentices. "Excellent." He turned to me, noting the look of longing on my face. "Come, I have need of your newfound Word." With that, he walked into the dark and I followed.

Maybe his eyewear was a form of night vision, or maybe his blue-white eyes could see in the dark, but I was forced to hold onto his shoulder until he produced a mini-flashlight and flicked the switch. I could have used Vision, but I wanted to hoard my power for the trial to come.

An eight by five wooden crate rested a few feet away, a crowbar leaning against the rough planks. "If you would do the honors?" Cain asked.

Nodding, I hefted the crowbar and started prying the crate open. After a couple of minutes' worth of effort, the side panel fell to the concrete with a resounding crash.

"What the hell?" I said.

"That is why I needed you and your new Word. These are our re-enforcements."

A few short hours later Cain and I traveled to a private helipad where a copter and pilot waited. Maggie and Alan went to prepare for the ground assault on the hotel with our ... re-enforcements and to contact Earth so it could simulate a quake. A few minutes after we took off, Alan reported that Earth had shaken the hotel quite thoroughly, shattering window glass on all floors and cracking pavement. Earth had stopped just short of collapsing the entire structure.

"I just live to surprise you, Cain," I yelled back. To Maggie, "*Yellow, How's it going?*" All of us used aliases while on coms. I was Green, Maggie Yellow, Cain Blue and Alan Red.

Her voice came tinny and small through the earwig set deep in my ear canal. "The building shook like an epilepsy patient, Green. Now all the rich and famous are streaming out like rats leaving a ship." A pause. "Although with some of these folks, that's an insult to rats."

Alan chimed in. "It's not helping that Earth cracked all the cement in front of the hotel. The limos are having a hard time of it, Green."

"How much longer will the evacuation take, Red?"

"Everyone staying at the hotel has a limo, so it's making for a tight squeeze, but it shouldn't be too much longer."

"Cain, how long can we hover here?" I yelled.

He checked with a pilot. "We have world enough and time, my young friend." He dipped into a thigh pocket and pulled out two plastic vials. "Drink up; this will imbue you with the ability to withstand at least six or seven Words for about half an hour."

I waved it away. "Already made an ointment that does the same thing!" I bellowed. "It's smeared under my sweater and it lasts all day. Also, it absorbs at least a dozen if not two." My mind went back to when Julian hit me with a Word from the Silver. "Providing they're normal Words, that is."

Silence. From behind his goggles, I could feel his implacable regard. "What?" Was it my breath? I use mints.

Still nothing, until, "I have walked this earth for such a length of time that millennia have been forgotten, seas have risen and fallen. I have beheld the Flood that formed the Mediterranean and destroyed fair Atlantis beneath its turbulent waves, sending Noah and his Ark spinning. It has been my privilege and honor to have taught magi throughout the endless centuries from Abraham to Charlemagne." He sounded pissed.

"So?"

"So? *So,* I am the greatest practitioner of magic the world has ever known! Not even Merlin Demonborn, the Naphil of Camelot, could equal my status as a magi, yet you, you insolent little pup, have done something I had not even considered: create an ointment to counter magic that is of greater efficacy than any potion I could and have ever devised."

"Yeah, man. So?'

"Sometimes you really piss me off, kid!"

Ten minutes later, while Cain still fumed, Alan gave us the green light.

I hollered at my companion, "Ready?"

"Ready, on your mark."

"Go!"

We jumped.

Chapter Thirty

Morgan

Freezing wind tore at my face, trying to scour the flesh from my skull. The thin plastic goggles preserved my eyes so I could see the city lights rush at me with the speed of inevitability.

I'd fallen five hundred feet, arms and legs spread. Another fifteen hundred feet to go.

My mind quested down down down to street level where Maggie and Alan had already started the ground assault.

In the warehouse, Cain had given me another Word: Seeing, and it smelled like Old Spice. With a touch and a soft utterance, I could see through the eyes of the willing. Maggie had been kind enough to let me See through her eyes to help co-ordinate the assault, if need be.

It went something like this:

Four golems jumped like spiders over the cracked and broken pavement, the word "emet" (אמת) inscribed in the chamois on the back of their heads. Instead of sculpting the creatures out of clay, wood or stone, Cain had procured crash test dummies, their light weight and articulation giving them a mobility and speed greater than that of traditional stone golems.

Cain had told me that every magi could only Create a finite

number of golems. A Twelve Word magus, he said, could conceivably Create up to fifteen or twenty, but not all at once. Apparently the golems would become progressively weaker if the earlier ones weren't destroyed.

I had made two, using Create as well as certain herbs, the crafting requiring both Botanical and Word Magic. It was a sign of his trust that Cain had let me know which herbs to use.

Maggie and Alan raced like track stars, weapons at the ready, in the path of the golems, which had burst through the front doors. The heavy tempered glass shattered like thin ice at the impact of the speeding automatons.

The next five hundred feet of our descent passed quicker than I could've imagined as the rooftops of the city grew huge. My altimeter was ready to spring my chute at twelve hundred feet.

To my right, Cain's chute deployed and he shot out of sight.

I hoped mine deployed or I'd discover firsthand what the term 'road pizza' meant. Once again images from below spooled into the back of my mind:

The Dagger Men in the lobby looked up in shock as flesh toned mannequins leapt with obscene grace across marble tile, two jumping twenty feet straight up to clear the railing to the upper lobby. The other two ran straight for the human guards, who let go with twin Mac-10s they had slung under their armpits. Bullets streaked out of the roaring weapons, many missing, gouging the priceless floor, but many hit the golems, shredding soft leather skin, bouncing off of steel skeletons.

They were still firing, taking turns changing clips, when the golems tore into them. One golem grabbed an arm—crushing ulna and radius like rotten wood—and ripped it off at the shoulder. The Sicarius screamed once before fainting dead away to lie in widening pool of her own blood.

The second gunman was more fortunate; the golem that attacked him merely rammed an iron fist through the bones of his face, bursting the eyeballs before the metal hand gripped the brain and *squeezed*. Dagger Man and weapon dropped to the floor.

An elevator door *pinged* and six more Sicarii joined the fight. One golem was knocked back fifteen feet by Force, landing high in a chandelier; the other was swarmed under four Strength-enhanced assassins who tore it limb from limb. A storm of rounds nearly decapitated the one jumping at them from the chandelier, which was already falling to the black and white marble floor.

From the upper lobby, the first two golems landed among the six assassins like deranged clockwork beasts, rending and tearing. The final screaming assassin mercifully fell to the rain of bullets fired by Maggie and Alan, who watched from the dubious safety of the shattered doorway.

My chute deployed, rapidly slowing my fall. Only a few hundred feet to go. Thermals from the buildings slung me to and fro, but I managed to stay on point, guiding the chute toward the helipad on the roof of the hotel.

A hundred feet from my target and I saw a guard walking the perimeter of the pad. I knew right then that he'd see me before my feet touched down. Hoping against hope, I spoke Strength, trailing an ammonia stench through the cold night air.

Twenty feet and I pulled the quick release on my harness, dropping hard on the center of the pad, my Strength-enhanced legs absorbing much of the force, but I felt an ankle twist and snap sickeningly, shooting fire up my leg as I rolled.

I looked up, .45 at the ready, only to see the guard with his weapon, an M16A4, I dimly noted, pointed at my face. I was about to die. The scene from below and inside would take me to the grave:

Two golems scampered up the elevator shaft the Sicarii had used; the damaged one (missing an arm and a head half-blown away) took the stairwell, followed by Maggie and Alan, who quickly lagged behind the nimble construct. The fourth golem lay scattered in pieces on the blood- and brain-soaked marble in the lobby.

"If ... I wanted ... aerobics..." panted Maggie as she passed another floor. "I would've ... joined ... a gym."

"Just ... move your lard ass, woman." Alan puffed. His voice sounded raspy and ragged, as if he'd been gargling with broken glass.

"I ... am going to ... kick your butt ...when we are through here ... assface."

From above came the sound of screaming and gunfire. And more screaming. Something wet and blobby fell past them to spatter down below.

"What ... was that?" Alan asked, not bothering to look.

Maggie kept her eyes on the stairs. One after the other ... then a landing then more steps. "Something ... important to somebody."

I would've closed my eyes, but the barrel of the rife held me hypnotized. The guard's finger tightened.

Bullets landed all around, one grazing my calf. Quite a few did more than graze the guard, who crumpled in a heap, blood pooling around his lifeless body.

Looking up, I saw Cain drift the last few feet to the helipad, a Mac-10 in one hand and harness release in the other. As his feet touched down, he yanked the release and chute and harness disappeared into the night, carried away on the cold New York wind.

"It appears as though you should consider exercising more caution while approaching the enemy," Cain said. "Are you well?"

The grating pain, the *pressure*, in my ankle gave way to blessed relief as I moaned a Healing. The bones of my ankle ground together and shifted, re-aligning themselves. "Fine, fine," I said, rising when the last vestiges of pain melted away.

The roof access point was locked with an electronic keypad and card slot, but a quick search of the guard revealed a key card. A quick swipe and we were heading down a stairwell.

Cain pulled alongside at the first landing down, a door marked 55 in front of us. "Here?"

"No. Main access will be at the first floor of these three-story suites.

Julian has his 'offices' there and that's where Mike and the Primal will be."

"The Primal will be in a safe, a lockbox?" The black goggles were gone and he once again sported his mirrored Glaciers, looking like a black ops commando ready for a skiing holiday.

I shook my head. "No. Julian will have the Primal on him at all times. With Boris on hand and his own slew of Words, it's safer than any lock box." The molecular knife was a conspicuous lump in my hip pocket. "Let's go."

54 ... 53. The door opened with the key card revealing a long hallway carpeted in burgundy cut pile. A Sicarius in a black skintight one piece turned at the sound of the door opening. As my silenced pistol appeared in hand as if by magic, I had just enough time to think about how ridiculous those one-piece outfits were before two quick shots dropped him hard to the floor, bleeding from throat and skull.

I knew him. Another cousin, distant, a real asshole named Ulric known for such brutality that he made Burke look like an altar boy. His death brought no remorse, no sadness. The world was better off without him in it.

But there would be others, I knew, others who I *did* like and who would die, maybe by my hand. It was a sobering thought.

"It falls upon you to lead the way, my young friend."

"Just keep those Words and that gun handy and watch my back. Things are about to become real interesting." Once again, I thought of the other two inside:

"Why do the steps end here?" Alan complained, staring at a bloody door half torn from the hinges. Sounds of fighting came from beyond. A body lay on the landing, torn to shreds. "We're not high enough."

"Security," Maggie panted. "Staggered stairs, no through-access from top to bottom." Without another word she reached past Alan and grabbed the door handle, tearing the door totally free from the remaining hinge.

"C'mon, scaredy pants!" she laughed. "Get it in gear!"

"I'm a lover, not a fighter," came the reply as he followed her into the hallway.

Blood splattered the full length of the hallway, along with bits and pieces of flesh and bone. A golem lay scattered about—a head here, an arm there. Only a leg and torso remained whole, twitching with terrible purpose, still attempting to complete its allotted task.

"Holy shit," whispered Alan, eyes wide with horrified fascination.

Maggie stared at the blood and flesh, the toe of her black canvas shoe disturbing a shattered tooth. "You got that right."

Shots rang out and a Dagger Man came running around a corner some fifty feet way, eyes wide with fright, a pistol in one hand, the other hand flopping broken and useless at the wrist.

Before he even reached the halfway point, Maggie's Tec-9 stuttered twice and he fell, sprawling, spewing blood and gore. He twitched once, then twice and lay still.

Alan stared at the corpse. "What now?'

Dark blue eyes remained resolutely fixed on the blood-soaked hallway. "We follow the noise. The golems will lead the way to the next staircase or the elevators."

"I hope they handle the rest of the Sicarii."

She checked the remaining clips to the Tec-9, then reached behind her to the base of her neck, tearing a weapon free from Velcro. It was a hand-axe—a medieval weapon two feet long with a spike on top and one opposite the blade.

"I hate it when y'all use that," Alan complained.

"It doesn't use bullets."

Alan pulled a K-bar from a side sheath. The edge showed keen in the soft lighting. "This is better, faster."

She snorted. "Don't flatter yourself." A shot rang out followed by a scream that cut off abruptly.

Alan looked to the statuesque blonde at his side. "Ladies first."

She rolled her eyes. "Men!"

The two apprentices ran down the hall, leaping over wet red lumps and pieces of golem. They rounded a corner to see a golem finish strangling a Sicarius with its one remaining arm. It turned to look at them with its dead plastic eyes before leaping into an elevator. The doors closed on the two of them before they could arrive. Another golem lay scattered on the floor nearby.

"Damn," Maggie fumed and pressed the up button. "These must be the elevators to the upper floors."

A couple of minutes later the elevator gave a chime and opened. The two entered and Alan hit the button for the 53rd floor. Muzak started playing as the doors closed.

Alan looked up. "What's that?"

" 'MacArthur Park,' I think."

"Not the music, you blonde bimbo, *that*."

Maggie's eyes traveled up Alan's arm, past his pointing finger to a splotchy red stain on the ceiling tiles of the elevator. "Blood, I think."

"That's what I thought. I believe there's a body up there."

"Cool."

"What does it mean?"

"Someone may have already started to do our job for us."

Alan licked his lips. "Why do this, Maggie? What's your interest?"

The big blonde grinned. "I owe Morgan. He got me out of Valhalla's grasp." Her smile became wistful. "Besides, he's cute. Why are you doing this?"

His voice seemed to come from a faraway place. "For the magic, Maggie. That's what it's always been about." He licked his lips, tasting sweat and blood, his body tensing. A battle was raging across the muscles of his face. It looked like determination versus regret.

Determination won.

His pistol came up.

He fired.

Chapter Thirty-One

Mike

Boris stood there and smiled at me. Not a nice smile, but the kind reserved for serial killers and politicians. It scared the hell out of me, but he didn't move, instead he continued to smile, savoring my fear like a fine wine.

A tonfa lay on the floor near my feet, probably dropped there by the Sicarii in their rush to pursue me. The club had been stained dead black and didn't really look like much, but in the hands of an expert, it was a deadly weapon. I knew just enough about its use to hurt myself.

When I picked it up and held it in one unsteady hand, Boris' smile grew wider, which frightened me even more. Slowly, sure I couldn't interfere; he reached under his suit jacket, drew forth a 9 mm pistol and shot me in the leg.

The bullet tore into the outside of my left thigh, through pants, skin, fat, muscle and out again, flinging blood and tissue out the back. It felt like being hit in leg with a baseball bat.

Next thing I knew, I was tasting carpet as screams tore at my throat like shards of glass, the hot pounding of my heart pushing more and more blood through the hole in my thigh.

Oh, Lord, it hurt so much!

My hands became warm, red and slick as I tried to apply pressure, to keep myself from bleeding to death. Not the first time I'd been shot, but on top of my other injuries, the beating I'd taken earlier, it was all too much. I lay there, sobbing.

A voice emerged from the depths of Boris' chest as he walked toward me, holstering his weapon. "You knock me down and make me much angry. Mr. Julian does not need you anymore, so he give you to me."

This just kept getting better and better.

"Don't do this Boris, please," I moaned, trying not to sob. "You don't have to do this."

"You are right. I *want* to do these things to you." One of his size twelves lashed out, catching me in the chin, and I saw stars.

Just as he drew his foot back again to give me another taste of shoe leather, the world decided to come apart around us.

A violent lurch had Boris on his butt in an instant. All I could do was curl up in a ball as the floor rippled, tossing me up and down, from side to side. A dull, deep, bone-rattling roar that I could feel in the roots of my teeth bounced around the suite.

A rush of bitterly cold wind bellowed through the room as windows shattered, tempered glass fragmenting into thousands of shards before falling out into the night air. The deep cold ate at me like a cancer, numbing my nose and fingertips. It also reinvigorated me, giving a jump-start to the old circulatory system.

With my leg hollering at me, a multitude of aches and pains plaguing me, and the floor rolling and humping, I still managed a one-legged frog-jump. My chin hit carpet I don't know how many times; only dogged persistence allowed me to hop and crawl on over to Boris through the snow of powdered plaster that fell from the ceiling while my nails scraped, scraped, scraped across the floor.

Through the surreal nightmare of popping light bulbs and heaving floor, the tonfa was an anchor to the reality of my escape, that and my faith. God had brought me this far, so I reckoned he still had a plan or two left for me.

Boris had his own plans. A white haze obscured my vision for a split second as a scarred fist clipped my cheek, splitting skin and spilling more of my precious blood. His other hand, grasping a 9 mm, swung about, ready to put a round between my eyes.

I swung the tonfa, hitting the gun hand below the thumb and sending the 9 bouncing away across the mat. My bloodied hands fastened on his arm, holding it steady long enough for me to sink my teeth in.

A warm salty flow of blood slid across my tongue as my teeth clamped down hard on the bones of Boris' wrist, worrying, tearing. Again and again his other fist smashed into my temple until finally he tore loose from my grasp in a gout of crimson.

Before I could roll away, the shaking stopped, leaving nothing but an eerie silence, broken here and there by the occasional pop and groan.

A big patent leather sole found my left hand and stamped down *hard*. Amid the gut-wrenching agony, I heard the crack of my own bones breaking like matchsticks. When Boris' clodhopper moved away from my hand, I saw pinkish gray sticks poking through my flesh.

And I thought the gunshot hurt.

Boris' shoe slammed into my already broken nose and that was lights out.

The Dreaming City Lounge was full near to bursting and I felt uncomfortable as hell walking in wearing civilian clothes. Five dollars cover charge! I felt like a rube for paying, but did anyway, attracted by the lure of a Def Leppard cover band.

Damn I felt old, shoving my way through writhing bodies and cigarette smoke. My time in Iraq was starting to feel like a dream … a dream of a brotherhood I wished I hadn't left.

Muscling between two beefy types with pop-collar rugby shirts, I arrived at the bar and held up a hand, a sawbuck between my fingers to flag attention.

"Whatcha need?" Yelled the pretty little bartender with teased hair and too much lipstick.

I hollered back over the raucous crowd, "Draft!" pointing to a tap.

"Light beer?"

"No! Real beer!"

She smiled and reached into a cooler for a frosted mug.

The band came on stage the same time the pretty bartender came back with my beer. The lights dimmed and "Rock of Ages" slammed out of the speakers. Too loud, not even Def Leppard would subject their fan to that kind of auditory overload. People drifted onto the dance floor to gyrate to the beat.

As I stood there, drinking ice-cold beer and listening to music through what felt like bleeding ears, the incongruity of me being there while many of my men were laid out in private lots or Arlington made me want to cry. It didn't seem fair that blood still thrummed in my veins while theirs had been spilled onto desert sand.

Damn, I was uncomfortable. My polo shirt and khakis felt prickly on my skin and, while I loved the music, the people there put me on edge … too carefree, blithely ignorant of the horrors the world had to offer. Or maybe they did know what lay around the corner, what lurked beneath the bed late at night waiting to strike. Maybe that's why they partied so hard, drank so much, treated sex like a sport instead an intimate act.

I didn't belong. Not there, not with those happy, desperate, dancing people, drinking, shouting, flirting, sweating, and cussing. That place was, those people were, too loud, too … too … lost.

I was lost, too.

"Hey, Sergeant."

Sergeant? I hadn't been a Sergeant for three months. Turning around, cold beer sloshing over the rim of the mug onto my fingers, I smiled in pleasant surprise at the short, stocky man in desert gear standing not more than three feet away.

"Hi, Corporal, what are you doing here?"

"Question is, Sergeant, what are *you* doing here?"

Strange, I didn't wonder why an armed and geared man was standing in a rock-n-roll bar smack dab in the middle of Omaha. Nobody looked at the Corporal, no one even came close to him and the place was packed elbow-to-cheek.

The truth came to me slowly, easing into my mind as if through osmosis. "You're dead, Corporal."

He smiled. "That's right, Sergeant."

Goekenhauer. That was his name. Ben Goekenhauer. "You took a round to the neck, Ben," I said slowly, almost in a stupor.

"Right again, Mike." The desert gear was gone, replaced by a navy blue Van Hagar t-shirt and ripped blue jeans.

"Am I dead?"

"Are you?"

The beer slid past my teeth and I gulped at the brew as if it contained the answers I needed. "Don't feel dead. Feel fine." Physically I felt great.

"Well, then, Mike. That's your answer."

"What are you doing here, Ben?"

The Corporal gently took the cold mug from my hand and took a drink, then gave it back. "Ah, that's good. I missed beer something awful."

"You didn't answer my question."

"I came to see you, Mike.

A girl bumped into me, a soft hip against my thigh. An innocent looking strawberry blonde in white shorts offered a sweet smile of apology before moving on. The band started up with "Let's get Rocked."

"That girl. I know that girl."

"Yeah, Mike. You met her here and went home with her when the bar closed."

I smiled. "That's right. Jenny … She was so sweet."

"You dated her for about three months before you realized the calling you felt was for the Church."

My voice became distant as memories slowly bobbed to the surface. "She cried when I told her. I think she really cared for me, maybe even loved me a little, but she said she understood."

"She did, Mike, although it broke her heart. A couple of years after you two broke up she met a man named Herrick and married him.

They had three kids and, for a while, were happy. She died of breast cancer last year."

Oh, damn. I felt a lump in my throat for a woman I'd only known for a few months but had cared deeply about—only not as much as I cared for the Lord.

"It was at St. Frances Cabrini Catholic Church near the river where I heard my calling for the first time," I mused, mind skipping and jumping like droplets of water on a hot griddle. "Tuesday. Yes, a Tuesday when the traffic was light and the sun was bright. I was fixing to head to Council Bluffs, but I saw that old building and it sang to me." The memory moved sluggishly through the cotton that shrouded my mind. "I just parked the car and walked in, lost in a world of emotions and thoughts I couldn't articulate. Pews, the carpet of the nave, nothing registered except the altar and the image of Christ on the cross." My voice grew thick. "I think that before I even made it to the altar I knew. I knew—the way I knew the feel of desert sand in the palms of my hands—that service to the Lord was my calling, my truth … and I was no longer lost."

"I like that Sergeant. I really do." Ben was now dressed in denim shorts, a green t and Converse sneakers.

"Am I dying?"

"Didn't you just ask me that?"

"No, earlier I asked you if I was dead. Dying is a whole different deck of cards."

"True, true." He snagged a cola-drink from a passing waitress, who ignored him just as everyone else did. "No, Sergeant, you're not dying."

"Then what is all this?" I gestured to the bar, the people, to the band that was playing "Pour Some Sugar on Me."

"I don't know. This is your place, your construct, not mine. For some reason this place holds significance for you."

"Hmm. Strange."

"Listen, Sergeant, I'm here to tell you something. Something important."

"Is it urgent?"

"Nothing is urgent in this place. Here we are between tick and tock of the clock."

"Good. Good." I took a long pull from the still-cold mug. "I want to listen to the music."

"Sounds good, Sergeant. Sounds good."

So we listened to classic '80s rock while drinking cold ones, feet tapping to the beat. The band did a credible job and the crowd was relatively well behaved. It was nice, standing there amid a sea of people who just wanted to have a good time and relax. As for myself, the thought of the real world didn't intrude on my consciousness, almost as if it couldn't. There was no urgency, no pain, no Boris.

The house lights came on, the band left the stage and the bartenders hollered out "last call." A momentary spike of pain, like a flash headache, ran from temple to temple and I knew my brief moment of piece was at an end.

Ben tapped my shoulder. "Ready, Sergeant?"

My heart sank. It was time, I guessed. "Yes, Corporal."

"Scream, Sergeant. Scream loud and long."

Scream? "What d—"

Pain, blinding and harsh in my side, a digging, slicing, and hot sear that brought me full out of whatever la-la land I had been in.

Boris' nasty face was inches from mine and he smiled into the teeth of my agony, enjoying every nerve-twitching moment. "I give you pain you don't believe, God-man."

I looked down and nearly gagged. Hands bound behind my back, I was once again in that damn ugly chair placed in the center of the exercise mat that dominated the main floor of the suite. Cold air from the broken window froze the sweat on my naked skin and my Danzinger's shirt had been torn from my body so I was naked from the waist up. The capper to this whole situation was my left side. Boris had sliced me open a treat and had jammed a pair of pliers into the wound, grasping a rib with the filthy metal. I could *feel* the ragged ridges of the gripping appliance tearing at the bone.

Boris laughed at the horrified look on my face.

"What you say, God-man? What you say now?"

A voice of a comrade came through the fog of pain in my side.

Scream, Sergeant. Scream loud and long.

My eye rolled to meet Boris' mad gaze and I screamed.

Loud and long.

Chapter Thirty-Two

Morgan

Alan fired, but Maggie's head wasn't where it had been just a moment before. From the corner of her eye she'd seen the sick greed on Alan's face, had seen the pistol come up, barrel aimed straight at her head.

Head rocking back, she felt the bullet whisper past her nose, the heat of it making her skin tingle.

"Son-of-a-bitch!" she spat, making a grab for the pistol.

Both apprentices uttered Strength at that same moment. To Maggie, it smelled of oatmeal raisin cookies, to Alan clove cigarettes. Each glared at the other with raw hatred, knowing that only one would leave that elevator alive.

"Why?" grated Maggie, a big hand gripping the barrel of Alan's weapon, the metal hot against her palm.

Face red, a pulsing vein showing large in his forehead, he answered, "W-what the Valhalla League offered ... couldn't pass it up ..."

Instead of responding, Maggie shouted Vigor, inhaling the sweet odor of strawberries and Alan yelled Grace, releasing the musky smell of a great cat.

He let go of the weapon and immediately Maggie took swing, trying to punch the butt of the pistol through her opponent's skull, but missed. She tried again and again, but Alan was always just out of reach, ducking and weaving with uncommon fluidity.

Back and forth, back and forth they danced in the elevator's confined space, Maggie striking with unflagging stamina and Alan dodging with preternatural elegance.

The elevator doors opened.

More blood and gore was smeared about the hallway, marking the remaining golems' movements. Alan, leaping over a sweeping leg, made for the opening. He almost made it.

No matter how graceful he might have been, once his back was turned in flight, Maggie had her chance and she made the most of it.

One muscular hand clamped down like a vise on the calf of the fleeing man and Maggie, standing a good six foot two, weighing 190 pounds, a one-woman battalion, fell on him like the wrath of God.

Maggie had been a champion in the League of Valhalla for two years running, fighting men much bigger and stronger than her to the delight of the Asgardians and their noisome crowd. One of her opponents described her as "the she-wolf from hell." She won so many fights that she'd become the darling of the Asgardians, that is until she had used magic in one of her bouts. That had landed her hard into trouble and a concrete cell under a League warehouse.

Alan kicked, thrashed and bucked, but he couldn't escape her furious grip, not even with Strength. A sledgehammer elbow broke two ribs on his right side, caving them like rotten sticks, puncturing a lung. Alan opened his mouth to scream, but his tortured midsection wouldn't let him. Maggie's follow-through once again tore into the damaged ribs and the convulsion that followed threw her clean off.

Alan folded in around himself, blood spraying from his gaping mouth as the life left his body.

"You stinking piece of garbage!" Maggie screamed, rising to her feet and giving the body a swift kick. It flew through the air and splattered against the wall, leaving a red imprint like an all-red Matisse cutout.

Eventually the Strength leeched from her system and she began to calm, staring at the shattered remains of what was once a trusted comrade. "Aw … shit," she moaned. "Why did you have to go and do that, you bastard?"

Her head came up as a scream of frustration split the air.

It wasn't Maggie's scream that filled my head at that moment, but Mike's, I knew it. It went on and on, a deep roar of pain that shriveled my balls.

"Follow me," I shouted, not waiting for Cain as I tore off down the hallway.

Everything blurred as my focus became diamond-hard on saving Mike, my friend. How strange was that? A *friend*, a comfort I'd gone the first two decades without, believed I didn't need. Now, in an effort to save one, I stormed the ramparts of evil with equal parts fear and dread running rampant in my veins.

I rounded a corner in time to see a crash test dummy, most of the chamois flesh stripped from its metal frame, burst through a door as if it were made of tissue paper. The scream came loud through the open doorway.

Chapter Thirty-Three

Mike

I screamed and screamed into Boris' face, screamed until my lungs burned with the effort, screamed until my throat burned with acid, scouring my vocal cords.

Boris seemed to drink it up, enjoying the spectacle immensely.

Crash! The door flew off its hinges, barely missing Boris and flying through the open space where one of the floor-to-ceiling windows had been.

We both stared in disbelief as a cross between a crash test dummy and the *Terminator* leaped through the doorway, metal hands outstretched for Boris' throat.

As a former soldier, I'd had some curiosity about my Soviet counterparts, the Spetsnaz. Highly trained, brutalized until pain was just another feeling to be dismissed, they were the bogeymen of Red Army, the best (or worst) of the best.

Boris proved equal to his calling because there was no hesitation as he met the mechanical monster, grabbing a metal arm and twisting his body to throw the thing over and across his hip. The monster flew through the air, landing near the broken windows.

All I could do was watch, dumbfounded, as Boris charged the dummy. It stood there waiting, arms stretched wide while the

Russian leapt. Apparently the creature didn't have the brains to figure the odds, because the outcome of a two-hundred-fifty-pound man taking on what I took to be a one-hundred-eighty-pound mannequin head-on seemed easy to calculate.

The soles of Boris' size twelves impacted solidly on the dummy's midsection, sending the thing sailing out past the broken window and into the night, where it quickly dropped out of sight.

Just as the giant Russian turned back to me, I heard the most wonderful voice in the world say, "Don't you dare move, Boris."

Chapter Thirty-Four

Morgan

I didn't pull the trigger. Don't get me wrong, I wanted to. The sight of Mike—battered and bloody, sitting on an ugly steel chair looking like death warmed over, face beaten into shapelessness—froze my blood, but something stayed my finger. Maybe it was the incredibly efficient, graceful way Boris had disposed of the golem, the terrible beauty of his lethality. Whatever it was, I let him live for that moment.

"Don't you dare move, Boris." I really, really wanted to shoot him in the worst way. It was like an itch you just had to scratch before it drove you mad. "You okay, Mike?"

My friend laughed, a sad, sick sound. "Depends on your definition, I guess."

I wasted no time in laying Healing on him, keeping one eye on Boris, who was glaring hot death at me. I could feel Mike grow stronger, but not enough, so I laid on another and another until the bruises on his body faded and his face became recognizable again.

Fatigue pulled at me, but I didn't care. Mike was alive. A flick of a K-bar and the zip ties holding his wrists together parted.

"So this is the infamous clergyman who causes the Sicarii to quail and quiver in their boots." Cain stepped into the suite, smiling at

Mike with what seemed to be genuine affection. "And I note the figure of a surly Russian who must be the dreaded Boris of whom such tales are spun as to unman ordinary mortals."

"Interesting turn of phrase," began Mike, rubbing some life back into his hands. "I vote we delay any further discussion until we are safe. Let's get out of here *now*."

"Sit, Boris," I commanded. The Russian just glared, so I shot the cuff of his expensive slacks. "Sit, or I take out your ankles, like last time." That put him on his butt right quick. It was then I noted we were standing on several wrestling mats. We had to be in a training suite where the guards kept their skills sharp. That meant Julian was close by.

"Hey, boss. Hey, handsome," Maggie's deep but very feminine voice came from behind. "Is this tall drink of cute the priest you were after? Too bad he belongs to God."

Mike's expression at seeing Maggie for the first time was worth the price of admission. She was a lot of woman to take in all at once.

Cain gave her a once over. "Alan?"

Her face closed down. "He was on the League's payroll. Tried to do me in."

I cast my mind back to the Seeing, the second half of which I had paid scant attention to while searching for Mike, and gave Cain a nod.

Mike cut in before Cain could reply, sounding more than a little frustrated. "I don't know what's going on, but we have a psychopathic Russian to deal with. Anyone have a pair of handcuffs or three?"

"Sorry, man," I said, not taking my eyes off of Boris. "You're right."

"Actually, a better idea springs new-formed to mind," Cain mused. "Mr. Heart should pursue the perilous quest while Michael, Maggie and I provide our overlarge friend here with some much needed containment." His shades moved my way. "Go. Find the Primal and set it free. Michael will be safe in our august company."

"Mike, you mind, man?" I was half-afraid he'd fall over despite the Healings.

"If you trust these people, then it's okay with me. Do what you must do. I'm pretty sure Julian is on the opposite side of the building, well past the elevators."

"Thanks, man." To Cain, "Be careful, Boris is the most dangerous non-magus I've ever met." That earned me a smile at full power. I was about to run out, but an impulse that had nothing to do with danger seized me. Grabbing Maggie by the shoulders, I laid a big one on her moist lips.

For a moment I thought she'd clean my clock right there, but instead her arms encircled me and she returned the kiss with interest.

When we both finally came up for air, lights sparkled in her baby blues. "Let's go, gorgeous."

I shook my head. "Sorry, Blondie, but this is a Family thing. I have to fly solo."

She scored quite a few points by nodding, instinctively understanding. "If we survive this, handsome, you're taking me someplace nice."

I kissed the end of her nose and she dimpled prettily. "You got it, Blondie." And with that I ran out, looking for Julian. I had to put an end to all this before New York paid the price.

Chapter Thirty-Five

Mike

Morgan was dressed like an SAS commando, all in black, with a black knit cap and blackout makeup on his face. He bristled top to bottom with weapons. The other man, a lean, strong figure, towered over him. He gave the impression of solidity, so much so that you would imagine the Washington Monument crumbling before he did. He wore the kind of sunglasses favored by skiers, and when he spoke, the lilting style was a mixture of colonial and southern formal that made my ears want to pack it in for the evening.

The woman was dressed the same, but looked like she'd be more comfortable with a sword in hand, collecting the souls of the dead from the battlefield for transport to Valhalla. When Morgan kissed her, I saw a real spark there between the two, a glimmer of something … divine.

After Morgan ran off, the woman turned my way and gave me a once-over. "Get a good eyeful, tall, dark and priestly?" she asked sourly.

I rubbed my moustache. "Was it at first sight? Or while you were planning this little shindig?" It was a random shot, but by the look of her, it scored.

"How did you—?"

"I may be priest, but I'm not blind."

The long, lean man broke in. "As illuminating as the new-found romantic nature of my apprentice may prove, I do believe that introductions are in order. The lovely lady whose resemblance to a Valkyrie is more than coincidental is Maggie. I, sir priest, am Cain." At my startled look he nodded. "Yes, *that* Cain. Brother of Abel. And while I realize that a priest may be brimming with questions both practical and philosophical for a gentleman such as myself, we have other, more pressing, concerns." He waved a pistol at the Russian, who had remained seated throughout.

Cain? *Cain?* A few weeks ago the revelation would have had greater impact. Considering everything that had happened, it now seemed par for the course.

"Okay ... Cain. Let's tie him up." What I wanted was to fillet Boris into Russian cutlets, but I was still a man of God.

The tall man flashed a huge smile. "When I arrived upon the scene, young ... Morgan was in the process of providing you several Healings. Would it be incorrect to assume that you have suffered most egregiously at the hands of the infamous Boris, the Mad Russian?"

"If you're asking me if he beat the living daylights out of me, then yes."

Maggie cut in. "He looks nasty."

I snorted. "Nastiest piece of work I've ever come across."

She aimed a Tec-9.

"Stop!" I shouted, appalled. "We don't kill prisoners."

Her look told me I was a few cans short of a six-pack, but I just stared her down until she lowered her weapon. "What do we do with the bastard, then?" she asked.

Before I could answer, Cain stepped forward, coming within three feet of Boris. "I have been informed that you are a force to be reckoned with, an extraordinary fighter of incalculable skill."

It took Boris a moment to digest that, but when he did, he tipped a spare nod.

"Wonderful!" Cain replied. "In my time I have studied the manly arts of the squared circle and consider myself a pugilist of no mean ability. To this end I have but one question." He stepped back, lowered his weapon and smiled like a shark sizing up its breakfast. "Do you want a shot at the champ?"

Boris stood, his smile matching Cain's mean for mean. "Oh, yes."

Chapter Thirty-Six

Morgan

Down the hall, past the elevators, not slowing, not stopping, I had to go in straight and quick, no hesitation. I was twenty years younger than Julian, but I was certain he'd be no pushover. He'd be aware that we were in the building and therefore on guard.

I skidded to a stop in front of the door to the suite and, as loud as I could, summoned Force. The metal door burst from its hinges, flipping end over end into the room; I followed right after.

Crack! A hit to my right thigh and I went down, blood spraying.

Crack! Another shot to the thick meat of my left thigh.

Crack! My right arm sprouted gore and the pistol fell from nerveless fingers.

Crack! My left arm became an unfeeling lump of meat dangling from my shoulder. Blood trailed down my chin from where I'd bitten my lip and fire consumed my thrashing limbs.

"I have to say, I very much enjoyed that." The voice, snide and gloating, came from behind.

Healing/cinnamon, Healing/cinnamon again and again. Bullets spat out of my body in rapid succession and the awful pain of torn flesh and shattered bone faded quickly, a sweet relief.

"Well, Oliver," said Julian from somewhere out of sight. "Not very original, charging into the fray like that."

"Oh, man ... that smarts." I slowly rose to my feet to see Annabeth at the broken doorway with twin 9s pointed at me, both barrels still smoking, a self-satisfied smirk on her face. The sight of her made me livid with rage and sick to my stomach. She must have seen my anger because she smiled even wider, with even more cruelty.

"Take off your Kevlar, Olivier," Julian said. I turned to see him lounging on the stairs leading to the second story. He was dressed immaculately in a dark Saville Row suit, every stitch, every hair perfectly in place despite the earthquake. In fact, the whole suite looked untouched by violence, a haven of normalcy in a mad world.

Slowly, I shrugged out of the vest.

Julian took a step down. "You know, I have read that silly little memoir your friend the priest was carrying with him." He laughed, an ugly sound. "You certainly think the world of yourself, do you not? No, do not bother answering. I was much amused at your conclusions, wrong as they were.

"You believe you are the last of the Line? And that that little fact will afford you some measure of protection? Let me set the record straight, young man." All trace of amusement fled his face as he stopped ten feet away and drew a pistol from a shoulder holster. A Sig Sauer P229. "You are not the Redeemer, you are just a talented magus who thinks too much of himself. Now shed your weaponry. Slowly."

I complied. "Then how come I knew all thirty of the Terrible Words the Silver offered?"

Julian shook his head dismissively. "It is not the quantity of the Words, it is the ability to use them without killing yourself." At my puzzled look, he sighed. "The Words the Silver offered exacts a toll from a body, depleting it of vital energy. The Redeemer would be the magus who could use the Silver without slowly killing himself. Is that not correct, sir?"

From hidden speakers all around came a familiar voice. "Correct, Julian. Hello, Olivier."

Well, hell. The Voice. My stomach took a plunge.

The speakers squawked, then that same terribly beautiful voice continued. "Trust me, my boy, you are *not* the Redeemer. You are *not* the last. There are always others. Tell him everything, Julian."

Chapter Thirty-Seven

Mike

Cain stripped to the waist after handing me a pistol, a Glock. I liked a heftier weapon, like a .45, but at that moment I would have been happy with a peashooter.

The Russian kept grinning like a wolf and it took every ounce of self-control not to unload, but I sent a prayer to the Lord for strength and remained true to my calling. Besides, I'd already killed a man that day and that was burden enough—more terrible than I could explain.

Boris stripped off jacket, tie and shirt, revealing a massive torso covered in black hair. Scars crisscrossed skin stretching tight over great slabs of muscle that moved like greased ropes. Black tattoos, Cyrillic characters, covered shoulders and belly. He looked like a fair-skinned gorilla with a bad attitude.

In contrast, Cain looked puny, almost skinny, but almost anyone would next to Boris. If you took a close look, you could see the sharp definition in Cain's muscles.

Then he took his sunglasses off. I longed for a rosary but had to be content with crossing myself. It was driven home to me that this man was *the* Cain, the first murderer. Off-white, slightly blue irises centered with pitch-black pupils. A cold shiver ran up and down my spine, matched by the freezing wind entering the suite.

Cain started removing his boots and that's when Boris attacked, leaping like a gazelle, great fist slashing forward toward Cain's skull.

It never connected.

If it had, Cain's neck would have no doubt snapped like a twig, but the tall man had simply flickered as if he had been edited from reality for a moment. The knobbly fist swished past Cain's nose by a whisker. Boris almost overbalanced, but righted himself quickly. That didn't stop Cain from taking advantage. One long arm shot out and tagged Boris on the nose, a tap, or so it seemed.

Blood gushed from the big man's nostrils and he recoiled in surprise. Clearly getting tagged was a rare experience for him. He licked the blood from his lips and waded in, fists and feet flying.

Cain didn't give him a chance to score. Moving like mercury across a plate, he rolled and slipped everywhere, always one step ahead of the increasingly furious Russian. Every now and then he'd throw a jab—nothing painful, but after a couple of minutes they began to tell. Boris started to slow, his own jabs becoming more and more wild and unfocused as rage and exhaustion began to take their toll.

"Stop moving!" he yelled, face red with fury, spit flying from his lips.

Cain did, his smile unwavering, and spread his arms wide. An invitation for Boris to do his worst.

The two stared at each other for a few tense moments; Boris, harried, wild, and Cain, calm, collected. "You fight good," Boris panted, unfazed by the other man's eyes.

"I've had time to practice," replied Cain almost amicably, lowering his arms.

Boris nodded and casually placed his hands in his pockets. "Why should I fight, then?"

"Because if you don't—"

Swift as a snake, one of Boris' hands whipped out, holding a knife. Before Maggie and I could blink, the blade sprang free with a hiss, flying faster than thought toward Cain's throat.

Chapter Thirty-Eight

Morgan

"There are ... crèches all over the world, places where the direct descendants of the Founder are raised," Julian said behind the safety of his Sig. Annabeth leaned against the wall beside the doorway, a smirk on her lips and the glint of madness in her eyes. "You thought Henri, Julian II and Philip where your only brothers, but the truth is you have dozens. You have met several, including Fergus and Burke."

"B-Burke?" I killed my brother? I committed fratricide? Nausea assaulted my belly.

"Quite. The truth of the matter is you have no cousins. Every one of those you've met are your siblings. Including Annabeth."

I couldn't help it ... I puked all over my shoes while my sister stood there and laughed. The Voice joined her, sounding like sugarcoated shit.

Chapter Thirty-Nine

Mike

In the milliseconds before Boris pushed the button on the ballistic knife, Cain said a Word.

The blade, that paper-thin projectile, bounced off of thin air ten inches in front of Cain's unprotected throat and shattered with a faint *tink*. My mind boggled. What was I seeing? Beside me, Maggie breathed, "I gotta learn that one … smells like honeysuckle."

Again and again Boris pushed the button on the ballistic knife, two more fine blades springing free to pierce the air toward Cain. Twice more the blades shattered musically in front of Cain.

Boris' shoulders slumped and Cain's smile, which had been plastered to his face the entire time of the fight, left his face. "You tortured a man of God. You work for the most evil people on the planet, people with demon's résumés, and you have been content to do so. You, sir, offend me!" It was Cain's turn for red-faced fury. He took a step forward, body trembling with the force of his anger.

"I have lived longer than a man should and I have done things of which I am certainly not proud of, but you … you …" Words seem to fail him, which I gathered was a rare event. *"You really piss me off!"* he screamed.

Chapter Forty

Morgan

It was the laughter that galvanized me, especially that of the Voice with its creepy humor and slime-covered hilarity. As I knelt there, wiping vomit from my lips and listening to them enjoy my humiliation, rage and frustration built up to a point where I just exploded.

Nothing wrong with Annabeth's reflexes, I soon discovered. As I sprang toward her, she put two rounds into my midsection that ripped through both intestine and stomach. The acid pain of it nearly took my breath away.

As my knuckles connected to the point of her chin, another round ripped through my torso, shredding a lung. Feeling her sag, I screamed a Healing, and as I pulled her away from the wall, twisting my body behind hers, I screamed another. One of her 9s hit the floor with a *thud*, but I had the other in my grasp before it could slip through her limp fingers.

Julian's Sig barked three times in rapid succession. All three found Annabeth's torso without penetrating her Kevlar. Had she been conscious, the shots would have hurt like hell.

I returned fire. Like Julian, I squeezed the trigger three times. One round clipped his ear, coloring his graying hair red. The other two bullets missed. At least his ear now matched mine.

Eyes wild with fury, Julian fired again, this time hitting Annabeth between the eyes, a shot that exited the back of her skull. The flattened and fragmented bullet scraped across my cheek and decorated my face with blood, bone and brain.

What had been a semi-conscious handful was now dead weight, and I had to snap off a Strength to hold her upright as my shield. The beginnings of Backlash tugged at my muscles, warring with the adrenaline coursing through my veins.

We both fired again simultaneously, his round catching me in the knee with sickening force and mine taking him in the groin, ruining his chances for future good times. As I folded, dropping Annabeth in a heap, I shouted another Healing. The cracking pain of my shattered kneecap had nearly made me lose consciousness.

From Julian all I could hear was a whistling whine, high pitched and agonized, while I watched the bullet pop out of my knee. The shards of the patella shifted and flowed together as it healed and I bit my lip at the itchy pain of it.

I rose jerkily to my feet and moved to where Julian writhed and bled, too agonized to mouth his own Healing. My vision went in and out, blurring as Backlash started to take hold, the pull of unconsciousness almost too strong to withstand.

"Stop right there, Olivier," the Voice piped up with a screech of feedback. "We can arrange something equitable here. Don't do anything stupid."

I didn't take my eyes off Julian. "I'm way past intelligent. Stupid is all I got left." Backlash sweat coated my cheeks and forehead and I realized that I was a far cry from okay. It was absurdly easy to fall to my knees at Julian's side and grab his lapels.

"Where is the Primal, you son of a bitch?" I snarled.

All he could do was gasp and cry.

"What do you care about a Primal, Olivier?" The Voice said casually, as if ordering breakfast.

"If I don't get the Primal back, Earth will swallow New York whole to retrieve it." Things went sideways for a moment as I almost succumbed to oblivion. Sheer force of will kept my eyes open.

"Between you and me, Olivier, we can take care of Earth. Just put an end to Julian and you can assume the mantle of the Patriarch."

Just the thought of that made me want to puke up my shoes. Instead of answering, I mouthed a Vigor and the rush of magic stabilized the world around me. I knew I'd pay for that later.

Taking a deep breath, I directed Truth at Julian and inhaled garlic. "Where is Primal Water, Julian?"

I watched as his eyes went from a pain glaze to the glassy look of the half-asleep. "Jacket pocket," he slurred.

Of course he would have it on him.

Chapter Forty-One

Mike

From Maggie's reaction, I could tell she had never seen Cain angry. For my own part, I never wanted to see it again.

Cain and the Russian came together swift and hard. I fancied I could *feel* the thunder of their impact down to the roots of my teeth.

The two heaved, twisting their bodies to and fro for leverage, the muscles of their torsos and arms standing out like cables. Grunting and sweating, they remained fused together in combat, neither achieving the upper hand.

When the end came, it was as brutal as it was swift. One second the two combatants were locked together like pieces in a jigsaw puzzle, the next Boris was flying across the mat to slam headfirst into drywall, cracking the sheetrock and leaving a red smear. He fell to the floor in a stupor.

"You must realize, Boris," panted Cain, slowly wobbling toward the fallen man. "While I am indeed a murderer, a man who despicably slew his own brother and who had the audacity to lie to God about it, I never in all my long history on this fertile earth have ever tortured another human being. I find the notion loathsome, repugnant."

"Cain—" I began. A raised hand stilled my tongue.

"You see, Boris," he continued as if I had never interrupted. "I regret what I have done, not because of the curse I find myself under, but because it was wrong, evil. I choose to shy away from evil, to set my feet upon the path that God has laid down for mankind. God may never forgive my worthless soul, as is his right, but that will never stop me from seeking forgiveness.

"You, however, have willingly chosen the road to darkness." He loomed over the Russian, who lay moaning. "Evil is your *choice*." He fastened his big hands onto Boris and heaved.

Maybe Cain used Strength, although I didn't hear him actually say the Word. Whatever the means, the outcome was the same; he lifted Boris like a sack of wet cement over his head, swaying slightly with the strain.

"It is … a war … between good and … evil," he gasped, turning slowly. "In …war there are … *casualties*."

With that he threw Boris screaming through the shattered window.

Being a priest, I should have felt horrified by the act, but Cain was right about one thing: in the war between good and evil, there's bound to be casualties.

Chapter Forty-Two

Morgan

Jacket pocket. Check. Something hard and cold met my fingers. A vial. A simple vial made of black plastic. So small. How could something so devastatingly powerful reside in such a small space?

I guess size doesn't matter after all.

A wave of dizziness swept over me as the Vigor started to fade around the edges.

"Put that back, Olivier," the Voice said equably. "Don't make me stop you."

I stood, running the cold bottle over my steaming forehead, the sensation almost as pleasurable as an orgasm. "Oh, why don't you shut up?"

"Olivier!"

"Go pound sand."

A hand like granite with joints clamped around my ankle, squeezing, and the world went white as bones shattered like glass.

A voice like crushed gravel rattling in a tin box came from Julian. "You should have listened, little meat puppet." Eyes black as sin stared out from a familiar yet distorted face. The face of a demon pressing through Julian's flesh.

Oh shit …

The Julian demon smiled with a thousand needle teeth, a grisly grin of hate and dark joy that I could feel even through the world of agony in my ankle.

I raised the 9 and pulled the trigger. One black eye exploded in a shower of dark fluid that spattered the carpeting, hissing and sizzling. The hard hand let go of my leg and I scrambled away, a Healing bursting from between my teeth.

Tearing pain like the mother of all ulcers speared my gut as Backlash took me, but my ankle writhed and set itself so I was able to stumble to my feet. The open doorway beckoned.

Before I staggered out of the suite, I stole a look behind me. Big mistake. The thing that had been Julian was on its hands and knees, ready to rise, its eye already whole. It gave me a look as it slowly gathered itself and I could feel its power, the unimaginable evil and spite. This was no mere demon, not just a cancer on the world. What shone through the thin tissue of what used to be Julian's flesh was the essence of one of the original fallen angels who had followed Lucifer to the Abyss. A Duke of Hell, the Devil's right hand.

The cold of the vial was matched by the ice that ran through my bowels and down to the soles of my feet. With horror at my back and fear fueling my feet, I attempted a run down the hallway toward my companions, toward some semblance of safety. Water needed to be freed and if I could throw the vial out the window, it would shatter on the concrete below and the Primal would be released to run into the storm drains and eventually out to sea.

Good plan; too bad I felt too much like a pile of refried crap to outrun the awful thing that pursued me. I could feel its attention on me, its repulsive regard. My shoulder hit the wall as I stumbled and my vision clouded as more of the Vigor receded, leaving me weaker, more prone to the ravages of Backlash.

I made it to the elevators before my Strength gave out and fatigue attacked, forcing me to my knees.

"OLIVIER!" The shout shook the hallway and I felt impossibly heavy footsteps draw close. It came to me then that I should've found a sink in the suite and poured the Primal out, but I hadn't been thinking that far ahead.

Nothing to do but go for it; I used Strength then vomited blood onto the elevator doors as nails raked my stomach. Getting to my feet was a no go, so I stuck my fingers into the crack of the elevator doors and *pulled*. I guess I used too much force because the doors *slammed* open, revealing the darkness of the shaft before me.

"Morgan!" cried Mike from the end of the hall. Good ... alive and away from Boris. That made me happy, but I was too tired to appreciate it much. He seemed alarmed for some reason. A hard footstep from behind told me why. My chickens had come home and roosting wasn't on their psychopathic minds.

Who wants to live forever anyway? I bet Cain would say it ain't so hot.

I pitched forward into the darkness.

Chapter Forty-Three

Morgan

A girl I dated once told me that slow motion was a favorite technique of filmmakers during the '60s and '70s, that if you choose a dozen films at random from that period, more than half would contain a slo-mo sequence.

That's what it felt like, falling down the elevator shaft, the rectangle of light from the doorway above growing steadily smaller. Strangely, I felt okay about the whole affair; my body was giving out anyway, ravaged by Backlash.

I thought I heard my name echoing down the shaft, but I had my mind on other things, like the vial. Before I fell, I had started to remove the lid, by the time I'd fallen twenty feet, it was to my lips and I was drinking.

Another twenty feet and absolute zero shot down my throat into my gut, freezing it solid. Wow … you'd think that would hurt, but all I felt was a numbing slosh in my stomach, followed by lassitude.

Two more floors. Long shaft, the cables blurred past my shoulder. At least the end would be quick. From far away came a roaring like the end of the world. It came to me that I felt pretty good; the Backlash was easier on me than I expected.

Thump.

Why wasn't I dead? I'd hit hard enough. Oh, a body beneath me. That was lucky, a soft-landing that kept my brains from decorating the elevator top. Couldn't feel my legs, though.

Then the world unfolded before my eyes.

Chapter Forty-Four

Mike

Maggie led the way down the hall, with me hot on her heels. Cain said a Word and exhaustion melted from his features. Vigor, I guess. He could have passed us both, but he stayed by my side, perhaps as a protector.

"OLIVIER!" The shout rang through our bones; sounding like it came from the pits of the Abyss. We redoubled our efforts and arrived in time to see Morgan, bloodied and torn, kneeling at the entrance to the same elevator shaft I'd used earlier.

Behind him, not five feet away, loomed Julian, but it wasn't Julian, not exactly. Some awful thing pressed against the inside of his face, distorting it into a monstrosity, and his clothes were far too small; the thing inside was too big for his mortal form. Both eyes glowed black, a negation of light that drank the color from everything around. Black fluid dripped from its chin.

Morgan looked at me for a brief moment, and I could tell from his face he knew that we wouldn't arrive in time to keep him from being mashed into jelly. A faint smile flickered across his face and I knew what he would do. The moment stretched, time becoming rubbery and plastic. Then he fell.

Maggie and I screamed our denial. The thing that was Julian

roared its anger through hundreds of slim, silver teeth. It made as if to jump after Morgan, no doubt undaunted by the prospect, but Cain shouted a Word that caused it to stumble backwards ten feet.

While I ran toward the shaft, Cain leapt forward as if jet propelled, hammering both feet into the thing's chest. It hardly budged and Cain fell to the floor to the sound of snapping bones. I didn't pay attention after that; I was too busy staring down the shaft looking for some sign of my friend. Maggie also stared into the darkness, tears streaming from her sky-blue eyes.

"Do you think he—?" she began.

"No. I'm afraid not." A fragile thing inside me broke with the sound of snapping wire. My friend was dead and there was nothing I could do for him.

There was, however, something I could do to avenge him.

AD 590, Pope Gregory revised a list of sins first linked to the fourth-century monk Evagrius Ponticus: Lust, Gluttony, Greed, Envy, Pride, Discouragement, and Wrath. It was this last that filled me to the brim, but I wasn't sure it was a sin because in my hands it became a weapon.

God used His wrath to smite the wicked, the evil ones, with a cold clean precision like a scalpel made of ice. That's how I felt—icy and calm but consumed with an anger I'd never known. I had no cross, no rosary to focus my ire, but I didn't care.

As I turned to face the Beast, Cain flew past, hurled with contemptuous ease by the Julian-thing. He landed forty feet away and rolled bonelessly, coming to rest broken and bleeding.

"Back!" I screamed, holding out a hand, palm forward, at the thing. It flinched. "In God's name I cast thee out!" Once again it flinched but didn't move from where it stood. It was taller and more massive than before; Julian's suit jacket was torn at the shoulders. Bullets spat from Maggie's Tec-9, riddling the creature, but it shrugged them off as if they were bothersome flies.

"Little priest," the thing drooled, dark spit hissing on the carpet. "You are only human. I AM MEPHISTOPHELES!"

All my anger evaporated in an instant, blown out by the force of the fiend's presence. Mephistopheles, Arch-Devil of Hell, one of the original fallen angels of Lucifer's cadre.

I bit down on my fear and persevered, absently noting a faint shimmer of heat encircling my hand. "The power of Christ compels you!" I continued in Latin:

> May the holy cross be my light. May the dragon never be my guide. Begone, Satan! Never tempt me with your vanities. What you offer me is evil. Drink the poison of yourself.

Each word caused the monstrosity to flinch, each syllable was a knife in its flesh, but that didn't stop Mephistopheles from stepping forward, his burst patent leather shoes with their exposed taloned feet gouging the carpet. Another step, then another against the hail of bullets from Maggie's weapon. It shrugged off both her bullets and my words. Slowly we backed away, keeping out of the thing's reach as it staggered forward against the force of God's power flowing from my hand, the heat-shimmer becoming larger, distorting my view.

Julian's tailored shirt and jacket were reduced to ribbon-like shreds, the flesh beneath bluish gray and heavily muscled. Its face had become long and mottled, the color of half-healed bruises.

From behind me came a shout, a Word that slammed into the monster. Unlike earlier, when it had been hurled back, it staggered momentarily and then kept coming. "Banishing won't work on me anymore, ape," it hissed in a voice full of blood and razor blades. "I have become too invested in this body, in this world. I am part of it now." Its eyes focused on me as Cain shouted another Word to no effect. "And you, little monkey, cannot channel the energy to *dispel* me!"

A sound like liquid thunder came from behind the monster, resolving into a contemptuous voice. "You've got nothing on me, dickhead."

Chapter Forty-Five

Morgan

Sixty percent of an adult human male is comprised of water. That means my body, at 175 pounds, contained 105 pounds of water. Water in the blood, in the cells, in the eyes, in the brain and in bone. Not pure water, for sure, but water nonetheless.

Imagine that water becoming *sentient*.

Every nerve, every cell in my body vibrated like a tuning fork, impelling me into some otherworldly realm of darkness inhabited only by brief flashes of light that seared into my mind with the force of a hurricane and the roaring of waves. There came a peculiar *shift*, like someone was rifling through the garbage can of my memories.

SO THIS IS LANGUAGE. INTERESTING.

What? Where did that voice come from? It came to me suddenly that I wasn't in my body anymore. I'd been evicted like a bum tenant and that pissed me off more than a little.

YOU WERE ALREADY DYING.

Not so loud; you're killing me. Who are you?

Once again that shifting sensation, accompanied by another flash of light.

[Better now?]

The voice was much like mine had been, but deeper and with a liquid gurgle running through the words. Sort of like gargling and talking at the same time.

Much, thank you. Who are you, again?

[I am Water, what you referred to as Primal Water.]

What?!

[You drank me. Rather a foolish thing to do, but I know now you really had nothing to lose. Still, from my perspective it was a bit disgusting.]

How ... what ...?

[Primals have no language; I had to take it from your mind, as well as your memories. I believe that now I am the only Primal that can communicate with humans, which puts me in an interesting situation, Olivier Deschamps. Or should I say, Morgan Heart.]

Olivier Deschamps died a long time ago. I never really liked him.

I felt a little sad. I'd wasted twenty years being someone I didn't like much. So much time tossed in the garbage bin.

How did Julian manage to capture you?

A pause, then [Better I should show you.]

The darkness around me receded, replaced by the bright light of the sun and the sound of the waves lapping the shore. My mind rang with the Word of God, that sound that brought me to consciousness. I felt Earth beneath me, surrounding me, sleepy and somber. Above Air laughed and capered. The light of the sun was part of Fire, warming me. All these, my brothers, my opposites, in conflict and balance.

Time passed and I ate at the Earth that thrust up through me, creating fjords and sculpting shorelines. On Earth I dug vast ravines, while animals drank of me. Soon Mankind came along, created by another Word more beautiful than the last. Its note echoed for ages. More time passed and I flooded an impossibly large valley, impelled by the will of God. My waters drowned cities, civilizations, and covered them completely. This later become known as the Mediterranean Sea.

The world changed, became colder. I froze, covering the land in ice, killing and killing with my frozen self. It was then I grew tired. My children were there to maintain the balance, and I felt so … unnecessary.

I pulled myself, my awareness into a small, cold, spot and floated away to where the ice never melted and it was there I slept. Until recently. Then I was awoken by Man, trapped in a container too dense to see or feel through. It was dark, and I grew angry.

Sudden warmth as an animal drank my essence, but it wasn't an animal, it was a man, a dying one at that. I called to the water in his body (I sensed it was a male) and was answered.

Suddenly, I was wrenched back into darkness, aware of my own self again.

Whoa! Are you telling me Julian found you in the North Polar ice cap? How the hell did he do that?

[I do not know. Perhaps he was led there by the one you call the Voice.]

Gunfire. *What?* Mike! It had to be Mike, Cain and Maggie. They were fighting the Julian demon.

[Mephistopholes. Or should I say the Angel Formerly Known As Maphriel.]

Whatever, you have to help Mike!

[I'm really not—]

I wasn't in any mood to take backtalk from fluid.

Without me you would still be in a plastic bottle! Now are you going to help me, or what?

[You seem to think that I suffer from the same motivations as humans.]

Christ! Indifference was the last thing I needed.

Do you understand revenge?

[No.] A note of finality.

How about gratitude? A sincere 'please' with a cherry on top?

A babble of humor swept over and through me. It took me a moment to realize that the Primal was *laughing*.

[The imagery that produced is most amusing.]

I thought of one argument that might work.

Does it amuse you enough for you to help restore balance to the world?

[?]

Isn't Mephistopheles' presence here an imbalance?"

[Clever human. If I agree to do this, your life will be forfeit. I can either take the time to heal you or I can give you the power to save your friend.]

No real choice at all. *Let's go.*

[I can even heal you of Backlash. You will not lose any Words.]

We're wasting time.

[Why sacrifice yourself for that man?]

He's my friend.

[That is important?]

He's my friend.

[Very well.] The gurgly voice sounded sad but resolute.

I waited in the dark, enduring the flashes of brilliant white light, waiting for the Primal to do something, anything. It grew worrisome, this waiting. I was sure Mike was in danger and the Primal was *taking too damn long*!

[What's the phrase? Oh yes ... Hold your damn horses. We are experiencing time differently. Only a few seconds have passed while I have made ... adjustments that will allow you to do this ...]

Roaring became my world.

And power. Oh, such power, like I had inhaled the sun. My body dissolved into liquid, its solid matter left behind on top of the elevator. Looking down, I saw legs as well as a torso, arms and hands composed of rippling water. Memories of flesh sculpted in liquid, liquid I could bend to my will. Inside my "chest" was a cold spot, so cold, in fact, that it was well below zero, but it remained liquid. The Primal, now quiescent, its power mine.

All around me I felt water, a connection to something that was part and parcel of my being. Water through the plumbing, traveling up and down the entire building ... It was like feeling the hot rush of blood travel through your veins. I called to the water … and it responded.

Pipes burst. PVC, copper, it didn't matter, water exploded through as if they were constructed of tissue paper. I continued to call, the invisible tether of my will pulling water to me. Within seconds I was bathed in crystalline sprays, which I absorbed, becoming greater and greater, sucking in more and more.

By force of will I kept the water from running down the sides of the shaft; instead I absorbed it all and began to rise, a liquid giant, a fluid behemoth. Above, the rectangle of light came closer and I could sense the monster above, its evil pulsing against my … self, my consciousness. I extended my senses and the fiend became a black star shining above. I could feel its anger, its endless capacity for hatred. Three souls glowed near the fallen. Each had a unique signature, an essence I could discern. Cain shone with vitality and magic, while Maggie gleamed with the fires of her passion.

Mike eclipsed them both with the Power of God made manifest; however, the dark star surged and flared with ravenous hunger, a spiritual black hole. It came to me that Mike couldn't channel any more energy without burning to ash on the spot.

No way was I going to let that happen.

I rose high enough and looked into the hallway, every molecule of water adhering to my form, totally under my control.

"And you, little monkey, cannot channel the energy to *dispel* me!" The fiend roared.

I felt horrendous anger and contempt. "You've got nothing on me, dickhead!"

Chapter Forty-Six

Mike

Dickhead? Whoever, whatever had said that had certainly captured the monster's attention. It spun, facing the speaker, its bulk preventing us from seeing who had insulted it.

"Begone!" I yelled, my hand flaring with the heat shimmer of power that sent burning pain through my fingertips. At that same moment Cain shouted another Word. This time Mephistopheles wasn't prepared and was hurled twenty feet down the hallway, tearing furrows into the drywall with its three-inch black nails. It landed with a floor-rattling thud that felt like a mini-quake.

There in the shaft was a turbulent column of water, and emerging from that column was the figure of a giant sculpted entirely out of translucent pale blue liquid, a water-man whose subtly shifting features were hauntingly familiar.

With a feeling of dread I recognized him. Morgan. My friend was … water? Beside me, I heard Maggie gasp as she recognized him as well.

"That is not something you see every day," breathed Cain in wonder.

Maggie's voice was full of tears. "You got that right, boss."

Bellowing, Mephistopheles bounded to its horned feet, tearing even more clothing from its bluish-gray flesh. "I am the right hand of the Morning Star!" raged the demon. "I am an Arch-Fiend of Hell, monkey. You can't possibly hope to stand against me!" One great claw flashed and passed harmlessly through my friend, who frowned at the demon.

"You were the Arc Angel Maphriel," burbled Morgan calmly, his voice like water rushing over rock, "one of the Powers who chose to side with Lucifer. That makes you pretty much an asshole."

The demon bellowed in defiance, slashing again and again, even chomping at Morgan with its needle-like teeth, to no effect.

"You are a Duke of Hell," Morgan said, sounding almost bored. "But you are *my* world now." His smile was a gash of disgust. "Here I rule water, like the water in your body." He made a small gesture.

The demon began to scream, then screamed louder, the noise piercing and vibrating in my skull. All three of us clapped our hands to our ears as Mephistopheles sank to its knees, pain racking its body. Its skin grew glassy with fluid as it threw its head back, bellowing in agony, more and more liquid building up. Its skin, defying gravity, became a watery shell.

It shrank, but only a little at first. As the fluid shell grew, the demon continued to … collapse, shrink in upon itself, the bruised-looking skin becoming wrinkled and shriveled.

One drop flew from the demon's shell, then another and another until it rained toward Morgan, who absorbed the liquid into … himself, I guess. As Mephistopheles shrank, my friend grew until he had to lean over or pierce the ceiling.

As its body shrank the Julian demon's voice grew softer, diminishing to a low keening, then a pathetic whine and finally a whimper. When the last drop of moisture pattered into Morgan's substance, all that was left of the demon was a husk that flopped lifeless to the floor and began to quickly decompose. Its smell was sulfurous, nauseating, the stench of a rotting corpses and vomit, only a thousand times worse.

"You know what his big mistake was?" Morgan asked in a silky voice that flowed like a mountain stream. "Once he took Julian's form, he was subject to the rules of this world, he should've remembered that. Then again, the fallen aren't that bright."

I stepped toward my friend, staring up at his watery, blue face. There was a certain ... *contentment* reflected in his features. I reached out and slowly ran a hand into his chest. Cold, like arctic runoff. In the center of his torso rested a soft, glowing pulse.

"That's the Primal, man," he remarked, as if reading my thoughts. "It's quiescent right now, but when I give its power back, it'll wake again."

"Morgan—"

"It's okay, Mike. It worked out better this way, I think."

Maggie stepped close, tears flying from her eyes and becoming one with his elemental body. "Aw, hell, handsome," she sobbed.

"Hey, Blondie, I'm sorry I won't be able to take you out."

"You're probably a lousy tipper, anyway." Her words were brave, but her face had contorted into mask of sorrow.

Morgan looked over my shoulder. "Cain, take care of them both, please."

The big man removed his glaciers and rubbed his strange eyes. "I will, my young friend. You have my oath on it."

"Boss," Maggie whispered, amazed. "Your *eyes!*"

I took a look and felt my legs wobble. A dark, soft brown circled the irises, a sharp border that hadn't been there before. Those orbs were still unnerving, but the impact of their regard was lessened somehow.

Cain reversed his glaciers, looking deep into their mirrored lenses and gasping in shock, the sound almost a sob.

Morgan smiled. "You weren't cursed for killing your brother, you know."

"Huh?" replied Cain, eyes riveted to the mirrored lens.

"God knew you felt true regret at the murder of your brother. What really pissed Him off was the lie."

Cain nodded.

"The Lord asked, 'Where is your brother, Abel?' and you replied—"

"'I know not. Am I my brother's keeper?'" finished the big man.

"Yes. The first lie. You are its inventor. By telling that lie (and to

God, no less!) you gave birth to an evil that warmed Lucifer's cold and jealous heart."

"Does this mean I am forgiven?"

"Not entirely, but it looks like you've finally made some headway. Cheer up; it only took several dozen millennia to find your answer. The rest should be cake."

I started to feel overwhelmed. "Morgan, how do you know all this?"

"Easy, man," he replied with a lighthearted, burbly laugh. "Merging with a Primal has some benefits. Did you know that the Earth's core is Primal Earth? And that the ozone layer is Primal Air?" He laughed louder with the sound of breakers. "Guess what's Primal Fire!"

Maggie snapped her fingers. "The sun!"

Morgan winked at her and then lowered his head, as if heeding an internal monologue. "Have to run, guys. Cain, call Fire, burn this place to the foundations, then go to the roof. Air will give you a lift to the nearest building. You'll be safe."

"Did you arrange it?" I asked.

He nodded. "The elements are grateful for the return of Primal Water. Balance can be restored. And this world needs a *lot* of balancing." Once again that internal monologue. "I have to go, but first, Mike ... take this." He held a silvery cylinder in the palm of his watery hand.

The molecular knife. I took the device and the metal was cold, so cold. "Morgan!" My throat tore at the lump that had formed there.

He took me into an all-enveloping, liquid, embrace.

[You're the best man I've ever known, Mike] came his voice into my head. He sounded like his old self again. [I don't want to go, man, but I have to.]

I know, but I don't want you to go!

[I'm going to be fine. Going to miss you, man.]

Aw, heck. I could barely think, I felt so alone, so empty. *Love you.*

A sob splashed against my mind. [I love you, too, Mike.]

And, like that, he was gone ... away down the elevator shaft and out of my life. A horrible spasm tore at my chest, as tears dripped off my chin. Beside me, Maggie surrendered to her own grief, a long low keening that raised the hair on the back of my neck with its abject sorrow. I gathered her into my arms for what comfort we could share. We sagged to our knees, tears mingling.

We stayed like that for a while lost in the labyrinth of our mutual grief until Cain gently lifted us to our feet and led us away. Acrid smoke curled about us as Cain led us to the roof, where Air gently lifted us to safety.

Fire burned the hotel down to its foundations, erasing all evidence of the conflict that had taken so many lives. We watched into the wee hours of the morning until the building collapsed in on itself, burning so hot that no firefighter would risk drawing near. By midday we were on a private jet bound for home.

That was two months and a lifetime ago. I resumed my duties at St. Stephen's, Maggie left for parts unknown, a little sadder, perhaps a little wiser. As for Cain, he's decided to stick around for a while, claiming that Omaha's pace suited him just fine. I think he wants to stay near me, to see if I hold the key to the forgiveness he seeks. I don't have the heart to tell him that he should seek forgiveness from within. I doubt he'd listen anyway; he's got a blind spot the size of Montana when it comes to introspection.

The newspapers and other media never followed up on the "big" Missing Heir story. Cain thinks the Sicarii are licking their wounds, keeping their collective heads down. I think they're truly afraid, perhaps for the first time ever. Good, they should be.

Sometimes, late at night, I think about why God sent an angel to save one, lonely, corrupt man and I remember what Cain said to me recently, that He uses a screwdriver, not a sledgehammer. Maybe God knew that young Olivier needed a push in the right direction, all so he could make the decision to save millions of people from Earth's fury and return Primal Water to where it belonged. Maybe.

Whatever you may think of Olivier Deschamps, he did try to do some good in this world.

And in the end, that's about all anyone can ask.

Born in Helsinki, Finland, **Mark Everett Stone** arrived in the U.S. at a young age and promptly dove into the world of the fantastic. Starting at age seven with the *Iliad* and the *Odyssey*, he went on to consume every scrap of Norse Mythology he could get his grubby little paws on. At age thirteen he graduated to Tolkien and Heinlein, building up a book collection that soon rivaled the local public library's. In college Mark majored in Journalism and minored in English. Mark has published two other books with Camel Press, *Things to Do in Denver When You're Un-Dead* and *What Happens in Vegas Dies in Vegas*. Coming soon: the third book in the *From the Files of the BSI* series, *I Left my Haunt in San Francisco*.

Mark lives in Denver with his amazingly patient wife, Brandie, and their two sons, Aeden and Gabriel. You can find Mark on the Web at:

markeverettstone.camelpress.com
www.markeverettstone.com.

Other Books by Mark Everett Stone

Coming in 2013

I Left my Haunt in San Francisco

Chicago, The Windigo City

Omaha Stakes